continued on the next page . . .

"Mary Jo Putney is a gifted writer with an intuitive understanding of what makes romance work."

—Jayne Ann Krentz

"Dynamite!"

—Laura Kinsale

"A delightful tale with wonderful historical details. A sweet and satisfying read." —*Literary Times*

"A transcendental piece of art that deserves a keeper shelf all its own." —*Affaire de Coeur*

"A complex maze of a story twisted with passion, violence, and redemption." —Nora Roberts

"*The Wild Child* may be the historical romance of the year . . . an enchanting tale that will captivate readers . . . superb . . . magical."

—Harriet Klausner, *Painted Rock Reviews*

The
SPIRAL
PATH

MARY JO PUTNEY

BERKLEY BOOKS, NEW YORK

F
Put

THE SPIRAL PATH

A Berkley Book / published by arrangement with
the author

ISBN: 0-7394-2051-8

BERKLEY®
Berkley Books are published by The Berkley Publishing Group,
a division of Penguin Putnam Inc.,
375 Hudson Street, New York, New York 10014.
BERKLEY and the "B" design
are trademarks belonging to Penguin Putnam Inc.

PRINTED IN THE UNITED STATES OF AMERICA

To the memory of Melinda Helfer,
whose passionate love and understanding of romance
touched countless writers and readers. We miss you.

❧ Acknowledgments ❧

Under the glamour of moviemaking lie amazing amounts of hard work. For helping me understand the creative and technical aspects of film, special thanks go to Julie Ganis for her sharp eye, tremendous knowledge, and wonderful stories. Thanks also to Barbara Ankrum and Shannon Katona for helping me understand the process, and Laura Resnick for sharing her memories of theater training, English style.

❧ *Prologue* ❧

Being a sex symbol was a hell of a lot of work. Kenzie Scott came in from his morning beach run panting like a racehorse and covered with sweat. Some days he reached the euphoria of a runner's high. Other times exercise was pure torture, and this was one of them.

His all-purpose household help, Ramon, silently handed him a cool glass of juice and disappeared back into the kitchen. Kenzie dropped onto the sofa in the family room, sipping his drink and watching the waves roll toward the beach. He could gaze at the sea forever, he sometimes thought. Wave after wave, eternally. Hypnotic, mindless peace.

There were a couple dozen things he should be doing, but he wasn't in the mood for any of them, so he took a videotape from the haphazard stack teetering on the end table. Oscar voting time was coming up, and studios were inundating Academy members with screeners of nominated films. He glanced at the box. *Home Free*, featuring a nominee for Best Supporting Actress. Raine Marlowe.

He'd heard good things about Raine Marlowe, but hadn't seen any of her work. He popped the tape into the VCR, then returned to the sofa with the remote.

He felt a tingle of anticipation as the opening credits appeared. He'd never outgrown his blind love of movies. The best memories of his childhood were the hours he spent mesmerized in the dark safety of movie theaters. Though becoming an actor had seemed impossible, he'd made it. Along the way he'd learned a lot about the complex skills required by filmmaking, yet he'd never lost the sense of wonder that movies always stirred in him.

Home Free, a low-budget family drama that had done unexpectedly well, was just getting interesting when the phone rang. His assistant, Josh, wouldn't have let the call through if it wasn't important, so Kenzie hit the VCR mute button and lifted the phone.

His manager, Seth Cowan, said, "Morning, Kenzie. Have you looked at any of the scripts I sent over?"

"I looked at them, they looked at me. So far, nothing else has happened."

"Never mind. I've just got a call about a role I'd really like you to think hard about. Have you heard that a remake of *The Scarlet Pimpernel* is in the works?"

"Vaguely." Though Kenzie had always liked the story of Sir Percy Blakeney, who pretended to be a fop while risking his life to save French aristocrats from the guillotine, at the moment he was more interested in the silent characters on his wide screen television. "*Pimpernel* is one of the all-time great adventures, but it's hard to see how a new version could be better than the one with Anthony Andrews and Jane Seymour. Why another remake?"

"For starters, this is a feature, not a television movie. It also has a terrific script, as good as the Andrews-Seymour version." Seth paused dramatically. "Plus, Jim Gomolko is directing, and he wants to open the bedroom door for the love scenes, which hasn't been done in earlier versions."

Kenzie rolled his eyes. "Sex does not automatically improve a movie."

"In this case, it adds dimension to the relationship. Sir Percy and Marguerite are married, after all. If that physical bond is made clear, the pain of separation and distrust will be that much more vivid."

"Good point."

"Plus, costume dramas are hot, and this would be a nice change for you. You can be dashing, romantic, and eighteenth century all at once." Seth finished by rattling off the names of the producer, the cinematographer, and the others involved in the production. All top people. "They really, really want you for the Pimpernel."

"Everyone wants me," Kenzie said dryly. When he'd dreamed of movies in smoky British theaters, he'd had no idea how exhausting success would be. "But you're right, it might be a nice change of pace. Who do they want for Marguerite?"

While Seth listed the names of several well-known young actresses, Kenzie watched a battered car pull up to the curb on his television screen. The family's prodigal daughter was returning. The camera cut to a pair of excellent female legs swinging from the driver's side of the vehicle, then panned slowly up a slight figure. Clothes hanging a little loose, brown hair pulled starkly back . . .

Kenzie sucked in his breath as the camera reached the girl's face. This had to be Raine Marlowe. She had "star" written all over her, effortlessly dominating the screen even in her drab costume.

Why was she so compelling? Not from beauty, though she had a face the camera loved. But mere beauty was boringly common in Hollywood. There was something much rarer about Raine Marlowe's presence, a quality that struck to the soul, or would if he had one. A combination of fierce intelligence, honesty, and aching vulnerability. He wanted to pull her out of the screen for a conversation. He wanted to stroll with her across Pacific sands. He wanted . . .

"Kenzie, have you heard a word I've said in the last five minutes?" Seth asked.

His gaze followed Raine as she walked down a shabby city street toward a reunion she knew would be painful. Even with her back to the camera, she drew the eye. Fear and determination were visible in every step she took. "They're hot to get me for the *Pimpernel*, they're willing to pay an indecent amount of money, and you think I should take the role."

Seth laughed. "Someday you're going to have to show me

how you always know exactly what's going on even when you seem to be out to lunch. If you're interested, I'll send the script over. It's damned good."

Kenzie watched the tense female figure disappear into a run-down apartment building. "Tell the *Pimpernel* people I'll consider taking the part if they get Raine Marlowe for Marguerite."

Seth hesitated. "I don't know, Kenzie. They've been looking at English actresses. Plus, Gomolko wants a lot of screen chemistry between his two leads."

The camera moved in for a close-up as Raine Marlowe paused outside an apartment door. She was lovely in her bones. "I think chemistry can be arranged," Kenzie said thoughtfully. "If they want me, they get Ms. Marlowe. If they prefer another Marguerite, I'm sure there are plenty of other actors who will do splendidly as Sir Percy Blakeney."

After a calculating pause, Seth said, "The girl is supposed to be a good actress, so she should be able to handle the accent. She's also new enough that she might come cheap. I'll tell them what you said." The negotiating process had begun.

"Thank you." Kenzie hung up the phone and restored the sound to *Home Free*. Raine Marlowe's voice was exactly what it should be, a flexible instrument full of aching hope as she hesitantly greeted the mother she hadn't seen in years. Her soft tones flowed over him like brandied chocolate, sinking into his mind and emotions. She'd make an excellent Marguerite.

This version of *The Scarlet Pimpernel* would open the bedroom door?

Hollywood power was a very useful commodity.

ACT I
Setting the Stage

❦ 1 ❧

Broad Beach, California
Spring, Present Day

The trouble with reality was that it was so damned *real*. Stomach churning, Raine Marlowe punched her security code into the control box of the beachfront mansion's private gates. If Kenzie had changed the codes, she'd have to come up with a new plan.

Not that her husband had any reason to be paranoid where she was concerned. Their separation was terribly, terribly civilized. No property disputes, a nice little no-fault divorce that should be final in a few months. The tabloids had been reduced to making up quotes out of whole cloth to make the story more interesting.

Motors purred and the ironwork gates swung smoothly open. As she drove her Lexus through, she gave a sigh of relief. She'd made it over the first, and easiest, hurdle.

She parked in front of the sprawling house's entrance and climbed from the car. Even for a professional actress, the performance she was about to give would be hideously difficult.

As she walked up the expensively landscaped path, she girded herself for the coming encounter. Her carefully chosen costume consisted of a briefcase-sized shoulder bag and a black Armani suit to show she meant business, with enough discreet cleavage to show she was a woman.

On the front steps she halted, unexpectedly paralyzed by the endless rush of breaking surf. The sensual sound snapped her back to nights when she and Kenzie lay side by side in bed. Though she missed the lovemaking desperately, even more she missed the conversation. In the stillness of night there'd been no stardom or competition or tabloid reporters. Just the two of them—a man and woman linking hands as they talked lazily about their days, the work they both loved, how much they'd missed each other during their frequent separations.

She wondered with clinical detachment how long the pain would be so devastating. In time, she supposed the anguish and gut-wrenching loss must fade because no one could live at such a level of misery. But relief wouldn't come any time soon, particularly not if Kenzie agreed to her proposition.

Face set, she tapped in her code to unlock the front door. This one hadn't been changed, either.

She stepped into the foyer and immediately checked the discreetly hidden security panel. Unarmed. Kenzie had always been careless about arming the system when he was home. Sometimes she wondered if he'd come to believe his own invulnerable movie roles, where he could decimate whole armies of villains without receiving more than a few bruises and maybe a carefully placed flesh wound.

This early on a Sunday morning, the house was silent. The Filipino couple who lived in a separate cottage and cared for the house and its occupant would be at mass now, but Kenzie should be home. She'd charmed his schedule out of his assistant, Josh Burke, who'd always liked her. Since her husband was in the final stages of shooting an exhausting action picture, he planned to spend a quiet day at home. Perfect for her purposes. "Kenzie?"

No answer. She checked the spacious kitchen, whose tiled floor and backsplash had the rich warmth of a Tuscan villa. Empty, and no signs that her husband had made breakfast here.

He wasn't in the living room, nor in the ground floor exercise room. Damn. He was probably still sleeping.

Hoping to God he was alone, Rainey climbed the sweeping staircase. The house was contemporary, designed to capture sunlight and take advantage of the magnificent, staggeringly expensive beach frontage. Kenzie had already owned the house when they married, and she'd been happy to move in.

He loved the sea. In fanciful moments Rainey had wondered if he might be a selkie, one of the legendary Celtic creatures who lived in the ocean as seals and on land as mysterious, dangerously attractive men. The legend certainly explained a lot, such as the fact that sometimes she felt as if she and Kenzie came from different planets.

Would it have made a difference if they'd bought a new house together and entered as equals? Probably not. He'd encouraged her to redecorate to make this place as much hers as his. They'd had great fun choosing carpets and furniture . . .

Hell. When would she stop thinking of them as a couple? She reminded herself that it had only been a few months since their marriage had exploded, so neurosis was natural. She headed to the master bedroom suite. With every step, her stomach knotted tighter. She considered bolting and contacting Kenzie through Seth Cowan, but the manager would be against Kenzie taking this job. She must risk a personal meeting if she was to have any chance of getting what she wanted.

A rap on the bedroom door produced no reply. Steeling herself, she opened it.

She sighed with relief to see Kenzie sprawled on the bed alone. Given the way women pursued him, there could easily have been an eager film student or ambitious starlet sharing the wide mattress, and Rainey would have had no right to complain. Months had passed, divorce papers were wending their way through the courts, and it wasn't as if either of them had ever claimed to love the other.

She entered the bedroom, letting her high heels click on the Spanish tile floor like castanets. Kenzie's eyes opened. Despite the instant recognition and wariness visible in the green depths, he didn't move a muscle. He simply lay as still as a lion. "Good morning, Rainey." So blasted civilized.

Keeping her distance, she said, "Sorry to disturb you this early, but I have a business proposition for you."

Kenzie propped himself up against the headboard, bare to the waist. His dark hair was tousled with a sensual abandon that a stylist would have been proud to produce. "Indeed? Tell me about it."

She was going to have to make her pitch to a naked man. Well, she'd done stranger things. She paced across the vast bedroom, tension reflected in her short, quick steps. "You know I've been working on a screenplay."

"Hard to overlook the endless series of yellow lined tablets you consumed in your trailer when on location," he said dryly. "You finished it?"

"Done, and almost through preproduction." She'd buried herself in the project in a frantic attempt to hold pain at bay. Every penny she could spare had gone into setting up a production company to do the prep work. "I've got most of a cast and crew lined up, and a financing package put together. With a bankable star, I'll get the green light."

"I presume this is where I come in."

"Your signature on a letter of intent would secure all the financing I need," she said bluntly. "I hear your next movie has fallen through so you have the time free, and God knows you love to work." That had been one of the problems in their marriage. Despite his laidback appearance, Kenzie was a workaholic.

"I doubt you can afford me. What's your budget for the film?"

"The total budget is about half the salary you're getting for the movie you're shooting now." She rubbed damp palms on her skirt. "Though I can't afford your usual price, I've built in a million dollars for salary, plus major profit participation. With even modest success, you'll do very well." A lot better than she would. "It won't hurt your market value to work on a little picture like this. People will know you're just helping your ex-wife out." Her voice turned sardonic. "That will enhance your nice guy image."

"So I'll make money, and look like a gentleman," he said, unimpressed. "I don't need either, and the drawbacks of working with you greatly outweigh the advantages."

She caught his gaze. "You're perfect for the part, Kenzie. And it's the kind that wins Oscars."

Though he didn't move so much as an eyelash, she had his full attention. After a long silence, he said, "Let's talk about it in the gym. A couple of your exercise outfits are still down there."

She was going to have to continue her pitch while doing leg lifts and bicep curls? Well, if that's what it took. . . . "Okay. I could use the workout."

She left before he climbed from the bed, unable to bear the intimacy of seeing him casually naked. As she headed for the gym, she wondered for the thousandth time if they'd had a real marriage. At the time she'd felt close to him, despite the subjects undiscussed and the declarations unmade. They'd managed to get beyond the movie star thing.

Yet even at their closest, she'd never truly understood Kenzie. He was as much a mystery to her now as when they'd met. Even more so, perhaps.

Rainey had been jubilant when her agent called to ask her to read for the part of Marguerite St. Just in *The Scarlet Pimpernel*. Though she loved making small, quirky movies and had built a decent career with them, *Pimpernel* was the big-time: big budget, big names, and a rousing classic story.

She immersed herself in the script for days before her audition, until she knew exactly who Marguerite was. She even booked sessions with a dialect coach to help her create an alluring French accent, and a movement coach to teach her to curtsy and dance in proper eighteenth-century style.

As she arrived at the studio, one of Hollywood's hottest young female stars was leaving the audition room. Well, she hadn't expected the competition to be easy.

As always on such occasions, the room was full of people evaluating her as if she were a slab of overdone steak. She recognized the film's director, two producers, a famous casting director, and half a dozen executive types.

The director, Jim Gomolko, looked as if he'd bitten into something sour when he told her to go ahead with the test scene. But she'd come prepared. Dressed in a flowing dress with a period flavor, she curtsied gracefully to the executives, using her carefully practiced French accent as she thanked them for their kind consideration.

An expressionless male assistant fed her lines as she performed the scene where Marguerite first meets Sir Percy. She began the scene coolly, for as the most acclaimed actress in Paris Marguerite was used to men wanting to bed her. She'd learned to keep admirers at a distance.

Yet there was something about this Englishman, a hint of steel beneath his languid manners and wicked wit. As the scene progressed she gradually realized that this was a man of surprising depths and passions, one who could keep a woman intrigued. . . .

When she finished her reading, the executives were nodding approval. Gomolko said, "I want you to read again with someone else, Ms. Marlowe."

One of the suits spoke into a cell phone and five minutes later Kenzie Scott ambled into the room. Rainey caught her breath, electrified. Though Scott was rumored to be on board for *Pimpernel,* her agent had told her the deal wasn't set yet.

Rainey had kept her fingers crossed because she was a great admirer of Kenzie Scott's work. And—well, of his looks, too, she was only human. But even more, she respected his acting. Though she preferred his early work, before he'd become a major star, he brought depth and nuance to even the most macho action roles.

He looked across the room at her as if she was the most fascinating, desirable woman he'd ever seen. Every cell in her body kicked into overdrive. Tall, dark, and charismatic, he was almost supernaturally handsome. He was often mentioned in the same breath with Cary Grant, and not only because of his chiseled features and the faint cleft in his chin. The real similarity lay in his easy, aristocratic British charm. On screen he could project strength, intelligence, wit, vulnerability—all at once if the role called for it. Those qualities were strikingly vivid in person.

Kenzie bowed, a perfect Georgian gentleman despite his khakis and polo shirt. "Mademoiselle St. Just, your performance tonight was brilliant."

With a pang of regret she realized that the admiration in those amazing green eyes was because he was in character. Since he was working from memory, she slid into Marguerite. Recklessly she tossed her script over her shoulder, pages fluttering to the floor while she prayed she'd remember her lines.

She responded to Kenzie's dazzled Sir Percy by playing the scene ardently instead of the coolness of her first reading. They were from different nations, different ways of life. To a loyal daughter of France, this languid aristocrat was all she was taught to despise, while she was an actress, a woman to be bedded, not wed. Yet they both were caught up in a blazing attraction too powerful to deny, no matter how much it cost them.

When they finished the scene, the executives were sitting upright in their chairs. One of the producers muttered, "Jesus, who knew she was so *hot*?"

Gomolko made a rueful face. "You were right, Kenzie, she's Marguerite. You've got your deal. Do you want the part, Ms. Marlowe?"

"Yes!"

"I'll contact your agent right away to work out the details."

As she stammered her thanks, the room erupted with excited talk, leaving her and Kenzie in a small zone of privacy. Now that they weren't acting together, she felt shy with him. Reminding herself that soon they'd be rolling around on a mattress together, she asked, "What did Gomolko mean about the deal?"

He smiled, tanned skin crinkling around his eyes. "I told him I wouldn't take the part unless you were cast as Marguerite."

No wonder the director had regarded her with misgivings—

he'd been afraid he might have to choose between the actor he wanted and an actress he didn't want. "Then I owe you quite a thank-you. Why did you want me in particular? We've never even met."

"I've seen most of your work, and knew you were right for Marguerite."

She groaned. "Please don't tell me you saw *Biker Babes from Hell.*"

He laughed. "That movie proved you could handle Marguerite's adventurous side. But I was already convinced. You should have won that Oscar for *Home Free.*"

She thought of the awards ceremony wistfully. Attending dressed to kill and not showing a shred of disappointment when she didn't win had been a major test of acting skill. "There was a strong field of nominees."

"You were the best." He touched her hair with gossamer delicacy. "This red-gold is your natural color?"

She shivered, a little breathless. "Yes, but usually I play drab, worthy brunettes."

"The time has come for you to play a glamorous woman of the world, Raine."

"People who know me well call me Rainey."

He repeated that in his beautiful deep voice. He'd trained at RADA—the Royal Academy of Dramatic Art in London—which gave him an unfair advantage, she thought dizzily. Earlier he'd been Sir Percy admiring Marguerite, but his expression now made it clear he hadn't insisted on her for this movie solely because of her acting.

So be it. She'd attained success through discipline and unrelenting work, not wasting her time on high-profile affairs to get her name into the gossip columns. But a life without occasional recklessness wasn't worth living. Kenzie Scott was gorgeous, likable, and attraction crackled between them like a high-voltage current. If they had a fling, it would be by mutual choice.

How much simpler life would have been if he'd only wanted an affair. . . .

❧ 2 ❧

Kenzie warmed up in the gym as Rainey changed in the dressing room. He was insane to listen to her proposal, but when she'd marched into his bedroom, cool as an ice queen, he'd been struck with such longing that he'd have agreed to anything to keep her there a little longer.

He was on the elliptical cross-trainer when she joined him. Her lovely apricot hair tied back, she was dangerously attractive in a spangled green leotard and tights that revealed every inch of her slight, elegantly proportioned and toned figure.

They'd shared countless exercise sessions in the last three years. An actor's body was a primary tool of expression and required relentless work to maintain. The grueling fitness regimen had been a lot more fun when Rainey shared the sessions, bantering, discussing the news of the day, and improving the scenery. Now and then discipline had gone out the window and they'd exerted themselves differently, teasing and laughing until they ended up in a sweaty, relaxed tangle of limbs.

As she began her warm-up stretches, he said, "Tell me about your movie."

"It's based on an obscure Victorian novel that I fell in love with years ago." She bent over and placed her palms flat on the floor. "*The Centurion* was written by a fellow called George Sherbourne who'd been an army officer in strange corners of the British Empire. It was considered strong stuff when it was published, practically treasonous, so it never became well-known."

"What's the book about?"

"Torture, guilt, and despair. The high price of empire for the soldiers who do the dirty work in distant, dangerous places. The saving power of love."

"What's the storyline?"

She sat, then locked her hands around her ankles and laid her forehead on her knees for a slow stretch. "John Randall is a British Army captain in the 1870s. Your classical hero—strong, absolutely sure of himself, a little arrogant. A decent fellow, but not exactly a deep thinker. On leave home, he falls in love with a young neighbor, Sarah Masterson. Since she's the prettiest girl around, naturally he feels he deserves her, while she's dazzled by him. They become engaged, and he promises to leave the army and take up life as a landed gentleman after one last campaign in North Africa."

"Where do the torture, guilt, and despair come in?"

Rainey stood and disappeared into the locker room, returning after a moment with a script. "You can read all about it here. The short answer is that Randall is captured by Arab rebels in an attack where all of his men are killed. He's beaten and abused, and is finally released, a broken man.

"Ironically, England is looking for something to be happy about in the wreckage of a nasty little campaign that went badly, so he's given a hero's welcome when he returns home. As Randall is dying inside, he's lionized, presented to the queen, and generally treated like the greatest thing since sliced bread. No one wants to hear about what really happened, and besides, he can't bear to talk about it."

Kenzie felt a chill of recognition. This was a character he could understand. "Presumably things get worse before they get better."

Rainey lifted hand weights and started slow bicep curls. "He doesn't want to marry Sarah because he feels tainted and unworthy, but there's so much momentum behind their engagement that before he knows it he's standing at the altar.

"The marriage starts disastrously, but even though Sarah is young and wildly naïve, she's not stupid, and she truly loves him. Gradually she comes to understand what torments her husband, and her love pulls him back from the brink of destruction. At the end, she leaves everything she's ever known to accompany him to Australia so they can begin a new life in a place where there are fewer rules and family expectations."

Frowning, Kenzie gazed out the window, where a famous neighbor walked along the sand with two golden retrievers. Though Rainey's project would be an interesting change of pace from his usual heroics, making a movie with her would be hell, and this particular story might cut too close to the bone. "You don't really need me. There are plenty of actors who could do the role well."

"I had you in mind the whole time I was writing the screenplay. John Randall has a tremendous emotional range from arrogance to despair to hope, and I can't think of another actor who could do it as well." Her voice turned persuasive. "You'll get a chance to stretch acting muscles you haven't used in ages. You've been getting restless with all of these big budget thrillers. This is your chance to do something different, and knock a lot of critical socks off."

His soon-to-be-ex-wife knew how to bait a hook. She was a great fan of his work, claiming that he made acting look so easy that it was always the people around him who won the awards. She might be right, and while he didn't need an Oscar, he was human enough to want to be considered good as well as successful. "Are you playing Sarah?"

She shuddered theatrically. "No way. She needs to be painfully young and innocent. I was never that young."

"Maybe not in your personal life, but you could play nineteen with the right lighting and makeup."

"I've already got a terrific young English actress, Jane Stackpole, to play Sarah. I'll be plenty busy directing."

"Directing is a popular ambition."

Though his tone was neutral, she reacted vehemently, setting down her weights and stalking to the glass to stare out at the ocean. "When I was young, I wanted only to act. Now that I've done that for years, I want more. I want to tell *my* stories *my* way instead of being a puppet playing out someone else's vision. But you know how hard it is for a woman to get a chance to direct." A tremor, instantly suppressed, sounded in her voice. "I want to make this story, now, and to do that I need you."

The rigid set of her shoulders showed how much it was costing her to ask for his help. "Who else is involved?" he asked.

"Marcus Gordon will be the executive producer."

"Impressive. If he's on board, you shouldn't have any trouble with financing."

Her hands clenched. "He's always had a soft spot for me, but he's a businessman first. Even though he thinks the script is terrific and that I can probably do a decent job of directing, he wants a bankable star like you to ensure that the movie at least breaks even."

He studied her slim silhouette against the window, alarm bells going off in his head. Agreeing to this project would be a very, very bad idea. They'd rub against each other painfully every minute of every day. The odds were high that they'd end up in bed together again, which would mean another excruciating separation when shooting ended. He'd be tempted to forget common sense and try to get her back, while she'd probably want to strangle him, especially when he was making cinematic love to the toothsome young Sarah.

But he couldn't resist Rainey. The fierce clarity of her will had attracted him from the moment he first saw her screen image. She had dreams and passions and the willingness to work to achieve them.

He'd also worked hard, achieving great success in worldly terms, but he hadn't been building toward a goal like Rainey. He'd been running from life. He flowed while she burned. They were complementary personalities, and together they'd produced blistering, dangerous steam. He knew in his bones that they were better off apart, but that didn't prevent him from missing her like an amputated limb.

The rationalizing part of his brain pointed out that even

though making this movie was a terrible idea, there was no risk it would change their situation, since Rainey was resolved on divorce and nothing would change her mind. He'd be able to do one last project with her, and in the process help her achieve her dream of directing. If at the end he was crippled by sorrow—it wouldn't be that different from how he felt now. "Very well. I'll make your movie."

She whirled to face him, startled. "Without even reading the script?"

"I'm willing to trust you and Marcus Gordon that it's good." Wryly he paraphrased the words English judges had used when pronouncing the death sentence: "And may God have mercy on our souls."

Rainey climbed into her car, still dazed by Kenzie's agreement. At heart she'd been sure he'd refuse, but once again, she'd failed to understand him. Maybe he felt he owed her for breaking their marriage? Or maybe he just wanted a shot at an Oscar.

Whatever his motives, *The Centurion* was in business. As the realization sank in, she threw back her head and gave a triumphant biker babe war whoop, feeling like herself for the first time in months.

Grinning, she put her car into gear and set off. Time to seal the deal with Marcus Gordon. She'd chosen her words carefully to give Kenzie the impression that Marcus was definitely set as executive producer, but she'd been stretching the truth to the breaking point. A sure sign she'd spent too many years in Hollywood, where the art of the deal had been raised to heights that would make a camel trader blush.

She swung onto the freeway, hoping she'd reach Marcus's home on time for their meeting. Negotiating the details of Kenzie's contract had been time-consuming, especially since they'd continued exercising the whole time. For her, settling everything without the intervention of Kenzie's sharp-toothed lawyer had been too good an opportunity to pass up.

By the time they finished, she'd been sweating and unfit for the sight of a man from whom she wanted a lot of money. She showered in the locker room of the gym, then swiftly redid her hair and makeup before racing out.

She was looking forward to being a director and not having to worry every minute about how she looked.

Bending the speed limit, she reached the Gordon estate only a couple of minutes late. The butler buzzed her through the gate and she parked in the shade of a stone wall. As she entered the sprawling house, she mentally prepared herself for the role of Successful, Confident Businesswoman and Director. Compared to her meeting with Kenzie, this one would be easy, though equally critical.

The butler led her out to a multilevel patio with a spectacular view over the Los Angeles basin. As she stepped into the sunshine, Marcus rose from a poolside dining area shaded by a bougainvillea-covered arbor. Wiry, balding, and barely average height, he didn't look like one of Hollywood's most powerful independent producers, unless one looked into the shrewd gray eyes. "You're looking remarkably fine, Raine."

Recognizing an oblique reference to her impending divorce, she hooked her arm through his and headed to the arbor area where his wife waited. "Nothing like hard work and clean living to keep a sparkle in the eye, Marcus."

No trophy wife, Naomi Gordon was frankly plump and silver-haired. She and her husband had maintained a famous partnership for almost forty years. Rainey kissed the older woman's cheek, leathery from decades of sun-loving. "Hi, Naomi. I hope you don't mind my letting business intrude on Sunday brunch."

Naomi laughed and gestured to one of the chairs. "When do we ever really get away from business? At least you've never shoved a script under the door of the stall when we were both in a ladies' room."

"Good Lord, has that happened to you?"

"Seven times. And Marcus has even more lurid tales." Naomi smiled affectionately at her husband.

Rainey set down her briefcase and settled into a chair as Marcus poured her a mimosa. The tangy fresh-squeezed orange juice was delicious, but she only sipped from the tall glass. She didn't want the champagne in the drink to fuzz her wits.

Though Marcus Gordon could be tough as nails, he'd always gone out of his way to help her, possibly because he'd known her mother. In his studio head days, he'd had Clementine under contract for a movie about a self-destructive rock star when the singer had self-destructed herself. Rainey remembered him vaguely from then. A father himself, he'd always been kind to her. Not like some of Clementine's visitors.

One of Naomi's house rules was no business talk until the food had been consumed, so conversation was casual as they ate exquisite napoleons made of sautéed vegetables and puff pastry, followed by a heavenly fresh fruit compote.

As the dishes were cleared away, Marcus leaned back in his chair. "Time for your pitch. We like your script. Now what do you want from us?"

"The money to make this movie." Rainey passed out copies of her detailed proposal. She'd hired several very sharp people to help on the preproduction, painstakingly working out the details of budget, locations, and shooting schedules. "And a distributor who will market it well."

"You don't ask much," Marcus said dryly. "Let's look at what you've got."

Naomi raised her brows as she skimmed through. "You've certainly done your homework on the prep. You can start shooting as soon as you get the green light?"

"I hope to begin within the next few weeks."

Marcus pursed his lips as he looked at a page. "The battle scene in New Mexico will be expensive."

"Yes, but it's essential to show this ugly, chaotic little war a long way from John Randall's home, and it will cost a lot less to shoot in New Mexico than in the Sudan. The big welcome home scene is another money shot that's needed to demonstrate Britain at the height of her power and prosperity."

Marcus nodded agreement and flipped to another page. "Clever to keep all of the English location shots in one general area. That will save money. It's still a tight budget, though, in both dollars and time."

Rainey gave him her most confident smile. "I wouldn't propose it unless I was sure I could make it work. I've got great people in all the key positions. They don't have the biggest names, but they're first-class talents."

"You've chosen well." Naomi exchanged a glance with her husband.

He nodded slightly and turned to Rainey. "Your figures look realistic and the script is first-class, but you don't have a leading man listed here, and I suspect there's something else you aren't telling us."

Marcus had a well-earned reputation for uncanny perception. It was time to reveal her deal-breaker. She'd start with that, then hope that Kenzie's consent would make it all possible. "As the director, I want final cut."

He whistled softly. "The top directors in Hollywood fight to get that. Explain to me why you think you deserve final cut on your very first production."

"I know I'm asking a lot, but I won't settle for less." She leaned forward, her intense gaze going from one to the other. "I've got a clear vision of what this movie should be. I don't want to make blockbusters—I want to do small, character-driven stories that are ultimately hopeful. This kind of movie isn't particularly fashionable, but there's a solid market for stories that aren't all guns and gloom. Stories with heart. Think *October Sky, The Winslow Boy, Crossing Delancey.* I want to make these kinds of movies, and I want to do it my way, not risk being overruled by some studio executive who thinks he knows better than I."

"Sometimes the suits are right." Naomi's eyes were troubled.

"Saying I want final cut doesn't mean that I won't listen to anyone else's ideas. I've put together a team of top creative people—including you, I hope—because I *want* good input. But ultimately this is *my* movie, and I want the final say. That's why I've kept the budget so tight—to reduce the risk."

"We're still talking millions of dollars in production costs, and even more millions for promotion," Marcus said. "Always assuming you can make a movie that's fit for release."

Matching his bluntness, Rainey said, "I can and I will. If I have to, I'll finance this myself even though a flop means I'll have to spend years working to pay the debt off." And that was if her career stayed healthy enough to make the kind of money that could pay off that much debt. In the entertainment business, there were no guarantees.

"Raine, Raine, the first rule of moviemaking is to use other people's money, not your own," Marcus said with a smile. "But even if you know exactly what you want, the story hinges on having an actor who can successfully play John Randall. You haven't listed anyone in your proposal. Who are you considering—another relative unknown?"

"Not at all. I got a commitment this morning, too recently for me to add his name." With a flourish, Rainey pulled her trump card from the briefcase and laid it on the table. "Here's a signed letter of intent from Kenzie Scott."

Naomi whistled as she scanned the letter. "Are you insane, child? Trying to direct a man you're divorcing will be so crazy-making you won't be able work."

"Kenzie and I are both professionals." Meaning she could work even with her heart bleeding. Ditto for Kenzie, though she suspected his heart was barely dented. "He's perfect for this role, Naomi."

Marcus took his turn at scanning the letter of intent. "He scratched out the salary, and I can't quite read what he wrote in."

"Another change for the better. Kenzie said that rather than demean himself by working for a paltry million dollars, he'd do the picture for union scale." And a sizable piece of any profits the film would make, of course, but it had still been generous of him to forgo the up-front money she'd offered. He was always such a blasted gentleman. "Doing that frees up almost a million dollars for unexpected contingencies."

"You've thought of everything." Marcus exchanged another wordless glance with his wife. "All right, you've got your deal. I can find you the money—I'm pretty sure that Universal will bite, and if they don't, another studio will. I'll act as executive producer, and I'll even guarantee you final cut. In return, I reserve the right to close down the production or prevent release if costs spin out of control or the movie is a dog that would damage all of our reputations."

"Fair enough. You won't regret this!" Exultant, Rainey hugged first Naomi, then Marcus. She'd gotten everything she wanted—and she prayed she didn't live to regret it.

~ 3 ~

*By the time Rainey reached home, her exhilara-*tion had been joined by a healthy dose of terror. Dear God, after all her hard work and planning, she was really going to be able to make her movie the way she wanted to! This was a tremendous opportunity—and if she blew it, she might never get another chance.

At least she didn't have to risk her house by financing the movie herself. She'd bought this canyon cottage with her first real money, and it was the truest home she'd ever had. Tucked into a secluded corner of Laurel Canyon, the simple cedar structure was fragrant from the tangy eucalyptus trees that shaded it, and brightened by sun-baked drifts of drought-resistant flowers. She'd fallen in love the moment she drove up.

Luckily she'd trusted her instincts and not sold the cottage when she married Kenzie. At heart she'd known their hasty marriage wouldn't last, so she'd rented out her place to a charming pair of production designers who'd taken good care of it. They'd just bought a house of their own when she left Kenzie, so she'd been able to come home. It had been like finding refuge in the embrace of a beloved friend.

Kenzie hadn't been in the cottage often, so she had few memories of him here. They were uncomfortably happy memories—she'd had no idea he knew how to make great salads until a poignant day when he'd helped her pack her most personal possessions—but the house had remained hers, never theirs. The Broad Beach estate had briefly seemed like it was joint property, but no longer. In the best civilized fashion, each of them was taking from the marriage exactly what they'd brought in, and no more.

She entered the living room and kicked off her high heels. The shoes rolled across the polished oak floor, one coming to rest on the thick, richly colored Tibetan rug splashed in front of the fieldstone fireplace. That rug figured prominently in her memories. With his uncanny perception, Kenzie had known she was a little sad to be leaving her loved home, so he'd seduced and made love to her with exquisite tenderness, reminding her why she'd taken the terrifying leap of faith into matrimony.

By the time she reached her bedroom, she'd stripped off her Armani suit. After hanging it in the huge closet, she paused to study the famous poster of her mother that hung above the love seat. This was the clearest image she had, since her childish memories were blurred by time.

Clementine at the height of her fame had been all passion and fire, a candle burning at both ends. Her wild mane of red hair was backlit by spotlights as she sang her signature anthem, "Heart Over Heels," a searing confession of a woman who fell in love too often, and always gave away more of herself than she could afford to lose.

I'm making it, Mama. I'm achieving success on my own terms without destroying myself. Her mother probably would have been glad to know that. But would she have approved of the tense, wary creature her daughter had become?

Rainey peeled off her stockings and slipped into cutoff jeans and a black T-shirt with a picture of the Buddha on the front. Then she flopped onto the waterbed and reached for the phone. Who to call first? Since her personal assistant, Emmy Herman, the world's greatest organizer, was out of touch on a sailboat with her husband, she'd call her coconspirator in Maryland.

She hit the autodial button. When her friend picked up on the second ring, she said, "Val, it's me. How are things in Baltimore?"

"The sun is shining, the weeping cherry is trailing gorgeous pink blossoms outside my kitchen window, and *how did it go?*"

Rainey grinned. Val Covington, a friend who dated back to elementary school, had been invaluable in developing *The Centurion.* She'd read numerous versions of the screenplay, and though she was a lawyer, not a writer, her comments had always been right on the mark and refreshingly un-Hollywood. Together they'd brainstormed the practical and legal difficulties involved in producing Rainey's dream. "You're going to get a production credit on a movie, Val."

"Hot damn!" Val whooped. "So you've got your deal?"

"Yep. Marcus Gordon will be the executive producer, he agreed to let me have final cut, and my soon-to-be-ex-husband will star."

"So Kenzie said yes. I almost wish he hadn't, but with him involved, there's no way you'll lose money. Congratulations, Rainey—your career as a director has begun."

"I still have to actually make the movie."

"You can. You will."

Val's warm voice carried the unconditional confidence that was supposed to be offered by mothers. Sometimes Rainey wondered what kind of relationship she and her mother would have had if Clementine hadn't died. Would they have been friends? Rivals? Enemies? Would she have taken her problems to her mother and known she'd get wise, womanly advice? Impossible to say. Clementine had been an erratic mother. When she wasn't doing concert tours, she was sometimes devoted and playful, other times stoned and inaccessible.

Feeling her stomach knotting, Rainey said, "Will you be able to visit me during shooting? It would be great to see you in either New Mexico or England."

"I think I can make it. I have a ton of vacation I haven't taken."

"I'll expect you then. Heck, I'll cast you as an extra if you want."

"Short, Rubenesque redheads do not make ideal extras. Too conspicuous."

"You're not Rubenesque—you have a great, curvy female figure. You'd make a nice Cockney flower girl in one of the London scenes."

Val hooted. "Better yet, hooker. Or would that get me disbarred?"

"Propositioned, maybe, but not disbarred."

After they hung up, Rainey called her lawyer. She wanted Kenzie's contract drawn up and signed quickly, before he could have second thoughts.

She needed to call her cast and key crew members to tell them the project was definitely a go. Instead she stayed sprawled on the bed with the phone resting on her midriff. Since it was impossible to keep thoughts of Kenzie at bay, maybe it was easier just to give in and get them out of her system.

"Since we're going to work together, how about joining me for dinner so we can get better acquainted?" Kenzie suggested as they left the studio where Rainey had won the role of Marguerite St. Just.

She accepted with giddy pleasure, and he took her to one of

the fashionable restaurants where you had to be Somebody to get a table. Kenzie's fame was the kind that got them instantly escorted to a private corner booth. For three hours they talked back and forth over trendy food that she barely noticed. She asked questions to draw him out, since she'd never met an actor who didn't love talking about himself. He turned the tables by asking about Rainey, and had been genuinely interested in her answers. He had the deeply flattering ability to give a woman total attention, as if nothing in the world was more important than her.

Soon they were trading stories about the ups and downs of their careers. She described almost getting herself killed riding a motorcycle for *Biker Babes from Hell,* while he hilariously explained the difficulties of emoting to a blank wall that would later acquire a monster created from special effects.

Rainey hadn't had so much fun in years, and she didn't hesitate when he suggested they go to his house to rehearse their parts. It was as obvious a pickup line as she'd ever heard, but she felt reckless and willing to take events as they came.

Outside the restaurant, several paparazzi immediately closed in, cameras flashing and questions snapping. Rainey flinched at the abrasive intrusion on their evening. On her own, she never attracted this much attention. A photographer called, "Hey, Kenzie, who's the classy babe?"

"We should have gone out the back," Kenzie said under his breath. He put a protective arm around her shoulders and said more loudly, "My cousin, Lady Cynthia Smythe-Matheson. We were childhood playmates."

The reporters laughed. "No way!" one said good-naturedly. "I know I've seen her around town."

"I doubt it. Lady Cynthia has been doing relief work with African orphans."

"Yeah, and Queen Elizabeth is your grandmother!"

The valet drove up in Kenzie's Ferrari. He helped Rainey into the car, and they drove away while the reporters were still debating her identity. Bemused, she said, "I know you're fa-

mous for never giving a straight answer about your personal
life, but really—Lady Cynthia Smythe-Matheson?"

"Would you rather have had your name linked with mine in
all the gossip columns tomorrow?" he asked dryly. "It would
be good publicity for you."

"I thought tonight was personal, not professional. I'd like to
keep it that way."

"So would I, for as long as possible."

She settled back, enjoying the sensation of being swept
along in one of the world's most extravagant cars. Kenzie
drove with effortless control, rather like his acting. They hardly
spoke on the drive to Broad Beach. As they glided past the endless lights of Los Angeles, Bach's Brandenburg Concertos
played softly on the compact disk player.

She felt as if she'd fallen into a dream and would wake to
find herself in her first drab Los Angeles apartment, with her
recent successes and Kenzie Scott mere wishful thinking. But
he was too masculine, too intensely real to be a figment of her
imagination. She really was inches away from one of the
world's most recognizable and desirable men—and he liked
her. Or perhaps just lusted for her, but it was heady stuff
nonetheless.

Surf drummed in the background when he stopped at his
gatehouse to punch in a security code. Within the walls, subtle
lighting highlighted the palms and flowers of California landscaping in a fair approximation of fairyland. When they parked
in front of the house and he came around the Ferrari to help her
out, she slid out with impeccable grace, no mean feat in a
sports car.

The biggest shock came when they went inside. He really
did want to rehearse.

In a softly lighted family room overlooking the Pacific, he
handed her a copy of the *Pimpernel* script and they set to work.
He already knew all the lines, damn him. She felt awkward
using the script, but relaxed as they began running through
their joint scenes. He'd had longer to think about the story, so

she welcomed his suggestions about what might work for Marguerite. Wonder of wonders, he listened thoughtfully when she made her first hesitant comment about Sir Percy, then tried her idea and agreed that it worked.

After that, it was like being in drama school, happily batting ideas back and forth as they became comfortable with the characters. The creative thrill of that was more intoxicating than the wine she'd drunk at dinner. Perhaps his desire to rehearse was a subtle and very effective form of seduction, because there was great intimacy in playing lovers, and in the fitting together of their minds and acting styles.

Things were getting very tense between Sir Percy and Marguerite when Rainey flipped a page halfway through the screenplay. "The ballroom scene. It will be fun to learn the minuet. I wish I knew it now."

"Fake it." Kenzie opened a cabinet to reveal hundreds of compact disks. Selecting one, he put it in the CD player and the room filled with the delicate precision of late eighteenth-century dance music. He held out his hand. "Will you dance, my lady?"

He spoke coldly, a man who loved a woman he couldn't trust. Knowing the request was really an order, Rainey gave him her hand but lifted her head haughtily, a woman who didn't understand her husband's withdrawal, and was too proud to show her pain.

In stony silence they circled each other, gazes locked. Rainey felt a disorienting mixture of Marguerite's emotions and her own. Each of them was unsettled by her partner. In Marguerite's case, the reasons were obvious and would be resolved by the end of the movie, but Rainey's situation was far more uncertain.

Kenzie Scott was dangerously attractive, and he knew it. There was something very real here, yet he was a stranger to her, a man famously protective of his privacy. A man who could injure her deeply if she wasn't careful.

To relieve the electricity crackling between them, she said,

"You're really good at this. Do they teach period dancing at the Royal Academy of Dramatic Art?"

"Yes, we learned all the major dances in movement classes."

"I envy your education." She spun away from him, their hands still linked. "The RADA graduates I've met are such good actors, prepared for everything."

"It's ultracompetitive—hundreds of hopefuls audition for a handful of places." He drew her toward him again. "The rejection is good preparation for an actor's life."

"You've known less rejection than most."

"I was a good instinctive actor, but instinct will only take one so far. RADA taught me the craft and discipline of acting. How to let a character play through me, rather than me playing the character. How to hit the same emotional point again and again and have it ring true each time. How to be a professional."

"You're making me even more envious. I learned piecemeal in various acting classes and workshops."

"Wherever you studied, you learned well, Rainey. I imagine that RADA students and atmosphere weren't much different from your workshops."

She laughed. "Everyone obsessed with acting, wildly melodramatic about their lives, and half the class sleeping with the other half, with partners changing regularly?"

His eyes glinted with humor. "Acting classes are the same the world around."

The music ended and they both slid back into character. "Farewell, my lady. I do not know if I shall return. "

Since the script called for a kiss, Rainey went into his arms. "Don't leave me like this, Percy! What have I done to deserve such coldness?"

Instead of Sir Percy's swift, unhappy kiss, Kenzie's mouth met hers with gentle exploration. She fell into him like a thirsty woman discovering water in the desert. He was so close that she saw he wasn't wearing contact lenses—that incredible green was real.

Hollywood had changed her from a rebellious girl to a self-protective woman. She had avoided casual affairs because it wasn't her nature to be casual and she couldn't afford distractions. But dear God, how she had hungered for warmth. Amazingly, under Kenzie's movie star glamour he seemed to yearn for intimacy as much as she did.

His hands skimmed her back as the kiss deepened. Soft, expert, passionate. Weak-kneed, she whispered in a last half-hearted effort at defense, "I can see why you have a reputation as a terrific lover."

"If I slept with even a quarter of the women the gossip columnists claim, I'd have died of exhaustion years ago." He tugged her down onto the sofa so that she was lying full-length along his strong, beautifully fit body.

She buried her hands in waves of dark hair grown long for the part he was going to play. Too many men looked on kissing as merely a step on the road to intercourse. Not Kenzie. His mouth and hands learned her with luxurious patience. No attempts to rip off her clothing or rush to greater intimacy.

His restraint made her feverish with longing. Even as a hormone-crazed adolescent, she hadn't felt like this. As he kissed her throat, she said huskily, "So we're going to have an affair?"

"Yes. But not until we've finished shooting *The Scarlet Pimpernel*."

"You're kidding!" She pulsed her pelvis against his. "Granted, it's been a while since I had a personal life, but you feel quite ready now."

He caught his breath, then lifted her so that they were reclining side by side in the deep cushions. Stroking back her hair, he said, "Think of what waiting will add to the sexual tension in the movie."

She erupted into slightly hysterical laughter, torn between intense frustration and deep relief that matters would go no further tonight. She wasn't ready for what she sensed lay ahead. "That's diabolical—but you're right. Very well, Kenzie, we have a hot date for when this movie is over."

He raised her hand and kissed her fingers tenderly. "And, I hope, some warm and friendly ones before then."

That was when she lost her heart to him. But it was a long time before she admitted that, even to herself.

The phone on her stomach rang, jarring her back to the present. Putting the past where it belonged, Rainey began the next phase of work. She would create a movie, and with it a new direction for her life.

❧ 4 ❧

Kenzie entered his trailer and flopped onto the bed, bone tired after rising at an obscene hour to shoot several scenes with a costar who had to be elsewhere in the afternoon. He'd be glad when filming ended; by this time, cast and crew were heartily sick of each other. Not to mention the fact that it had been difficult to play a lighthearted rogue while in the midst of a divorce. But he'd soon be working with Rainey again.

On the verge of dozing off, he made a mental note to call his English friend and mentor, Charles Winfield. They chatted regularly, but he'd been so busy lately that by the time he thought of calling, it was too late to place a call to London. Today would be a good time. . . .

Rinnnnnng!

The phone jerked him awake. Yawning, he lifted the handset without opening his eyes. Hearing his manager's greeting, he said, "Go away, Seth. The star's brain has quit for the day."

Undeterred, Seth said, "Sorry to wake you, but I just finished reading the screenplay of *The Centurion.*"

The tone jerked Kenzie into wakefulness. "What did you think of it?" He hadn't had the time or energy to read the script yet himself, but surely Rainey wouldn't have taken revenge by persuading him to do a bad movie. That would rebound disastrously on her own career, and besides, Rainey was never petty.

"It's a terrific script," Seth said. "I had no idea Rainey could write so well. But Jesus, you really want to do this movie?"

"What are your objections?"

"John Randall isn't exactly a heroic figure. If this flick gets made and more than ten people see it, it's going to do strange things to your image."

Stonewalling with the skill of long practice, Kenzie said, "Sorry you feel that way, but I've given my word and signed the contracts."

"Contracts can be broken."

"But not my word. Good-bye, Seth."

He hung up, feeling a chill of apprehension. He hadn't wanted to admit to his manager that he'd been so careless as not to have read the screenplay himself. Besides not having the energy, he trusted Rainey's professional judgment. When they had been together, her advice on which scripts to choose and which to refuse had been impeccable. She wouldn't be passionate about making this movie if the material was weak.

So why had *The Centurion* upset Seth? It was time to dig the screenplay out of his briefcase, and actually read the damned thing.

Tires squealing, Kenzie slammed his Ferrari to a stop in front of Rainey's canyon cottage. He stalked to the door and hit the doorbell. After the opening chords of Beethoven's fifth symphony rang inside, Rainey opened the door, wariness in her eyes. "What an unexpected pleasure. Just passing by?"

He swept past her into the living room. "I can't do your movie, Rainey."

She spun to face him, eyes wide with shock. "But you promised! Why are you having second thoughts?"

He hesitated, wondering how to explain himself without saying too much. "I just read the screenplay."

"Today? You've had it for three days. There was plenty of time to read it before signing the contract."

"I was busy, and I took your word for it that the script was good."

Her face tightened. "Now you've read it and think it's dreck?"

"It's not dreck. Seth called and was impressed by your writing, but thought that my making this movie would be bad for my career. So I read the script, and realized I didn't want any part of it."

"Why not?" she asked, expression stony.

"You told me John Randall was tortured. You didn't mention that he was raped repeatedly, or that he fell in love with his captor."

"I told you he was abused and tortured, which is accurate, and he doesn't fall in love with Mustafa," she retorted. "It's all going to be a lot subtler and more impressionistic than that, especially the abuse scenes. Is that why you and Seth have panicked—because Mr. Action Hero isn't ever supposed to be a victim?"

How the hell was he supposed to answer that? He certainly wasn't going to explain his horror of being helpless, even if it was only acting. Tamping down on his temper, he said, "I can't do the role justice. As you said, Randall is a complex man who has to show a tremendous range of emotion. I'm not the best person for that. If you like, I'll help you find someone better for the role, but I can't and won't do it."

"You can't back out now! Everything is in place to start shooting." She glared at him. "You signed a contract, Kenzie. If you don't go through with this, I swear to God I'll sue you for your perfectly capped back teeth."

"Sue and be damned!"

Her face paled. "Did you agree to take the part with the idea of pulling out to torment me? What did I ever do to you to justify that?"

"Damnation, Rainey!" he snapped, angrier with her than he'd ever been. "What have *I* ever done to make you think that I could be so maliciously cruel?"

"Do you want me to answer that?"

Lord, no. He couldn't bear to increase the poisonous tension in the room. Then he saw tears in her eyes. His indomitable wife, who never cried except when a script required it, was on the verge of breaking down. "I don't want to fight with you, Rainey," he said wearily. "I'm not trying to make your life difficult. I just . . . can't do this movie."

She closed her eyes for a moment. "To be an actor is to be insecure. You think I don't know that? Every time we take on a role that's radically different from what we've done, it's like jumping off a cliff. But the roles that really make us grow and produce the finest acting are exactly the ones that are scariest. Though you've never played anyone quite as tormented as John Randall, I *know* you can do it, and brilliantly."

"Pushing limits is all very well, but every actor has a range of things he can do, and things he can't do. I can't be John Randall. I'm not talking actor nerves, Rainey. This role is beyond my range."

"I don't believe that. Some of your early BBC work hit the same notes needed for John Randall." She gazed at him earnestly. "You can do this, Kenzie, and I'll help every way I can. Is there any rewriting that would make you feel better about the script?"

"Are you volunteering to remove the sexual assaults and Randall's complicated feelings about Mustafa?"

Rainey sighed. "Those are the core elements of the story. The reason Randall is so torn when he returns home is because he's discovering more ambivalence inside himself than his rigid world view allows. Take that away, and there's no movie."

"Then find an actor who really enjoys playing tortured characters."

She offered a hesitant smile. "If you're feeling tortured about taking the part, you should be very convincing in it."

Exasperated, he began to prowl the living room. Rainey had decorated the place in her own charmingly eclectic style, but it was too small. Suffocating. "You don't know what you're asking."

"Apparently not, but it's clear from your reaction that this is way outside your comfort zone. What exactly bothers you about this story? Is it something personal, maybe the fact of playing a character so vulnerable when I'm directing? Or is it professional anxiety, the fear that you'll fail?"

He didn't want her to think more about personal reasons, though she was painfully accurate in guessing that he hated the idea of being stripped bare emotionally in front of her. She already knew him too well. "The personal and professional intersect. The combination of this particular role and working with you is more than I can handle. You've created a great opportunity for yourself. Don't ruin it because of some misguided belief that I'm essential to your success."

"Unfortunately, you *are* essential."

He turned to face her. "Truth time. Are you sure your conviction that only I can play John Randall doesn't have anything to do with our disintegrating marriage?"

She flinched as if he'd slapped her. "You think this is all an excuse to spend time with you?"

His smile was wintry. "Nothing as simple as that. I won't pretend to understand the workings of your convoluted mind. Only you can say for sure."

She bit her lip and thought about his question. "To the extent that being married to you gave me a better sense of your talent and potentials, it's personal that I want you for this movie. And . . . there's a small, sick part of me that loves the idea of working with you again. A much larger part would rather dodge trucks on the Santa Ana Freeway."

As always, her stark honesty undermined his defenses. Taking another tack, he asked, "Is the potential payoff for this movie worth the psychic cost of working together?"

"I think so, or I wouldn't put us both through this." Her changeable eyes were pure, cool gray as she regarded him. "Let's take it one day at a time, Kenzie. Don't think about the whole movie all at once. A day's shooting only amounts to a few minutes of usable film, and surely for those few minutes you can handle this role. There's nothing like slicing a story into hundreds of takes to grind the primal fear away."

She had a point. If he thought of this strictly as a matter of craft, performed one take at a time, it was more manageable. Acting didn't have to be personal, and probably was better if it wasn't. Maybe American Method actors felt the need to immerse themselves in ice water before playing a winter scene, but no well-trained British actor had to do that.

You're kidding yourself. The voice in his mind was the one that couldn't be denied, that knew him in all his weaknesses. He *was* kidding himself, but he was caught between a rock and a hard place. Wanting to help Rainey, he'd given his word without checking the project out carefully enough. It had never occurred to him that the story would be one that gave him cold chills.

But he couldn't back out now without causing enormous damage to Rainey, and that he couldn't bear. He'd have to make the blasted movie, no matter how painful the process. "You win," he said reluctantly. "I won't quit, but don't blame me if my performance doesn't live up to your expectation."

"Thank God. You had me scared out of my wits." She approached and laid a hand on his wrist. "I'm sorry I didn't handle this better. I should have made sure you'd read the script before sending the contracts."

"The fault was mine." He looked down at her hand, feeling her touch burning through him. More than anything on earth, he wanted to take her in his arms. Just . . . hold her, as they'd once held each other at the end of long, exhausting days.

Impossible, of course. Someday, when the fires of passion had burned out and she'd married someone else, it might be possible to embrace as friends, but not now.

With effort, he moved away. "Even though I trust your judgment, ultimately the responsibility for reading the work was mine."

"Apart from horror at having to play Randall, what did you think of the script?" There was more than a trace of uncertainty in her voice.

"Very powerful. Good characters, good structure. Classic storytelling, which the movies need more of. I'd love to see it with, say, Laurence Olivier in his prime playing Randall."

"I'd have taken him if he was thirty and available. You're the next best thing."

"Compliments will get you . . . somewhere." Wanting to compliment her work in return, he said, "Your dialogue is excellent. Very incisive and British. Often witty."

"Most of the dialogue came from the book. I'm no writer. I just pulled the best bits out of the novel."

"There's an art to adapting a novel into a script. Give yourself credit."

"That's hard when I remember how insane I am to tackle a project this large and expensive with so little directing experience. Did I mention that I insisted on final cut?"

He rolled his eyes. "No wonder you needed a name brand actor to get financing. Why didn't you try to produce the movie in a smaller way, or for television? It would have been a lot easier."

"I wanted to make the best possible movie, and reach the largest possible audience. There's great, creative work being done for cable, but the budgets are usually tight and the audiences smaller. Doing it this way may be hard, but if it works, the result will come much closer to my vision of how the story should be made."

Gloomily he addressed the wall, which was covered with a mixture of paintings, framed prints, and flattish objects like antique rug beaters. "Why did I have to choose a profession where I'm surrounded by obsessed creative types?"

"Because you're one of us, of course, even when you try to pretend that acting is just another business. Movies are more than that. They spin dreams and hopes and fears. So do the actors who make them, which is why you're recognized all over the world."

"The downside of success." There were actors who enjoyed having women plead for sex, but Kenzie wasn't one of them. He loathed knowing he was a fantasy sex object for God knew how many women. And men.

He said good-bye and left, thinking how he'd arrived at her house determined to withdraw from her project. Yet here he was, still committed.

What the devil was it about Rainey that always made hash of his intentions?

She dropped into a chair, shaking, after Kenzie left. For a terrible few minutes, she'd thought her movie was doomed. She didn't understand his reaction to the script, but his distress was quite genuine. Odd. He was one of the least temperamental actors she'd ever met, saving his emotions for the camera. But John Randall had gotten under his skin badly.

Though she'd been able to talk him into continuing with the project, she could see that she'd have to chivvy him along every step of the way. Just what a new director needed—a skittish lead who was in virtually every scene of the movie.

She'd take it one day at a time. Kenzie might have to be encouraged or threatened to keep going, but she'd get a great performance out of him if it killed them both.

Needing to burn off some of his restless frustration, Kenzie spun his car eastward out of the driveway to head deeper into the hills. Damn Rainey. Her creative passions and her willingness to put herself on the line for what she believed in still entranced him.

His response to her celluloid image was pallid compared to the impact when they met at her audition for the *Pimpernel*. Acting with Rainey was like playing tennis with a champion who anticipated his every move and returned each shot with something extra. They brought out the best in each other, both professionally and personally. With her, he was someone he'd never been before. A man who was almost free.

He thought back to the evening they'd spent together after she won the role. The excitement of discovering a uniquely compatible spirit had been mellowed by a sense of familiarity, as if they'd known each other for a dozen lifetimes. Though he'd been alarmed by the way she slid past his defenses as if they didn't exist, that night he was almost reckless enough not to care.

He'd deliberately avoided seeing her again before production started. The next time they met was in the wardrobe department when they were being fitted for *Pimpernel* costumes. Garbed as Sir Percy, he wandered into the room where the costume designer was supervising as her assistants tucked and tacked a low-cut chemise and frothing, lace-trimmed petticoats around Rainey. The effect was deliciously provocative even though the garments covered her far more thoroughly than modern clothing.

"Your unmentionables look very authentic," he observed.

Rainey grinned. "I'll bet you learned a lot about period undies when you did work for the BBC. These have to be right since they're going to appear on camera."

The knowledge that he would peel that chemise from her slim body accelerated his pulse, even though there would be a production crew present when that happened. "Making a television version of *Les Liaisons Dangereuses* was a graduate course in eighteenth-century lingerie. In the process I learned that it's powerfully arousing to remove layer after layer to find the hidden woman."

"Really? I thought men found it powerfully arousing when females wear only about two ounces of nylon."

"That, too."

A young female assistant wrapped a boned corset around Rainey and began tightening the laces. "Now we'll fit the ball gown over this, Miss Marlowe."

Rainey gasped as the corset tightened. "I may die of suffocation!"

"There's a trick to corsets," Kenzie said. "Inhale deeply while she pulls the laces, and you'll have an inch or so more room in the gown."

She promptly sucked in a lungful of air to expand her chest and waist. The costume designer on the other side of the room said disapprovingly, "An inch more on the corset will look like two inches on camera."

"Better a live, chunky actress than a thin, dead one," Rainey retorted.

The designer smiled at the idea that Raine Marlowe could ever be considered chunky. "You can see why women in this era weren't very liberated. It took most of their energy just to breathe."

"The men weren't much better off." Rainey studied Kenzie's long satin coat, striped waistcoat, tight breeches, and high, gleaming boots with more than professional interest. "Amazing how long it took the human race to invent jeans and T-shirts."

Kenzie gave her his best courtly bow. "Ah, Marguerite, much elegance has been sacrificed to the squalid little god of comfort."

She immediately dropped into her role. Expression sultry, she lifted a carved ivory fan from a table and waved it languidly. "I vow, my lord, that you quite outshine me, as the glorious peacock outshines his drab peahen."

"My plumage has but one purpose, and that is to attract the most desirable female in the land." On impulse, he pressed his lips to the slender nape exposed by her upswept hair. Her skin was warm and silky firm.

She shivered and caught her breath, yearning and vulnerability apparent on her face. When he stepped back, their gazes caught as wordless messages hummed between them. Messages, and promises.

A poster of a similar kiss was used to illustrate the movie. It embodied such tender, erotic power that it ended up in the bedrooms of hundreds of thousands of schoolgirls. Critics raved that the onscreen chemistry between the *Pimpernel* leads threatened to melt the film stock.

But that was later. At the time, Kenzie had known only that Raine Marlowe was like a spun glass butterfly—delicate, strong, and utterly captivating.

He rounded a tight curve and found a straight, empty stretch of road ahead. He accelerated the Ferrari in a long, smooth surge of power, wishing he had the time to drive to the Mojave. There was something deeply purifying about the desert. But for now, the Santa Monica Mountains would do.

Flashing lights appeared in his rearview mirror. *Bloody hell.* Swearing at himself, he pulled onto the shoulder.

Behind him a motorcycle cop braked in a shower of gravel. After checking Kenzie's license tag in his computer, he swung from his bike and swaggered to the car. No doubt he was enjoying the prospect of proving that a badge was more powerful than an Italian sports car. Kenzie opened the driver's window and resigned himself to receiving a richly deserved speeding ticket.

"Do you know how fast you were going, sir?" The patrolman loomed over the low car, his tone less polite than his words. His name tag read SANDOVAL.

"Not exactly, but certainly far too fast."

Officer Sandoval, rather young under his helmet, looked nonplussed at such ready agreement. "Your record is pretty clean for someone who drives as if he's looking for a runway to land on."

"Usually I only do this in rather remote places." Kenzie handed over his license and registration.

Sandoval looked down at the documents, then his head snapped up and he stared. "My God, you're Kenzie Scott!"

Since the fact wasn't news to him, Kenzie merely nodded.

"I love your movies, sir," the young man said, his bravado replaced by bashfulness.

"I'm glad you enjoy them, Officer Sandoval."

"Especially that one where you played a cop whose partner was killed." His face darkened. "The way you kicked in the wall after his death—it's exactly like that."

"Have you had a partner killed?" Kenzie asked quietly.

"Yeah." The patrolman looked away. "You made it so . . . real."

"Movie deaths should never be presented as without consequences. It's important to remember the tragedy and pain involved." Many movies forgot that, but Kenzie didn't. He'd never taken on a role that had him killing people as if they were only targets in a shooting gallery, with no dignity or value.

"Anyone who's ever pulled a burning body from a car knows how painful and messy death really is." Sandoval lowered his ticket pad. "Would you mind giving me your autograph, sir? Not for me, but for my wife. She's a big fan of yours, too."

"Of course." Kenzie pulled a small notebook from his glove box. "What's her name?"

"Annie Sandoval."

Kenzie scribbled a note to her. "Here you are. My regards to Annie."

"Thanks, Mr. Scott." The officer reverently folded the page and tucked it inside his jacket. "It's been a real pleasure to meet you, sir."

As he turned to leave, Kenzie asked, "What about the ticket?"

Sandoval grinned. "I'm letting you off with a warning. Have a good day, Mr. Scott."

"You do the same, Officer." Kenzie waited until the patrolman roared off, then pulled the Ferrari onto the road, his mouth twisted.

He never asked for special treatment.

He didn't have to.

❧ 5 ❧

Val scowled as she hung up the phone. As if Rainey didn't have enough troubles at the moment. She hit a button on her autodialer. A few seconds later, the phone was picked up in California. "Hello, this is the office of Raine Marlowe."

Recognizing the voice, Val said, "Hi, Rainey. I thought your faithful minion would answer. You must have a zillion things this close to the start of production."

"Emmy had a doctor's appointment, so I'm answering the phone myself. The production designer and English location manager and I are trading frantic calls to find a new manor house for the Randalls, since the one we were going to use fell through."

"Surely England is rife with photogenic manor houses."

"Yes, but we need one close to base camp since it would add time and money to move to a new location for those scenes."

Reminding herself that she hadn't called to talk about the movie, Val said, "There's some bad news here in Baltimore, Rainey."

"Oh, no! Has something happened to Kate or Rachel or Laurel?"

Val should have realized that Rainey would immediately think of their old gang, the "Circle of Friends" forged during their school days. "We're fine, but your grandfather was in a bad car accident. I gather the prognosis isn't good. I thought you should know."

After a long silence, Rainey said, "Yes, I suppose I should. Did my grandmother ask you to call?"

"Hardly. I run into her occasionally at the supermarket, and she looks as forbidding as ever. It was a friend who works at GBMC Hospital who saw that your grandfather had come in and let me know so I could call you. Apparently your grandmother hasn't left his side."

"After fifty-plus years of marriage, even someone as stoic as Gram is bound to be upset when threatened with losing her husband." There was another silence. "You think I should come back to Baltimore, don't you?"

"That's your decision. I just didn't want you not to hear he was ill until . . . until it was too late."

Rainey sighed. "It was always too late for me and my grandparents. They think I'm the bad seed. In two days, I have to be in New Mexico to begin shooting, and I'm up to my ears in last-minute crises. What would be the point of visiting? Will I have a touching deathbed reconciliation with my grandfather?"

"Not likely. That sort of thing is more Hollywood than real life. But . . . I think you should probably come, because if you don't and he dies, you'll almost certainly regret not doing it. Your grandparents had all of the warmth of frozen cod, but they weren't evil. In their way, they did the best they knew how."

"Damn you, Val," Rainey said, voice unsteady. "I'll bet you're lethal when you argue a case in court. Very well, I'll come—I can work on the trip so it won't cost me too much time. But you have to let me stay with you. I'm going to need a friendly face if I'm visiting the grandparents."

"You know you're always welcome here, Rainey. I'll pick you up at the airport."

"No need—I'll call a car service." Rainey's voice lightened. "At least I'll be able to see you and Kate and maybe Rachel, so there are compensations."

"See you soon, then." Val hung up the phone. It would be

nice to have her friend in Baltimore, but this was the wrong reason.

Rainey should have been working on her laptop computer as the hired town car carried her directly to the suburban hospital where her grandfather was being treated, but her concentration evaporated as soon as her plane landed. Her mind kept going to the first time she'd flown into Baltimore, when she was six years old.

After Clementine's spectacular rise and tragic death, it was the Marlowes who'd inherited her illegitimate daughter, father unknown and legal name Rainbow. Rainey had been put on the plane in Los Angeles as an unescorted child, and a warm-voiced flight attendant looked after her during the long flight.

The trip took her from summer to winter both physically and metaphorically. Icy February winds shook the jetway as the attendant led her into the terminal, but far colder were the expressions of the Marlowes as they collected the granddaughter they'd never met. Clutching a white teddy bear, Rainey stared at her grandparents, not quite believing that she now belonged to these people. Both were lean and erect, with lines of permanent disapproval marking their faces.

"She has red hair, like her mother," William said with a frown.

"Not quite as red. That's something," his wife replied. "She doesn't look much like Clementine. Such a skinny little thing. I wonder who her father was."

Rainey's eyes filled with tears as she hugged her bear tighter. A sign of affection from one of the Marlowes would have won her heart forever, but all she got was a terse, "Come along, child. We'll take you home now." Virginia glanced at her husband. "I can't call her by that outlandish name her mother gave her."

And she hadn't. For as long as she lived with them, Rainey had been *you* or *her* to her grandparents. Her first weeks in Baltimore, she cried herself to sleep every night.

As an adult, she'd come to respect their fairness. They wanted her no more than she wanted them, but they had been conscientious. She'd been well-fed and well-clothed and never physically abused even when she was in her rebellious high school years. And luckily, they'd enrolled her in the local Quaker school, where she would get a good education with the moral grounding they thought she needed.

At Friends' School Rainey met the girls who had become her true family. She spent more of her waking hours with Val and Kate and Rachel and Laurel than she did with her grandparents. Slowly she'd learned to play, to laugh with her friends, and to confide in Julia Corsi, Kate's unflappable mother, when she needed womanly advice.

Like Clementine, she'd flown far and fast as soon as she was old enough. Her grandparents had undoubtedly been relieved. She occasionally sent brief notes with changes of address and phone numbers so they could contact her if they wished, but they hadn't wished. Nor had they sent felicitations on her marriage. Prescient, perhaps.

The only time she'd seen them since moving to California was the year before when she'd come to Baltimore for Kate's second wedding. Feeling that she should make an effort, she'd visited her grandparents. They greeted her with stiff surprise and no sign of pleasure. She left after a polite but uncomfortable half hour, wondering why she had bothered to come.

It was almost dark when the town car pulled up in front of the Greater Baltimore Medical Center, a sprawling complex of buildings surrounded by hills and trees. Rainey remembered it well. She'd visited the emergency room regularly after falling from trees, being whacked by a lacrosse stick, and similar misadventures. She'd been a sore trial to grandparents who'd planned on a peaceful retirement.

The hospital was a maze, but Rainey found her way to her grandfather's room with only a few missteps. She paused in the doorway. William Marlowe lay still as a waxwork, only the beeping monitors showing signs of life. Virginia sat next to him, eyes closed and face drawn with fatigue, but still erect in her chair.

How had William and Virginia Marlowe created a daughter as vital and flamboyant as Clementine? Once when Rainey was eleven and exploring the attic on a wet day, she found an old photo of her mother singing in a church choir as a teenager. Even in a choir robe, Clementine's red hair and voluptuous body had made her more sinner than saint. Rainey took the photo and hid it in her treasure box. She had it still.

"Gram?" Rainey asked quietly.

Virginia opened her eyes, startled. "What are *you* doing here?"

"My friend Val Covington called when she heard about Grandfather's accident." Rainey studied his long face, almost as white as the pillows. Even sleeping, his expression was inflexible. "How is he doing?"

Her grandmother shrugged. "He's still alive." Her flat tone couldn't quite disguise her despair.

Rainey felt an unexpected pang of sympathy. Her grandparents' relationship had been so deeply private that she'd half assumed they stayed together from propriety and habit, but there was real grief in Virginia's eyes. "Does he know where he is?"

"He knows I'm here, but not much more, I think." Virginia twisted her hands together with uncharacteristic nervousness.

"Then come down to the cafeteria with me. I just landed and need a meal, and I'll bet you haven't been eating much since his accident."

Virginia glanced at her husband, on the verge of protest. Then she sighed. "I suppose you're right. I must keep up my strength."

She stood, inches taller than her granddaughter. Together they walked out of the room and down the hall. Word must have spread that Raine Marlowe had arrived because a cluster of nurses and aides had gathered at the departmental desk, but no one approached or asked for an autograph. Rainey was grateful for their tact.

All she could face eating was vegetable soup and crackers, but she was glad that her grandmother got a hearty plate of meat loaf and mashed potatoes. The woman looked far too thin. Though they'd never been close, their relationship had been less strained than the one between Rainey and her grandfather. Seeing Virginia so vulnerable brought out an unexpected protective streak.

She waited until her grandmother pushed away her meal half uneaten before asking, "What happened, exactly? And what do the doctors have to say?"

Virginia's mouth twisted bitterly. "He was on his way to play golf when his car was hit by a drunk driver. At nine o'clock in the morning!"

"How bad were his injuries?"

"He has lacerations and broken bones, with a collapsed lung and a head injury."

"Is the head injury serious?"

"A concussion. Not too bad." Virginia's hands locked around her cup of tea. "But when they gave him a CAT scan to look at the skull injuries, they found an inoperable brain aneurysm that could rupture at any time."

"I . . . see. But an aneurysm could also hold for a long time, couldn't it? Years?"

"William's doctor seems to consider it unlikely in this case. His attitude is that I should prepare myself for the worst."

Rainey frowned. It might not be a doctor's place to offer false hope, but neither should he make patients feel doomed. Life was uncertain, and hope could be healing. "Have you gotten a second opinion?"

"There hasn't been time to think of such things."

Rainey thought of a New York surgeon friend. He owed her a favor. "Would you mind if I called in a neurosurgeon that I know?"

Virginia shrugged, not agreeing, but not denying.

"I'll call him then."

"I hear you're getting divorced from that movie star husband of yours."

Rainey winced. "Yes. It's uncontested, so there won't be any lurid headlines."

"Hollywood actors shouldn't be allowed to marry. Especially not to each other. Drinking, drugs, orgies." Virginia shook her head grimly. "Though I suppose that's what you're used to."

Biting back anger, Rainey said, "Kenzie is British, and they tend to be less crazy than American stars. Neither of us do drugs or drink more than socially. Once at a party I stumbled into what would probably be considered an orgy. I left." On that subject, she couldn't speak for Kenzie, though if she had to guess, she'd say that orgies weren't his style. "We're people, not stereotypes."

"No drugs?" Her grandmother looked disbelieving.

"My mother died of an overdose. I've never so much as smoked marijuana."

"If that's true, you're wise." Virginia swallowed the last of her tea. "I have to get back to William."

"Is there anything I can do, Gram?"

Her grandmother shrugged again. "We've gotten along without you very well. We don't need anything now."

Stung, Rainey blurted out, "Why do you both dislike me so much? I tried so hard not to be a burden. To . . . to make you proud of me for my grades and school activities. But no matter how well I did, I still knew you didn't want me. Was it because you thought the sins of the mother should be visited on the child?"

For the first time, her grandmother's gaze focused on her. "We didn't dislike you, and it certainly wouldn't be fair to blame you for Clementine's behavior. But it's true we didn't want you with us. We both felt too old to cope with a child." She hesitated, then added painfully, "You were a reminder of the worst failure of our lives."

Startled by the candid answer, Rainey asked hesitantly, "Clementine?"

Virginia nodded. "She was born late, after we'd given up hope of having a child. She . . . she was like a flame, all burning life, and just as impossible to handle. We tried so hard to raise her as she needed, but we failed. When she left college to join a rock band, I knew she was doomed. Maybe not right away, but eventually."

Rainey swallowed, her throat tight. "That self-destructive streak was part of her, I think. I doubt anyone could have cured it."

"It's the duty of parents to raise their children right!" Anguish showed in the faded blue eyes. "But we didn't, and she died not even thirty years old."

Rainey had never seen such powerful emotion in her grandmother. On the verge of tears, she asked, "Why didn't you show me how much you cared about her? She was my mother. We . . . we could have mourned together."

"You looked just enough like Clementine to be painful, yet you were also a little stranger, with traits that were totally alien. And so we failed again."

Painful though the conversation was, for the first time ever they were actually talking to each other. "You didn't fail entirely. I'm not self-destructive like my mother."

"But you're still a stranger."

Rainey was unable to control her bitterness. "Whose fault was that?"

"Ours." Virginia's face was bleak in the harsh cafeteria light. "By the time you arrived in Baltimore, we had nothing left to give."

"What about today? Are you sorry I came here?"

"No, you're William's only grandchild. It was right for you to come." She stood, pushing her chair back from the table. "I must go back to him now. You might as well leave. The nurse said he won't wake up for hours."

A hint that heavy was impossible to overlook. Suppressing

a sigh, Rainey got to her feet. "I'll stop by in the morning before I go."

✥ 6 ✥

On the way to Val's house, Rainey used her cell phone to call Dr. Darrell Jackson in New York. Luckily, he was home and answered his private line. When she heard his deep voice, she said, "Hi, Darrell. It's Raine Marlowe. How are Sarah and the kids?"

"Raine! Great to hear from you. They're fine. Bobby's grown six inches since you saw him last. How's my favorite actress?"

"I'm afraid I have a big favor to ask."

"If I can do it, you've got it." His voice softened. "I'll never forget how you came to visit my mother. She died with a smile on her face because of you."

"That smile was because she was so proud of her children and grandchildren." Angie Jackson had worked hard as a domestic to raise her children. All had gone to college on scholarships with her encouragement. She'd deserved to live until she was ninety, pampered by her adoring family, but fate hadn't been kind.

Angie had been dying when Darrell contacted Rainey's office and said that Raine Marlowe was his mother's favorite actress, and would she consider visiting? Since Rainey was shooting a movie in New York City, it had been easy to fulfill the request. Her first visit had been from altruism. The half dozen other visits she'd made had been because it was impossible not to love Angie Jackson. If only William and Virginia Marlowe had possessed a tenth of Angie's warmth.

"What's your problem, Raine?"

Tersely she described her grandfather's injuries and the

aneurysm. "I don't know if you'll be able to help, but maybe what's inoperable to the average, garden variety brain surgeon is something you can pull off."

"I'm not God, but if you have the CAT scans sent up, I'll take a look."

"Thanks. If you can't help, nobody can."

"You didn't listen when I said I'm not God. We'll see."

After signing off, Rainey called Emmy in California to make arrangements to get the CAT scans from Baltimore to the neurosurgeon. How had she survived before the invention of the cell phone?

She leaned back in the seat, drained. The ringing of the phone jerked her up again. Retracting her prior kindly thoughts about cell phones, she opened it. "Hello?"

"How are you doing?" Kenzie asked. "I had to call Emmy, and she told me about your grandfather's accident. I'm sorry. Hard for him, and very bad timing for you."

As always, his rich, beautifully modulated voice soothed her. "I don't know quite why I'm here in Baltimore, given that he always wished I'd disappear."

"No matter how difficult your relationship with your grandparents, you're connected to them, and connections are what keep us anchored in life."

"True. Plus my friend Val—you've met her, the sexy redhead—guilted me into making the trip. I'm glad I came, actually. I was just at the hospital, and my grandmother and I had the closest thing we've ever had to a real conversation. That was worth flying cross-country for."

"Indeed."

Was that wistfulness in his voice? Kenzie had a hundred colorful tales about his father, the colonel, or perhaps the viscount, and his mother, who'd been debutante of the year, or maybe a big game huntress in Kenya. But if he had any real relatives, Rainey had never met them. He was a man without a past. It was something they had in common—she had only half a past herself.

"Sometimes I wonder about my father, and what family I have on that side," she said slowly. "I probably have cousins, maybe even half-brothers and -sisters. Would I like any of them if we met? If I needed a bone marrow transplant, would one of them be a match? But I don't know. I'll never know."

"Have you ever thought of hiring a private investigator to find your father?"

She stared out the window of the car at the dark streets, still familiar more than a dozen years after she'd left. "I doubt that even my mother knew who he was. She lived one of those very liberated '70s rock-and-roll lifestyles. There must be plenty of candidates for the sperm donor who absent-mindedly created me." Had her mother been glad to have a baby? Rainey didn't know that, either.

"She may have had several lovers around the time you were conceived, but the number is finite. Five? Ten? Twenty? Not beyond investigation. If you find a likely candidate—well, these days DNA testing can verify who a father is."

"I never thought about searching." Knowing her mother's promiscuity, seeking her father had seemed like a waste of time. Kenzie was right, though—the number of candidates couldn't be that large. Even if she found her father, it would be unrealistic to expect a warm embrace from a man who probably didn't know she existed. And yet . . . "I'd probably regret it if I tried."

"At least you might be able to satisfy your curiosity."

Deciding she'd think about it, she switched the subject to business. "Are you set to start shooting?"

"As ready as I'll ever be," he said without enthusiasm.

"Do the script changes I made help any?"

"A little."

If only he cared about this movie. He was too much a professional to give a bad performance, but he might give one that was without heart, and that would be almost as bad. Well, it was a director's job to coax, threaten, bully, or do whatever was necessary to get the best possible performance from her actors.

By the end of *Centurion,* she'd know how good a director she was. "I'll see you next week in New Mexico, then."

"Maybe I'll come down a day or two before you start shooting my part. We've wrapped on my currently untitled opus."

And Kenzie hated not being busy. "If you decide to come early, just let me or Emmy know so we'll have your suite ready."

He thanked her and signed off. It had been thoughtful of him to call. How could a man so sensitive in many ways be such an unacceptable husband?

Foolish question. She'd known from the beginning the marriage wouldn't last. The mistake was hers for saying yes when he asked her to marry him. They should have stayed with a grand affair, then gone their separate ways with only a pang or two.

But maybe he had a point about trying to identify her father. Her marriage was over, she was embarking on a new venture that could change her career. She'd even had a real conversation with her grandmother. Maybe it was time to see if she could find her father. The trail was cold after so many years, but it would only get colder. If she was successful—well, as Kenzie said, at least she'd satisfy her curiosity.

The car pulled up in front of Val's attractive old brick row-house near Johns Hopkins University. It was a peaceful neighborhood of mature trees and carefully tended yards. Welcoming. Seconds after ringing the bell, she was being greeted with a rib-crunching hug. "I'm so glad to see you," Val said warmly. "How are you feeling?"

"Tired." Rainey slung an arm around her friend's shoulders and they entered the house. "Since you're wearing a navy suit and your hair is forcibly restrained, I assume you just got home."

"I walked in the back door about thirty seconds before you rang the bell." Val peeled off her tailored jacket and tossed it over the back of a chair, then yanked out some pins and freed her hair into a curling red frenzy. "What will it be—wine or ice cream?"

"Ice cream, with as many extra calories as you can pile on."

"I'll make you the Sinner's Special." Val shook her head. "How does an ice-cream addict like you stay so slender?"

"Remember that I was unfashionably skinny when I was a kid—all bones and eyes. I just got lucky that skinny is now trendy."

"Slim, yes. Skinny, no." Val disappeared into her kitchen.

As Rainey sat down, her black cat jumped onto her lap and began to purr. As she scratched the sleek, furry head, her nerves began to unknot. A cat was better than a psychotherapist.

Coffee ice cream, hot fudge, nuts, and whipped cream helped even more as she described her visit to the hospital. "Here's hoping Darrell Jackson can help my grandfather. I wouldn't miss him much if he dies, but Gram certainly would."

"To success, or a miracle, whichever is required." Val savored a spoonful of ice cream and fudge sauce. "Was Mrs. Marlowe impressed that you're on a first-name basis with one of the most famous brain surgeons in America?"

"We didn't get into that." Rainey doubted that Virginia Marlowe would have been impressed even if her granddaughter *was* the famous neurosurgeon. "How are things going for you?"

Val turned sideways in her overstuffed chair so that her legs draped over one arm. Petite and curvy, she looked more like someone who should be jumping out of a cake than a razor-brained lawyer. "Same old, same old. I'm getting pretty tired of celibacy, but I haven't seen anyone to tempt me from it in months."

"This is sounding serious."

Val closed her eyes, her levity dropping away to reveal bleak unhappiness. "It is, Rainey. I've begun to think I'm incapable of having a healthy, normal relationship."

"That can't be true, Val. You're warm, smart, funny, and

kind. You have plenty of friends who value you deeply. You just haven't found the right man."

"Therein lies the problem," Val said self-mockingly. "My judgment about men is terrible. I meet a guy who seems different—nice, devoted, interested in a relationship—and sure as God made little yellow canaries, he'll turn out to be an alcoholic, or in love with his ex-wife, or a compulsive Don Juan, or some other kind of loser."

Rainey had heard enough about Val's boyfriends over the years to know that was true. "I wish I could say something useful, but my own track record is nothing great."

"Better than mine." Val stroked the calico cat that had joined her in the chair. "Actually, celibacy does have its points. It's nice not to have my emotions roller-coastering all the time, and with two cats, I don't have to sleep alone."

They drifted into easy conversation as they'd done regularly for the past quarter of a century. In the months since Rainey's separation, they'd talked even more than usual, because Val had the time, the willingness, and the understanding Rainey had needed. It would have been harder to talk with Kate Corsi, who'd been bubbling with happiness since her remarriage the year before.

They progressed from ice cream to chardonnay and were deep in a discussion about aromatherapy when Rainey's cell phone rang. She wrinkled her nose as she pulled it from her pocket. "I suppose I'd better answer this. Hello?"

"Hi, Raine." It was Emmy. "There's good news and bad news. What's your preference?"

She frowned at the tension in Emmy's voice. "Start with the good news."

"The CAT scans for your grandfather are on their way to New York by special courier. Dr. Jackson should be able to study them first thing in the morning."

"Definitely good. What's the bad news?"

Emmy took a deep breath. "I'm pregnant again; I've made it to the fourth month—but my doctor says I can't go on location with you. The work is too strenuous. I might lose this one, too, if I don't take it really, really easy."

Rainey bit back an oath. Emmy was her right hand, and she'd been counting on her help during the shooting. But Emmy had already miscarried twice, and she and her husband wanted this child desperately. Putting enthusiasm into her voice, she said, "That's wonderful news! Since you're four months along, I'm sure this baby will make it to term, but of course you can't take any risks."

Emmy's voice caught. "I'm sorry to let you down, Rainey. We weren't going to try again until after *Centurion* was shot, but well, things happen."

Rainey felt a powerful, unworthy stab of envy. How marvelous it would be to have a loving husband who wanted children. Well, Emmy deserved that. "Location work is brutal. Your doctor is right to put it off limits. I can find another assistant, even though she won't be as good as you."

"I can still handle the Los Angeles office. Will that help?"

"That will be wonderful, as long as you don't work too hard. Maybe we can have calls and mail forwarded to your place so you can work at home and get as much rest as you need."

"That would be *great*." Emmy sniffled back tears. "Damn, ever since I got pregnant I'm crying all the time. Thanks for being so understanding, Rainey. I was almost afraid to tell you."

"Babies come before business. Give David a hug and my heartiest congratulations." Rainey sighed as she said good-bye and shut down her phone.

"I gather that Emmy is pregnant and grounded?" Val asked.

Rainey nodded. "Wonderful for her, of course, but terrible timing from my point of view. I was counting on her to watch my back while we're shooting. At least she'll still be running the business office, but now I have to find a good location assistant."

"You've overcome far worse obstacles than losing an assistant." Val refreshed the wine in their glasses. "Have some more chardonnay to mitigate the shock. Or does this call for a second round of fudge sauce?"

"Things aren't quite that bad." Rainey gazed at her friend through the balloon of her wineglass. Nice to have Val to commiserate with her.

Wait, a minute, *Val.* The idea was absurd—or maybe a stroke of genius. "Will you take Emmy's place, Val?"

"Me!" Val's voice rose to a squeak. "That's absurd. I'm a lawyer, not a moviemaker. There must be herds of personal assistants who'd jump at the chance to work with you. People with production experience."

Warm with wine and excitement, Rainey swung her feet from the sofa to the floor and leaned forward earnestly. "Don't underestimate your experience. You've visited me on plenty of movie sets, you've been my sounding board while I prepped *Centurion*, and you're one of the best organized people I've ever met."

"I've got a job here! I can't just flit off."

"It's only a couple of months. Didn't you say earlier that you have a ton of unused vacation and sick time?" Rainey grinned wickedly. "Time to fish or cut bait, Valentine. You're always complaining about how much you hate being a lawyer. Or have you outgrown your famous impulsiveness?"

"I hope not, but . . . but what about my cats?" Val clutched the calico so close that it meowed and slithered from her lap.

"That's really feeble. Leave them with Kate and Donovan—they adore cats and wouldn't mind a couple more for a few weeks. I think you'd be terrific at the production end of moviemaking. In fact, you already are—I'd never have gotten through the prep as quickly without your help."

Val ran a hand through her hair, standing the red curls on end. "This is a rotten trick, Rainey. You're handing me a golden opportunity, and if I don't take it, I'll forever lose the right to complain about my job."

"This is pure selfishness, not a golden opportunity. I'd just really like to have you there." Rainey's teasing faded. "Making this movie with Kenzie will probably be the hardest thing I've ever done. I'm going to need someone who doesn't think of me as the boss who must be placated to her face and cursed behind her back. I need a friend."

After a silence, Val said, "Since you put it that way—it's a deal. But if I'm awful at assisting, for heaven's sake hire someone who knows what she's doing, and I'll just hang out and be available if you need someone to vent to."

"You won't blow it. This will be fun, Val, you'll see. A lot of work, but fun." Rainey smiled mischievously. "I guarantee you'll meet a lot of fascinating, maddening men who are totally ineligible and would make you miserable if you got involved."

"Well, hell, Rainey, you should have said that first. How can I turn down such an offer?" Val raised her wineglass and clinked it against Rainey's. "Here's to the movie that will change your career, and maybe mine, too."

"I'll drink to that." Rainey swallowed a mouthful of wine, feeling happier than she had all day. The prospect of directing *Centurion* had just become a little more manageable.

ACT II
Cameras Rolling

❧ 7 ❧

One of the worst parts of moviemaking was the insanely early hours required. Kenzie yawned, then swallowed another mouthful of scorching coffee. John Randall and his native cavalry rode at dawn.

All around him, the chilly New Mexican night reverberated with the sounds of recalcitrant horses and tense riders trying to position themselves to the assistant director's satisfaction. Luckily his own mount was a placid beast, specially chosen so as not to risk breaking The Star's neck.

Rainey, who was buzzing around like a wasp at a picnic, materialized in front of him. Dressed in jeans and the official *Centurion* show jacket, which was a shade of British military red that had not been chosen to go with her hair, she radiated a mixture of excitement and nerves. "Ready to go, Kenzie?"

He nodded. "It's nice that my first scene doesn't require me to say a word. I can ease my way into the part." Rainey wore no makeup except for a little lipstick and mascara. The result was very close to the natural bedroom look he'd always liked best. Not the face of the glamorous actress, but his wife.

The divorce would be final a week or so after they finished shooting her movie.

She looked anxiously upward. "I hope those clouds don't move in. This is the first morning since we arrived with a decent sky."

She was poised to dart away when he caught her shoulder. Awareness crackled between them like static electricity. "Relax, Rainey. You've got a great crew and everything that needs to be done is being done. Fussing will just put everyone on edge and increase the chance of mistakes. Have some coffee."

"More caffeine is hardly likely to make me relax." Nonetheless, she drank deeply. They both liked coffee the same way—scalding hot, milk only. "Thanks."

She glanced up, and for an instant they were caught in one of the unsettling flashes of intimacy that persisted even though the marriage was over. He was grateful to have the moment interrupted when Josh, his sharp-eyed assistant, rushed up with fresh coffee. Taking the cup, he asked, "Why did you choose this area to stand in for North Africa?"

"Mostly because it fit my budget. I had some license because the military campaign in Sherbourne's novel is imaginary, though it was inspired by a real campaign in the Sudan that involved angry Arabs who wanted to drive out the Europeans. One of Queen Victoria's messier little wars."

"The one where the noble General Gordon died at Khartoum a mere two days before a relief army arrived, I presume? One of the famous Victorian military martyrdoms, though I seem to recall that an officer who knew Gordon said the man wasn't worth the camels lost in the rescue attempt."

"I never cease to be amazed at your memory. Sherbourne's novel specified a remote, desolate setting, and this canyon fits the bill." She gestured at the stark landscape. "I also needed dozens of good riders for the skirmishing between Randall's patrol and the rebels, and it's easy to hire them around here. Since they all wear scarves wrapped around their faces, we don't need real Arabs, just people who look like they were born in the saddle."

"You got your money's worth. The dailies I saw yesterday are first-rate. Plenty of fierce, chaotic action. When it's cut together, viewers will feel like they're in the middle of the battle. My stunt double did a good job of going down fighting bravely."

"At this stage of the story, John Randall has the courage of the unimaginative." She checked the lightening sky again. "Almost time. Make sure you don't fall off your horse. We might not have another chance to get this shot right."

"I shall endeavor to stay on my horse." He handed his coffee cup to Josh, and swung onto his mount. "Don't worry, Rainey. We rehearsed this ride six times yesterday. It will be fine."

"From your lips to God's voice mail." She jogged over to her Jeep and drove off to join the camera crews on the other side of the hill.

As Kenzie waited for the signal to start moving, he became John Randall, erect and arrogant, an officer of the empire on which the sun never set. He and his patrol would ride west over the hill, appearing as silhouettes against the rising sun. Though his men were in drab khaki with faces swathed against the dust and heat, Randall wore his regimental uniform. The blood-red blaze of his tunic would be the only color in the dun landscape as they descended the hill to their fate.

The second assistant director who had been organizing the scene used his radio to announce that all was in readiness. Another two minutes of increasing light passed before the first assistant director's voice crackled back over the radio, "Rolling!"

Kenzie set his horse into motion, letting it choose its own footing in the dim light. Shoulders square, face determined, a man as at home in the saddle as he was in the world. These rough hills held nothing that a true-born Englishman need fear.

In typical movie fashion, this scene came before the battle scene that had been shot over the previous days. Rainey had set up the schedule to allow him to start as late as possible, in case his previous film ran longer than it was supposed to. It hadn't, though. He'd arrived in New Mexico two days before, using the time to visit the set and take long drives along remote roads.

The shooting schedule was a tight one. Since John Randall was in almost every scene, from now on he'd be working six days a week. After the battle and capture exteriors were done, the production would move to England for location work. The final phase would be shot on a London sound stage.

Kenzie crested the hill and rode down toward the cameras, accompanied by the thunder of hooves, the jingle of harness, a trailing haze of dust. Below, Rainey stood with the two cameras and crews recording the approaching riders. One caught the whole scene while another zoomed in for close-ups. Randall and his patrol rode forward steadily, not expecting trouble but ready for any that might show up.

"Cut!"

Just short of running over the cameras, Kenzie and his patrol reined in their horses. Rainey called, "Great job! You all looked fantastic against the sunrise. Dramatic. Ominous. Doomed."

She grinned. "Now get back over that hill as fast as your horses will take you, and we'll do a second take, just in case."

"Cut!" The marker snapped shut on take sixteen.

Kenzie sighed. They were trying to get the master shot of the first, critical scene between Randall and his charismatic captor, Mustafa, leader of the rebels. It took place moments after Randall was captured, and had to establish the complex interplay between the characters.

Kenzie prided himself on his professionalism, always knowing his dialogue. Usually he could nail a scene on the first take. Unfortunately, Sharif Asuri, the young Pakistani-British actor playing Mustafa, seemed incapable of walking and talking at the same time. Though Sharif had done well in rehearsal and had the physical presence to play the rebel leader, he'd flubbed every take so far. Tension was rising among the crew, and Sharif was a nervous wreck.

Rainey was admirably patient. "Take a few deep breaths and we'll try it again, Sharif. Forget the cameras and act like you did in rehearsal."

Sharif nodded and took his place. Kenzie was lying half-propped against a pile of rocks, wrists tied in front of him, bruises and smudges of blood artistically scattered over his face and hands.

"Now." Rainey gave the signal to start another take.

Lithe and cruel as a panther, Sharif knocked aside the spear one of his men was about to drive through Randall's chest. "Don't! This one is an officer." He kicked Kenzie's carefully padded ribs. So far, so good. "I shall find a use for him."

"You might as well kill me now, because I'll do nothing that might help you," Kenzie spat out. Randall was fiercely defiant at this point, sure he could face death with courage, not knowing that dying would be simple compared to what lay ahead. "Or if you're the warrior you claim to be, cut me loose so we can fight like men!"

Sharif smiled with vicious anticipation. "There's m-m-m-more . . . " His words trailed off in a stutter.

"Cut!"

The youthful cable puller gave an audible groan. Sharif flushed violently. Rainey took one look at his face, then whirled and stormed over to the culprit. "You're off the movie. Now!"

He gasped. "But . . . but . . ."

"It's not your job to judge performances," she snapped. "If you want to continue working in this business, remember that in the future. Now *go!*"

The boy left in the midst of paralyzed silence. Even his boss, the head of the sound crew, didn't protest. Rainey was well within her rights to fire the idiot, and she'd proved to the crew she was tough enough to be the boss. But something had to be done to get production back on course.

Kenzie scrambled to his feet. "Someone take these damned ropes off me. We all need a break."

Seeing his expression, Rainey said, "Kenzie's right. Take ten."

As the first assistant director, Bill Meriwether, called the break to the crew, Kenzie said to Sharif, "Let's take a walk. Stretch a few of the knots out of our legs."

Looking like a lamb on the verge of being sacrificed, Sharif nodded. Kenzie fell into step beside him and headed away from the trucks and cameras. In the desolate canyon, it took only a dozen paces to start feeling alone in the wilderness.

Sharif had his head down as if he was walking through a minefield. Despite his height and a splendid beard that made him photograph older, Sharif was quite young, Kenzie realized. Early to mid-twenties, which explained a great deal. "Is this your first movie role?" he asked conversationally.

"Yes, sir. I graduated from the Central School of Speech and Drama last spring. I've done several small television and stage parts, but nothing like this." Though he used an accent for Mustafa, his natural speech was as crisply British as Kenzie's.

Central was one of London's top drama schools, so Sharif obviously had ability and good training. While Kenzie was wondering what might get him to relax, Sharif blurted out, "I'm so sorry, Mr. Scott. I thought I had my lines down perfectly, but . . . " He made a helpless gesture with his hands.

"Being in a Hollywood movie terrifies you."

"That's part of it." Sharif swallowed. "And . . . and it's also you, sir. I saw you play Romeo at Stratford. The way you made him come alive . . . You lit up the whole stage. That's when I knew I had to become an actor."

Ah. As a RADA student, Kenzie had once shared a stage, in a very minor role, with Sir Alec Guinness. He'd almost expired from awe. Though he was hardly in Guinness's class and only a dozen or so years older than Sharif, an idol was an idol. "So I'm your hero?"

"Yes, sir."

Kenzie swung around and faced the younger man. "I'm not your hero," he snarled. "I'm a son-of-a-bitch Englishman who knows I'm superior to you and your whole filthy country."

Sharif stared at him, shocked. "What . . . why are you saying that? I was born in Birmingham and I'm as English as you are."

Kenzie pushed harder. "My people have better guns and a

better God, so that makes us a better race. You miserable hea-
then savages should be grateful that a Christian nation even
bothers with you."

"You arrogant Pommy *bastard*." Sharif's British civility
vanished in a surge of fury.

As the younger man's fists clenched, Kenzie balanced on
the balls of his feet so he could dodge if necessary. Then Sharif
caught his breath, rage vanishing into understanding. "I see, sir.
You mean I should stop being distracted by heroes and Hollywood and just do the job. Be Mustafa instead of a nervous
actor."

"Right. But I'm not 'sir.' I'm a swine. An arrogant unbeliever—and I definitely don't belong on a pedestal."

"Yes, si . . . Sir Swine." Sharif smiled. From now on, he
would regard Kenzie as a fellow actor, not a paragon.

Kenzie clapped the young man on the shoulder. "Let's go
back and try it again, and this time, send chills through John
Randall's unimaginative heart."

Take eighteen was filmed without a hitch.

❧ 8 ❧

After the final scene of the afternoon, Rainey
rolled her tight shoulders. It had been a long day, but a good
one. After filming the close-ups of Randall's first meeting with
Mustafa, they'd gone on to an earlier scene where Randall
risked his life to save one of his men from a poisonous snake.

Kenzie had been wonderful—tight-lipped, fearless, utterly
competent. She hoped there would be room for the incident in
the final cut because it demonstrated Randall's courage, his
marksmanship, and his dedication to his men. Since Randall's
rigid world view might be hard for modern audiences to relate

to, it was important to show that by the standards of his day, he was an exemplary officer.

Walking up to Kenzie, she said, "You're doing great."

Looking tense and tired, he unbuttoned his heavy red wool uniform tunic, revealing the very modern white T-shirt underneath. "This is only my first day. It's going to be a long couple of months." Rubbing at the red marks left by his tight collar, he headed for his trailer.

She followed, stretching her steps to match his. "Thanks for settling Sharif down. Since you talked to him, he's been terrific."

"He's very talented. The perfect blend of danger and disturbing appeal."

"The tension between the two of you is complex enough to make everything that happens later believable."

She was about to say more when Kenzie paused, tall and intimidating in his uniform. "Is there a good reason why you're following me around?"

Rainey stopped in her tracks, flushing scarlet. "As . . . as your director, I wanted to see how you're doing."

"As your soon to be ex-husband, I find too much proximity exhausting."

She felt as if she'd been slapped. "I . . . I thought we were getting along pretty well. I'd hope we could work together as friends."

A muscle jumped in his cheek. "Friends. A woman's idea of a good solution, and a man's nightmare. You are not my friend, Rainey. You are my wife, at least for now. While you're thinking amiability, I'm thinking how much I enjoyed sleeping with you. I can't help it, I'm a man and we're made that way. Usually we hide our base natures, but when I'm making a movie, I haven't much energy left over for maintaining a civilized facade. Not where you're concerned."

"You think only men obsess about sex?" she retorted. "How very retrograde."

His brows arched. "Is that a declaration of interest?"

"It's a declaration of memory." She sighed. "We both knew this would be difficult. I didn't mean to make it worse by following you around. I'm just worried. About you, the movie, everything."

He gave her a wintry smile. "A little worry is useful, but too much is destructive. Don't overdose on anxiety before we even get to England."

"You're right, of course, but relaxation is hard to do on command." She saw a gleam in his eye and belatedly wondered if he was going to suggest that sex was a famously effective stress reliever—one that he'd used with her in the past when she was tied in knots.

A memory seared through her of the two of them lying in bed together after making love, a pine-scented candle burning on the bedside table. She couldn't even remember where they were—an inn on the coast of Brittany, maybe, because waves had been crashing on the headlands outside. But she remembered how she'd felt: utterly tranquil, her busy brain almost still. So this is peace, she had thought with wonder.

Kenzie had been equally relaxed, his arm around her and his face buried in her hair as he molded her against his body. There had been no need to talk. They had fit together so well it was impossible to imagine anything ever separating them.

She swallowed as she realized she was staring at the thinly covered chest visible under his open tunic. Wrenching her mind back to business, she asked, "Do you feel any better about doing this story?"

"No," he said bluntly. "I feel worse because it's becoming more real in all its awfulness. But don't worry. I'll do my best."

"I know that. I'll see you tomorrow morning." She turned and walked back to the shooting area, where equipment was being broken down and stored for the night. Time to return to the small, off-season ski resort where the cast and crew were staying, so she could spend the evening working.

If she worked hard enough, maybe her sleep wouldn't be haunted by dreams of Kenzie.

• • •

After removing his makeup and changing into his own clothes, Kenzie collected the rented SUV that was one of his few perks on this production, and roared away from the desolate canyon where they were shooting. How the devil was he going to survive two months of this? A single day had gone by, and already his nerves were frayed to the point where it was hard to be civil to Rainey. He would continue because he'd given his word— but he hated to think what kind of shape he'd be in by the end of shooting.

Driving through the open countryside soothed him. Since arriving in New Mexico several days earlier, he'd spent every spare moment exploring, from rugged mountain peaks to hidden lakes, solitary meadows to dramatic ski slopes that teemed with people during the snow season. He'd stopped for coffee in a truck stop with an espresso machine, visited Indian ruins and modern pueblos. He'd even found a bed-and-breakfast establishment carved into a rocky escarpment, like the homes of ancient cliff dwellers. The place had so intrigued him that he'd booked it for Saturday night, so he'd have the experience of sleeping inside stone.

He wanted to absorb everything, because New Mexico spoke to him, even the barren canyon where they were filming. He'd visited areas of Arizona that looked similar, but they'd felt different. New Mexico had a spare, clear energy unlike anything he'd ever experienced. If forced to describe his reaction, he'd have to say this land touched his soul. A pity the whole movie wasn't being shot here.

About two more hours until dark. That should be enough to get him into balance, at least for tonight. He turned right onto a minor road, hardly more than a trail.

Which was worse, playing John Randall or being around Rainey? At the moment, Rainey was worse, he decided. For a novice director, she was doing well, authoritative without being intimidating, and clear about what she wanted. She was also an actor's director, inviting comments and collaboration when a scene was being developed. Her earnestness and passionate commitment entranced him as they always had. No wonder his mind was flooded with memories.

The Scarlet Pimpernel was a lavish production with a large cast, and it had required five solid months of shooting in France and England. During production, he and Rainey maintained their pact not to become lovers, though it became harder and harder. The filmed passion was real, not feigned, and more than once he'd almost asked her to carry what started on the set to its natural conclusion in private.

Yet he didn't. Not only was there a perverse pleasure in denial when they both knew it was only a matter of time until they came together, but they were learning so much about each other. The pressures of making a movie tended to strip away facades and show an actor's real temperament. Rainey, he discovered, had a bone-deep sense of fair play, and good temper even under grinding stress. Though she was often intense, she also had an irresistible sense of humor.

He particularly liked the courtesy and consideration that were as natural to her as breathing. The crew members worshipped her. Though he abhorred prima donna behavior, got along well with coworkers, and was famous for the generosity of the crew gifts he gave during shooting, he would never have Rainey's relaxed, natural friendliness. He always stood two steps apart from the normal world.

Except with Rainey. He couldn't imagine that there were any similarities in the way they grew up, yet the two of them resonated together.

By the time of the wrap party at the end of production, exhaustion was universal, and emotions flowed as deeply as the champagne. Moviemaking transformed cast and crew into a temporary family, though sometimes a highly dysfunctional one. Since *Pimpernel* had been a good shoot, with few major blowups and considerable satisfaction, the knowledge that the family was about to be broken up produced teary farewell hugs even between people who'd occasionally threatened to throttle one another.

He and Rainey had exchanged a few smoldering glances across the London restaurant hired for the party, but he didn't try to approach her until the party was well advanced. Halfway across the room, he was intercepted by the director. Gomolko hugged him exuberantly. "You were everything I hoped for and more, Kenzie. You're the best damned Sir Percy ever."

Not fond of being hugged by men, Kenzie gently disentangled himself. "You get the credit, Jim. You handled every aspect of the story beautifully, from the romance to the adventure sequences." He and Rainey had had to fight Gomolko to keep the love scenes more evocative than graphic, but things like that were forgotten once the film was in the can. "This will be the definitive *Pimpernel*."

Beaming, Gomolko headed off toward the attractive female production designer to express his thanks for her undeniably brilliant work. Kenzie resumed his course toward Rainey, avoiding eye contact with others so he wouldn't be sidetracked again. He'd said his good-byes, and now she was the only person he wanted.

She greeted him with a dazzling smile despite the circles under her eyes. After her last scene, she'd thrown her hated corset away with a whoop of pleasure, leaving her in Marguerite's lace-trimmed shift. If Kenzie hadn't had one more scene of his own to shoot, he'd have carried her off then.

The dress she wore tonight was shiftlike, a flowing green, gauzy fabric that swirled around her ankles when she walked. Stretching out her hand, she said, "I owe you for all of this, Kenzie. Thanks for wanting me in this movie. It's been one of the best experiences of my life."

He wanted to wrap himself around her in an embrace that would make them both weak in the knees. He settled for kissing her hand, as courtly as Sir Percy. "It wasn't only the movie I wanted you for. We had a date for the end of filming. Are you still interested?"

"Oh, yes." Her voice became husky. "But I warn you, what I really want to do is go to bed and sleep for a week."

"What a coincidence. That's close to what I had in mind." He swept her up in his arms and carried her through the restaurant. After a surprised instant, she settled into his embrace, head resting on his shoulder.

Accompanied by hoots and applause from their colleagues, he took her outside to the white limousine he'd ordered. Laughing, Rainey slid across the leather seat. "The modern version of being carried off on a white horse. You have style, Scott."

He cupped her face, admiring the delicate bones and the honesty of her gray-green eyes. Then he pressed his lips to hers. The last five months of kisses had been for the camera. This one was for them—slow, intimate, unhurried.

When they separated, she released her breath in a sigh. "Nice. A necking session. Almost as romantic as when we solemnly exchanged blood tests last month."

"As you said, I have style," he murmured against her throat. Though he wanted her intensely, fatigue had the advantage of muting his desire to the point where he could enjoy the foreplay without wanting to rip her clothes off. There would be time enough for that later.

They had reached London City Airport before Rainey broke free long enough to stare out the window. "What on earth are we doing here?"

"Flying back to California."

"But I haven't packed! I don't even have my passport."

"Don't worry, I suborned Emmy. All your things are waiting for us."

Rainey fell back onto the white leather seat, laughing. "I'm being abducted! What a fabulous way to end a job. I trust we're flying first class?"

"Better than that."

Kenzie's assistant was highly efficient, and the arrangements for this escape had been planned meticulously. As they approached the private jet, Rainey's eyes rounded like saucers. "Kenzie, do you own this plane?"

"Yes and no. I own a couple of shares in a network of private jets. When a shareowner wants to fly somewhere, the network arranges to have a plane available."

They climbed the steps and entered a cabin arranged as a comfortable lounge. A flight attendant approached and said with a musical French accent, "Monsieur Scott, Mademoiselle Marlowe. I am Rochelle. May I get you anything?"

He traded glances with Rainey, who was drooping under his arm. "We both just want to go to bed and sleep until somewhere around Boston."

"Of course, Monsieur. I shall tell the captain it is time to depart. As soon as the seat belt light goes off, you may retire."

As Rochelle went forward into the cockpit, Rainey said, "There's a bed?"

He nodded toward the wall behind them as he sat down in the deep leather lounge chair and fastened his seat belt. "There's a nice little bedroom and bathroom back there—I ordered this jet especially for that reason."

She settled into the seat next to him, fastened herself in, then reached for his hand. "This makes first class seem like steerage."

He interlaced his fingers with hers. "Private jets do rather spoil one."

They didn't speak as the jet taxied down the runway and took off. When the plane leveled, Rochelle appeared again and escorted them to the bedroom. "Monsieur, mademoiselle, please ring for me when you are ready for breakfast."

After the door closed, Rainey studied the queen-sized bed, which had a lace-trimmed satin comforter and mounds of pillows, vases of roses secured in wall brackets, and plush scarlet carpeting. "It's a flying bordello."

He grinned. "But a very high-class one."

She smothered a yawn. "I wasn't kidding about needing to sleep."

"Agreed. But won't it be nice to sleep together?" He nodded to the door behind them. "There should be a nightgown waiting. You wash up first and go to bed."

"I'll be asleep by the time you join me."

"Not to worry. Sixty seconds later I'll be sleeping as well." He turned off all of the lamps except for a dim night-light, suddenly so tired that he ached.

Rainey emerged from the bathroom in the cream-colored silk negligee he'd bought for her. With her fine features and tumbling apricot hair, she was a sight to raise dead men from their tombs. Yawning again, she slid into the bed. "I can't believe you coordinated the nightgown with the bedding."

"Anything worth doing is worth doing well." Removing his gaze from her with difficulty, he went into the bathroom and stripped off his clothing, not bothering with pajamas since he didn't own a pair.

As promised, her breathing was slow and regular when he climbed into the bed beside her, but she turned toward him drowsily. Soft and female, hair scented with rosemary, she fit into his arms as if they were two halves of one whole. He gave a deep sigh of release as layers of stress slowly fell away and . . . Rainey . . .

He awoke hours later when she rolled onto her back and stretched like a cat. The comforter slid down to her waist, revealing the flex of her lithe body under the negligee. "I feel remarkably rested. How long since we left London?"

He glanced at the wall clock. "About five hours."

She propped her head up and regarded him thoughtfully. "How awake are you feeling?"

"Quite." He didn't move.

Their gazes locked. "Strange," she whispered. "I've been looking forward to this for months. I've had crazed, lustful dreams of ravishing you or vice versa. Now that we're finally together—I feel shy."

"So do I." He hesitated. "I want everything to be perfect, and that's impossible."

"Lovemaking doesn't have to be perfect. It just has to be real." She leaned forward until their lips touched, soft and sweet.

The passion he'd been banking for so long flared into life. They'd learned much about each other's bodies while filming. He knew the texture of her silky skin, the curve of her shoulder, her individual scent, provocatively female.

Yet all that was mere prelude to joining physically and emotionally. They explored each other's bodies with increasing intimacy, learning rhythms and signals with startling swiftness, building desire into searing mutual fulfillment.

Until, in the end, it was perfect *and* real.

Afterward they lay in each other's arms for a long time, not needing to speak. His mind drifted, refusing to think of past or future, wishing he could stay in the present forever. "This was worth waiting for."

"Yes—but I'm glad we didn't wait any longer. I might have succumbed to spontaneous human combustion." She nuzzled his throat. "There's something powerfully erotic about being surrounded by jet vibrations."

"Vibrations, vibrators. Surely there's a connection."

"What a wicked thought. I'm sure you're right." She trailed her hand over his torso. "I'm glad you don't shave your chest like some actors do."

He cupped her breast. "And I'm glad these are soft and real, not improbable silicone."

"I considered implants, but finally decided that if I couldn't get work on my acting ability, the silicone wouldn't make much difference."

"Anyone can augment a body, but few people can match your talent."

"You certainly know the best kind of compliment." She grinned. "Isn't there a saying that a man should compliment beautiful women on their brains, and brainy women on their physical attractiveness?"

"Since you have both, does that mean I can't compliment you at all?"

"A true master of flattery." She rolled onto him so that her legs bracketed his and her silky hair brushed his chest. "I like the idea of a week in bed."

"So do I." He stroked his hands down her back. She was beautifully fit, her muscles taut under creamy skin. "Actually, I've got two and a half weeks before I have to leave for Argentina for my next job."

"Damn." She gnawed her lower lip enchantingly. "I'm due in New York in two weeks, and I have to spend at least a few days vertical and doing business before I leave."

He felt a stab of disappointment. He'd hoped she would come to Argentina with him, because already he hated the fact that they would have to separate. He kissed her navel. "We'll just have to make the best of the time we have."

And they did.

Kenzie found that he'd pulled off the road, face sweating and pulse accelerated. Damnation, ever since Rainey filed for divorce, he'd tried not to think of those first glorious days, all pleasure and no pain.

Because remembering was all pain and no pleasure.

❧ 9 ☙

*Since they were shooting in remote areas, trans-*portation for cast and crew was done with rugged four-wheel-drive vehicles rather than the plush cars used on most productions. Rainey didn't care—to a tired woman, the backseat of an

SUV was plenty good enough for sprawling out and gathering strength.

The first requirement for a director was high energy, because the work was never done. After dinner each evening she watched the dailies that had been shot the day before, flown to Los Angeles for processing, then returned to New Mexico for viewing. Watching dailies took intense concentration as she made notes on the scenes and takes that worked best. Her editor back in L. A., Eva Yañez, would rough out a preliminary cut as they went along, which would save time and money in postproduction.

Before bedtime, she studied the next day's shooting schedule to decide if she wanted to go with the angles and shots she'd planned, or if her thinking had changed. It was essential to show up on the set completely prepared, because an indecisive director wasted time and undermined the confidence of cast and crew.

Her cell phone rang. She groaned. Not opening her eyes, she flipped the phone open. "Yes?"

It was Marcus Gordon. "How are things going, Raine?"

"Pretty well." Most of the calls she received increased her stress level, but talking to Marcus usually relaxed her. Now his imperturbable good sense soothed the disturbance in her psyche produced by Kenzie. "We're on schedule, and the film we're getting is first-rate. Greg Marino is doing a great job as director of cinematography. He's getting exactly the look I want—beautiful but desolate. A long, long way from Randall's idea of civilization."

"You must be doing something right, since the biggest part of your job is inspiring the rest of the crew to do their best work. How about Sharif?"

"Amazing. He has so much charisma that he'd blow anyone less than Kenzie off the screen."

"That good? I can't wait to see this movie. Speaking of which, I'm flying in tomorrow night for a couple of days."

Her eyes snapped open. "Is that necessary? An executive

producer usually has better things to do than hang around a set."

"One of the conditions for getting the money was that I keep close tabs on what you're doing. Investors are a skittish lot, especially with a first-time director."

Especially with a first-time female director, though Marcus was too polite to say that. "I look forward to seeing you. Is Naomi coming?"

"Not this time, but she hopes to visit during the English location shooting."

Rainey finished the call, glad Val would be arriving in a few hours. It had taken several days for her to arrange a leave of absence, and Rainey's temporary assistant had a lot to learn. Val did also, but Rainey had infinite faith in her friend's organizational skills, and her ability to master a job quickly.

The phone ran again. "Hello?" This time it was Virginia Marlowe.

Rainey sat up guiltily. She and her grandmother had talked after Darrell Jackson examined her grandfather's medical files and decided that he might be able to repair the aneurysm, but Rainey had been so busy she'd forgotten that this was the day of the surgery. "Hello, Gram. How did the operation go?"

"Very well. They say your grandfather's prognosis is excellent."

Rainey was surprised at the amount of relief she felt. "That's wonderful news."

Virginia cleared her throat. "Our family doctor told me that Dr. Jackson managed a miracle. Thank you, Rainey. If not for you . . . "

She blinked, unable to remember another occasion when her grandmother had used her nickname. "The credit goes to Darrell and his willingness to attempt such a risky procedure. I'm just glad I happened to know him."

"He told me how you met, and how much time you spent with his mother before she died. You . . . you have a generous spirit, Rainey. Like Clementine."

The few times in the past that Rainey had been compared to her mother, the intent had not been flattering. "I owe you whatever help you might need. After all, you two raised me, and taught me a lot of things worth knowing, like the value of hard work and honesty." She hesitated. "People in my business are wildly overpaid. If you want a larger house, or a different car, or a cruise around the world, I'd love to give it to you."

"We don't need your money," Virginia said with her usual tartness. Her voice turned uncertain. "But maybe when you're through with this movie of yours, if you have time to stop in Baltimore for a visit, we . . . William and I would both like to see you."

Rainey swallowed hard. "I'll be there. It will be a couple of months or so, but I'd love to come under less stressful circumstances than the last trip."

She ended the call as her driver pulled up in front of the hotel. It was far too late for her to develop a daughterly relationship with her grandparents. But maybe they could become friends.

When his emotions were under control again, Kenzie resumed driving. His map showed that eventually this small dirt road would connect with a larger one leading back to the hotel. Not that he was in any hurry to return.

He swung around a curve, and slammed on his brakes as a screaming horse reared up in front of him. The vehicle slewed sideways and shuddered to a halt as the horse's rider crashed to the ground in the middle of the road. Swearing, Kenzie leaped from the SUV, hoping to God he hadn't hit the fellow.

The man lying motionless on the road had silver hair and a face weathered by decades in the open air. For a horrible moment Kenzie feared he was dead. Then the old man coughed and his eyes flickered open.

Kenzie knelt and looked for signs of injury. "Are you hurt?"

"Don't . . . don't think so." The rider pushed himself cautiously to a sitting position, waving off Kenzie's attempt to make him lie still. "Not the first time a horse tossed me, and if I'm lucky it won't be the last."

"I'm sorry. I should have been driving more carefully." Kenzie stood and helped the man up, then retrieved his fallen hat.

"My fault. Only a fool rides in the middle of a road with his mind wanderin'." Carefully he settled the battered hat on his head. "You aren't from around here."

"I'm British originally. These days, my official home is in California." Kenzie scanned the countryside. "Your horse seems to have vanished. Can I give you a lift?"

"Wouldn't mind if you did. My horse will get home before I do, but it's a long walk for an old man. My name's Grady." He offered his hand.

"Mine is Scott."

"Pleased to meet you, Mr. Scott." Grady might be an old man, but he had a powerful grip. And, pleasantly, he didn't seem to recognize Kenzie.

They climbed into the SUV and Kenzie set off, following his passenger's directions. A couple of miles along, Grady directed him to turn left onto a primitive road that led under a sturdy archway built of weathered timber. Across the top, the name CÍBOLA had been shaped from wooden letters. Kenzie searched his memory as he drove through the arch. "Didn't the Spaniards explore this area searching for the legendary Seven Cities of Cíbola?"

"Yep, that's the tale. The Cities of Gold. The conquistadors hoped to find the kind of wealth they'd looted from the Aztecs. They never found what they were lookin' for, but I did. That's why I named my place Cíbola. Forty-seven years we've lived here."

Kenzie crested a small hill, then halted to admire the valley below. Carpeted with grass and wildflowers, it lay serene and lovely as a Chinese landscape painting. On the opposite side of the valley, a sprawling adobe house nestled into a hillside among a scattering of outbuildings. Away to the left, light glinted from the surface of what looked like a small lake. Above, jagged mountains loomed against a sky of breathtaking blue. "What incredible beauty. Do you own this whole valley?"

"Yep. Not the best spot for ranchin', but there's not a prettier place on God's green earth." Grady sighed. "We're going to have to sell up soon."

Guessing the other man wouldn't have mentioned the subject if he hadn't felt the need to talk, Kenzie asked, "Why do you have to leave?"

"Too much work, not enough money. Had to take out a mortgage when my wife was ill a few years back. When we sell and pay that off, there should be enough left to buy a little place down in Chama. It'll be a lot easier life." He frowned at Kenzie. "Don't know why I'm tellin' you all this."

"Some subjects are easier to tell a stranger than a friend."

"True, and you're a deep listener."

"Listening is a large part of my job." A good actor had to be a good observer. Even as Kenzie sympathized with the old rancher's plight, he was taking mental notes of what dignified despair looked like.

He put the vehicle in gear and slowly crossed the valley on the rutted drive. As they pulled up in front of the adobe house, a pleasantly round woman with snowy hair and tanned skin came out to greet them, accompanied by a dog with some border collie in its family tree. "Glad to see you back, Jim. Figured it was a bad sign when Diablo showed up alone." She couldn't quite conceal the relief in her voice.

Grady climbed stiffly from the SUV. "Luckily, Mr. Scott was there when Diablo and I parted company. Mr. Scott, my wife, Alma, and my dog, Hambone."

As Hambone trotted forward, tongue lolling, Alma studied Kenzie, her eyes narrowed. He probably looked familiar, but she couldn't quite place him. "Thanks for bringing my wanderer home, Mr. Scott."

"That was the least I could do when it was my vehicle that startled Diablo." Her face suggested Indian and Hispanic blood. Like the house, she belonged in this place. His gaze moved across the adobe and its surroundings. "Your home is very lovely, Mrs. Grady. It could be on the cover of a book about New Mexico."

She smiled. "Spoken like a tourist. The house may be picturesque, but to me it's a run-down old place that needs one repair after another. I'd trade it for a nice new double-wide trailer with good plumbing and heating and not much to clean."

Wondering if she was saying that to prepare herself to leave her longtime home, he said, "Please don't shatter my illusions. Like all tourists, I like to think that now and then I find something authentic."

"Oh, Cíbola is authentic enough. Not convenient, but authentic." She hesitated, then asked shyly, "Would you join us for supper? The food's simple, but . . . authentic."

"I'd be delighted." He liked the Gradys, and dining here would keep him away from the hotel—and the shadow of Rainey's presence—a while longer.

Grady ruffled Hambone's ears. "How about I show you around while Alma finishes cookin'?"

It was another offer Kenzie had no desire to refuse. Just as people interested him, so did their settings, and the Gradys fit this ranch the way well-worn tools fit a hand.

Hambone at their heels, they visited the stables, where Diablo was placidly eating dinner. A small gelding was the only other occupant of the dozen stalls. Grady produced a sugar cube for the gelding. "When the kids were growin' up we had half a dozen horses. I hope we'll be able to take these two along when we move. Like us, they're too old to learn new tricks."

As they moved among the outbuildings, Kenzie spotted a small satellite dish. Grady said, "The kids chipped in to buy us that for our forty-fifth anniversary. Authentic means satellite dishes and four-wheel drive, not livin' in a museum."

"I should think a museum would be boring." Cíbola wasn't—it was a living entity, well-cared for despite signs that money was in short supply. The adobe buildings looked as if they'd grown from the soil and had the spare, pure elegance of function and simplicity. Kenzie studied everything, an idea tickling the back of his mind.

The small, postcard-perfect lake wasn't visible from the house, but it was only a five-minute walk away. When they reached it, Grady said, "Alma wasn't kiddin' about the double-wide trailer. When we find a buyer, I might ask if he'd sell us a lot so we can put a little place here on the lake. More private than Chama. Shouldn't think a new owner would want the old ones around, though."

"None of your children want to take over the ranch?"

"Not a rancher in the lot, but we're proud of 'em." Grady gave a fleeting smile. "A teacher, an air force pilot, and a nurse. Do you have children?"

"No." Kenzie softened the edge in his voice. "No children, and once the courts finish their business, no wife."

Grady gave a sympathetic nod. "There's all kinds of hard luck."

When they returned to the house, Grady sent his guest inside while he took care of some chores. Kenzie saw when he entered Alma's kitchen that she hadn't exaggerated about the work that was needed. Though immaculately clean, the appliances were old and rickety, the sink marred by permanent stains, and the cabinets cheap and inadequate.

Yet that hardly mattered, for the kitchen had the warmth of a mother's smile. The irregular beams in the ceiling had been shaped by hand, and the quarry tile floor was softened by Indian rugs whose colors were muted with age and honest wear. He held his hands to the rounded adobe oven built in a corner, feeling the warmth of whatever was baking inside. "I've been in Southwestern-style houses in California, but they're only pale imitations of this. Would it be too forward of me to ask for a tour?"

"I'd be happy to show you around." When he smiled, she

added, "Better watch that smile, Mr. Scott. Anyone ever say you're too handsome for your own good?"

"Frequently," he said with great dryness.

Chuckling, she showed him through the adobe. High ceilings and spacious rooms that had been designed to keep the house cool in summer gave the structure an airy feel. He liked the serenity of the white stucco walls and mellow pine floors, and the warm promise of the massive living room fireplace. The windows in the room looked across the valley and showed the sun sliding behind stark mountain peaks. He paused to admire the blazing colors. "Does it snow much here?"

"Some, but usually we don't get a lot. We're at the perfect elevation—high enough not to scorch in summer, low enough not to be buried with snow in winter."

The bathroom was as primitive as the kitchen, but like the bedrooms, it was generously sized. The smallest of the four bedrooms had been converted to a computer room. "E-mail sure is handy for keeping in touch with the kids and grandkids," Alma said. "When we first came here, Cíbola seemed like the end of the world, but not now."

"How do you feel about moving?"

Instead of telling him to mind his own business, she shrugged. "This house is too big now the kids are gone, but I'd be lying if I didn't say it'll be hard to leave. No use complaining about what can't be helped, though." Briskly she turned back to the kitchen. "This is my favorite part of the house."

She opened a back door and stepped into a small garden surrounded by high adobe walls. Stone paths wound between vibrant flowers and shrubs, while in one corner vines were trained over an arbor to shade a table and chairs.

Kenzie caught his breath. "A secret garden."

"Like the movie? I watched it with my grandkids, but this garden is walled to keep the wild pigs from eating my herbs and flowers."

"You've made the practical into a thing of beauty." He touched the ripening sphere of a tomato. A tabby cat poked her head out from under a shrubby rosemary bush, surveyed Kenzie thoughtfully, then began washing one of several plump, furry kittens. Above the walls, craggy mountains floated majestically. What would it be like to live amidst such peace?

Dinner was classic Southwestern fare, with corn tortillas, beans, rice, and salad. It was also sensational, though if the peppers had been any hotter, Kenzie would have been in trouble. After washing down the last bite with coffee, he asked, "Is New Mexican cuisine different from other regions, or is this so good because of the cook?"

"Both." Grady smiled fondly at his wife. "New Mexican food is better than Texas or Arizona to begin with, and nobody makes it better than Alma."

Placidly she topped off everyone's coffee. "He learned early that the best way to eat well was to flatter me shamelessly."

Kenzie laughed, feeling as if the Gradys were old friends. He hoped their children appreciated how lucky they had been to be raised in this place, by these people. "You're serious about selling?"

"Dead serious," Grady replied, his light mood vanishing. "I'm calling a real estate agent this week."

Kenzie hesitated for an instant, checking to see if he was really sure about this. He was. "I want to buy Cíbola."

Absolute silence. The Gradys stared at him.

"Since I travel a great deal, I don't know how much time I'll be able to spend here," he continued. "So I'd like to work out an agreement with you. In return for my building you a house on the lake, will you stay on and watch over the place?"

Alma clunked her coffee cup onto the table. "Are you *serious*?"

"Completely."

Alma's eyes widened with shock. "You're Kenzie Scott, the actor! I knew you looked familiar, but it never occurred to me a big Hollywood star could just wander in!"

"I'm shooting a movie about twenty miles away." He looked down at the beautifully woven old Indian rug, knowing he must reveal something of his private self in return for their honesty. "I have a home I love on the Pacific, but in Southern California one is always aware there are millions of people nearby. Cíbola has the serenity of solitude. Since you're planning to sell, maybe . . . maybe it was meant for us to meet."

"Do you have half a dozen homes all over the world?" Alma asked.

"Not half a dozen. Just the California house, which I'd keep because of the amount of time I have to spend in Los Angeles, plus an apartment in New York."

Overcoming his initial shock, Grady said, "The place on the lake—would you put us out if you decided you wanted a new caretaker?"

Kenzie thought a moment. "You would own the house and the land it's on, but we'd need an agreement that I'd have the right of first refusal, at a fair market price, if you ever decided to sell. I wouldn't want strangers there."

Eyes sparkling, Alma said, "So I get my double-wide trailer!"

"Actually, I was thinking of one of those prefabricated redwood homes with a nice deck." Kenzie smiled. "Since I'll be looking at it, I want the place to be attractive."

Alma and her husband looked at each other, and she gave a faint nod. Grady offered his hand to Kenzie. "If you're not a raving lunatic, you've got yourself a deal."

After two hours of working out details, Kenzie headed back to the hotel. In the morning he'd call his business manager and put the legal wheels in motion, but that handshake was the real contract.

Money could make things happen very quickly, and he wanted to be able to come here to reknit his raveled nerves when he finished shooting *The Centurion*. A prefab house wouldn't be quite as easy as a double-wide trailer, but it would still be fast, and the Gradys could choose a house that appealed to them. Alma had happily agreed to do light housekeeping and some cooking when he was in residence; he suspected she missed having a house full of children to care for.

Buying a ranch on impulse might seem eccentric, but he had no doubts at all. He looked forward to retreating to this place of tranquillity whenever he wanted—and it would have no memories of Rainey.

❧ 10 ❧

*As nightfall obscured the spectacular New Mexi-*can scenery, Val's eyes drifted shut. She hadn't gotten much sleep since agreeing to work on *The Centurion.*

She'd been on the verge of backing out daily, but kept returning to the fact that she needed a change. And maybe Rainey really needed her as well. In the meantime, if being picked up by a Lincoln town car in Albuquerque and carried to the door of her destination was typical of the movie business, Val could get used to it.

The movie was headquartered in a sprawling, lodge-style resort hotel in the middle of nowhere. A very upscale lodge, she saw when she checked in. Yes, she could get used to this.

The bellman was whisking her luggage away when Kenzie Scott walked in the front door and headed toward the front desk. Val struggled with an impulse to go over and deck him. Not that she'd be successful, unless maybe she stood on a chair for a better shot. Unlike many stars, Kenzie Scott was tall and strongly built, not pumped up like a bodybuilder, but with the overall fitness of a decathlete.

He was also surreally handsome, with perfect, ruggedly masculine features. Though she'd met him once when visiting Rainey, she'd forgotten the impact of his looks, which had to be seen to be believed.

But he'd made Rainey miserable, which deserved a decking

in Val's book. Though as a lawyer she knew that every dispute had at least two sides, probably more, she turned off objectivity when her friends were involved. Especially when the friend in question was Rainey, who'd bailed Val out more than once.

Since Kenzie was the Big Star of this picture, Val would have to be polite to him, but she'd save that for the next day, when she'd had a good night's rest. Quietly she carried her hand luggage to the elevator so she'd be gone by the time he finished his business at the front desk.

The elevator doors had almost closed when they suddenly snapped open and Kenzie Scott stepped in. Val withdrew to a corner as he glanced at the control panel. There were only four floors and apparently they were both going to the fourth. His gaze touched her absently. Then, dammit, he said, "You're Rainey's friend Val, aren't you?"

She nodded. "I just got in." Irritated by his lighthearted expression, she added, "I suppose you've been out tomcatting around." The sound of her words appalled her. She hadn't even started work, and she'd just gotten herself fired by breaking the first rule of moviemaking, which was that The Star was never, never to be annoyed.

Kenzie looked startled instead of angry. "Actually, no. I did see a cat, but even though it was female, I had no designs on its virtue."

Flushing, Val said, "I'm sorry. I had no business saying any such thing."

"Probably not, but you're Rainey's friend. It would be odd if you weren't partisan." The elevator glided to a stop. He stepped back politely so she could exit first.

Wishing she could sink through the floor, Val stepped out, then had to pause to figure out which direction her room was. Behind her, Kenzie said, "Do you need help with your bag? It appears to have a rock collection inside."

Why did he have to have that wonderful British voice? She pivoted and started down the left-hand corridor. "I'm fine, thanks. I'm used to hauling heavy loads around."

"And wouldn't accept my help if I were offering free water in Death Valley." He fell into step beside her.

She smiled reluctantly. "Probably not. I'm famously stubborn. But I'll do my best to be polite." Reaching her room, she slid the card key into the slot. "Good night, Mr. Scott."

"Kenzie." He smiled. "I always envied Rainey her friends. Good night, Val."

Wishing she hadn't seen that smile, she darted into her room as he continued down the corridor. His charm could melt asphalt shingles off a roof. And those green eyes! No wonder Rainey had married him against her better judgment. Of course that easy charm, lavishly spread around, had been the problem, but it was hard to dislike him in the flesh as much as Val did in the abstract. Which was just as well, since they'd be working together.

Flopping on the bed, she lifted the phone and asked the switchboard to connect her to Rainey's room. She half expected not to be put through, but Rainey picked up immediately. "Hi, Rainey. I'm here." Val covered a yawn. "Do I start work immediately, or do I get a good night's sleep first?"

"You made it! Come up to my room for a hot fudge sundae." Rainey chuckled. "I'll fill you in and even give you an official red *Centurion* show jacket, which won't go with your hair any better than mine, so I guess you start work tonight."

Val's doubts about the wisdom of this job evaporated. She might be in for a wild ride, but she wouldn't be bored.

Kenzie smiled to himself as he entered his suite. Val Covington was a small but not-to-be-underestimated wildcat. He wondered how much Rainey had told her friend about their marriage. Probably not a lot—Rainey was almost as reticent about personal matters as Kenzie—but enough that Val seemed to be ready to scratch his eyes out.

Saying he envied Rainey her friends had been the honest truth. Women were so much better at sharing their feelings and supporting each other than men. That was something he'd never been able to do, and not only because he was male and British. Despite all Trevor had done for him, they'd never had a confiding relationship. Even with Charles Winfield, there had been subjects untouched. A good thing he had acting as an outlet for past angst.

Though he almost never drank alone, he found some wine in the suite minibar and poured a glass, then went onto his balcony without turning on the light. The moon had risen, silvering the landscape. He tried to guess where Cíbola was among those folded mountains and valleys.

The exhilaration he'd felt at buying the ranch was fading now that he was back in the hotel, overshadowed by the fact that Rainey was within a couple of hundred yards of him, and untouchable.

He sank into a chair and sipped at his wine. Offering for Cíbola had been the most powerful impulse he'd had since his proposal to Rainey. He hoped to God that Cíbola worked out better.

Instead of returning to Los Angeles after the *Pimpernel* filming ended, he'd had the private jet take them to a small airport in Northern California. There he loaded Rainey and the luggage inside a nondescript rental car that awaited them.

As they pulled onto the coast highway, she loosened her seat belt enough to lie down and pillow her head on his thigh. "It's been dark for a long, long time."

"The drawback to flying west with the night. Soon the sun should start rising behind us." Since the car was an automatic, he had a hand free to rest on her shoulder.

"Is it permitted to ask where we're going?" she asked drowsily.

"An inn on the coast where I stayed a couple of years ago. Very peaceful and private."

"You can certify it as an ideal love nest?"

Feeling tension in her shoulder, he explained, "I stayed

there alone to get away from the world for a few days. I remember thinking it would be a wonderfully romantic place if I knew someone I liked well enough to take there."

Relaxed again, she curled a hand over his knee. A good thing they'd had such a passionate flight, or her touch might start to interfere with his driving.

"I'm almost afraid to go to bed properly and wake up later," she said quietly. "Fear of the Gilda phenomenon."

"You mean when Rita Hayworth said that men went to bed with the glamorous, fictional Gilda, but woke up with the real Rita instead?"

"Exactly."

"Since we both have to deal with that, I expect the effects to cancel out." He stroked along her side, unable to get enough of touching her. "I'm not worried. We've had months of working together to get beyond the images."

"Actually, to me you seem much like your public image. Intelligent. Enigmatic." She hesitated. "A little tragic."

The trouble with actors is that they observed too closely. "Enigmatic—the quality of keeping silent and making people wonder if one is stupid rather than opening one's mouth and removing all doubt."

She laughed. "What's your real history, Kenzie? You've told so many wild tales that I figure the truth is something really boring, like your father was a solicitor, you went to a good but unexceptional school, and have absolutely nothing colorful to talk about."

A chill entered the warm sanctuary of the car. "Don't ask me about my past again, Rainey. I don't want to have to lie to you."

She was silent for the space of several heartbeats. "Very well."

He'd liked her acceptance. Most women were like curious cats, determined to tease information out of him, but Rainey never raised the subject again.

The inn had a guest cottage isolated from the main building, and they stayed there for a glorious, absurdly romantic holiday. Long walks on the beach in sun, fog, and rain, sometimes all in the same walk. Drives through the mountains. Lazy evenings in front of a fireplace or in a hot tub. Watching videos of bad movies and becoming helpless with laughter as they made wicked comments about the acting and production values. Making love, sleeping in each other's arms, then waking to make love again. He'd never been so happy in his life, and Rainey glowed, more relaxed than he'd ever seen her.

Seven days flowed past swift as a heartbeat. Five more days until they must leave. Four. Three. His gut knotted at the knowledge that soon he must be in Argentina while Rainey flew east to New York. It would be weeks, perhaps even months before they could get together again, and who knew what might intervene?

Two days before departing, he reluctantly called his manager. "Kenzie! Dammit, where are you?" Seth roared. "Every reporter in America is trying to find you."

"Which is why I haven't told anyone where I am. Why are the reporters slavering? I haven't broken any laws that I know of."

"Because Raine Marlowe also dropped off the face of the earth, and was last seen with you playing Tarzan to her Jane."

"Ah. I should have guessed. Is there any critical business I should know about?"

"Just the usual minor crises—nothing to worry about. You haven't told me where you are, or if Raine is with you."

"I'm in the Pacific time zone, and the other matter is really no one's business."

"So you're together. Hope you're having fun. But you will be in Argentina next week, won't you?"

"When have I ever broken a contract?"

"As long as this time isn't the first," Seth said, mollified. "In your spare time, you might draft a press release about your relationship with Ms. Marlowe. As soon as you show your face in public, you'll have to say something."

"You do it. Tell the world we are merely great and good friends." As Seth snorted, Kenzie ended the call.

Rainey asked, "A media feeding frenzy?"

"If Seth is to be believed."

She reached for the phone. "I think I'll start with Emmy rather than my agent."

The call to her assistant confirmed what Seth had said. Fevered speculations about their relationship were front-page news. The world was starting to close in on them, as threatening as wolves circling just beyond the firelight.

The night before leaving the inn to drive down the coast, they made love with special intensity. Useless with words when it mattered most, he tried to show with passion and tenderness what she meant to him. Tried to brand her with a rapture so intense that no other man would ever satisfy her so well. In return, without saying a single word, she slid past his defenses, melding so deeply into his spirit that he feared he would wither away when she left.

He lay on his side while she rested on her back, the elegant curves of her body gilded by firelight. "You look like a perfectly composed camera shot of the most beautiful, erotic woman in the world."

Though she smiled, it didn't dispel the sadness in her eyes. "I don't want to go back to the real world."

"I don't either. But all idylls end."

"So true." Her gaze moved to the fire and she began to sing "Heart Over Heels," the signature song of Clementine, one of rock music's great, tragic superstars. He'd been only a boy when he first heard it, but the plangent emotion had struck him to the heart. Singing sweet and true, Rainey's voice hit with the same force as when he'd first heard the song.

*"Thought this battered heart of mine would never mend.
Yet here I am, heart over heels again.*

Heart over heels, moth to the flame.
Maybe this time, Lord, maybe this time . . ."

In the faint light he saw tears glimmering on Rainey's cheeks. He kissed them away. "I didn't know you could sing. You sound very like Clementine."

Gaze still on the fire, she said, "I should. She was my mother."

"Your mother? Good God, I had no idea. Wasn't her last name Bartlett?"

"She was married briefly at twenty, and she kept her husband's name. It's not exactly a secret that she's my mother, but I haven't made a point of telling people, either. Since I'm an actress, not a singer, I thought being her daughter wouldn't do me any good professionally, just turn me into a curiosity. There probably aren't more than a dozen or so people in California who know about our connection."

"Wise to be quiet about it. Not only would there be eyes watching to see if you'd crash and burn, but you'd have been pestered by people wanting money."

"Because they'd assume I inherited Clementine's estate, like you just did?"

"You weren't her heir?"

"She never updated her will after I was born, and almost everything went to good causes. Save the whales. Battered women. Animal rescue. My grandparents disliked what she did so much that they refused to contest the will on my behalf." Rainey smiled. "I'm glad, actually. Clementine did set up a small trust fund when I was born, and the income from that helped me support myself when I first moved to Los Angeles. I think if I'd inherited her whole estate, it would have been a straitjacket."

He envied her casual dismissal of a fortune. For him, money was his shield and fortress, protecting him from the world. "You inherited her voice, which is quite a legacy. You could be a singer if you wanted."

"Not really. Clementine's voice was much bigger, and she was a real musician who sang from her soul. I'm not on that level."

He compared her delicate features with what he remembered of Clementine, who had been a robust, earthily sensual woman. "It's not obvious, but now that you've told me, I can see some resemblance to your mother. You must look more like your father, though."

Hearing the unspoken question, she said flatly, "Haven't the foggiest idea who he was. Maybe Clementine didn't, either. She had a very . . . liberated lifestyle."

"And it cost her her life. Such a great, great waste."

"Indeed." She gave a humorless smile. "I was the one who found her body after her drug overdose."

"Dear God, Rainey." He pulled her close, aching to dispel the terrible pain expressed in her taut body. No child should have to endure what she did. Yet she had survived, and successfully engaged with life on her own terms.

Now he understood the mysterious resonance between them. Coming from different countries, different social levels, unimaginably different upbringings, nonetheless they had much in common. No wonder she affected him as no other woman had. Maybe . . . perhaps with Rainey . . .

Swiftly, before he could remember all the reasons this was insane, he said, "Marry me, Rainey. We can drive to Nevada tomorrow and be married by dinnertime."

She pulled away and stared at him. "Marriage? Why, because you pity me?"

"No. Because becoming husband and wife says we want to be together whenever we can. Isn't that true?"

"I . . . I thought we were just having a fling. Fun, no complications, and go on our merry ways."

"Is that what you think the last week has been about?"

She bit her lip. "No, but I'm not the marrying kind, and neither are you. Our careers are too demanding to have time for family life. What kind of marriage starts with the spouses halfway around the world from each other?"

"One where they both intend to get together again as soon as possible." He kissed her breast, feeling the nipple tighten against his tongue. "Maybe it won't work, but isn't risking failure better than not trying at all?"

A week of sensual abandon had taught him exactly what she liked best. How to touch, how to kiss, how to build desire until she cried out uncontrollably.

Until she whispered, voice breaking, "If it's what you truly want—yes, Kenzie, I'll marry you."

It took ten minutes to get a marriage license—thirty-five dollars, cash only—at the Washoe County Courthouse in Reno, Nevada. The process would have been quicker if the clerk hadn't recognized them. "Oh, my God, it's Raine and Kenzie!" she gasped as her gaze went from the application to their faces.

Kenzie repressed a sigh. Celebrity meant having everyone call you by your first name. "Indeed. Is there a wedding chapel you would recommend where we might be able to married without waiting?"

"Celebrate Chapel is real nice and only a couple of miles away. I'll call and see if they could fit you in," the clerk offered.

The chapel was not only available, but could provide rings and flowers, and it turned out to be in a pretty Victorian-style house. Under the excited gazes of the husband-and-wife proprietors, Rainey chose a beautiful bouquet of white roses and silver ribbons. She was almost as white as the flowers, but her eyes glowed.

After they selected plain gold wedding bands from a range of sizes, it was time. Kenzie's memories of the actual service were sketchy, apart from the fact that he had a death grip on Rainey's hand, fearing she'd change her mind. This was the most foolhardy thing he'd ever done. He'd never wanted anything more.

Voice resonant, the minister intoned, *"I now pronounce you man and wife."*

In the flowing green dress she'd worn at the London wrap party, Rainey was the most beautiful bride Kenzie had ever seen, but she was trembling when he kissed her. He enfolded her in his arms, stroking her amber hair until the shaking stopped. "We'll make this work, Rainey," he whispered. "We can, and we will."

Smiling tremulously, she took his hand, and they walked outside into a seething crowd of reporters and onlookers. Kenzie swore to himself. Either the courthouse clerk or the chapel owners must have called every TV and radio station and newspaper in the Reno area, then every one of their friends and neighbors.

Microphones stabbed toward them like spears and questions pounded in from all directions. The loudest voice bellowed, "How did you get Kenzie Scott to marry you, Raine?" The tone made it clear that he was a prize, and she was a nobody.

Swearing to himself, Kenzie wrapped an arm around her shoulders, walking them both toward the car. "That's the wrong question. The correct one is how did I manage to convince the loveliest, most intelligent woman in the Northern Hemisphere to be my bride? And I think the answer is that I was very, very lucky."

Rainey gasped when a particularly aggressive reporter shoved her aside, crushing the bouquet against her chest as he jammed the microphone in Kenzie's face. "Where have you two been hiding for the last week?"

Seeing no reason to reward rudeness, Kenzie ignored the man and answered a question from a woman with better manners. The crowd was coagulating in front of them, and Rainey halted, unsure how to proceed. More experienced with press mobs, Kenzie cleared a path with his free arm, surreptitiously crunching down on the foot of the rude reporter. "Keep moving," he murmured in Rainey's ear. "If we stop, they have us."

She nodded and managed to answer the next question, an innocuous one about making *The Scarlet Pimpernel* together. As they neared the car, a cloud of soap bubbles drifted toward them, blown by a group of giggling teenage girls. Surrounded by fragile, popping bubbles, Kenzie used the keyless remote to open the passenger door. He bundled Rainey inside and locked the door instantly so no one could open it again.

He'd have liked to drive over the whole damned lot of them, but experience had taught him that a measure of cooperation worked much better. Before getting into the car, he said in his best stage-trained voice, the one that could carry to the cheapest seats in the back of a theater, "Ladies, gentlemen. This is a very special day for Raine and me. I hope we have your best wishes."

That disarmed the reporters enough that they allowed Kenzie to slowly maneuver the car away. He turned at the first corner into a residential area, weaving among the streets until he was sure they weren't being followed.

When they were safely away, he glanced at his bride. Rainey was staring down at her crushed bouquet, her face pale. "What have we done, Kenzie?" she asked in a low voice. *"What have we done?"*

"The right thing, I hope." He captured her tense left hand and carried it to his heart. "Thank you for marrying me, Rainey. Wife."

She gave him a fragile smile. "Will it always be that bad?"

"No. We're a new item, and far more interesting as a couple than either of us were individually. Soon we'll be old news."

"I hope you're right." They had survived the first assault on their marriage. But they never quite recaptured the uncomplicated joy of that week on the California coast.

The New Mexico night was turning cold. Wearily Kenzie rose from the balcony chair and went back inside. It would have been better by far if he and Rainey had never married. For himself, he couldn't be sorry, despite the agony of losing her. Better this pain than emptiness.

It was subjecting her to equal pain that was unforgivable.

❧ 11 ❧

*Naturally, the day Marcus Gordon arrived every-*thing went wrong. The truck carrying the cameras broke down on the rutted road leading to the morning's location, delaying shooting so much that they lost the light for the scheduled scene and had to postpone it.

Rainey then called for a scene planned for two days later—and found that Sharif didn't know his lines yet. Sweating and swearing it would never happen again, he asked for an hour and disappeared into a trailer to memorize his part. More delays.

A complex sequence that she'd painstakingly storyboarded in advance turned out not to work well in practice. She went into a huddle with her director of photography, assistant director, and production designer, and they devised a new sequence that worked beautifully. But by the time that was done, it was too late to shoot Sharif's scene.

Marcus had been quietly observing in the background, making use of the slack periods by working on papers he'd brought in a voluminous briefcase. As they shared a car back to the hotel, Rainey observed, "I think you brought us bad luck, Marcus."

"It's the same principle as bread always falls butter-side down—as soon as the producer shows up, everything falls apart. Don't worry, you're only a half day behind, and you should be able to make that up easily enough. Considering the number of action scenes you've shot, you're doing amazingly well." He glanced at the papers on his lap. "You're staying on budget, too, which proves you've got some of the qualities of an effective director. Now all you have to do is produce a great movie at the end."

Though his comment was intended as a joke, Rainey was too frazzled to be amused. A movie was a terribly fragile creation that could be wrecked in ways too numerous for counting. They'd finish up in New Mexico within the next couple of days, and if she hadn't captured the right images on film, it would be too late.

Marcus continued, "I want to talk to you and Kenzie half an hour after we get back to the hotel. Just a short meeting in the production office, mostly about some promotional ideas I'd like to kick around."

"Fine." She guessed that Marcus wanted to see how much cooperation Kenzie would provide for publicizing the movie when it was released. Having Kenzie on a few major talk shows would be invaluable. Ordinarily publicity was spelled out in a contract, but since Kenzie hated doing such things, Rainey had avoided the subject when she worked out their initial agreement. Now Marcus had to coax his star into a commitment. She'd have to do promo gigs herself if she wanted *The Centurion* to do any business, even though she hated them as much as Kenzie did.

"There's been some bad news on the financial front."

That caught Rainey's attention. "How bad?"

"Two million dollars of money that was promised has fallen through."

Her fists clenched. "That's a big chunk of my budget."

"I think I can find at least part of that amount elsewhere, but you might want to consider if you really need all the more expensive scenes, like the welcome at Victoria Station when Randall returns from his captivity. Crowds of people in a large location—that sort of thing is a nightmare to shoot, which can mean extra time, and more money."

"I have to do that! The welcome home shows how appalled and overwhelmed Randall is to find himself being greeted as a hero when he feels like a disgraced failure." She'd written that scene from memories of the suffocating panic she'd felt when she and Kenzie were mobbed in public.

Marcus frowned. "I see your point. Very well, see if there are a couple of smaller scenes that aren't essential." They rolled up in front of the hotel, and he assisted her from the car. "I'll see you in the office in half an hour."

Rainey would have loved to take a shower, or better yet, a long bath, but the day was far from over. She headed straight to the production office, a conference room on the ground floor of the hotel. Val was already there sorting through Rainey's mail. She handed over a sheaf of papers. "This report is personal business."

Scowling, Rainey dropped into a chair. By the time she finished skimming the pages, Val had made a cup of mocha latte and placed it by her hand. Rainey took a deep swallow, needing the combination of sugar, caffeine, and blessed chocolate. "You'll have noticed that this is from an investigator researching who my father might be."

"Yes, but you don't have to tell me anything about it." The espresso machine made gurgling noises as Val processed another shot of coffee. "All I saw was the first paragraph. I didn't look any further."

"Such restraint must have been painful for someone of your curiosity."

Val grinned. "Damn right it was, but the last thing you need is more stress."

"Since you've known me forever, you might as well hear what Mooney has to say. He doesn't have any definitive answers—just a list of contenders for the honor of having fathered me, rated in rough order of likelihood and with notes on which are dead and beyond DNA testing."

Val sipped a cappuccino, delicately licking a line of cream off her upper lip. "Are you that curious about your father?"

"I'm not obsessed, if that's what you mean. It's more that this is a . . . a piece of unfinished business. Maybe I'll never find out who the bastard is, and if so, fine, I've survived this long without knowing. But I figured that if I wanted to know, I'd better get cracking. The trail is already over thirty years old."

"Since your mother was famous, plenty of people must remember her."

"They certainly do. According to Mooney, he's established that Clementine's likely partners around the time I was conceived are in the range of eight to ten."

Val winced. "She lived up to her reputation as a hard-lovin' woman."

Rainey consulted the report. "If the semen contributor was a one-night stand at a club or concert, he'd be virtually impossible to trace, so Mooney sticks to potential daddies who had something resembling a relationship with her. Two were Asian and one black, so they're rated low probability, given my rather Celtic coloring."

She flipped to the next page. "There were three musicians, one of them part of her backup band, a rather mediocre bass player. She had a fling with the star of a hit cop television show of the time. I've seen it in reruns—the guy couldn't act his way out of a canary cage. There are rumors that she was involved with a studio executive, and/or a recording company honcho, but Mooney hasn't any names on that.

"The highest probability listing is for her drug supplier. They apparently consorted regularly for some months, but he met an untimely end from lead poisoning—the kind that comes in concentrated pellets that do bad things to one's anatomy. That happened when I was about six months old, and if he was my father, I can only rejoice. That's all Mooney has for now. If I want to continue, he figures he can narrow the field down to more manageable numbers."

From Val's compassionate expression, Rainey knew she was overdoing the brittle humor. She slid the report back into the FedEx envelope, wondering if she really wanted to know more. Probably not—but she did want to tie up the loose ends of her life, and this was a big one. When the investigation was over, she could file the findings away and forget the matter of her father.

Seeing the tawdry details of Clementine's life made Rainey appreciate her grandparents more. They were cold, strict, and humorless, but at least she'd never had to worry about strangers emerging from their bedroom in the morning.

Marcus and Kenzie entered the conference room together. Val made cappuccinos for both of the men, which gave Rainey time to bury the past again. The stresses of a bad day of shooting were mild compared to her early childhood memories.

Kenzie leaned against a wall, self-contained as always, but Marcus sat down and helped himself to one of the sandwiches Val had ordered. "I need to talk to both of you about blocking out time for promotional appearances."

The phone rang, and Val caught it on the first ring. After a moment of listening, she said, "It's Emmy and she says it's really important."

"Go ahead and take the call," Kenzie said. "Marcus is trying to do an end run by acting as if I've already agreed to the promotion he wants and it's merely a matter of scheduling."

"Round one to Kenzie," Marcus said. "Shall we move on to round two?"

"Is that the one where you say I owe my fans more public appearances, and I reply that overexposure destroys a star's aura of mystery?"

Marcus grinned. "Okay, we'll jump to round three."

Ignoring the banter, Rainey said, "What's up, Emmy? Are you okay?"

"I'm fine. The good news is that I think I felt the kiddo kick this morning. The bad news . . . " She took a deep breath. "I didn't call earlier because I thought maybe we could turn this around, but after a day of fighting, I think the situation is hopeless. Jane Stackpole is dropping out of the production."

"*What!*" Rainey dropped her half-eaten sandwich and

jerked upright in her chair. "She can't do that! Next week she's due to meet us in London."

"She can do it, and she has."

Rainey rubbed her pounding temples. "Why? Is she ill?"

"She got a better offer—the chance to be the love interest in a big Hollywood thriller. She almost got that role in the initial casting, and when the star decided he hated the girl who was first choice, they called Jane back."

"She practically kissed my feet when I offered her the part of Sarah," Rainey said numbly. "Swore that it was the most wonderful role she'd ever seen, and it was the opportunity of a lifetime."

"That was then, this is now. Being a bimbo pays better and offers more visibility," Emmy said cynically. "If I ever meet that ungrateful, anorexic traitor in person, I'll kill her, but in the meantime, is there someone I can call as a possible replacement?"

Rainey gloomily thought of all the actresses she'd considered and rejected. "I'll talk it over with Marcus and get back to you."

When she hung up, Marcus said, "We lost Sarah?"

"Jane Stackpole got a better offer. Can we sue her for her back teeth?"

"Unfortunately, no. The final contracts are still at her agent's—maybe he was stalling in the hope that this other role would come through. Better we put our energy into finding a replacement." Marcus glanced at Kenzie. "You know the British actresses better than I do. Do you have any suggestions?"

His gaze went to her. "Rainey."

She gasped. "I can't play Sarah! I've already got a job on this movie."

"Plenty of actors have directed and starred in their own productions. No reason why you can't do the same."

"Male actors do it regularly. Females almost never." She

groped for more reasons. "Besides, I'm not English, and I'm too old for the part."

Marcus was studying her with narrowed eyes. "Kenzie may have a point. With the right lighting age won't be a problem, and you do a fine English accent. Actually, when I first read the screenplay I thought you must intend to play Sarah. It's a terrific role, and you'll be able to handle it at least as well as Jane Stackpole."

It had been a long, difficult day, and facing two men trying to convince her to play a role she didn't want pushed Rainey to the snapping point. *"No!"* Barely managing to restrain herself from throwing her coffee cup across the conference room, she pitched her voice with ear-splitting clarity. "I am not going to play a simple-minded teenage virgin!"

Her uncharacteristic outburst produced startled silence. Then Kenzie straightened from his lounging position against the wall and crossed the room. "You need a time-out."

Before she realized his intentions, he unclipped the cell phone from her belt and tossed it to Val, then scooped Rainey up in his arms and headed for the door. Appalled, she struggled to free herself. "Damn it, Kenzie, what the hell do you think you're doing?"

"Abducting you," he said calmly. "Before you shatter into little pieces."

"Marcus, *stop laughing!*" She wriggled furiously but Kenzie had done a thorough job of pinning her arms so she couldn't get loose. "Are you going to let him do this?"

Her producer tried to look serious. "You could use a break, Rainey. A few hours away will be good for you."

Less amused, Val grabbed the phone. "Shall I call security?"

"Yes!" Rainey thought of the uproar that would cause. The security men would probably ask Kenzie for his autograph and laugh heartily about his masterful way of dealing with the little woman. "No!"

Before she could decide on the best course, Kenzie had carried her from the conference room. It was only a dozen steps to a side door. He turned and shouldered the door open, keeping a firm hold on Rainey. His rented SUV was parked just outside.

He opened the vehicle door, and had her inside in seconds. She grabbed for the handle while he circled to the driver's seat, but he'd locked her door with his remote. She was searching the unfamiliar controls when he started the ignition and they roared down the hotel driveway to the main road.

Her resistance collapsed and she buried her face in her hands, struggling not to weep with stress and frustration. A warm, familiar hand rested on her shoulder. "Relax, Rainey," he said quietly. "It's Saturday, and there's nothing that has to be done for tomorrow. Take a few hours off. You haven't seen anything of New Mexico that wasn't through a camera lens."

She wanted to jerk away, but she couldn't bear to sever the contact between them. "This compulsion you have to play Tarzan has gotten old."

"I dislike repeating myself, but direct action seemed a better approach than trying to talk rationally when you were freaking out." He released her shoulder to change gears, keeping both hands on the wheel after he shifted. "If you want to go back to the hotel, say the word. But why not slow down and get things back into perspective? I think I know some pretty good medicine for what ails you."

Did she want to go back to the hotel? Truthfully, no. Knowing their marriage was unfixable offered a weird kind of freedom. She'd enjoy spending some time with Kenzie, and it wouldn't be any more painful than working with him every day. She studied his calm, perfect profile, wishing again that he wasn't such a damned nice guy. There was a deep kindness in him that she hungered for. Yet he'd broken their marriage as casually as someone tossing out a magazine, and never offered regret or apology.

She fastened her seat belt, but said in a warning tone, "Okay, it's break time, but if the medicine you have in mind is seduction, forget it."

"Actually, what I had in mind was kittens."

"Kittens?" she repeated blankly.

"I have to visit some nice people, and their cat has kittens. Very soothing."

She loved cats, but wasn't home enough to have one of her own, so borrowing someone else's kittens would be a nice break. She settled back to enjoy the scenery. She'd always liked New Mexico, but Kenzie was right—on this visit she hadn't seen any of the beauty around her except in terms of how it would work in the movie.

There was something to be said for a friendly abduction.

❧ 12 ❧

Rainey dozed a little, wondering how many hours she'd spent in a car with Kenzie behind the wheel. He didn't have a macho thing about being in control—he simply liked driving more than she did, while she enjoyed letting go and letting him do the work.

The sun was still well above the horizon when he turned under a sign that announced CÍBOLA. Deciding she wouldn't give him the satisfaction of asking where the devil they were, she held her tongue as they rattled down a long entrance road and pulled up in front of an adobe ranch house. It was a pleasing structure, perfectly formed from its setting.

Kenzie took a folder from the backseat, then came around the SUV and helped Rainey out. A dog trotted up and greeted him adoringly, then turned to study Rainey. She was cautiously extending her hand when a comfortable-looking older woman emerged from the house.

"Hi, Mrs. Grady. Here are the brochures I promised you." Kenzie gave the woman a hug. "This is Raine Marlowe. I brought her here to see the kittens."

Mrs. Grady's eyes widened a little, and Rainey knew that the woman recognized her as Kenzie's wife, and probably even knew they were getting divorced. But she only said, "They'll be happy to meet you, Miss Marlowe. The little devils have worn everyone else out with their playing."

The interior of the house was cool and restful after the heat of the day. Mrs. Grady said, "Would you like some lemonade?"

"That would be lovely."

Mrs. Grady rattled ice into a tall glass, then filled it with lemonade from a pitcher in the refrigerator. "The kittens are out in the garden. I don't let 'em run outside—they'd be a quick bite for a coyote. This way."

A door opened to a walled garden fragrant with flowers. Wondering if the small fruit tree trained against one wall was an apricot, Rainey walked out into the late-afternoon sun. As a tiny tabby roared across her foot, Kenzie said, "Enjoy."

He withdrew to the kitchen, leaving her alone in the garden with the kittens. A little gray guy trotted up and tilted its head back to study her. Rainey dropped to the ground and crossed her legs, scooping three kittens onto her lap. Their placid mother lay by a rosemary bush with a fourth kitten dozing under her paw.

The lemonade had the fresh, tangy flavor that came only when it was made from scratch. After a long, deep swallow, she gathered the kittens in her hands and rubbed her face against the soft baby fur. The tabby began licking her ear, the gray guy purred at a high pitch, and the third, mostly white with tabby patches, scrambled onto her lap and started to gnaw at a shirt button.

Peace. She petted the gray kitten when it settled on her shoulder. Kenzie was right—this was a way to regain perspective. Things always went wrong during production, and this movie was actually going rather more smoothly than most. Only the fact that she bore so much responsibility was making her nuts.

She still felt like spanking Jane Stackpole, but the girl

wasn't the first to back out of a deal when a better one appeared, and she wouldn't be the last. It was a pity—Jane had a wonderful combination of fragility, grace, and inner steel, perfect for Sarah.

Casting was one of the most important parts of moviemaking, and the wrong person in a part could destroy the whole production. But there would be another ingenue who could do Sarah justice. Tomorrow morning, when it was a decent hour in England, Rainey would call some of her London contacts and set the wheels turning.

In the meantime—she had kittens.

The sun was dropping below the adobe walls when Kenzie looked out into the garden. "Ready to move on?"

Rainey sat cross-legged among kittens, looking lovely and relaxed. Like herself again. "I only wish I could take a couple of these little sweethearts with me." She kissed the tabby on its tiny nose before setting it on the ground, then rose lithely and followed him into the house.

Inside, she gave Mrs. Grady a warm smile. "Thank you so much. You could patent those little fellows as the Kitten Cure."

"Do you want a kitten or two? They'll be old enough to leave their mother in a couple of weeks."

"If I weren't going to England next week, I'd take you up on that," Rainey said.

"There are always more kittens in the world when you're ready. It was nice to meet you, Miss Marlowe."

"Please call me Raine. Thanks so much for letting me visit." With a last smile, Rainey accompanied Kenzie out to the SUV. As he drove across the ranch, she asked, "How do you know Mrs. Grady?"

"I'm buying Cíbola from her and her husband."

She stared at him. "Just like that, after only a few days in New Mexico?"

"Just like that. The Gradys will move to a modern redwood house, which will be built on the little lake to the west—you might not have noticed it. I came by today to drop off the brochures for some very nice factory-built houses. While you were kittenizing, Mrs. Grady was choosing the model she liked best. If her husband agrees, construction will get underway immediately."

"So you get caretakers, and they get a low-maintenance retirement home. Sounds like a good deal, but I never thought you'd buy a place so far from the sea."

He turned onto another road. In the distance, a cluster of lights marked a small settlement. "Neither did I, but I like New Mexico."

"I'm surprised you took me to Cíbola. I'd have thought you might prefer not to contaminate the place with my presence."

Sometimes she was a little too perceptive. "I can live with the memories of you and the kittens in the garden." In fact, that image was burned into his brain to the point he'd never be able to enter the garden without thinking of her. A bittersweet memory. Maybe in time the sweet would outweigh the bitter. "Are you hungry?"

"Ravenous," she admitted. "I'd just started my sandwich when Emmy called."

"There's a barbecue place up ahead. I ate ribs there a few days ago—greasy, fattening, deeply unwholesome, and delicious. Are you up for it?"

Her face lit with laughter. "How could I resist such a description?"

The small, casual restaurant reeked of authenticity, not to mention barbecue sauce. When they entered, the hostess glanced sharply from Kenzie to Rainey, but she made no comment, just led them to a corner booth. The other customers were casually dressed and weathered by wind and sun, working people who belonged to this part of the world as thoroughly as Cíbola did. Several glanced in their direction, then returned to their own meals, respecting the couple's privacy as the hostess had.

As they waited for their orders of ribs and a pitcher of beer, he said quietly, "People leave one another alone here. It's another thing I like about this part of the world."

Rainey settled into the booth appreciatively. "I could get used to this. Generally I don't mind signing autographs, but I hate having my meals interrupted."

Steaming platters arrived promptly, and Rainey fell on hers like a swarm of locusts. Besides eating her share of ribs, along with coleslaw and potato salad, she still had room for a slab of apple pie.

After rendering her side of the table a wasteland, she leaned back happily and wiped her hands with a paper napkin. "I didn't realize how hungry I was. What a great place. A good thing I don't live nearby—I'd look like a blimp."

"Not any time soon. You've been losing weight since shooting started, and there wasn't much of you to begin with."

She smothered a yawn. "As soon as we get back to the hotel, I'm going to go to bed and sleep at least eight hours."

"We're not going back to the hotel."

She snapped to full alert. "Enough already, Kenzie. You've abducted me, cut my electronic leash, and gave me a forced lesson in perspective, but it's time to get back."

"Several days ago I booked tonight at a rather unusual bed-and-breakfast near here. Since tomorrow is Sunday, you can afford to stay away a little longer."

Her eyes narrowed to slits. "I thought you said no seduction."

"Nary a bit." He hoped the regret didn't show in his voice. "It's an apartment, so you can have the bedroom while I sleep on the foldout sofa in the living room. All very proper."

"Does the bedroom door have a lock?"

"I think so." He drained the last of his beer. "Your faith in me is touching."

She gave him a crooked smile. "What if it's me I doubt? This won't be the same as having separate rooms at the hotel, Kenzie."

"Nothing will happen unless it's what we both want."

Her gaze dropped to the check. "I'm buying dinner."

Which was, perhaps, her way of saying that they might both want it, but it wasn't going to happen.

"How far down is this place?" Rainey asked.

"One hundred and ten steps. We're almost there." Kenzie was just below her, leading the way along stone steps carved from a rugged cliff. Though the steps were wide, Rainey gave thanks for the handrail on the left that separated her from a sheer drop of three or four hundred feet.

Kenzie hadn't been kidding about this place being unusual! He'd picked up keys at the nearby home of the man who owned the bed-and-breakfast, then drove them to a place of serious emptiness. One key had unlocked a massive door that was set in solid stone. It opened to reveal the top of this staircase. A switch turned on low lights set on every sixth step of the alarmingly long descent. As he closed the heavy door behind them, Kenzie said, "I think we'll be safe from autograph hunters here."

In true gentlemanly fashion, he went first with his duffel bag, presumably to break her fall if she collapsed into a maidenly faint. She wasn't about to do that, but she stayed as close to the cliff as humanly possible.

Finally the staircase flattened into a long, tiled balcony. To the right, sliding glass doors were set into the cliff. Kenzie used the keys again to let himself in. Turning on a light, he asked, "What do you think?"

"I've never seen anything like this." Rainey halted on the threshold, stunned by the room carved out of living stone. Walls and ceiling curved to suggest a natural cave, yet underfoot was thick, plushy white carpeting. There wasn't a lot of furniture, but it was well-chosen and comfortable. The overstuffed sofa was angled to take advantage of both a fireplace and the view out the glass doors.

"Quite something, isn't it? Inspired by the cliff dwellings of the ancient Anasazi Indians, I understand. I was lucky to be able to book the place for tonight—there was a cancellation."

Kenzie dropped his duffel behind the sofa and gestured for her to explore. The bedroom was beyond, with a luxurious bathroom that included a steam shower. In a corner of the living room was a kitchenette. Kenzie opened the door of the small refrigerator. "Care for some white wine?"

"That would be nice." She accepted a glass, thinking that even though he hadn't planned on seduction, this place was damnably romantic. Uneasily she walked back onto the balcony and halted with one hand on the railing.

Kenzie flipped off the staircase and interior lights and came outside to stand a careful yard away from her. As her eyes adjusted to the darkness, she began to pick out details of the moon-washed landscape. At the foot of the cliff a small river glinted, while rugged rock formations loomed on the far side of the canyon. The only sounds were wind, water, and the rustle of a small beast higher up the cliff.

"This is definitely something special," she said, voice low because noise seemed wrong in the cathedral stillness of the night. "I'd love to work it into a movie."

He laughed. "You're a born director, Rainey. Every sight, sound, and idea is grist for your mill."

"I think you're right." She took another small sip of wine. The last thing she needed was to drink enough to weaken her judgment. "As much as I wanted to act, I always had a vague sense that there was something for me beyond acting. Do you have any desire to produce or direct? Most actors do sooner or later."

"Not me. Acting was the only thing I ever dreamed of doing. It's what I am."

"It isn't what you are. It's what you do."

"Speak for yourself. If I'm not an actor, I'm nothing."

In the moonlight, his features had the cool symmetry of carved marble and the air of mystery that always made her yearn to get closer, to try to grasp that elusive essence. Despite their years of marriage and the ease between them at the moment, she still didn't know what made him tick. Maybe no one did.

"What I'd like to know is why you flipped out at the suggestion of playing Sarah," Kenzie remarked. "It's a wonderful role, and you could do it well."

Her tranquillity vanished. "For God's sake, Kenzie, what part of 'no' didn't you understand?"

"The irrational part."

"I'm not going to play Sarah, and that's final!" She spun on her heel and marched back inside, seething.

Kenzie followed. "It's chilly. I'll light the fire."

"Don't bother for my sake. I'm going to bed." She rinsed out her wineglass and set it to drain, then rubbed her arms, shaking from cold.

Wood was already laid in the round pueblo-style fireplace, so Kenzie had only to set a match to the paraffin-saturated fire starter. As the first flames flickered upward, he asked quietly, "What about Sarah bothers you so much?"

Why did she hate the idea so much? Sarah was a good character who grew from a sheltered innocent to a strong, nurturing woman. When Rainey wrote the screenplay, she'd sweated blood to capture the nuances of Sherbourne's heroine, and thought she'd succeeded pretty well. "I . . . I think it's because Sarah is so incredibly innocent and naïve. I can't identify with her. Even at six years old, I wasn't that innocent."

He sat back on his heels, watching the growing flames. "That innocence is the source of her strength. It doesn't occur to her to leave Randall, even though he's an emotional basket case when they marry."

"The nice thing about fictional innocence is that the writer can turn it into a virtue instead of the weakness it is in real life."

"You're certainly no sheltered Victorian virgin, and every time we take on a role that's radically different from what we are, it's like jumping off a cliff." He gestured toward the sliding doors and the vastness beyond. "But the roles that make us grow, and produce the finest acting, are exactly the ones that are most frightening. Though Sarah's innocence might make you feel uncomfortably vulnerable, you're quite capable of playing her, and doing it well."

She crossed the room and sank wearily into the sofa, absorbing the warmth of the fire. "Pushing one's boundaries works to a point, but we all have a range of things we can do effectively. Sweet little Sarah is out of my range."

"Then don't think about the whole movie at once. A day's shooting is only a few minutes of usable film, and surely for those few minutes you can manage Sarah and her naïveté. There's nothing like slicing a story into hundreds of takes to grind the primal fear away."

Everything he said made sense, yet she shivered at the thought of playing Sarah with anyone, much less with Kenzie. "You don't know what you're asking."

"I think I do." He gave her a sidelong glance. "It's hard enough working together, but to play lovers? Husband and wife? Of course it will be difficult, but for the sake of the movie, you have to do this. You won't find a better actress in the time available."

She started to reply, then stopped dead as she realized the conversation was eerily familiar. "You're using the same arguments I used when you tried to back out of the production!" In fact, with Kenzie's flypaper memory, parts of the conversation were word for word.

He chuckled. "I wondered how long it would be before you noticed. The arguments are as valid now as they were then. How does it feel to have them thrown at you, rather than doing the throwing?"

She didn't know whether to laugh or swear. "It feels rotten, especially with you taking an indecent amount of pleasure in making me sweat."

"I can't say I enjoy watching you suffer, but the situation is not without humor." He caught her gaze. "I have a stake in this movie, too. I'm putting in my time, energy, and reputation. My

name will go on the theater marquees. I want this production to
be as good as it can be, and that means we need you as Sarah."

"There has to be an English actress who can play her as well
as me. Probably better."

"If there is such a person, which I doubt, what are the
chances of finding her in a week, and her being available?" He
smiled faintly. "Having loftily told me that suffering through a
painful role would be good for me and my art, can you justify
taking the coward's way out when the tables are turned?"

Her eyes narrowed. "Are you trying to use emotional black-
mail?"

"I have a much better weapon. Your sense of fair play."

She swore under her breath. "You certainly know what buttons to push."

"Thank you."

"That wasn't intended as a compliment." She rubbed her
temples, thinking how much she didn't want to do this role. But
karmic justice had struck with a vengeance. She let her breath
out in a long sigh. "Very well, damn you. I'll play Sarah."

❧ 13 ❧

Kenzie gave her the smile that always tied her
stomach in knots. "I'm glad. Acting together will be stressful,
but that's not a bad thing for the movie, since the characters are
saturated with stress."

"You're grasping at straws, Kenzie. We're going to drive
each other crazy. But you're right, the movie will probably
benefit by having both of us, even if the camera guys have to
work twice as hard to make me look young enough." She rose
from the sofa. "I think I'll call it a night."

"Isn't it a little early? We could do some rehearsing."

They'd rehearsed together many times since that first night

with *The Scarlet Pimpernel* at Kenzie's house, but so much had changed. So damned much . . . "I haven't got a copy of the script."

"I do. I'd planned on working tonight. We can manage with one copy. I've learned just about all of my lines, and since you wrote the screenplay, you must know it almost by heart."

He'd booked this exotic hideaway for a Saturday evening of work? "Sometimes, Kenzie, you're downright inhuman."

"You've finally discovered my deep secret—that I'm a space alien who learned to act so I can pass as human."

Though he said it jokingly, there was a strange kind of truth in his words. Not that he was from outer space, but that he felt like an outcast. Many actors felt like outsiders, herself included. She knew the source of that primal sense of disconnection in her own life, but not in Kenzie's. He'd posted the subject of his childhood off-limits at the beginning of their relationship, and she'd respected that.

But she'd wondered what influences had shaped him. His voice, accent, sophistication, and confidence indicated an upper-class British background. Yet he had an almost complete lack of ego, which didn't jibe with a privileged upbringing or his phenomenal success. In the most narcissistic profession in the world, he was profoundly unassuming. He accepted that he would receive star treatment, but never seemed to want or expect it.

Nor did he have the vanity that was usual with most beautiful people. Neither did she, but that was because she hadn't been a particularly pretty child. With her skinny frame, thin face, and odd red-blonde hair, she'd been passable at best. She'd stared into mirrors and brooded on the unfairness of fate for not giving her Clementine's lush beauty. In time she'd learned to play up her good features and carry herself as if she were beautiful. That illusion had worked for her as an actress, but it wasn't the same as being born with traffic-stopping good looks.

She deduced that Kenzie's childhood had been very difficult, maybe an alcoholic or abusive parent. Maybe, like her, he hadn't been a very attractive child. If he'd been overweight, it explained the lack of vanity and his rigorous physical fitness regimen—access to a gym was a standard clause in all his movie contracts.

Or maybe he'd been dumped into a boarding school and forgotten, or been a short skinny kid who'd been bullied mercilessly. Whatever the details, that upbringing had been so painful that he wouldn't talk about it to anyone, not even to her. Maybe he'd anticipated that they wouldn't stay together, and she might tell his story to the tabloids after they parted. Life had made him extremely wary.

One of the things they had in common.

Though she would prefer to put a door between herself and her husband, it would be foolish to waste several hours of uninterrupted working time when the movie had such a tight production schedule. "I suppose we could do a read-through of the script, though I don't want to get into serious acting."

"Agreed. I figure I'll only be able to manage Randall and his problems for one or two takes per scene, so I'm not going to waste the emotion at this early stage." He pulled a copy of the screenplay from his duffel bag and handed it to her. "But a read-through will help us to get a handle on playing these characters together."

She'd loved working with Kenzie on the two movies they'd made before this one. Not only was he incredible to act with, but it had meant spending more time together. Conflicting obligations had kept them apart for half their marriage, and that had contributed to their breakup. How many times had she talked with him on the phone when the hunger for his physical presence had been so great she'd almost moaned from the pain of separation?

Forcing her mind back to the present, she flipped through the script. Every scene between Sarah and Randall was either romantic, charged with heavy emotion, or both. It was difficult directing Kenzie through this material—acting with him would be hellacious. It was a good thing that Sarah was on the verge of tears half the time—*that* Rainey could handle.

She began to read her first scene, when Randall asked Sarah to marry him. Miss Naïveté at her most credulous, full of wonder that the handsome, dashing officer she'd adored from childhood wanted her as his wife. Rainey kept her voice flat, and suppressed the memory of Kenzie proposing to her in California. He read his part with matching neutrality.

After the engagement came Randall's African campaign and imprisonment. He dreamed of Sarah during his captivity, her innocent beauty becoming an emblem of his homeland, but they didn't see each other again until he stepped from the train at Victoria Station and found himself a hero.

Though her parents didn't approve of a gently bred girl meeting her fiancé in such a public place, Sarah insisted on going to the station. She was waiting with her protective father as Randall emerged from the train. They couldn't speak properly in the middle of the turbulent crowd, but she was close enough to see the longing in Randall's eyes when he saw her, then the panic as journalists and hero-worshippers closed in on him.

Line by line Rainey and Kenzie worked out the rhythms of the dialogue so that the formal Victorian language wouldn't sound stiff. The characters had to be convincingly historical, yet the language must not distance the audience. That was why Rainey had wanted an English actress with classical stage training. Luckily, she'd spoken the dialogue as she wrote it, so she could manage the high-flown sentences.

Besides running the dialogue, they began to roughly block out movements. She had clear mental images of how far apart they would stand, how they would look at each other—or avoid a glance.

Despite her intentions, she began to slip into her character. Rainey had written the final shooting script in a white haze of pain after she and Kenzie split up, and it was impossible to separate herself from Sarah when they shared the anguish of losing a beloved man for reasons they couldn't understand.

Kenzie wasn't doing much better. His natural fluid movements had been replaced by the rigidity of a repressed, tormented Victorian officer, and he was acting out every sentence as if they were on camera. By the time they reached the scene where Randall tried to break the engagement, Rainey's nerves were raw, and Kenzie was darkly convincing in his portrayal of a man on the edge.

Desperate because of the social pressures that were inexorably forcing them to the altar, Randall asked his fiancée to walk with him to the village. She accepted happily, prattling on about aspects of their wedding until he said harshly, "Sarah. My dearest girl. I . . . I can't marry you."

"Not marry?" She stopped dead, horror-struck. "You can't mean that! Are . . . are the preparations too elaborate? If you prefer, we can have a simple ceremony."

"No! It's not the ceremony, but the marriage itself."

Two beats of silence before she whispered, "What have I done, John?"

"The fault isn't yours, but mine." He turned away, his movements brittle. "I am . . . flawed. Broken. Unworthy to be your husband."

"That's not true! You are a gentleman, a soldier, a hero. You are worthy to marry any woman in England." She caught her breath. "There's someone else, isn't there? A grand lady better suited to be your wife."

"There is no other woman. There never will be." He gazed at her, his soul aching in his eyes. Was that Randall's pain, or did some of it belong to Kenzie?

"Then *why*? I don't understand."

"Thank God you don't." A muscle jumped in his jaw. "The world is a place of great wickedness, and it has . . . destroyed my honor. I cannot marry."

Heart hammering, Rainey realized they were acting a scene she hadn't had the courage to face in real life. "But we pledged ourselves to each other! Even if you won't be my husband, in my heart I am your wife. I love you. I always will."

"How can you love me when you don't even know me? I'm not the man you think I am, Sarah. I never was." He touched her hair with yearning, a gesture so eloquent it must be duplicated on camera. "You mustn't marry a stranger."

But Rainey had, and with her eyes wide open. "Aren't men and women always strangers to each other? You dreamed of valor and honor, while I dreamed of creating a home for you and bearing your children." Her voice broke as she thought how much she'd wanted to have Kenzie's child. "Two years I waited and prayed for you, and half that time I thought you were dead. Never once did I look at another man. Do you think I can stop caring simply because you bid me to?"

"You *must* leave me," he said with barely suppressed violence. "For both our sakes."

"To say that, you are more honorable than you believe." More Rainey than Sarah, she stepped nearer, struggling with the desire to touch him. "I will release you if you truly wish it—but only if you will swear that you don't love me."

"This isn't about love!"

"How can marriage not be about love?" She stopped so close they were almost touching. "Persuade me that you don't love me, and you are free."

"Free?" His mouth twisted. "You were with me every moment I was in Africa. In the bleakest hours, thoughts of you were my only link to sanity. You were my salvation then. I can't drag you down into my darkness now."

"As long as we're together, I won't mind the darkness." Rainey turned her head and kissed his hand, tears stinging her eyes as she abandoned all pretense that she was acting. "Why, Kenzie? I don't understand any more than Sarah does."

He flinched, retreating into his role as a shield against her loss of control. "Don't cry, Sarah. I can't bear to think I'm hurting you."

She choked back a sob. "But you are."

The script called for him to kiss her tears away. For a taut moment they stared at each other, caught between the force of the story and painful reality. She thought he'd withdraw without touching her, but he bent into the kiss. The frayed line between characters and actors dissolved and she tilted her head back. Their lips met, his salty with her tears. It was not the kiss of a Victorian soldier with his innocent fiancée, but the embrace of a husband desiring his wife.

The script fell from her hands as she clung to him like a drowning woman to a life line. For months she'd hungered for his touch. This was insane, but she didn't want to think or judge, only feel. "Ah, Kenzie, I've missed you so much. . . ."

"Not as much as I missed you." His arms encircled her and they kissed with explosive force. She wrapped herself around him, trying to melt into his body, until he released her, swearing under his breath. "I should never have suggested rehearsing in such an isolated place."

Shaken by his withdrawal, she said acidly, "You mean this isn't a planned seduction?"

"Hardly. I've hurt you enough. The last thing I want to do is hurt you again."

"Like John Randall, you're painfully honorable, at least in this." She placed her hands on his shoulders, slid them down his arms, feeling his muscles tense at the caress. What did she want tonight, wisdom or passion?

She began to unfasten his buttons. "I already feel miserable. At least if we sleep together, there are compensations."

He caught her hand. "Strictly temporary ones, with a fierce morning after."

She tugged his shirt loose. "I've read that it's pretty common for couples in the process of getting divorced to sleep together, so this is normal behavior."

"Normal, maybe, but not wise."

"To hell with being wise." She kissed the hollow above his collarbone, enjoying the shiver that went through him.

"Are you sure?" His hands slid down her back to cradle her hips, drawing her tight against him.

She hesitated, knowing she should take this chance to change her mind. But she wanted him so much it was a physical ache, and they would never have such privacy again. "I'm sure. This will change nothing, but . . . I want to be with you one last time." Perhaps a final intimacy was needed to say good-bye.

"Then let's make it a night to remember." He caught her up in his arms and carried her into the bedroom, enfolding her body after he laid her on the bed. As he kissed her throat, he murmured, "No past, no future. Only now."

"This won't even have happened." She buried her hands in his hair and released the doubts and fears that ruled her life. For now they were lovers, and nothing else mattered.

They came together with fierceness and tenderness, ravenous hunger and taut restraint, knowing each other so well that no words were needed. She cried out when he entered her, wanting to weep at the familiarity and rightness of their joining. Why had he thrown away something so precious? She buried the thought, concentrating on the fever in her blood, the rising urgency that drowned out mind and pain and anger.

Until in the firestorm of fulfillment, she was free.

❧ 14 ❧

An apartment carved from a cliff was as deeply silent as a tomb. So silent that Kenzie thought he could hear the beating heart of the woman sleeping in his arms.

Faint light glowed from the living room to show the elegant contours of Rainey's shoulder and torso. Her body wasn't as dramatically sexy as some, but discipline and hard work had made her supple and perfectly toned, and she radiated the allure of passionate honesty and deep feeling. He wanted to lean forward and lick those soft curves and hidden places until she woke with slow-building desire.

Swearing silently, he slipped from the bed. Exhausted by days of grueling work, she didn't stir. He wondered how long it would be until she regretted succumbing to their mutual craziness. Probably about half a second after she woke up.

He pulled on his jeans and shirt and left the bedroom, crossing the living room to go out onto the balcony. Sharply cold night air on bare skin dispelled the physical languor of lovemaking. He braced his hands on the railing, wondering why the devil he'd let them end up in bed.

Because he had no willpower where Rainey was concerned, which was the underlying reason for letting their marriage end. Tonight's intimacy would rip open the wounds of separation all over again. Even so, he couldn't make himself regret what had happened. For a brief spell, he'd been . . . happy.

He'd even been weak enough to wonder what Rainey would do if he begged for forgiveness and another chance. Probably she'd say no, but the chance that she might be willing was dangerously tempting.

Luckily sanity returned when his blood cooled. Sex, no matter how great, changed nothing, except maybe to make matters worse. They were still bound for divorce, still facing weeks of painful proximity. Working together had been hard when the barriers were firmly in place between them. Now the treacherous, illogical part of his brain would want to be with her all the time even though tonight's lapse was an unplanned aberration.

He wrapped his arms around himself, shivering from the cold. Maybe he should blame John Randall, whose helpless longing for Sarah had oozed into Kenzie's brain and emotions. Yes, he'd blame Randall—if they'd been rehearsing a different story, he wouldn't have lost his control so disastrously.

Uneasily he wondered where Randall would take him next.

•   •   •

They'd been working on different continents for a month, with Kenzie in Greece and Rainey in California. Even daily phone calls didn't ease the bitter ache of separation. It would be at least another couple of weeks until they could see each other again, and she thought there was a very real chance that she'd perish from longing. Not for sex, even though every night brought scorching dreams, but because she missed the emotional intimacy. The knowledge that Kenzie understood and accepted, and was always on her side. She supposed that kind of closeness was why the institution of marriage survived.

If she hadn't wanted him so much, she wouldn't have blurted out what should have been said face-to-face, and only when and if the right moment arrived. During one of their daily phone calls, she said, "Maybe it's time to have a baby— I could keep it around for company when we're working at opposite ends of the world. Maybe two babies, so we could each take one on location."

The silence was palpable even across thousands of miles. They'd never discussed children, and now she knew why—her instincts had tried to warn her that the subject would be a source of conflict. She was about to start babbling to fill the blankness when he said, "An interesting thought, but cats housebreak much more easily."

Though they'd never had a real fight, his tone put a wall between them more frightening than an argument. "I was just kidding, Kenzie. Kids have their points, but they don't make really good pets."

More silence. "You wouldn't have mentioned a baby unless the subject was on your mind. It's perfectly reasonable to want children. Most people seem to."

Before she could reply, a knock sounded on the door of her trailer, followed by the director's personal assistant. "Miss Marlowe, you're needed on the set."

"I'll be along in a few minutes."

The assistant looked worried. "You need to come right

away. He wants to shoot against the storm clouds, and the sky is changing fast."

She clutched the phone, torn between the need to talk things out with Kenzie and the demands of her job. Duty won. She said into the phone, "I'll call you back later."

"It will be too late—a ten-hour time difference, remember. I'll talk to you tomorrow. Good night, my dear."

Then he was gone. She followed the assistant outside, biting her lower lip so hard the lipstick needed renewing. Luckily this scene called for her to stand around looking soulful rather than actually act, because her concentration was nonexistent.

Her anxiety grew until, at the end of the day's shooting, she asked the director to rearrange the schedule to give her three days off. After an initial howl of protest, he cooperated. She'd never requested special treatment before.

Kenzie was starring in a big, splashy action movie currently shooting on the island of Crete. Since he'd given her a shockingly expensive share in the private jet network for her birthday, she had Emmy arrange a flight to Greece ASAP.

Two hours later, she was in the air. She debated letting him know she was coming, and decided surprise was best. If he had time to rehearse a response, she'd never find out what he really felt about children, and they desperately needed to have an honest conversation on the subject.

She flew through the night and into morning, landing in Crete near noon. A hired car waited to take her out to the movie location.

As the car wound through the stark, sun-saturated landscape, she stared out the window, wondering what she would say to her husband. All her life she'd wanted children—at least two, because she'd hated being an only child.

She had dreamed of having Kenzie's children in images so vivid she'd wake up reaching for a soft infant form. They'd have three, she thought, two girls and a boy. She could see their faces in her dreams. They would be raised with the sta-

bility she hadn't known with Clementine, and the warmth she'd never received from her grandparents.

But even more than babies, she wanted Kenzie. If he truly didn't want children—well, she would have to accept that. Heaven knew there were powerful arguments against having kids when they both had such demanding careers. But some actors managed it, and she thought they could, too.

Maybe he'd only been startled by her bringing up the subject of children so suddenly, and he'd like the idea after he got used to it? She suspected that was pure wishful thinking on her part.

She'd visited Kenzie earlier in the shoot, so it was easy to get admitted to the production site. Recognizing her, the security guard grinned toothily and pointed out the right trailer, assuring her that her husband was inside.

The trailer was parked in the shade of a cypress tree, its air conditioner roaring. Since the door was unlocked, she swung it open and climbed two steps into the cool interior. Blinking at the dimness after the brilliant sunshine, she called, "Kenzie? I hope you're in the mood for a surprise."

"Shit!" The voice was throaty and female.

Rainey's eyes adjusted, and she froze. Kenzie was sprawled against a mound of pillows on the bed, straddled by his mostly naked costar, Angie Greene. Her red-nailed fingers on his zipper, she made a rueful face. "You shoulda called first."

Rainey felt as if she'd been slammed in the belly with a baseball bat. This couldn't be happening, it was the stuff of cheap melodrama. Maybe they were rehearsing for a bedroom scene. But Kenzie made no move to explain or deny. After the first flash of shock, he just stared at her, his expression as unreadable as granite. She could almost hear wheels clicking in his brain over the best way to play this scene.

Angie sat back on her heels, her crotch still covering Kenzie's. Flipping her tumbling blonde hair over her shoulders, she said breezily, "Don't look so upset, Raine. This is just a location fuck. No big deal."

Maybe it wasn't for Angie Greene, a voluptuous chaser of men and headlines, but it was a big deal to Rainey. Unable to bear the thought of breaking down in front of them, she fumbled for control, and found her grandmother's cool detachment. "So inconsiderate of me not to realize that my husband couldn't be trusted out of my sight. I'd expected better of him."

Kenzie swung Angie to one side, setting her on the bed beside him. "I'm sorry, Rainey. But maybe this is for the best."

Any frail hope that they might survive this shattered. She tugged off her wedding ring and threw it on the floor so hard that it bounced and skittered across the trailer. "My lawyer will contact yours."

Then she spun on her heel and left, grateful she hadn't dismissed the hired car, even more grateful that she hadn't arrived five minutes later and caught them in the act. If that had happened, she'd have been violently ill.

Shock kept her impassive until she was back at the airport. Mercifully, the jet hadn't yet been assigned another trip, so she booked it for the return flight.

She cried for seven thousand miles.

Rainey awoke weeping to find Kenzie sitting on the edge of the bed, a gentle hand on her arm and his expression concerned. "Are you all right?"

She almost blurted out that she'd had a ghastly nightmare of him in bed with another woman, then bit off her words when she realized that she'd been dreaming the truth. Being with Kenzie had brought it all back, as agonizing as when it happened. He'd been right to warn her the night before that the joys of lust would be followed by a fierce morning after. She drew a shuddering breath. "I've been better."

His face darkened. "I'm sorry. I should have taken you back to the hotel after the spare ribs. Stupid of me not to guess what might happen here."

She weighed the pleasure against the revitalized pain.

"Maybe this was better. You were unfinished business. Now I think there will be some closure."

"How satisfying to know that the night's exertions weren't wasted."

He started to rise but she stopped him. "Since we're here with our hair down, this is a good time to ask why you were so willing to throw away our marriage. Was it that horrible?"

"Not horrible at all." He hesitated, choosing his words. "Like John Randall, I'm not fit to be a husband. The difference is that I was slower to realize it. Less honorable. It would have been better never to have married."

"For heaven's sake, Kenzie, this isn't 1880. Grand statements about honor don't cut it. You were a pretty amiable husband, and you didn't seem unhappy. Quite the contrary. Was that all acting?"

"I wasn't acting. But what we had was an affair, not a real marriage."

"So it was all sex."

For a moment she thought he was going to agree. Instead he said reluctantly, "There was more than sex. But a marriage requires two qualified and willing people. I proposed on a selfish impulse because I enjoyed being with you, but never really thought about what it means to be married."

"You could have found a better way of ending things once you decided you wanted out."

He grimaced. "I'm too right-brained for advance planning. Rather than thinking the situation through, I let events drift until they exploded into a situation that was far crueler than anything I'd have consciously chosen. That was unforgivable on my part."

"Few things are truly unforgivable." Painful though this discussion was, at least they were finally talking honestly. "If either of us had shown an ounce of common sense, we could have gone our separate ways after our post-*Pimpernel* fling, and avoided all of the painful messiness of marriage and divorce."

"Common sense has never been my strong point." He smiled faintly. "Think of the trauma of divorce as adding to your creative repertoire."

"I prefer to get my experience vicariously." But he was right. No matter how rotten an event, it could be thought of as fuel for the creative process.

"Some things should be experienced directly." He tugged her blanket down, exposing her to the waist. "I agree that once we go back, it should be as if this never happened. But common sense says that since tonight is off the clock, we ought to take full advantage of it." He bent forward to kiss her navel, swirling his tongue in a circle.

She gasped as her lower belly tightened in response. "If . . . if you do that again, I'm going to be in no condition to analyze whether your thinking is warped."

He did it again, and she stopped thinking entirely.

Val looked up from her desk when the office door opened, sighing with relief when she saw that it was Rainey, who seemed to have survived her abduction. Heading for the espresso machine, she asked, "Any catastrophes strike while I was gone?"

"Nary a one. Probably because it's Sunday, and at least some of the world isn't working."

"But you are. What about Marcus?"

"He's having lunch with friends in Santa Fe. I've been covering for you, in case you'd rather not have to explain your extended disappearance with Kenzie."

The espresso machine gurgled disgustingly as it delivered a shot into Rainey's cup. As she took milk from the refrigerator, she said, "You might as well ask what happened before you perish of curiosity."

"I could make a pretty good guess about what happened, but I wouldn't mind hearing the gory details."

Rainey scooped foamed milk into her cup, then settled into a stuffed chair. "Kenzie took me to see some kittens and to a great barbecue shack, then to an amazing bed-and-breakfast apartment carved into a cliff."

"I read about that place. I'd love to stay there sometime."

"It was incredibly peaceful—a world away from the stresses of moviemaking. We talked about Sarah, and Kenzie persuaded me that I'm the best choice to play her."

"Great! I've thought all along that you'd do a dynamite job in the role."

Rainey made a sour face. "Everyone seems to think that but me. However, the practical arguments are strong, so I guess I'll have to do it. Kenzie had a copy of the script, so we did a read-through."

"So you rehearsed. How staid."

"It was, until we jumped each other's bones."

"I thought you were determined to keep the relationship all business."

"We were struck by temporary insanity caused by playing two people who desperately long for each other." Rainey shifted to a cross-legged position in the chair. "Which is probably why I resisted the idea of playing Sarah so vehemently."

That made sense. It must be disorienting to play a woman who wants a man when one *didn't* want the man. Or wanted the man, but didn't want to. "I see the problem, but the jumping of bones is treacherous. It's the easiest thing in the world to go to bed with someone you're breaking up with. Familiarity, uncertainty, and yearning for better times are a great formula for wild sex. But in my experience, it screws your emotions up royally."

"Too true. We did some long overdue talking, which was good." Rainey drew her feet up onto the chair. "I even wondered for a nanosecond if I should ask him if it was worth another try, but luckily the moment passed."

Val shoved the papers she'd been working on out of the way and propped her chin on her hand. "Would you want to get back together with Kenzie?"

Her friend frowned. "If he was decent husband material, maybe. But how can I live with someone I can't trust?"

"Not even worth trying." Val debated whether to say more. She'd arrived in New Mexico wanting to despise Kenzie, but hadn't managed it. Underneath his distractingly good looks, he had a rare kindness and consideration. But it took more than that to make a decent husband. "Is Kenzie completely unreliable, or did he just screw up once, and doesn't want to ask for a second chance?"

"Last night he said in as many words that he isn't cut out for marriage, and ours was a mistake from the get-go."

"This is just an impression on my part, but when you're around, there's an awareness about him," Val said slowly. "As if he's always watching you, even when he isn't. It's not the reaction of a man who is indifferent to a woman."

Rainey sniffed. "Sex, pure and simple."

"It's more than that. There's a kind of . . . I don't know, protectiveness, maybe. Caring. Suppressed yearning."

"Even if you're right, which I doubt, it wouldn't matter. Do you know what it's like to be married to a high-maintenance charmer? Women lusting after him and trying to figure out how to ditch me. Teenagers waiting outside the gates of the house to throw their panties at him. People staring at me and wondering how I managed to capture such a prize, and how long it would be before the Sexiest Man in the World dumped me." Rainey set her cappuccino aside and wrapped her arms around her knees.

"Try to relax—you're on the verge of tying yourself into a pretzel," Val said. "I'd hate that, too, but it sounds like it's the world that's high maintenance, not Kenzie."

"Technically you're right, but it doesn't make much practical difference. He was just a speed bump in the highway of my life, and things are a lot simpler when he isn't around." Rainey rose and went to the fax machine, flipping through the new pages. "The sooner we get to England and finish shooting this movie, the better."

Val returned to her paperwork. Maybe Rainey was right about her husband, and he no longer had feelings for the woman he married. But Val couldn't shake a suspicion that there were some pretty complicated currents below the surface of that relationship. More complicated than Rainey wanted to admit.

❧ 15 ❧

Kenzie sipped on a cup of good English tea as Rainey rehearsed a scene with Richard Farley, the very distinguished actor playing Sarah's father. The combination of Marcus Gordon's contacts and a first-class script had given *The Centurion* an impressive lineup of experienced British character actors.

They were nearing the end of a week of intensive rehearsals in London before filming began again. Though the New Mexican shoot had been mostly action, with the only important talking scenes those between Kenzie and Sharif, the English portion of the movie was almost entirely character interactions so rehearsing was essential.

Sir James Cantwell, the aging and even more distinguished actor on Kenzie's right, said loftily, "Neither you nor Miss Marlowe are working terribly hard."

It was the sort of comment allowed a man who'd been a star when Kenzie was a very green RADA graduate, awed to be sharing a stage with a giant of the British theater. Mildly he said, "We're saving the raw emotion for the camera."

Sir James gave him a wicked glance. "Or you've been ruined by Hollywood. You were a promising stage actor as a lad, but after all those action movies, you need to be reminded how to act by some real players."

Kenzie grinned. "That, too."

Sir James's gaze went back to Rainey. Even casually dressed in slacks and sweater with her apricot hair tied back with a scarf, she had a compelling presence. "What is it like to be directed by a woman one is in the process of divorcing?"

"It's . . . interesting. Luckily, we're on good terms."

Though not as good as that one night inside a cliff. Now that they were surrounded by people, there was no chance that rehearsing would slide from professional to personal. Just as well, since he still hadn't recovered from the emotional backlash of one night's intimacy. Calm and controlled, Rainey gave no sign that she'd been affected at all. Perhaps that night had given her the closure she'd needed, and she'd put the marriage behind her. For her sake, he hoped so.

"I've never done a movie with a female director before," Sir James mused.

"Then it's time you did. Rainey's good. She has a clear vision of what she wants the movie to say, and she knows how to communicate that to cast and crew."

"She's learned to do that on her first production?" Sir James said, intrigued.

Before Kenzie could answer, Rainey glanced in their direction, saying hopefully, "Surely John's father will know, Papa."

"My cue," Sir James murmured, rising to join Rainey and Richard Farley. "I know that my son needs a sweet girl like you," he boomed, bluff and utterly sure of himself and his world. "I'll admit that being held captive by savages put the boy off his feed a bit, but don't worry. He'll be cured as soon as he's wed."

Kenzie settled back in his chair, enjoying the fact that Sir James was acting at full wattage, probably to show up lazy colonials who'd worked regularly in Hollywood. Responding to the challenge, Farley also began to emote as if the cameras were rolling.

Reacting to the men, Rainey moved fully into Sarah, capturing the girl's combination of innocence and determination. That lasted until her next scene with Kenzie. Rainey cut back from torch to pilot light. Kenzie was equally subdued as the two British actors sat down and looked pained.

Having his share of actor's pride, in Kenzie's next scene with Sir James he cranked up the emotional intensity. On the verge of breakdown, John Randall was struggling desperately to prevent himself from falling apart in front of his father, whose good opinion he craved.

Kenzie played the scene without histrionics or overwrought body language. Instead, every word was torn bleeding from his soul. The long, shabby room fell utterly silent. Even Sir James look impressed.

"Well done," Rainey said when the scene ended. "Another day of rehearsal and we'll be ready to roll." She checked her watch. "This is a good place to stop for the day. See you in the morning."

Scraping chairs and murmuring arose as cast and crew prepared to leave. Pulling on his jacket, Kenzie asked Rainey, "Are you satisfied with how rehearsals are going?"

"So far, so good, except for you and me. I trust that we'll both hit the marks when it counts." She smiled faintly. "One of the pluses for casting you in the lead is that you're so good at nailing the first take. Very economical."

"I'm quite the bargain, especially on a tight budget," he agreed. "Sir James was wondering how you learned to direct so well on your first project."

"When you were shooting that film in New Zealand, I directed a couple of episodes of *Star Pilgrims* for television."

"Really? I've never seen your name on the credits, and I don't think I've missed any." They used to tape the show and watch it together, since the science fiction series was well-written, well-produced, and highly escapist. It had been a ritual that involved large bowls of popcorn and turning off professional judgment so they could simply enjoy.

A flicker in Rainey's eyes indicated that she also remembered those evenings. "Exactly. Did you know that the *Star Pilgrims* executive producer is an old buddy of mine? She was willing to give me a chance to get some experience. Since she didn't mind me using a pseudonym to avoid publicity, I became 'R. M. Jones.' My first day on the set I was terrified, but pretty soon I developed quite a touch for coaxing good performances out of blue-skinned aliens."

"R. M. Jones? I remember seeing that name. *Where Angels Dance* was one of yours, wasn't it? That was the best episode of the season."

"That was because of the script." But she smiled, and for a moment their gazes caught with unwanted intimacy. Popcorn and pleasures.

The moment ended when Val called, "Rainey, Kenzie, your limo is waiting outside. You go on back to the hotel, Rainey. I'll close up here."

"Thanks. I'll see you later then."

Kenzie followed Rainey, opening the door for her. "Why Jones?"

Her smile faded. "When I was a kid and wondered about my father, I'd think of him as Mr. Jones. My mysterious progenitor. Jones was as good a name as any."

As they went down the stairs, he wondered if it was possible not to be haunted by speculations about an unknown parent. Probably not.

They passed the porter at the building's front door, and stepped out into shouts and electronic flashes. "Miss Marlowe, what about the reports of feuding on the production?"

"Did you fire Jane Stackpole because she and Kenzie were having an affair?"

"I've heard talk of a reconciliation between you two. Care to comment?"

Kenzie's jaw tightened. Usually celebrities were photographed arriving and leaving London and largely left alone otherwise, but his and Rainey's personal situation had created extra interest. They'd both given interviews about the production, ignoring questions about their relationship and talking about what a great film *The Centurion* would be. That was the protocol—no matter how much one might want to be somewhere else, one didn't bad-mouth the current production. Until now, that had been enough to keep the tabloid press happy.

Guessing there were about two dozen reporters and photographers waiting, he said under his breath, "It must be a slow news day, with no royal scandals."

"Or they want to get an easy story before we move to the country."

Since congestion forced the car to wait halfway down the block, he placed a protective hand on Rainey's back and they began walking steadily through the crowd. Kenzie was acquainted with most of the reporters, so he smiled lazily at the man who'd asked about feuding. "You need to find better sources, Henry. The production is going very smoothly. Not a prima donna in sight."

The reporter grinned, unabashed. "Of course you'd deny any trouble."

"Cooperation doesn't make much of a story," Rainey said sympathetically. "But what can I say? This is a great group of people to work with."

A tall blonde called, "Are you glad to come home to England, Kenzie?"

"Of course, Pamela." He gave her the smile guaranteed to scramble female thinking. "Where else can one get a proper cup of tea?"

Pamela gulped before shifting her attention. "Raine, is it true you put this production together just to get Kenzie back?"

Rainey's eyes narrowed. "Nonsense. I started work on *The Centurion* long before I met Kenzie, though I'll admit I'm delighted to have him as the lead. He's doing a marvelous job."

As similar questions were tossed at them, they continued toward the car. They'd almost reached it when a tall man with a sharp face barked out, "Where were you born, Kenzie? Where did you grow up?"

Thinking there was something familiar about the man, Kenzie slipped into a Scottish accent. "I was born in the Outer Hebrides, and my father says I'm the legitimate Stuart heir to the throne of Scotland. Bonnie Prince Charlie married Flora Mac-Donald, you know, by traditional Scottish handfast. They had a son, and bonnie Flora concealed the lad to save him from the Sassenach, giving him the name Scott. As the direct descendant of that son, I'll thank you to call me 'Your Royal Highness.' "

His statement produced roars of laughter. "That's a good one, Kenzie." Henry grinned. "What a headline that will make: 'Kenzie Scott Is the True King of England!' "

The sharp-faced man refused to be amused. "What's the real story? You've always hidden behind a pack of lies, and it's time to set the record straight."

Startled by the naked hostility in the reporter's voice, Kenzie said, "Sorry, I don't recognize you. What's your name and who do you represent?"

"Nigel Stone of the *London Inquirer.*"

The tabloid was probably London's tawdriest daily, but it was the name that caused Kenzie to catch his breath. No wonder the reporter seemed familiar. They'd known each other once long ago, when Nigel Stone had been a feral, rat-faced boy called Ned. As a scandal-chasing reporter, he'd found the perfect profession.

Knowing the other man couldn't possibly recognize him, Kenzie smiled charmingly. "I'm a mere player, a projection of the audience's whims and fancies. Why spoil that with tedious reality?"

They reached the car, and the driver flung the door open. Kenzie bundled Rainey in and followed quickly, but before the door closed, he heard Nigel Stone bark, "You've got away with lies in the past, but no longer. I'm going to find out who you really are!"

Rainey slid across the seat to make room for Kenzie. As the car pulled away from the curb, she asked, "Your Royal Highness?"

His expression eased. "See what you're giving up by divorcing me? The chance to be the next queen of England."

"As if I didn't have enough problems with publicity!" She frowned. "If that Stone fellow tried, would he be able to uncover your mysterious past?"

"He might be able to back to my time as a student at RADA. No further."

Thinking Kenzie sounded very certain, she asked, "Did you spend your childhood abroad so there's no paper trail in Britain?"

He looked out the car window. "That's one possible explanation."

In other words, back off. Moving to safer ground, she asked, "What is it like to return to England? You seem very British to me, but I've always sensed you have some ambivalence about visiting here."

He exhaled, still avoiding her gaze. "Britain is home in a way nowhere else can ever be, but not all the memories are good ones."

Everyone had painful childhood memories. His must be exceptionally bad to provoke such a reaction. "The movie business brings you back here regularly."

"And I come. Ambivalently."

Yet he'd never become an American citizen even though he'd been a legal resident for more than ten years. She supposed that said something significant about his feelings for his native land.

Once she'd guiltily examined his passport when he left it lying on his dresser after a trip to Cannes. The document said he'd been born in London on the February day and year he claimed, but she wondered if the information was true. Would Kenzie's determination to conceal his past extend to falsifying documents? Maybe.

Realizing she'd probably never know the truth, she settled back in her seat. Because Kenzie hadn't demanded a separate driver, they shared a car to and from the hotel. It saved a little money, and she enjoyed the treacherous pleasure of riding with him. As promised, they'd both pretended that night in the cliff

house had never happened—but the sensual awareness between them had been off the charts ever since. "The rehearsals
are going so well that I'm getting cautiously optimistic about
the results, even though I know there's many a slip twixt the
camera and the final edit."

He turned from the window. "Not to mention the fact that
the hardest part is yet to come. The rest of the production will
be difficult for both of us. One might even say 'excruciating.' "

She shivered at how menacing the word sounded in his
level voice. "Harder on you than on me, I'm afraid."

"You have to direct me, which you're going to hate, just as
you're going to hate playing Sarah's more emotional scenes."

"You're beginning to sound as ominous as Macbeth's
witches."

"They weren't only ominous. They were right."

She thought about the brilliant scene he'd just done with Sir
James. Kenzie knew the character of John Randall inside out.
If he said that the next weeks were going to be excruciating, he
was undoubtedly right. Now that it was too late, she wondered
if the end product of a movie justified what she was asking of
him.

Was it too late? As soon as the thought struck her, she dismissed it. Too much money, too many people, too much trust,
were bound up in this production. Marcus Gordon might give
her a second chance if she failed to deliver a movie as strong
as her vision, but he'd never forgive her if she turned coward
in the middle.

"You look like you just bit into an apple and discovered half
a worm."

Kenzie's voice snapped her out of her reverie. She said, "I
was having a horrified moment of wondering what I got myself into with this project."

"You'll survive, Rainey. You always do. It's a most intimidating virtue." Kenzie stretched out and closed his eyes, ending the conversation.

Maybe sharing a car wasn't such a great idea after all.

❧ 16 ❧

It didn't take long for Nigel Stone to move into action. The next morning Rainey and Val had a quiet breakfast together in Rainey's suite, both of them skimming the London newspapers to check coverage of the production. Val picked the *Inquirer* from the pile, then whistled softly. "Hell and damnation. Take a look at this."

Rainey accepted the tabloid with a sinking heart. The whole front page was a sinister-looking photo of Kenzie with a headline that screamed, "Do You Know Who This Man *Really* Is?" She flipped to the story inside. A double-page spread with a blaring head asked, "Rich Man, Poor Man, Beggar Man, Thief? Is Britain's Most Popular Movie Star a King or a Criminal?"

Half a dozen photos of Kenzie showed him in roles where he played dark and dangerous characters, or wearing as few garments as possible, preferably both. Since he was a workaholic who'd made a lot of movies, the tabloid had plenty of material. One shot was of her and Kenzie in a steamy embrace in *Lethal Force,* a thriller they'd made together the year before. The caption below asked ominously, "Did Raine Marlowe Leave Kenzie Scott When She Discovered the Real Man Behind the Handsome Mask?"

The sneering text said that Kenzie Scott claimed to be British, but his stories about his past were one long string of lies designed to make fools of his countrymen, who generously accepted him as one of their own. Stone challenged his readers to come forward if they'd known Kenzie Scott in his youth. The *Inquirer* would pay handsomely for early photos. Together, Nigel Stone and his readers would uncover the truth!

Rainey swore. "This makes Kenzie sound like an ax murderer. Can he sue the *Inquirer* for libel?"

Val shook her head. "Everything is done with questions and

suggestive pictures. They don't actually accuse him of anything, so there's no libel."

A pity. Knowing Kenzie wasn't much of a newspaper reader, Rainey stood, retrieving the tabloid. "I'd better show this to Kenzie so he's prepared."

His suite was just down the hallway from hers. She knocked crisply. "It's me."

A minute passed before the door opened to reveal Kenzie in a bathrobe and damp hair. A faint shock jolted along her nerves. Stupid, stupid, stupid. It was hardly the first time she'd seen his chest, and a great deal more.

He ushered her in with a courtly gesture. "I suppose the obvious, vulgar implication of your calling on me is too much to hope for."

"In your dreams, Scott." She handed him the newspaper. "You're not going to like this."

His levity vanished as he saw the front page. "You're right. I don't."

He turned to the story with the granite expression that appeared whenever the subject of his past came up. Hesitantly she said, "I've tried to respect your privacy, but under these circumstances, I need to know if anything illegal might turn up."

His mouth twisted. "You think I'm a criminal?"

"No, but I've had to wonder what you're so secretive about. If really catastrophic information might become public, I'd like some advance warning. It's my neck the investors will chop if the production is jeopardized by something you did."

"You can relax. There are no outstanding warrants for my arrest."

Which was not the same as saying that he had a guiltless past, but she didn't pursue the point. "Anything else that might cause trouble if it's made public?"

After a long silence, he said, "There are . . . incidents that would make splendid tabloid headlines, but no one will come forward to talk about them."

She sighed. "Why am I not more comforted by your confidence?"

"It's all you're going to get, but don't worry. Nigel Stone will be swamped with spurious leads that I'll be able to deny with complete sincerity." He handed the tabloid back. "If you'll excuse me, I need to get ready for the last day of rehearsal."

Troubled, she returned to her suite, hoping that whatever her husband wanted so much to hide would stay hidden.

Thoughts of Nigel Stone's crusade to unmask "Britain's most popular movie star" gnawed at Kenzie all day. There was almost no one left who could connect the boy he was with the man he became, and those few had good reason to stay silent. But . . .

When the rehearsal ended, he told Rainey, "You can have the hired car. I'm going to visit an old friend."

She managed not to ask where he was going, barely. "Have a nice evening."

Since reporters waited in front of the building, he used the back door and hailed the first taxi he saw. "Ramillies Manor, please."

A half hour ride in heavy traffic brought him to a quiet corner of Kensington. Though it had never been a manor, the sprawling Victorian brick house made a handsome retirement home. He entered the familiar beveled-glass front door. The elderly receptionist finished up a phone call, then greeted him with a smile. "Why, Mr. Scott, how nice to see you again. Mr. Winfield will be ever so pleased."

"How is he doing?"

She sighed. "He has good days and bad days, but he never complains. Such a fine gentleman. I believe he's taking the sun in the garden now. You know the way. Shall I send out a tea tray for the two of you?"

He agreed, knowing it would please her, then made his way through the house toward the rear exit. Would any of the employees of Ramillies Manor be tempted to contact Nigel Stone and tell what they knew about Kenzie Scott? Probably not; since this establishment catered to moneyed people, employees were chosen for discretion. Even if an employee revealed his regular visits to Charles Winfield, none of them knew anything about his past.

Charles Winfield sat in the shade of a rose arbor, a knee blanket tucked over his lap and a set of earphones on his head. Thinking it had been too long since his last visit, Kenzie approached, touching the old man's shoulder to get his attention. "Charles. Sorry I couldn't come sooner. How are you?"

Winfield tugged off the headset and stopped his tape recorder. "Kenzie, my dear boy, what a pleasure! No need to apologize—I know you've been madly busy ever since arriving in London." He spoke with the deep, sonorous voice of a stage actor. "Do have a seat."

"What are you listening to?" As Kenzie sat on the stone bench, the older man adjusted his wheelchair so that he could see his visitor with peripheral vision; macular degeneration had robbed him of most of the sight in the center of his eyes.

"That delightfully malicious Hollywood autobiography you sent me. Not so witty as the British equivalent, but quite amazingly forthright."

"You should dictate your memoirs. They'd be a best-seller."

Winfield shook his head regretfully. "As a gentleman, I'd have to leave all the best bits out, which would remove much of the appeal."

"Speaking of revelations, are you familiar with a reporter called Nigel Stone?"

"A miserable weasel of a fellow who's probably the most malicious entertainment reporter in London. I believe he's British born, but spent some years working in Australia. For our sins, he returned home a couple of years ago and became established at the *Inquirer*. He's known for his scandal mongering. You've met him?"

"Yes, and he's decided he owes it to the British public to reveal the truth about my background. He's made an open call for information and is offering money for early photographs."

"A dreadful man. Mean to the bone." Winfield's lips pursed. "He won't find anything, if that's what you're worrying about."

"I hope you're right. But if he does a good job investigating my years at RADA, he could learn that you helped me get into the school."

Winfield made an airy gesture. "Nonsense. It was your audition that got you admitted. I merely pointed you in the right direction and dropped a word in the ear of the principal." He gave the evil smile he'd used when playing Macbeth. "And if he tracks me down, I shall delight in sending him off in all the wrong directions."

Kenzie smiled. "Don't get too creative—Stone isn't stupid."

"Don't worry, I shall have only a small amount of sport. If you wish, I can also speak with the surviving members of the old circle. Not that any would reveal secrets to a low-bred reporter, but forewarned is best."

"Thank you. I'd appreciate that, especially since the production will leave London in another couple of days."

"Ah, yes, *The Centurion.* The novel was a favorite of mine. I'm glad that it's finally being made into a movie. I suppose it couldn't have been done properly before now." He cocked his head. "I hear the tea tray coming."

"They continue to take good care of you?"

"Yes, and well they should, given the absurd amount of money you pay them to look after this decaying carcass of mine."

"It's a small return for all you did for me." Charles had been quite successful in his day, but he'd lived lavishly, and working in the theater was less lucrative than television or feature films. One of the pleasures of money was being able to help friends, and Kenzie owed Charles his career.

Despite Kenzie's passionate love of movies and the theater,

he'd never dreamed it was possible to become an actor himself. Seeing his interest, Charles had drawn him out, then become his tutor when he recognized Kenzie's talent. Next to Trevor Scott-Wallace, the professor who'd taught Kenzie reading, manners, and the ways of society, Charles had been the greatest influence on Kenzie's life.

"Here you are, gentlemen." The young attendant set the tea tray down on the circular cast-iron garden table between the two men. After a lingering glance at Kenzie, she withdrew.

"You'd best pour, my boy," Charles said. "With my vision, I'd probably drown the cucumber sandwiches. Do tell me the latest gossip, and what it's like to be directed by that frightfully talented demi-wife of yours."

Kenzie had saved Hollywood and actor tidbits he knew Charles would enjoy. As he poured their tea, he thought how pleasant it was to be with the one man in the world from whom he had nothing to hide.

Charles tired easily these days, so it wasn't long before Kenzie left. As he walked toward Kensington High Street to look for a taxi, he realized he was passing the flat of one of his old RADA girlfriends, Jenny Lyme. On impulse he went to the door of the building and rang the bell, not really expecting to find her in.

He was turning to leave when the intercom came to life. "I don't know who this is," she said tartly, "but it's been a vile day, so unless you're prepared to buy me a frightfully expensive dinner, go away."

Jenny was in good form. "It's a deal," he said. "Where shall I take you?"

"Kenzie, is that you? You beast! Come up instantly."

She buzzed him into the building and kissed him with enthusiasm when he entered her second-floor flat. Tall, lush, and dark-haired, she had a thriving career as a television actress. "You're divorced now, aren't you? Have you come to seduce me with champagne and Belgian chocolates? Please?"

He had a swift memory of his night with Rainey. Gently he

disentangled himself. "Tempting, but the divorce isn't final yet, so technically I'm still a married man."

Her extravagant manner fell away. "Ah, it's like that. Fair enough." She hooked an arm through his and drew him down beside her on the brocade sofa. "What about that dinner?"

"Your choice. Anywhere we can get into on short notice."

"There's a magnificently trendy and insanely dear bistro in Chelsea. I'll give them a call." She looked up the number and called, using his name for the reservation.

"Success," she reported after hanging up. "They usually have a two-week waiting list, but for Kenzie Scott, they can find a table in an hour. So handy to have old classmates who've become wildly successful."

"You haven't done badly yourself."

She made a face. "After you, I'm probably the most successful from our RADA year. I think half the class has given up acting altogether, and the others are working sporadically at best. It's a terrible business, Kenzie. Why do we do it?"

"Because we're too odd to be employable anywhere else?"

"There is that." She curled up in the sofa corner and studied his face. "We have some time before we need to leave for Cachet. What's wrong, Kenzie? The divorce?"

Jenny had always been wickedly perceptive. They'd been friends and sometimes lovers through the RADA years, and kept in touch ever since. "Nigel Stone of the *Inquirer* is enlisting the British public in a full-fledged campaign to uncover my past. He's bound to investigate my time at RADA, so you might be hearing from him."

"I can't tell things about you that I don't know. You made the average oyster look like a blabbermouth." She looked hopeful. "Shall I make something up?"

There was something to be said for laying a false trail, and Jenny was less likely to go overboard than Charles. "What did you have in mind?"

"How about if I say that I'm not at all sure, because you were a very private person, but based on occasional bits and pieces, I deduced that you were born in England, then taken to Africa as a small child when your parents emigrated." Her mobile face transformed into a woman being forthright to an interviewer. "I'm not sure where—perhaps Zimbabwe when it was Rhodesia, or maybe South Africa. Your parents were massacred during the political unrest, so poor orphaned you returned to England, and entered RADA shortly thereafter. The subject of your family was so painful that you wouldn't ever discuss it. Dreadfully sad."

A good story that would explain the lack of school records before his time at RADA. "Clever. If you can convince Stone I grew up abroad, he could waste a lot of time searching the former British Empire for evidence of my existence."

"He'll believe me. I'm an actress; I can make anyone believe anything." She stood. "I'd better go change. I'm not going to Cachet in anything less than my glittering best." Halfway across the room, she hesitated. "If Stone is a big enough sneak, he might be able to get your records from RADA. Is there anything in your original application that might reveal more than you want him to know?"

"The application was as vague as I could make it—privately educated, no next of kin, and not much more." Charles Winfield's friendship with the RADA principal had helped with that. Old-boy networks were useful.

"One of the things I always liked about you, darling, was how very unobvious you are. Are you ever going to tell me the real story of your working-class past?"

He concealed the jolt of surprise. "What makes you say that?"

"You hadn't quite perfected that aristocratic accent when you started at RADA." Jenny drifted into her bedroom, dropping into the role she'd play if interviewed. "I've always had quite a good ear for accents. I do believe I detected a trace of South Africa in your voice when we first met."

She'd tie knots in Nigel Stone.

❧ 17 ❧

Knowing she should monitor the Inquirer, Rainey reluctantly reached for a copy to skim during her breakfast. The photograph splashed on the front page of the tabloid almost caused her to lose her eggs and British bacon. "Kenzie Steps Out" the headline screamed over a picture of him and a gorgeous brunette whose figure and cleavage could raise the dead.

Queasily she read the caption. The woman was Jenny Lyme, and she and Kenzie had dined at Cachet, an ultra-fashionable restaurant. Rainey studied the photo, recognizing Kenzie's protective posture toward his date, the surprise on both their faces as the photographer caught their picture. If they'd wanted anonymity, they should have gone to a less trendy eatery.

Jenny Lyme was a RADA classmate and longtime friend of Kenzie's, and Rainey suspected they'd been lovers, though Kenzie had never said that. So what were they now—friends or lovers?

Not that it was any of Rainey's business—she was just Kenzie's director. He had every right to boff old girlfriends as long as it didn't interfere with his work on *The Centurion*. If she could only convince her stomach of that. . . .

She closed her eyes and breathed deeply until her nerves settled down. It was fortunate that today would be spent preparing an old train barn for the biggest, most complicated scenes of the movie. She would buzz around monitoring details such as lighting, set dressing, and the crowd of extras, but she wouldn't have to really concentrate until they started shooting, which wouldn't be until after dark.

She flipped to the entertainment section, and saw that Stone had done an article on Kenzie's early BBC work, with quotes from people who'd known him then. It looked as if the reporter was digging for negative statements, but had trouble finding anyone willing to knock Kenzie. About the harshest words were, "He was real quiet like." At least the tabloid wasn't fabricating nastiness.

Yet.

Pulse racing, Rainey surveyed the vast train barn from her perch on a crane that held a camera and crew. Two hundred extras in period dress were being herded into position, while outside the barn a steam train rumbled expectantly.

They were about to do her "money shot"—the big, complicated, expensive scene that would eat up a huge chunk of her budget. She'd be glad to have this shot in the can before Marcus could have more doubts about the cost.

Her radio crackled to life with the voice of her first assistant director, who was responsible for setting up the crowd scene. "Picture's up in five minutes, Raine."

"The second camera crew is in position?"

"Yep."

"Good. Five minutes, then." She lowered the radio, her gaze sweeping the set again. The location manager had done well to find this long-unused train barn. Hard work and too much money had transformed it into a mock Victorian railway station. While the electricians had spent all day lighting the echoing space, set dressers worked feverishly on the period details like lampposts and railings that made the set look convincing.

Greg Marino was personally operating the main camera beside her, and he gave a thumb's-up when he saw her glance. She smiled, trying to look confident, then adjusted the belt that secured her in the seat, trying to reduce the pressure of the whalebone corset on her ribs. Damn Jane Stackpole for slighting her obligations. Since Rainey would be in several shots later, she had to wear full costume and makeup. Directing was much easier in jeans.

The radio crackled. "We're ready, Raine."

One last look, knowing that the weight of cast, crew, extras, and equipment all rested on her shoulders. Taking a deep breath, she said, "Roll 'em!"

The camera started to whir as Greg focused on the dark entrance to the train barn. Since modern London was directly outside, the shoot had to be done at night to avoid glimpses of a twenty-first-century city.

A beam of light slashed through the darkness, followed by the menacing bulk of the locomotive. Pistons churned, wheels whirled, and smoke poured from the stack as it rumbled to a halt with bone-vibrating power.

The camera was set low to emphasize the mass and power of the locomotive, so different from the sand and horses of the desolate land where John Randall had been imprisoned. Inside the cars, dimly visible moving figures prepared to alight.

The camera panned to the second carriage, fixing on a door as it swung open and passengers began to emerge. An elderly lady, a young couple. Then Kenzie, his scarlet uniform loose and his face haggard from captivity. Damn, Kenzie was good.

He stepped onto the platform, and a roar of voices greeted him. A brass band struck up as he looked around, shocked and confused. The crane began to smoothly rise and move backward, gradually revealing the massed people who'd come to welcome their hero home.

As they lifted, Greg and his camera crew maintained their focus on Kenzie, whose attempt at retreat was blocked by passengers behind him. The crane stopped so near the ceiling that Rainey instinctively ducked. Below, Randall had almost vanished among the crowd of his admirers, a man being eaten alive by celebrity. His scarlet uniform coat blazed like a splash of blood in a sea of civilian black.

Everything was just as Rainey had envisioned it years earlier when she'd first read the novel, and seen it in her mind as a movie. She felt a combination of exultation and terror. This was the essence of moviemaking—creating images that told a story. This was what she'd been born for. "Cut!"

After they returned to ground level, she and Greg studied

the video monitor replay. "It works for me, Greg. What do you think?" He gave a nod of approval, so she called, "Print."

A second take just in case, then on to the next setup. Vignettes were shot—the brass band, a child waving a Union Jack, the prime minister welcoming the hero home because an election was coming and he wanted good press. Some things never changed.

While the second camera crew shot crowd details at the other end of the barn, Greg filmed Randall woodenly meeting the prime minister. His father greeted him, beaming with pride and total insensitivity. After the official welcome, Randall began a painfully slow attempt to move through the crowd.

Then it was Rainey's turn. While lights and camera were reset, the head makeup artist did a touch-up, muttering fretfully at the challenge of making a woman over thirty look ten years younger. Rainey was equally anxious, though she tried to conceal it. She'd never directed herself before.

Despite knowing what she wanted on film, Rainey found it disorienting to sink into Sarah while at the same time having to remember to think like a director. She missed her marks on the first take, then blanked on the dialogue and blew the second take as well. "Steady, TLC. Just do it," Greg said quietly.

Rainey swore at herself and tried again. This time she nailed the scene, a simple one that showed her watching Randall's arrival. At first she was exhilarated, but her expression changed. "Papa, something is wrong. Why won't they leave him alone?"

Though Sarah had meant to stay at her father's side on the fringes of the crowd, once she saw Randall's face she plunged into the mass of people. As the chant, "Randall, Randall!" echoed through the vast station, she fought her way toward him, ignoring her father's calls to retreat.

Some men smiled indulgently and squeezed aside, while others frowned at her boldness. She scarcely noticed, all her attention fixed on Randall. She was perhaps the only one in the vast train station who saw the panic in his eyes. He looked as if he were being flayed alive.

Kenzie's frantic gaze touched hers, and she gasped. The horror in his face was so compelling that both Sarah and the director fell away, leaving Rainey, who feared for her husband. "John! *John!*"

Staring at her as if she were an angel descending from on high, he reached out. Her gloved hand stretched toward him until they clasped fiercely across three men, her green sleeve bright against the black coats.

For an instant the pressure of his hard fingers was crushing. Then his grip relaxed as his expression shifted to distress. Sensing that she was losing him in more ways than one, she tightened her grasp, refusing to let him escape.

They clung like that for long moments, until Rainey called, "Cut!"

She released Kenzie's hand, chest heaving in the tight costume after her struggle through the crowd, and joined Greg to watch the video. He'd done his job perfectly, zooming in until the clasping hands became an emblem of their relationship— the man in retreat, the woman determined to hold on no matter what dark forces tried to separate them. "Just what I wanted, Greg. Print."

While the crew did the next setup, she returned to Kenzie, who had retreated to the shadow of the steam locomotive, arms folded across his chest and expression remote. The extras had moved away, leaving the star his privacy.

Since he didn't seem to see her approach, she touched his arm lightly. "Kenzie, that was terrific."

He jerked his arm away violently, as if she'd attacked. It took a moment for his eyes to focus on her.

"Without a single word, you showed everything a viewer needs to know about Randall's state of mind," she said hesitantly. "A man returning from hell, and bringing it with him."

He adjusted the sleeve of his military tunic. "It's what you wanted, wasn't it?" He pivoted and stalked away.

She watched him go in dismay. She'd wanted him to stretch his acting to the limits. Be careful what you wish for. . . .

•   •   •

After the shoot finally wrapped for the day, Rainey found Kenzie dozing in the car waiting to transport her to the Dorchester. She almost fell over him when she climbed into the vehicle. "Sorry." As he moved across the seat to make room for her, she added, "I thought you'd have left by now."

"I needed time to unwind." As the car pulled into the street, Kenzie wearily rubbed his eyes. "I'm sorry I snapped at you, Rainey. I'm afraid it's only going to get worse between now and the end of the shooting."

"I think I'm the one who owes you an apology. I'm beginning to realize just what I talked you into."

"Does this mean you wish you'd found yourself a different John Randall?"

She bit her lip. "No. You're doing an amazing job with him. What I wish is that playing the role wasn't so upsetting for you."

"That's my girl." There was humor in his voice. "It takes your kind of single-minded determination to make good movies. Moviemaking is like war, and there are bound to be a few casualties."

"Now I really feel guilty."

"I expect I'll be among the wounded, not the dead."

"How very comforting," she said dryly. "By the way, Greg called me several initials I didn't quite catch, and I forgot to ask him about it. T-something. Is that some kind of director nickname that I haven't heard before?"

He laughed. "Back in New Mexico, the crew started to call you 'TLC.' "

"Tender Loving Care?"

"No. Tough Little Chick."

She flushed. "Any reason in particular, or general principles?"

"You got the nickname after you fired the cable puller."

"He deserved firing," she said defensively. "The last thing a struggling actor needs is someone being snide."

"Undoubtedly true, which is why TLC is a compliment. The crew likes a director who's in control."

Tough Little Chick. She supposed it could be worse. They might have called her BB for Bitch Boss.

Kenzie's amusement vanished. "Did you see that photograph in the *Inquirer*?"

Her stomach immediately knotted up. "Yes."

"Jenny is strictly a friend. I dropped by to talk to her about Nigel Stone, and we went out to dinner."

Rainey exhaled roughly. "Thanks for telling me. I know it's not my business, but it would be . . . uncomfortable if you were carrying on an affair with someone else right under my nose."

"I know." He reached through the darkness and touched her hand. "I promise—no affairs while we're shooting."

Like Sarah, she had an almost overpowering desire to grab onto his hand to prevent him from slipping away.

Being older, modern, and almost divorced, she didn't.

✺ 18 ✺

While waiting for shooting to begin, Kenzie paced back and forth along the west side of Morchard House. At times like this he almost wished he smoked. Maybe fiddling with a pipe would help him relax. The closer he came to Randall's disintegration, the tenser he became. He could feel the character sliding under his skin, suffocating him from the inside out.

At least the production had left London, which meant no paparazzi. Unfortunately, London newspapers were delivered locally so he wasn't free of Nigel Stone's crusade. Each day the reporter trumpeted some new piece of information about the lurid past of Kenzie Scott. So far, it hadn't been too bad. No one who knew Kenzie well had spoken up, and Stone hadn't found a shred of information from before the RADA years. Though the reporter presented every incident in the worst possible light, he hadn't printed any outright lies. Probably the man had a lawsuit-wary editor vetting his forgettable prose.

Kenzie looked down to where Rainey was conferring with Greg Marino about a complicated long shot that would require two cameras. Dressed in a flowing, virginal white gown, she looked like the ingenue, not the boss. Yet she'd taken to directing like a swan to water. Her grasp of her story and how she wanted to tell it was admirable, as was her respect for the expertise of her cast and crew. She never forgot that moviemaking was a collaborative process. Under different circumstances, he'd have really enjoyed being directed by her.

His restless gaze moved to the voluptuous green hills of Devon. If the dailies were to be believed, this movie was going to be achingly beautiful, a nostalgic portrait of a vanished England that had sent her sons to build an empire, and accepted their pain and sacrifice as her due. *The Masterpiece Theatre* audience would love it. He wasn't up to watching the dailies, though. He couldn't bear seeing himself as Randall.

Leaving the director of photography, Rainey drifted toward him, looking as young and innocent as this next scene required. "You're good, Kenzie—you even pace in the character of an uptight Victorian officer," she said cheerfully. "Do try to vary your path, though. If you wear holes in this lovely green turf, I'll have to pay the owner for restoration, and I suspect that pieces of lawn that have been pampered for five hundred years don't come cheap."

Her teasing relaxed him into a smile. "I'll bear that in mind."

"Let's walk around the house. By the time we get back, Greg should have the second camera set up to shoot the gazebo end of the scene." She took his arm. Feeling his tight muscles, she said quietly, "We're going to have to get used to touching each other on camera."

Thinking that bluntness was in order, he asked, "Does the

prospect of being cinematic lovers again bother you as much as it bothers me?"

"I'd rather shoot a stark naked sex scene with anyone else." She grimaced. "Even if we both play this as pure acting, without a particle of personal emotion, viewers will look at these scenes and think they see you and me. I hate the thought of that."

"So do I."

They rounded a corner and began paralleling the north face of Morchard House. "Apart from you and me being as nervous as ants on a griddle, production is going so smoothly it makes me nervous," she said. "Morchard House, for example—who would have believed we could find a manor house with two facades so different that we could use one building for both of the major estates? It's a real money and time saver."

The older section of the house was Jacobean in style, while a newer wing was Georgian. Careful camera placement would make them seem like two separate structures. Morchard also had several beautifully detailed interior rooms and extensive gardens with ponds, copses, follies, and other scenic settings. The estate was theirs for the next fortnight, since the owners had taken their immense rental fee and gone on holiday in France until the production left.

Rainey shaded her eyes as she peered into the distance. "The location manager said there's a labyrinth at the far end of the garden. I'll have to look for it, if I ever have a moment to explore."

"Do you mean a maze?"

"No, mazes are formed by banks of shrubbery and designed to confuse. A labyrinth is a two-dimensional pattern with only one path through. By walking the pattern from one end to the other, you—well, the idea is to find yourself instead of becoming lost."

The idea was to find oneself? He made a mental note to avoid the Morchard labyrinth at all costs. "How does it work?"

"Concentrating on the path is very relaxing, almost a form

of meditation. There's an outdoor labyrinth at Grace Cathedral, that big Episcopal church on Nob Hill in San Francisco. My friend Kate took me there one night after we had dinner, and to humor her, I walked the labyrinth. By the time I was halfway through, I was more relaxed than I'd been in days. I now walk labyrinths whenever possible."

"Beware of finding a Minotaur in the center."

She grinned. "Any monsters who got that far would probably be in a light trance and fairly harmless."

They turned the last corner and saw the production crew ahead. "Looks like it's time for you to chase me through the gardens," she said. "I've been thinking of using this sequence to open the movie and as a backdrop for the credits. What do you think?"

"Sounds plausible. This sets the tone for the movie, both the relationship and the idealized, picture perfect England that Randall is going to lose."

"That's what I thought." As they neared the crew, she said pensively, "As much as possible, I've set up the shooting schedule to keep the scenes in the order they fall in the story. I wonder if that will make any difference in the continuity of the emotions."

"It shouldn't. Any skilled actor should be able to nail his scenes no matter what order they're shot in."

"But I want more than skill. I want inspiration."

"Perspiration is more reliable than inspiration," he said dryly. Safer, too. The last thing he wanted to feel on this movie was inspiration, which would risk cracking the floodgates of memory. That way madness lay.

Her expression bright with laughter, Sarah Masterson caught up her skirts and darted across the velvety green grass. A quick glance over her shoulder confirmed that she was being pursued by Captain Randall, his laughter matching hers.

Their families had always been neighbors, but in the past he'd looked on her as a little sister. She'd grown since the last time they'd met, and he'd noticed. Oh, yes, he'd noticed. Since his return home on leave a fortnight earlier, he'd called on her daily. When they waltzed at a ball the night before, she'd come near to melting in his arms. Half the night she'd tossed and turned, wondering if she'd imagined that light in his eyes, but she hadn't. He really was interested in her, Sarah Masterson.

Afraid to carry the thought too far, she raced up the hill toward the gazebo, driven by the primal instinct that made a doe flee a stag so the male must pursue and win his mate. When she reached the small Italianate structure, she stopped, panting as her lungs fought the constriction of her corsets.

The captain joined her, his breathing hardly quickened. He could have caught her easily, she knew, but he'd also enjoyed the chase.

His tall frame seemed to fill the space between the entrance columns. He was the handsomest man she'd ever seen, and the light in his eyes made her excited and nervous all at once.

He took a step toward her. "Miss Masterson. May . . . may I call you Sarah?"

Absurd that he should feel shy of her. "You may," she said, blushing at the intimacy of allowing him the freedom of her Christian name. "You did when we were younger."

He drew another step closer. "Sarah, this may seem sudden, and yet I feel as if I've been waiting for this day my whole life."

He took her hands in his and looked at her with Kenzie's green eyes. Rainey blinked, disoriented, as her mind broke character. Hoping the camera outside the gazebo hadn't caught her lapse, she gazed at her suitor raptly, as Sarah would have.

"You were the sweetest and prettiest of little girls, and now you've grown into the sweetest, loveliest young woman I've ever known." He raised her hands and kissed them. "The only woman I can imagine spending my life with. I love you, Sarah. Will you marry me?"

She caught her breath, stunned by the words she'd dreamed of hearing. This magnificent man wanted her for his wife.

Didn't he know that she would give him anything he asked, even the heart from her breast? "Yes, Captain Randall," she whispered. "I will gladly marry you."

His expression turned from uncertainty to exhilaration. "What, no protestations that this is so sudden? No requests for time to consider the matter?"

"I've never been surer of anything in my life."

"Oh, Sarah, Sarah, that honesty is part of what I love about you." He drew her into an embrace. "You must call me John when we are in private."

She turned her face up for his kiss, not certain what to expect. The warm, gentle pressure of his lips was deeply pleasing. As her eyes drifted shut, she became acutely aware of him through her other senses. The taste of his mouth, the warmth of his body, the roughness of his breathing, his provocative male scent. From this day on, she would know him from every other man in the world even with her eyes closed.

The kiss lengthened, became joined by caresses that made her blood pump urgently through her body.

Once more her concentration broke. She'd been a fool to think she could play this scene without personal emotions erupting. Sarah's innocence took Rainey back to the night Kenzie had asked her to marry him, and for a brief, mad moment she'd dared hope it would work.

But it hadn't. The sorrow of that was so intense that even her actor's discipline couldn't keep tears from her eyes. When his hand brushed her breast, she lost Sarah entirely and stepped back with a gasp that wasn't in the script.

Kenzie's expression showed that he was also having trouble separating himself from the role. Improvising dialogue, he drew her down beside him on the bench that circled the gazebo. "I'm a beast," he said with suppressed violence as he stroked the tears from her cheeks. "You're so pure, so innocent, and I have frightened you."

"I'm not frightened," she assured him. "Just—overwhelmed by happiness."

Moving back to the script, he said, "I wish we didn't have to wait to marry, but next week my regiment sets sail for North Africa."

He would leave her so soon to go into battle? "How long will you be gone?"

"Only a few months. We're being sent to quell a rebellion by some fanatic natives, so it shouldn't take long. When we've rolled up the rebels, I'll resign my commission and come home to you." He smiled tenderly. "I've had enough of adventures. Now I'm ready to build a home and family with you."

Despite his reassurances, she felt an icy chill down her spine. Not sure if it was a premonition or simply concern, she said intensely, "However long it takes, I shall wait for you, John."

"My dear, dear girl." He kissed her again. This time, she kissed him back with a fervor born of fear.

After a few seconds had passed, Rainey pulled back and said, "Cut." Shaken by the emotions searing through her, she said, "Don't print this. We're going to have to reshoot from the time I enter the gazebo."

Greg frowned. "I dunno, Rainey, I thought it looked pretty good. Come check it on the video monitor."

No way was she ready to watch herself lose control, but neither could she ignore Greg's professional judgment. "Okay, print, but we'll do another take on the gazebo scene."

So low only she could hear, Kenzie said, "Doing several more takes should safely take the excess emotion out and reduce the scene to nice, clean actor's skill."

She scowled. "Don't try to tell me that you won't prefer that."

"I'd much rather act this role at arm's length," he agreed. "But will that give you the movie you want?"

"What I don't want is a devil's advocate!"

"Comes with the package, TLC." He gave her a wintry smile, then rose and left the gazebo while Greg prepared for the next take.

She sat unmoving on the bench, mentally cataloguing the number of scenes between Sarah and Randall yet to come. If she ever came face-to-face with Jane Stackpole in the future, she'd throttle the girl with her bare hands.

At least, she would if she managed to survive this movie.

By the end of the day, Kenzie felt as if he'd been drained dry and crushed for recycling. Each of the scenes between him and Rainey had required several takes, with the quality deteriorating every time. The first takes were invariably the best, but every one was wrenched painfully from his and Rainey's viscera.

His mood was not improved when he returned to the pleasant country hotel that had been temporarily taken over by *The Centurion*. His efficient, unobtrusive assistant, Josh, had carefully laid that morning's edition of the *Inquirer* on the antique desk in Kenzie's sitting room. Blaring across the corner of the tabloid was a flash proclaiming, "Kenzie's Past Revealed!"

Praying this was a false trail, he turned to the story inside. At the top was a sexy photo of Jenny Lyme looking misleadingly earnest and reliable. "Kenzie's longtime ladyfriend tells all!" If the *Inquirer* wasn't careful, they'd run out of exclamation points.

Jenny's "revelations" were the tragic, colonial past she'd invented the night they had dinner. Though she mentioned that she was only making an educated guess, Nigel Stone was willing to race off with her speculations.

He also managed to imply that Kenzie and Jenny had been lovers more or less continuously since their student days, including during his marriage, but once again the reporter avoided saying anything actually libelous. Kenzie tossed the newspaper aside. With any luck, Stone would follow that red herring off to Africa, and the newspaper campaign would gradually fade away.

But he couldn't escape the uneasy feeling that his luck wouldn't be that good.

❧ 19 ❧

*Kenzie stood at attention as organ music rum-*bled through the church. The elaborate arrangements for Randall's wedding reminded him of why he'd asked Rainey to elope. If he'd had to go through these complications in real life, he'd have lost his nerve and bolted.

Of course, even if he and Rainey had chosen a formal wedding, he wouldn't have received a personal message from Queen Victoria commending him for embracing wedded bliss, and looking forward to more fine sons to defend the Empire. Having been pressured to go through with the marriage by his beloved, both families, his sovereign, and the British press, John Randall was a basket case by the time his wedding arrived.

Flower girls, bridesmaids, a maid of honor. It was the Victorians who'd invented the modern white wedding. They'd even started the custom of having the bride dressed in a gown that resembled a wedding cake.

As the music crescendoed, Rainey appeared at the far end of the church aisle on the arm of Richard Farley, who looked mightily distinguished as her father. She was a beautiful bride, radiant with the absolute certainty usually found only in the very young. Kenzie forced himself into John Randall again.

As he watched his bride approach, guilt almost overwhelmed him. He was filthy, tainted, unworthy of this bright, pure girl. Allowing this marriage to take place was criminal weakness. As he took her small hand and they pledged eternal vows, his mind and spirit were hammered by the dark drumbeats of despair.

It was easy to express that. He'd felt the same at his own marriage.

The wedding scenes went so smoothly that there was time to return to Morchard House for more shooting. The production had made up the time lost in New Mexico, and gained a full day on the original schedule. To Rainey, having a cushion of extra time was better than money in the bank, though she wouldn't have minded some of that, too.

The wedding was followed by the wedding night. In an elaborately decorated bedroom, Sarah waited in a canopied bed, dressed in foaming layers of lace and virginal white silk sheer enough to hint at the equally virginal but eager body underneath.

She sat against the pillows, fingers locked tensely as the minutes ticked away. Her mother had told her what to expect of her wedding night. Peculiar though marital activities sounded, Sarah trusted her husband to guide her. But where was he?

She awoke from a doze with a start when he finally entered the bedroom. His hair and garments were subtly disheveled, his expression unbearably bleak.

He swallowed hard before starting to speak unthinkable words. He'd been wrong to marry her, and they must seek an annulment. He'd take all the blame, and she'd be left unsullied, free to marry another man.

Horrified, she slid from the bed and went to him, touching his chest as she begged for an explanation. His voice faltered, then died away as he stared down with hungry eyes. One shaking hand lifted to stroke her arm. Driven by Eve's instinct, she stood on her toes to kiss him.

His control shattered and he pulled her down onto the bed, kissing her frantically, crushing her with his weight. Alarmed, she resisted in an unspoken plea for him to proceed more gently. He halted, face frozen, groaning, "May God forgive me."

He rolled from the bed and stumbled across the room. Folding to the floor, he wrapped his arms around his belly and retched violently.

Kenzie was improvising again. Afraid to speculate what had inspired a gesture so powerful and disturbing, she joined him on the floor and drew him into her arms. Their wedding night faded out on the image of his head pressed against her silk-clad breasts as he wept with unholy despair.

By the time Rainey and Greg had all the coverage they needed for the wedding night scene, Kenzie's internal demons were out in full force, howling and slashing. Desperate to get away, he escaped from the house as soon as the shots were finished.

He was halfway to the gardens when the assistant director intercepted him. "There may be time to set up and shoot another scene, Kenzie. Will you be in your trailer?"

He bit back an oath. "If you want to shoot more, find another target." His assistant approached, but one look at Kenzie's face and Josh stopped dead in his tracks.

Kenzie cut into the carefully manicured woods. He'd walked this way before and knew the path led to the farthest reaches of the private park. To solitude.

Rainey had said that Randall's violently physical reaction to his wedding night was brilliant. Pure inspiration. Yet even as she praised his performance, Kenzie could see her worry about the murky depths that had spawned his inspiration. If only she knew.

Thank God she didn't.

He retched again as images of bare limbs and violated innocence swamped his mind. He clung to a tree, gasping for breath, until the cool air steadied his stomach, then he blindly continued along the path.

The wedding night scene was bad enough, and worse was yet to come. He hadn't the faintest idea how he'd get through the rest of the movie. Inhabiting John Randall was chipping away at the defenses that made it possible for him to function. But Rainey was right that this was the kind of role that won Oscars. John Randall was so tormented, so antiheroic, that the industry professionals who voted for the awards would be impressed at Kenzie's willingness to so degrade himself.

It bloody well wasn't worth it for a stubby little statuette.

Though John Randall was a neurotic mess, he was a better

man than Kenzie Scott, because he'd tried to resist entering into a doomed marriage. If Kenzie had rejected the impulse to propose, he and Rainey could have gone their separate ways, perhaps met now and then with fondness instead of living in purgatory. *We'll always have Paris.* Or in this case, the Northern California coast.

He reached the end of the path, and found himself in a sunny clearing rimmed with flowers. In the center circular patterns were embossed in the turf. This must be the labyrinth Rainey had mentioned. What had she said? That it was a path to finding oneself.

That was the last thing he needed—he knew who and what he was, and had spent a lifetime trying to bury that knowledge. He started to turn away, then remembered that she'd also said that walking a labyrinth was a way to find peace. That he could use.

As he located the starting point, he wondered what one was supposed to do during a labyrinth walk. Pray? Meditate? Try to empty the mind, zen-style?

He inhaled deeply several times, consciously letting go of the tension in his body. Then he started walking, looking downward to stay on the curving path. That simple act helped focus his mind and quiet his churning thoughts. His consciousness gradually narrowed down to the act of walking while physical awareness increased: the pulse of his blood, the steady pump of air in and out of his lungs, the woodland scents in his nostrils.

By the time he reached the middle of the labyrinth, his demons had largely fallen silent. That was good enough. He knew they'd never go away entirely, for they were the forces that defined who he was.

But he was also a survivor. Instead of self-destructing, he'd built a comfortable, satisfying life, and even achieved a bizarre degree of success. Every now and then the demons would wake and rip at him, but eventually they returned to their slumbers. They would this time as well. In a few weeks the *Centu-*

rion shoot would be over, and he could go on to his next project. He'd never even have to watch the finished movie.

Though he would miss Rainey bitterly, his life would be simpler. If there were none of the joyous highs he'd experienced with her, there would also be no crushing lows. He could have his comfortable, detached existence back.

Feeling relatively peaceful, he exited the labyrinth, and looked up to see Rainey. Tension returned with a vengeance. Still dressed in her layered Victorian nightgown, Rainey sat on the grassy embankment with her knees drawn up and her arms crossed on top of them. She looked like a lost waif.

A sexy lost waif. Despite his distress during the wedding night scene, his damned hormones had reacted to the fact that he'd been rolling around in a bed with the most desirable woman he'd ever known. "Have you come to find me, or lose yourself?"

"Some of both. I was worried about you—acting of the caliber you were doing comes out of one's marrow."

"You were doing some high-octane acting yourself."

"Which was why when I finished, I took one look at the paperwork Val had carefully laid out in my trailer, and decided to run away and hide. I can be a director, or an actress, but it's hard to be both at once."

He prowled across the clearing, keeping his distance. "Are you glad or sorry to be making this movie?"

After a long silence, she said, "Both."

"Nothing like a definitive answer," he said dryly. "What was it about this particular story that made you so determined to make it?"

"I have control-freak tendencies. You may have noticed."

He had to smile. "I've noticed. So?"

"This was a way of getting everything to come out right. The characters suffer a great deal, yet ultimately they not only survive, but are better, stronger people for what they've endured. They'll have a better, more honest marriage, too."

The parallel to their own failed marriage was painfully obvious. Changing the subject, he asked, "Have you seen the latest *Inquirer*? I haven't yet."

"Today's installment was pretty interesting. Nigel Stone had two photographs alleged to be you as a child."

Shock jolted through him. "Did they look like me?"

She shrugged. "The pictures showed a small, dark-haired boy with a face shaped approximately like yours and a hint of cleft in the chin. It could have been you, but it could have been any number of other men. The pictures were sent in by some fellow in Scotland who claims you're his long lost brother, Hugh MacLeod."

He exhaled with relief. "How did the man reach that conclusion?"

"Apparently his brother joined the army, became an elite SAS operative, and was in a helicopter that crashed into the Persian Gulf during some sneaky operation. There was no body identified, so the brother suspects that Hugh MacLeod was rescued but lost his memory, and went on to Hollywood success."

"It's a good story. What was Nigel Stone's take?"

"He rather liked this because it explains why you're so cagey about your past—you don't remember it."

"As I said, it's a good story. Tomorrow there may be one that's even better. Probably someone claiming I was born in Sherwood Forest and raised by wolves."

Her brow furrowed. "Are there wolves in Britain? I thought they were wiped out centuries ago."

"They were, but saying I was raised by terriers wouldn't have the same effect."

"I'm glad to see that you're recovering." She smiled, but it faded quickly. "Are you going to make it through to the end, Kenzie?"

"I don't know," he said honestly. "If I had the sense God gave a sparrow, I'd walk off the set while I still have my sanity. But the tradition that the show must go on was thoroughly ingrained at RADA. Having started this project, I have a responsibility to finish it." His strongest identity was as an actor. Quitting in the middle of production would betray his self-image of being a consummate professional, and that would be even more destructive than inhabiting John Randall's scalding skin.

"For the sake of the movie, I give thanks to RADA."

He studied her pinched expression. "You don't look very relieved."

"If you walked out, I'd be crazed, but a little relieved, too." She rested her chin on her crossed arms. "I don't want to be responsible for you having a nervous breakdown."

"I'm going to be rotten company until shooting is finished, but I haven't lost my mind yet, and I don't think I will."

"I'd like to believe you, but you're a mass of nerves. It's so unlike you to be pacing back and forth like a caged lion. You've always been so laid-back."

"I am pacing, aren't I?" He stopped halfway between the labyrinth and the encircling trees. "Is that better?"

"Not much." She patted the grass next to her. "Sit down and contemplate the daisies or something."

After a moment's hesitation, he did as she suggested. If she didn't mind the fact that she was wearing a semitranslucent gown that was sliding down one shoulder, neither would he. "You're looking as stressed as I am. Any reason in particular, or are you twanging on general principles?"

"I kept thinking about what you said about finding out who my father is, and finally hired an investigator. Joe Mooney sends weekly reports about his lack of progress so at least I'll know where the money is going. One arrived today." She hunched still further, her arms tightening around her raised knees. "He still has a few leads to follow up, but in his professional opinion, I probably won't ever have a definitive answer."

"Does that bother you?"

"It's a loose end I'd like tied up, but if the information isn't available, I'll just have to accept that I'll never know."

"Look on the bright side. If you did find your father, he might be a leech who'd want you to support him."

"I hadn't thought of that." She smiled faintly. "I could prove I was a tough little chick by telling him to get lost. But at least I'd know who he was. It's strange. I've gone all of these years without knowing, but having started to look, now I'd like an answer."

"Ambiguity isn't your strong point, Rainey. You're terrific in a crisis, but uncertainty sends you round the bend."

"You know me too well."

"The feeling is entirely mutual." He picked a small yellow flower from the grass and rolled it between thumb and forefinger. "A divorce decree should divide up not only marital property, but marital knowledge. I'd insist you return your appalling skill at reading my mind."

"I'd demand that you hand over your obnoxious ability to sense what I'm feeling, usually before I do."

They looked at each other, and burst out laughing. "You have to relinquish your knowledge of where I'm ticklish," he said.

"And you have to wipe from your mind what I look like in the morning when I first wake up."

He looked into her changeable eyes, green now in the grassy clearing, and realized that he was not the only one aroused by their on-camera grapplings. "My lawyer will tell you that I refuse to give that up."

"Then you don't get the tickle secrets back." She raised a hand and traced the edge of his ear with her fingertip. The effect wasn't ticklish; it was incendiary, and she knew it. He leaned forward and kissed her, his mouth slanting over hers hungrily.

She made a sound deep in her throat and moved closer. "We both deserve a reward after a difficult day," she murmured, "and there's no chocolate around."

He laughed, feeling better than he had since leaving New Mexico. Catching her around the waist, he lay back on the grass and pulled her on top of him. "Give the costume designer a bonus. This silk and lace thing you're wearing is even more irresistible than chocolate."

The looseness of the garment made it easy to slide his hands under as they kissed fiercely, the tensions of their work exploding into raw, needy passion. Her urgency matched his, and she tore at his Victorian buttons as he kneaded her silky skin under the lacy layers of the gown. When they came together, he forgot demons and shredding nerves and future loneliness in the intense reality of the moment. Though the past couldn't be mended, he could give her pleasure now, a gift of atonement for what couldn't be changed.

She cried out, grinding her hips against his in a long, powerful climax. He let himself surrender to annihilation, crushing her to him as he convulsed uncontrollably. Then he held her trembling body close, not wanting this precious interlude to end. If only they could have remained like this, been satisfied with the intimacy born of affection and rare physical passion. But she'd wanted and deserved more, and he was incapable of it.

Breathing nearly normal, she murmured, "We have to stop meeting like this."

Tenderly he smoothed back her hair. "Not a problem. This didn't happen."

She slid off him and rolled onto her back, expression troubled. "I wish I was better at convincing myself of that, or at least had better willpower."

He took her hand, lacing his fingers between hers. "Sleeping together while we're getting a divorce is bound to have painful emotional repercussions. But you must admit that we're both much more relaxed than we were a few minutes ago."

"Good point. I haven't a tense muscle left in my body. In fact, I might not have any bones, either."

"So the time hasn't been wasted."

"I suppose not," she said, but her expression was grave.

He wondered if the pressures of making this movie would drive them into each other's arms again. He hoped so, because physical intimacy had gone a long way toward repairing his tattered spirit.

A few more such encounters, and he might survive this movie after all.

❧ 20 ❧

Over morning coffee, Rainey read Nigel Stone's latest article on Kenzie's mysterious past. This time, "Morgan the Castle," the Welsh caretaker of an ancient ruined fortress, said he'd always suspected Kenzie Scott was really a classmate of his from a fishing village in northern Wales. Rhys Jones had been a handsome lad with a quick tongue and a taste for play-acting. After leaving school he'd joined the British Navy, then deserted and never been heard from since. Morgan's guess was that Rhys had decided to become an actor and taken the name Kenzie Scott, concealing his past because he didn't want to be court-martialed for desertion.

Morgan supplied another photo of a small boy, this one sitting on the back of a wide pony with his little legs sticking out. The child looked vaguely like Kenzie, but not enough.

She set the newspaper aside. As Kenzie had predicted, Stone was swamped with tips from an overhelpful public. The *Inquirer* printed only the most plausible possibilities out of the hundreds that had been sent in. If anyone had offered the truth, it was buried in a haystack of false sightings.

Which was good, because Kenzie had enough to worry about. Though he hadn't flipped out again in the week since the wedding scene, he looked as tense as a bowstring, and had withdrawn into monosyllables off the set. She wished he'd talk to her, but he was doing brilliant work, so she left him alone.

The production had rented him a sports car, and after shooting ended for the day, he would roar away, not to be seen until his call the next morning. Even though she knew he was a first-rate driver and had been raised in this country where they drove on the wrong side of the road, she had nightmare visions of him swinging around a curve on a narrow country road and smashing into a truck or tractor. Or speeding off a cliff into the sea.

His wanderings kept him out very late. Since the hotel's two best rooms were in the same hallway with facing doors, she would lie in bed and listen for him, unable to rest until she knew he'd returned safely. She wasn't sure if she was acting like his wife, his director, or his mother, but she couldn't stop worrying.

In another three weeks, shooting would be over and they'd go their separate ways. She'd feel as if an arm had been ripped off, but at least life would no longer be surreal. Post-production on *The Centurion* would keep her crazy-busy for the next several months, and by the time she surfaced again, she'd be a free woman, and over Kenzie. Mostly, anyhow.

Or at least, maybe by then she'd *want* to be over him.

"Cut!" Rainey's flat voice ended the take.

Swearing under his breath, Kenzie released Rainey's hands, then stood and rolled his tight shoulders, wondering if she was going to ream him out. Lord knew she had reason to, but in his present mood he'd explode if she took him to task for his failures. This was the eleventh take of this scene. Only two takes had been worth printing, and both were marginal. The fault was solidly his—he was getting worse and worse.

He prowled away from the camera, the sea breeze blowing his hair. The scene took place on a cliff where Sarah had stopped Randall from hurling himself onto the rocks below. As she gripped his hands, anchoring him to life, he stammered out the bare details of the atrocities he'd endured, saying enough for her to deduce why he was so profoundly disturbed and filled with self-loathing.

In other words, Randall had to spill his guts to his wife, but Kenzie was incapable of evoking the right emotions. When he wasn't blowing his lines, he was failing in his delivery. In contrast, Rainey was at her best as a young wife offering compassion and acceptance for a situation that she was barely capable of understanding.

Later the scene would be intercut with flashbacks of Randall and his captor that would be shot on the sound stage in London. Kenzie tried not to think about those last scenes, which came at the very end of the shoot and would be truly harrowing. Assuming he'd be able to do them at all. Based on how he was managing today, he might never make it as far as the bloody sound stage.

He expected Rainey to call for another take. Instead, she told her AD, "Break time," and took Kenzie's arm. He flinched at her touch, then felt oddly comforted.

"Walk with me," she said. "Maybe the sea breezes will clear our heads."

At least she was going to yell in private rather than in front of everyone. He was grateful for that, though he'd still bristle defensively. God knew he was trying, and Rainey ought to know it, too.

Silently they followed the path along the cliff, the wind blowing tendrils of her hair and fluttering her long, heavy skirts. When they were far enough from the production crew for privacy, she said quietly, "As this movie has progressed, you've had to reveal more and more of yourself, and you've done it brilliantly. This scene is the most intrusive yet, and it won't equal your other work unless you can allow that camera into your soul. It's a lot to ask of you, maybe too much." She glanced up into his face. "Think about it. When you're ready, we'll do one more take and print whatever we get. If you still can't hit the right notes, to hell with it. We'll do some editing magic with the film we have and fake it. Okay?"

He drew a shaky breath. If Rainey had tried to browbeat him, he'd have fought her, maybe even walked off the set—

something he'd never done before. Instead, she understood the hell he was going through, and would accept it if he'd reached his limits. Which meant he must do his damnedest to spill his guts for the camera. "You're one amazing director, Rainey," he said gruffly. "Give me ten or fifteen minutes alone, and we'll try it again."

She nodded, then shyly stood on tiptoe to kiss his cheek. "Thanks for doing your best, Kenzie."

His gaze followed her as she turned back toward the camera, graceful as any Victorian lady who'd been raised with corsets and full skirts. Then he turned and continued along the cliff.

She was absolutely right that the problem was one of self-revelation. He didn't know if he was capable of peeling any more layers away. It didn't matter that no one watching the film would know exactly what he was revealing—he knew, and he was already working way past his comfort zone. If he didn't go further still, he would fail the movie and the character he was playing. Authenticity was a subtle quality, but most viewers knew when it was missing.

A willingness to reveal oneself was essential to acting. He'd done a fair amount of that early in his career, when he was working in England. Then he'd gone to Hollywood and become an action star, where he could do a good job without ever having to push himself until it hurt. In fact, he'd avoided roles that might have made him uncomfortable, until *The Centurion.*

His thoughts circled back to the bedrock truth that if he was anything, he was an actor. He owed it to himself, Rainey, and his craft to do his best no matter how painful that might be. Which meant spilling his guts.

He spent the rest of his walk thinking about the scene and the character, then returned to the set. Rainey was frowning over the script, but she stood when he approached, her gaze questioning.

"Let's do it," he said tersely.

She nodded and set the script aside. As she took her position, she said, "You might want to try looking right into my eyes this time."

As he waited for the makeup girl to tousle his hair to her satisfaction, he realized that on the previous takes, he'd avoided looking directly at Rainey because of his desire to conceal himself from her. It took a lot of trust to reveal so much to a woman he'd wronged. He inhaled deeply, then gave her a nod of readiness.

"Now," she said, her voice gentle.

As the camera began to roll, he gazed into the infinite depths of her eyes, and revealed his bleeding soul, sentence by stammering sentence: the horror, the pain, the humiliation that had destroyed his sense of who he was, leaving . . . nothing.

He nailed the scene perfectly.

"Cut!" Jubilant, Rainey released his hands and threw her arms around him, tears streaming down her cheeks. "Kenzie, I've always known you were one of the best actors anywhere, but you surpassed yourself that time."

Though glad he'd finally got it right, he felt too raw to deal with anyone, even Rainey. "Twelfth time lucky." He disentangled himself from her hug. Trying not to sound too brusque, he said, "See you in the morning."

He broke away from her and escaped to his trailer, waving off a makeup girl and costumer. Usually he appreciated help in removing makeup and complicated period costumes, but at the moment he couldn't bear to be touched. Swiftly he cleaned off his makeup and exchanged his Victorian outfit for slacks, shirt, and sweater.

Josh had left a pile of messages, stacked in order of importance. He ignored them. Grabbing his car keys, he stepped from the trailer.

And ran smack into Nigel Stone. As a camera flashed in Kenzie's face, the reporter gave a smile that wouldn't have looked out of place on a snake. "You're raising the *Inquirer*'s circulation, Mr. Scott. Readers are fascinated by the hunt for the real man. Information has been flooding in. Care to make any comments? I thought the Welshman who suggested you were a naval deserter might be on to something."

To be accosted by this weasel *now*. Kenzie tightened his fist against a violent desire to smash Stone's ugly face, but he'd learned early that it was disastrous to allow a bully to know that he was getting under one's skin. Especially in front of a photographer who was busily recording every detail.

Collecting himself, he managed a piece of acting almost as difficult as what he'd just done for the camera. "A very entertaining series, Mr. Stone." Smiling with practiced charm, he walked past the reporter. "Some of your stories are better than the ones I've been spinning for years. I'm glad that such a good time is being had by all."

Stone pursued him. "I couldn't find a record of the birth of a Kenzie Scott on the date you claim, or for years in either direction, so you must have changed your name."

"One could assume that. Now if you'll excuse me, I'm late for an engagement."

As he unlocked the door of the Jaguar, Stone said sharply, "I know who you are, Scott, and I swear to God I'll find the evidence I need to expose you."

For an instant Kenzie froze. Reminding himself that Stone couldn't possibly be sure, he slid into the low car, quoting *Macbeth,* " 'Life's but a walking shadow, a poor player, that struts and frets his hour upon the stage, and then is heard no more.' I'm merely an actor, Stone, a creature of smoke and mirrors. There's no mysterious truth. Only what meaning or pleasure people find in my work."

He slammed the door, put the car into gear, and roared away, wheels spitting gravel back at the reporter and photographer. Kenzie's façade of composure lasted long enough to get him out of sight. As his underlying exhaustion took over, once more he wondered bleakly if he'd be able to finish the shooting schedule. He'd given the movie his best, and now, like John Randall, he was left with . . . nothing.

*   *   *

He drove west along the coast into Cornwall, then turned inland, following the old B roads, marked yellow on most maps, that wound their way through villages and towns far from the modern motorways. On the rocky coast route, he whipped the Jaguar around tight turns on steep winding roads.

Such driving required complete concentration, preventing his thoughts from circling obsessively. Inland he once had to slam the brakes on to avoid plowing into a herd of sheep, and later nearly smashed a bicyclist riding down the center of the road. After that, he slowed a little, but not much.

His only stop was for petrol. Probably he should eat, since he hadn't been doing much of that lately, but he dropped the idea when his stomach knotted.

Driving helped banish thoughts of Nigel Stone and John Randall and the carefully constructed being known as Kenzie Scott, but he couldn't escape Rainey so easily. He yearned for her as a dying man yearned for grace. Damnably, he knew that if he went to her for comfort, she'd give it with no questions asked. Yet he'd forfeited the right to ask for it.

So he drove through the night in a futile attempt to outrun the demons.

He returned late to the small hotel that was temporarily home. He'd barely slept for days, and wouldn't tonight despite his bone-deep exhaustion. He'd have to settle for lying down and relaxing, muscle by muscle, which experience had taught him would permit some rest. At least enough to face the next day.

His hand was on the porcelain knob of his room when he looked across the narrow hall at the door to Rainey's suite. She was just inside there. Soft, warm, accepting, with the generous heart she did her best to conceal in her professional life. So close . . .

More than anything on earth, he wanted to hold her. Reason and conscience debated instinct, and lost. There were a couple of paper clips in his pocket, so he dug them out and straightened them into lengths of wire.

The hotel locks were primitive, and he'd lost none of his old skill. It took less than a minute to pick the lock, and go in to his wife.

❧ 21 ❧

There was someone in her room.

Rainey jerked awake as years of urban fear sent adrenaline surging through her veins. It took a moment to remember that she wasn't in crime-ridden California, but the quiet English countryside. Not that location mattered if assault was imminent.

She was on the verge of screaming when a deep, familiar voice whispered, "It's only me."

"Kenzie?" Her heart was hammering so hard that she couldn't even manage anger over his intrusion. "What are you doing here?"

Soundlessly he crossed the room to her canopied bed, his taut face and figure faintly limned by moonlight. The mattress sagged as he sat next to her. She was about to ask what on earth he was doing when his questing hand touched her face. His fingers were cold as death.

She had a sharp memory of his appearance after the last take of the day. Whatever he'd done in the hours since had not improved his state. She slid her arms around his chest and pulled him onto the bed beside her. His whole body was shaking and chilled.

Wondering if he was coming down with some illness, she cradled him as if he were a hurt child. He released his breath in a long exhalation and buried his head between her neck and shoulder. She realized he wasn't here for talk or romance, but the basic human comfort of touch.

She tugged the edge of the duvet out from under his weight, flipped the soft covering over him, then enfolded him in her arms again. Between the cocoon of the duvet and her own body heat radiating through the sheets, he gradually warmed up, his tense body relaxing. His breathing became slow and regular, and eventually he slept.

It was ironic that she was doing the soothing. In the past, Kenzie had been the relaxed one who would calm her when she was wound up. But this movie was clearly stirring up the most hidden depths of his personality. Bleakly she wished that her passion to direct had fastened on a different project. One with no role for Kenzie.

Though she'd been prepared to meet the price of her ambition, she hadn't realized that he would end up paying it for her.

She was wakened by Kenzie's stealthy attempt to slide from the bed. She glanced at her bedside clock. Sunrise came early in an English summer, and it would be almost two hours before her day officially began. "Wait a minute, buddy." She caught his wrist, using a line from a thriller they'd made together. "Think I'm some kinda one-night stand?"

He smiled a little. "I was hoping if I left quietly, you'd forget I was ever here."

"Not likely when you scared me out of a year's growth." She settled back on her pillow, studying his face. He needed a shave, but he looked almost normal again. "How did you get in? I distinctly remember locking the door last night."

His gaze shifted. "It's not a very complicated lock."

"Don't tell me—you made that movie where you were a gentleman burglar, and you learned breaking and entering."

"One should never turn down the chance to acquire new skills."

She felt a touch of envy; she'd never gotten beyond picking a cheap padlock with a hairpin. Children were natural criminals, she suspected. "Are you feeling okay now? You looked like death walking last night."

"If anyone ever offers me the kind of role that wins Oscars again, I'll slam the door in his face."

She winced. "I'm truly sorry. I had no idea how hard this would be."

"Shooting will be over in a fortnight. I should be able to last that long." He sat up, his gaze flicking to her bare shoulders and away again. Dropping into Victorian gentleman mode, he said, "I'd best be gone before I ruin your reputation, my dear lady."

She laid her hand over his. "I don't think it can ruin a wife's reputation if her husband is seen leaving her room."

He didn't move. "For us, the issue isn't reputation, but gossip columnists."

Not to mention their ability to wound each other emotionally—yet she couldn't bear the thought of him leaving so soon. "It would be a waste to have the sexiest man in the world in my bed, and not do anything about it."

He tensed, his gaze traveling the length of her sheet-covered body. "Are you offering a medicinal fuck to keep me from falling apart?"

She flushed violently and rolled away from him, curling into a knot on her side. "What a rotten thing to say! If that's how you feel, get out."

He swore and lay down beside her, wrapping his arm around her waist to tuck her against the front of his body. "I'm really sorry, Rainey. Last night I . . . asked you for more than I should have. We've already had two incidents that didn't officially happen. Three would be pushing it." His voice became dry. "Especially if your motive is charity. I don't have a lot of pride, but I have enough not to want that."

"What makes you think my suggestion was about you?" She swallowed the lump in her throat. "Even tough little chicks can use some tenderness now and then. Unless . . . you really don't want to."

"Don't want to?" He exhaled against her nape, his breath warm and intimate. Then he kissed the juncture of her throat and shoulder in precisely the right point to send sensation blazing through her. "For a clever woman, you can be rather foolish."

He turned her onto her back and drew the sheet down to her waist. She was intensely, erotically aware that she was naked while he was fully dressed.

"You make an exquisite Eos, goddess of the dawn, all luminous skin and hair the color of sunrise." He began unbuttoning his shirt. "I'm glad to see that you haven't developed the unsightly habit of wearing a nightgown."

Suddenly giddy with anticipation, she attacked the zipper of his slacks. "That's because it's summer. If it were winter, I'd be wearing heavy flannel from ankles to chin."

"Then let us celebrate summer." He stood and stripped off his clothing.

She wished he'd undress more slowly, because she loved looking at his strong, beautifully proportioned body. Yet even more she wanted him with her. Eagerly she reached out when he joined her on the bed, as ready and hungry as she.

Unlike the intense, searingly passionate way they'd come together in New Mexico and at the labyrinth, their dawn lovemaking had a playfulness that she hadn't experienced in far too long. Once, they'd always made love with laughter. . . .

Not that passion was lacking, for Kenzie was the most generous of lovers. He also had the most sensual, skilled mouth in creation, a fact he demonstrated until she forgot the movie, the divorce, the guilt, and soared with joy and fulfillment. There was equal joy in returning the gift he gave her, drowning him in sensation until, for a handful of moments, he soared as freely as she.

Afterward she lay contentedly in his arms, listening to the beat of his heart and trying to pretend the clock wasn't ticking with equal regularity. How could they be so close, physically and, she'd swear, emotionally, yet be in the middle of a divorce?

Because he didn't want to stay married. Not once had he opposed the divorce, asked for forgiveness, or suggested that there was any reason to stay together. He'd said he wasn't suited for marriage, and apparently that was his final word on the subject.

Hearing her sigh, Kenzie murmured, "I presume that this morning is another one of those things that hasn't happened?"

"Denial is getting pretty silly, isn't it?" She rolled onto her back and stared at the ruffled canopy of the outrageously romantic bed, assessing the lava flow of pain that pulsed beneath her contentment. "I prefer keeping what happens between us private, but . . . well, as you said, it's only two weeks until the end of production. Obviously sleeping together makes us both feel a whole lot more relaxed and happy, at least in the short-term."

"And in the long-term?" His voice was neutral.

The lava would erupt into a volcano and burn her to her bones again, but that would happen no matter what they did during the next two weeks. "We'll go our separate ways when shooting ends, which will be . . . difficult, but no worse if we sleep together than if we don't. That being the case, the cost-benefit analysis favors continuing to sneak around and see each other." She darted a glance at him. "What do you think?"

"Cost-benefit analysis? What a very cold way of saying that we're happier together, and we'll probably work better for it." He smiled a little wistfully. "Our terms may be different, but we seem to be in agreement. Sneaking around it is."

She snuggled closer, knowing that later she would pay big-time for these two weeks of intimacy. But she'd enjoy herself while it lasted, perhaps find a sense of closure. The agonizing rupture after she'd discovered him with another woman had been too abrupt, the wound too raw to heal.

Remembering him with Angie Greene made her shudder. Noticing, he said softly, "Second thoughts, Rainey?"

Not wanting to think of his unfaithfulness during these golden moments, she offered a different truth. "I thought of

Sarah, which made me twitch. I still haven't got a handle on her. If I don't soon, it will be too late."

"Maybe you should get out of the way and let Sarah take over," he suggested.

"Very zenlike. Can you be more specific?"

"You probably know Sarah inside out, but you're still not comfortable with her. I don't think you like her very much."

Rainey started to protest, then stopped. "You may be right. I love John Randall because his problems and struggle to heal touch universal chords, but so much of Sarah seems specific to her own restricted time and place. I have trouble getting into her because the world is so much different now."

"She's loyal and loving, and those qualities are as universal as Randall's. It's interesting that you can relate to his pain more easily than her virtues."

If Rainey were a cat, her fur would be bristling. "She's a young woman with potential who is trapped in a world that gives her almost no choices! This benefits Randall, but I still feel sorry for her."

"Much harder to live in a time where divorce was almost impossible. How fortunate you are to be able to walk away from an unsatisfactory marriage, unlike Sarah."

Recognizing that they were on thin ice, she made herself step aside and study her reaction, as if she were learning a new character. "Maybe Sarah's situation makes me think of the years when I lived with my grandparents and felt so powerless."

"I can see why that would get in your way, but remember, Sarah likes herself and her situation very well. One of the things that makes her special is that she's completely comfortable with her place in life. Because she's working from a secure center, she can offer Randall strength and stability."

"You've really thought a lot about her, haven't you?"

"Of course. She's the lifeline for my character, and I need to know why."

Kenzie had always been terrific at figuring out characters.

She'd missed the intense discussions they used to have. Especially since those talks often took place in bed. "Any suggestions for how to come to terms with Sarah?"

He frowned at the canopy overhead. "Why not put yourself back into the most secure time in your life, and work from there?"

"There *were* no secure times."

He laid a gentle hand on her bare midriff. "That's a drawback. You'll have to build her out of pure craftsmanship."

"A lot of help you are!"

He grinned. "Time for a return to Drama 101. What's Sarah's secret?"

A profound secret that the character would never reveal to anyone was often a key to the character's personality, and added depth and a sense of mystery. "You know, I've never thought of a secret for Sarah. A sign of my distance from her."

"Find one," he suggested. "Maybe then you'll connect with her."

What shameful secret might honest, naïve Sarah Masterson be concealing?

The answer struck like a thunderbolt: Under that innocence, Sarah was deeply, physically passionate in a time and place where women were supposed to be demure, sexless "ladies." Sarah knew that about herself, and the realization shamed her.

She didn't love Randall just for his noble profile and heroic exploits, but for his virility and beautiful body. She'd instinctively recognized that he was a man who might match her in passion. That call of the blood gave an intensity to her love. Even though their marriage hadn't yet been consummated, she believed to her marrow that they belonged together—and she didn't dare let anyone, even Randall, know about her wanton nature for fear they'd despise her.

Her pulse accelerated. "By George, I think I've got it. Sarah's secret."

"And it is . . . ?"

"If I told you, it wouldn't be a secret."

"Maybe I can persuade you." He pounced, kissing and caressing and murmuring against her breast in a menacing growl, "Tell me her dark secret, or I'll drive you mad."

"I'll show you madness!" Laughing, she rolled him onto his back and pinned him to the bed with her hands and knees before nibbling her way down his body. The laughter bound them together as surely as passion, until levity vanished in hot urgency.

After total meltdown, she lay panting in his arms. *Don't think that soon this will be over—think about the two whole weeks that are left.*

After a luscious, lazy interval, Kenzie kissed her temple, then climbed from the bed and started to dress. "Time I crept back across the hallway."

Reluctantly she also rose and drew on her bathrobe. "I did some rewriting on a couple of your later scenes. I'll print out the pages and get them to you today." After he nodded, she asked, "With your dyslexia, is it hard to learn new dialogue?"

His hands froze on his belt buckle. "I beg your pardon?"

"You're dyslexic, aren't you? I've always assumed so."

He fastened the belt, the leather snapping like a weapon. "Why do you say that?"

"You have trouble with right and left, you reverse things, you don't read easily, and your spelling can be pretty creative." She regarded him uneasily. "Was I wrong to assume dyslexia, or is this one of those topics you really, really don't want to talk about?"

His expression became fractionally less taut. "Both. I thought I'd done rather a good job of concealing my difficulties. Does everyone know?"

"I doubt it. You compensate beautifully. I was just in a position to notice more." She'd noticed everything about him for more than three years.

He drifted to the window and stared out, shoving his hands into his back pockets. "I was quite hopeless as a child. Probably retarded. Certainly worthless."

The flat words chilled her. Though she'd figured out that he was dyslexic fairly early, she hadn't realized how profoundly the condition had affected his life. "England is a civilized country, and dyslexia has been well understood for years. Why weren't you diagnosed when you started school?"

He shrugged. "Britons aren't quite as keen on slapping labels on children. Plus, there were . . . other circumstances."

Such as having a very traditional family that didn't believe some children's brains were wired a little differently than others? No wonder he was surprisingly lacking in arrogance. He wasn't reserved and unassuming because he was "an English gentleman," but because it was difficult to develop arrogance after years of being treated as stupid. "I assume that eventually a good teacher figured out what was wrong."

"Yes. Luckily, intensive work can do a great deal to compensate for learning disabilities. But it doesn't cure them, of course."

Nor did it eliminate the years of shame he'd suffered. Looking for a silver lining, she said, "It's probably helped your acting. You have a phenomenal memory, not to mention perfect pitch for accents. And your discipline. You're about the best prepared actor I've ever met, and I suspect that was another way of compensating."

He nodded, still staring out the window. "It's amazing how clever one can become at hiding one's flaws."

"Dyslexia isn't that big a deal, Kenzie. I've had several friends with varying degrees of dyslexia. I sometimes scramble things myself. It seems to go with creativity, which you certainly have in spades."

"I'm glad it's not a big deal to you," he said quietly.

But it obviously was to him. "Okay, subject closed. I won't mention it again."

"I'd appreciate that." He turned from the window. "I'd also prefer this didn't become common knowledge."

She tried to make a joke of it. "Telling the tabloids that Kenzie Scott went to bed with three women and an Angora goat would be news, but a learning disability wouldn't interest anyone."

"If you're telling tales to tabloids, go with the orgy. It would be less uncomfortable." He left the room, closing the door behind him with unnerving care.

She tightened her robe around her, feeling depressed. Whoever had convinced Kenzie he was a worthless child deserved to be shot—and despite her pacifist leanings, she'd be happy to load the gun.

Kenzie's call wasn't until after lunch, so he showered and ate—the night with Rainey had done wonders for his appetite—then drove to Morchard House and walked through the gardens to the labyrinth. It had helped him before, maybe it would today.

Discovering that Rainey had recognized his dyslexia made him feel like a turtle whose shell had been ripped off. Intellectually, he knew his reaction was foolish. Learning disabilities were not uncommon. Many well-known people had gone public with their own struggles.

But he'd never wanted to be a spokesman for a cause, nor could he be detached about a condition that had shaped his childhood with the harsh finality of an ax. Even with Rainey, he'd felt gut-level fear when his weakness was casually mentioned.

If he'd had a normally designed brain, his childhood would almost certainly not have been the Dickensian horror that he'd barely survived. But his brain wasn't normal, and as a child he hadn't known how to conceal that. Thoroughly convinced of his worthlessness, he'd never looked for a way out, because it hadn't occurred to him that escape was possible. Mutely he'd done what he was told, and been dragged into an abyss that left him irrevocably scarred.

Movies and radio had saved him. Though he didn't master the written word until years later, as a boy he'd loved listening to beautiful language. He'd been nine when he first heard a

Shakespearean play performed on the radio. The rich, seductive power of *The Tempest* had taken him away from what he was doing, and what was being done to him.

While language was wonderful, the combination of word and image in the movies had been pure magic. Film had taken him to new worlds, created sanctuaries in his mind where he could withdraw from the sordid reality of his life.

He'd been very lucky to receive patient, intensive instruction while he was still young enough to benefit by it, but reading was still too much work to do for pleasure. He envied Rainey's ability to become totally lost in a good book. His undeserved reputation for being literate and well-read was a result of the countless audio books he'd listened to during the boring intervals of filming or while he was exercising.

He'd plunged into acting without fully realizing how much reading would be required. Hundreds of screenplays were sent to his office every year. More than most actors, he had to rely on other people to screen potential scripts for him. Once or twice, his manager and assistants had passed on a role that he later wished he'd taken, but overall the system worked well, except when he had to make a decision quickly.

That had happened with *The Centurion.* He certainly should have read it before agreeing to take the role, but he'd been busy, Rainey had explained the story, and he'd come to rely on her judgment about screenplays while they were married. So he'd agreed when he shouldn't have, and had only himself to blame.

He still wasn't sure whether or not he regretted being part of this movie. The night with Rainey had improved his mood. *The Centurion* meant time with her while having the safety net of a definite cutoff point. Of course he could endure two more weeks as John Randall.

But then he remembered how crazed he'd felt on Randall's wedding night, and wondered.

He reached the end of the labyrinth. Pivoting, he started through it again in the opposite direction. Maybe he should have one of these built at Cíbola, since the effect was definitely calming.

It appealed to his sense of irony to know that he and his wife would be having an affair. The situation was pure drawing-room comedy, as long as he didn't think of how soon she would cease to be his wife. Neither of them had pushed to make the divorce go through quickly. In fact, he hadn't pushed at all, merely told his lawyer not to oppose the suit, and to respond to Rainey's lawyer as needed. But divorce wasn't difficult in California, and in another few weeks, this one would be final.

Rainey would be free, and he'd be alone.

❧ 22 ❧

"Cut." Rainey set down her flower basket with a sigh. "Definitely don't print."

Greg frowned at the section of garden where they'd been shooting. "We should adjust the lighting."

"Go ahead. Maybe a break will be good for my nerves." Rainey smiled ruefully at the woman acting opposite her, Dame Judith Hawick. One of the British theater's most revered actresses, she'd agreed to play the small but vital role of Sarah's mother. Rainey had always admired the older woman immensely, which was probably why she was so nervous that she'd blown their first scene together four times running.

Dame Judith was too much a pro to comment on Rainey's fumbling, but she did arch her brows expressively. "Have a shot of whiskey, my dear. I always find that wonderfully good for nerves."

"If I blow my lines again, I might just do that." Wanting to stretch her tense muscles, Rainey moved away from the camera. It was amazing how quickly the last week had flown by.

Today was Saturday, the last day of location shooting before they moved to London for the sound stage scenes.

She was surprised to see Kenzie leaning against the nearest trailer, arms folded across his chest. She'd have preferred that he missed her clumsiness, but it was impossible not to enjoy the sight of him. Wearing a leather jacket and sunglasses, he was almost a caricature of gorgeous Hollywood cool.

She strolled toward him, wondering if everyone could see the heat sizzling between them. Carrying on a torrid, secret affair agreed with them both. The knowledge of how fleeting it would be lent a bittersweet intensity to their time together. She refused to think of how his infidelity had shattered the foundation of their relationship. What mattered was the moment, and how much good they were doing each other.

With his help, she'd learned how to get into Sarah's skin, while he seemed to have overcome his problems with Randall and was doing terrific work. If the dailies were to be believed, the movie that had once existed only in Rainey's mind was meeting and exceeding her expectations. Film was being flown regularly to Marcus in Los Angeles, and he agreed that they had the makings of a real winner.

When she reached Kenzie, she said, "Dame Judith is wonderful, and by this time she probably thinks I'm an idiot."

"I doubt that. She's pretty gracious with beginners." He smiled reminiscently. "She was with me. Years ago I played a tiny part in a play where she was the star, and fell over my own feet in front of her during the dress rehearsal. She looked down and said, 'My dear boy, being a footman doesn't mean you need to lie down to be walked on.' "

Rainey laughed. "Maybe I should try a pratfall to loosen things up. I'm too awestruck to be able to think of her as my mother, particularly since she has to give a lecture on wedding vows and 'till death do we part.' Pretty different from Clementine."

Mentioning her real mother caused a sharp, unexpected pang of loss. If Clementine hadn't died, what kind of relationship would they have now? Friends, probably, with her mother being warm and a little wacky, while Rainey would be the worrier of the pair. But—they'd be friends. Being a pal was a role that would have suited Clementine better than motherhood had.

Kenzie smiled. "Tell Rainey to go off somewhere, and let Sarah play the scene. Maybe she'll accept Dame Judith as a mother more easily."

"Why is it we have to be told the obvious over and over? Thanks." Rainey made a rueful face, then returned to the garden. She had had trouble maintaining her usual focus in this role, probably because of her dual duties as director and actor, but Kenzie could always get her back on track when she wandered.

The reflectors has been shifted and tweaked, and everyone was in position for another take. Rainey closed her eyes for a moment to summon Sarah. When she was sure her character was in control, she opened her eyes and spoke to her wise, practical mother, who was serenely deadheading roses.

The take was a print, and so was the next. The rest of the outdoor scenes with Dame Judith flowed smooth as cream. Barring a processing disaster, *The Centurion* was ready to move to London.

The last scene of the day included Kenzie. When the final "cut and print" was called, he bowed over the older woman's hand. "It's a pleasure to work with you again, Dame Judith. Especially since I have more than a single sentence to deliver this time."

Dame Judith laughed. "But you fell to the carpet with consummate style. I knew even then you'd go far, Kenzie. Perhaps we can do another play again someday. Oscar Wilde, perhaps."

He looked surprised, then intrigued. "I'd like that, I think. I haven't done a play since I went to Hollywood."

Dame Judith's gaze was calculating. "I'm going to be directing my first production in the United States soon, and hope to do a West End play in a year or so. Shall I have my agent call your agent if the right property turns up?"

"It's worth a try, though scheduling is usually a problem," he replied.

Rainey grinned. "I'd fly halfway around the world to see the two of you do a play together."

Dame Judith's gray eyes narrowed like a cat considering a mouse. "What about you, daughter? Have you done any theater?"

"Yes, Mama." Rainey dropped back into the character of a Victorian daughter. "Though I'm scarcely fit to trod the boards with two classically trained British actors."

"Nonsense, my girl. You can hold your own with anyone." Dame Judith smiled. "The chances of such a project happening are thin, but it's amusing to dream, isn't it? I'll see you both in London." She inclined her head graciously, then swept off the set.

Rainey spent a moment imagining what it would be like to share a stage with Kenzie and Dame Judith in some romantic venue like Stratford on Avon, where she and Kenzie might have another fling. Maybe an on-and-off affair was the most they should have tried for. But she'd wanted more, and at the beginning, so had he. Putting the thought aside, she headed toward her trailer, Kenzie falling into step beside her. Tired but pleased with the day's work, she murmured under her breath, "Your place or mine tonight?"

He gave her a sidelong glance that raised her blood temperature by several degrees. "How about my room? I like the idea of you breaking in and ravishing me."

The promise in his eyes made her want to ravish him on the spot. She was wrestling with temptation when Kenzie's assistant approached. "Kenzie, there's another message from London. Mr. Winfield's condition is deteriorating rapidly. If you don't visit soon, it might be too late."

Kenzie stopped dead. "What? Is Charles ill?"

Josh looked surprised. "Didn't you see the note I left for

you yesterday? The head nurse at Ramillies Manor called to say that he's suffered a sharp decline. They . . . aren't optimistic."

Kenzie looked as if he'd been punched in the stomach. "I didn't bother to look at any of my messages. Rainey, I'm driving up to London. You might have to shoot around me for the first day or two on the sound stage."

Before he could escape, Rainey put her hand on his arm, feeling the tight muscles. "Do you want me to go with you?"

He shook his head. "I can manage on my own."

She'd expected that—he was much better at giving support than receiving it. "I'm sure you can, but I'd be glad to come." She thought of her bleak flight to Baltimore after her grandfather's accident. "This looks like the sort of journey that shouldn't be made alone."

He hesitated. "Very well, if you can spare the time. Fifteen minutes to change. Meet me at the Jaguar." He spun away and headed to his trailer, rattling off orders to Josh over his shoulder.

Rainey headed for her own trailer as fast as her restrictive gown would allow. On the way, she grabbed a wardrobe assistant to help her out of her costume. As the assistant unhooked the gown and the blasted corset, Rainey hastily cleaned off her makeup. There was just time to toss a toothbrush and cell phone into her handbag and slide into a comfortable shirt, jacket, and slacks.

She was breathing hard when she reached Kenzie's Jaguar. Impatient to be off, he was pacing restlessly beside the car, but he still opened the door for her. His mother had trained him well. As he circled to the driver's side, Val raced up and handed a tote bag to Rainey through the open window. "Road rations."

Word got around fast. Rainey glanced down and saw a variety of food and drink. "Bless you, Val. Take care of whatever needs doing. I'll call you when I can."

Val nodded and stepped back from the car. Kenzie took off. After fastening her seat belt, Rainey combed her hair out of its complicated Victorian arrangement, glad to let it fall loose around her shoulders.

Kenzie was quiet, whipping the sports car along narrow lanes at a speed just short of total recklessness. He drove with absolute concentration, his profile as still as marble. He seemed so unaware of her that she began to wonder if she'd made a mistake to invite herself along. She waited until they emerged from the maze of local roads and roared onto the M-5 before asking, "Would you like something to drink? There's a thermos here that probably has coffee."

Her voice pulled him out of his thoughts. "Thanks. I'd like that."

She poured steaming coffee into one of two travel mugs Val had included. There were even small cream containers. After handing Kenzie the mug, she dug farther into the tote bag. "Val is wasted as a lawyer. She'd make a really first-class caterer. When you get hungry, there are sandwiches, fruit, shortbread, and what looks like a couple of still-warm Cornish pasties."

"Good. We won't have to stop to eat." He sipped his coffee, gaze on the motorway. "Do you recognize the name Charles Winfield?"

"The stage actor Charles Winfield?" When Kenzie nodded, she continued, "On my first trip to London, I saw him in *She Stoops to Conquer.* He was the best Mr. Hardcastle I've ever seen. He's a friend of yours?"

"More than a friend. A mentor." Half a mile blazed by. "The man who taught me to act, and convinced me that a theatrical career was possible."

Kenzie's sentences were short, almost brusque. Maybe that was because for the first time, he was actually revealing an important piece of his past. Winfield sounded like a surrogate father. "He must be well along in years now."

"His mid-seventies. He and his friends all smoked like fiends. He's outlived most of them, and his own health has been poor for years, so this isn't a surprise, but . . . I'll miss him."

"It's lucky you're in England. At least you'll have a chance to see him before it's too late."

"If I'm in time." His mouth tightened. "I should have at least looked at the damned messages Josh left for me yesterday."

"Don't blame yourself too much. It's easy to forget the outside world when filming." She lightened her voice. "I'm sure you'll have your chance to say good-bye. An old trouper like Charles Winfield isn't going to miss a chance for a grand farewell."

Kenzie glanced at her, his expression easing. "You're probably right about that. He's always loved an audience."

She smiled and rested her hand on his thigh for a moment. Conversation lapsed again, but she no longer wondered if it had been a mistake to come.

❧ 23 ❧

*They reached London in record time, and with*out a speeding ticket. Rainey figured that had to be divine intervention. If she didn't have absolute faith in Kenzie's driving skill, she'd have been cowering with her head under the dash.

When they entered Ramillies Manor, they were greeted by a dignified older woman who sat behind a wide desk. "I'm so glad you could come, Mr. Scott. Mr. Winfield looks for you whenever the door opens."

Kenzie relaxed at the news that his friend was still among the living. "I'm sorry I didn't get here more quickly. Mrs. Lincoln, this is Raine Marlowe." After an almost imperceptible pause, he added, "My wife. Rainey, Mrs. Lincoln is the matron here."

Mrs. Lincoln studied Rainey with interest. "He's awake now, so you can go directly to his room."

Kenzie started to go, then paused. "What's his condition?"

"Peaceful and pain-free." She sighed. "We've done all we could."

In other words, there would be no miracles for Charles Winfield. A light hand on Rainey's back, Kenzie guided her down a hallway that ran to the left. Quietly she asked, "Is this a hospice?"

"No, though they provide hospice care when necessary. This has been Charles's home for several years, and he wants to die here, not in a hospital. The staff will see that he does it in comfort."

Kenzie halted by a door at the end of the corridor. She asked, "Would you prefer to be alone with him?"

"I think Charles would like to meet you. What better way for an actor to go than talking shop with his own kind?"

When the time came, she'd probably be glad to go the same way. She followed Kenzie into a handsome corner room, where the last rays of the sun slanted through the windows. The handsome traditional furniture, polished oak floor, and Persian carpets glowed in the golden light. One whole wall was covered with framed photographs and posters and playbills that commemorated Winfield's career, while another was covered with well-filled bookcases.

The actor lay on his bed, pale and bone thin, but he managed a smile when Kenzie entered. "I knew you'd come." He had the husky rasp of a long-term smoker.

As a nursing aide who'd been sitting by the window quietly left, Kenzie went to Winfield and took his hand. "I should have been here sooner, but I was engaged in battle royal with the character I'm playing, and didn't bother to check my messages yesterday."

Winfield made a rusty, wheezing sound that must have been laughter. "I've done the same thing myself. When the Muse sulks, the world vanishes." His head moved back and forth as if he was trying to get a better view of Rainey. "Are you going to introduce me to your lovely companion?"

Kenzie drew her to the bedside. "My wife, Raine Marlowe." This time he called her his wife more easily.

"I'm sorry I can't bow properly." Winfield's tired smile still had the charm he'd displayed in all his roles. "You should have won that Oscar for *Home Free*."

She grinned. "I'd like to think so, but what actor doesn't believe that every performance is a winner?"

He gave his wheezing laugh again. "So true, so true." His gaze went to the awards on the mantelpiece. "I've had my share of winners, and a great deal of amusement along the way. Don't mourn when I'm gone, Kenzie. Just drink a toast to my memory." He began to cough convulsively.

"I'll get the matron," Kenzie said tersely. "Stay with Charles."

Rainey obeyed, her throat tight. It was easy to understand Kenzie's deep bond with Winfield. If only her grandfather had a fraction of the actor's warmth.

Hoping a drink would help, she lifted a water bottle with a straw from the bedside table and held it to Winfield's lips. He took a tiny sip, coughed, then drank again. The attack ended.

As she set the bottle down, he caught her hand in a bony grip. "Take good care of the boy. He's had much to endure. Too much."

Rainey bit her lip, not sure how to reply. Didn't Winfield know about the divorce? Seeing her expression, he said impatiently, "Don't let him drive you off, child. He'll try, you know, but you mustn't let him get away with it."

Was that what Kenzie was doing? Rainey wanted to ask Winfield more, but Kenzie entered the room with Mrs. Lincoln, who came to the bed and did a quick examination of her patient. Voice thready, the actor said testily, "I'm still dying, if that's what you want to know."

"We're all dying, Mr. Winfield." Unperturbed, the matron checked his pulse. "The question is when."

"I'll fade on the crowing of the cock," he murmured.

"Is that more of your Shakespeare?" She smiled affectionately. "It's been quite the education having you here."

Rainey recognized the twist on a line from *Hamlet*. She guessed that Winfield was forecasting accurately—he wouldn't last the night. He'd wanted to see Kenzie one last time so he'd held on. Now he no longer had to.

Mrs. Lincoln gave her patient a pill and left. Rainey began to browse the bookshelves so Kenzie could sit by the bed and talk privately with his friend. Winfield had eclectic tastes that went from drama to biography to fiction, with lots of mysteries. Audio books had kept him company after his vision began to fail.

She moved to the photos that surrounded the fireplace. Winfield had been on friendly terms with most of the British theatrical world for decades. He'd specialized in witty, debonair leading men, later turning to character roles.

There were three pictures of him with Kenzie, who looked younger, but not really young. Was he born with those ancient green eyes?

One photo included a third man about Winfield's age. He was balding, with a homely, intelligent face. Not an actor, she guessed—he didn't carry himself like one—but he was in several other pictures with Winfield. A close friend, apparently.

The sun had set, so she turned two lamps on low for a gentle light. Then she chose a lavishly illustrated history of the British theater and sat in the armchair by the fireplace to leaf through it. Though she tried not to listen to the murmuring conversation between the two men, her attention was caught when Winfield said in an effort-filled voice, "I've often wished I had a son. One like you."

"You were my father-in-theater," Kenzie replied. "That's almost as good."

"Better, maybe. Not many sons would support their fathers in such luxury."

Rainey kept her gaze on her book, not surprised to hear that Kenzie was paying for Ramillies Manor. She'd been married to him for two years before she'd learned by accident how much money he gave to charity. His preference was to help people, especially children, who were trapped by poverty and needed help to change their lives.

Winfield sighed heavily. "I always wanted to do a play with you. We won't have the chance now."

"We could do a reading," Kenzie suggested. "Is there something you'd like to perform one last time?"

"Splendid idea," Winfield said, his voice stronger. "Shakespeare, of course. *King Lear* would be the logical choice, but I'm not in the mood for a tragedy about a mad, foolish king." Another wheezing laugh. "I was always best in comedy. *Twelfth Night?* No, *Much Ado About Nothing.* I'll be Leonato, Constable Dogberry, and the friar, since I've played all of them. You did Benedick at RADA, so you know that, and you can do the other male parts. Raine can do the females. I think I know all my lines still. I've a couple of copies of *Much Ado* in the bookcase if you need help."

Kenzie raised his voice. "Rainey, are you up for this?"

Abandoning all pretense of reading, she set the theatrical history aside and rose to scan the bookcase. "I'd love to, and *Much Ado About Nothing* is a favorite of mine. I played Beatrice under a tent one summer." She struck a pose and declaimed, " 'But then there was a star danced, and under that was I born.' "

She found two copies of the play, one in Shakespeare's collected works, the other an illustrated volume of that play alone. Thinking of Kenzie's dyslexia, she gave him the single volume since it would be easier to read, then sat on the opposite side of the bed and flipped to the play in the *Complete Works*.

There was a spark of anticipation in Winfield's eyes, though he looked so fragile that it seemed a breath would blow him away. Rainey wondered if he'd last the length of the play, even though *Much Ado* was one of the Bard's shorter works.

She gave him her warmest smile. "I'll do the musical accompaniment." Trying to sound like trumpets, she sang a clarion fanfare. "Your cue, good Mr. Winfield."

In a frail but beautifully modulated voice, he spoke Leonato's first line. "I learn in this letter that Don Pedro of Arragon comes this night to Messina."

Since they'd all performed in *Much Ado,* the printed plays were needed only for checking the dialogue of secondary characters. Rainey loved the snappy verbal fencing between Beatrice and Benedick. Playing opposite Kenzie made it easy to create the undercurrents of longing and wariness between Shakespeare's frustrated lovers.

Despite the sometimes slapstick humor of the play, the circumstances lent power and poignancy to the reading. Winfield's love of his craft was obvious, the flowing beauty of the words weaving a garland of language.

But his voice became more and more labored. In the fourth act, he quoted the friar: "Then shall he mourn . . . if ever love . . . had interest in his heart. . . ." He drew a long, rattling breath before whispering hoarsely, "Dying . . . is . . . easy. Comedy . . . is hard."

When he fell silent, Rainey looked up in alarm, but his chest still rose and fell. Kenzie waited until it was clear his friend would not complete the speech, then took over Winfield's parts. He read as if his future career depended on it, his marvelous, flexible voice perfectly capturing the rhythm of the blank verse.

Somewhere in the last act, the spirit of Charles Winfield departed, though Rainey couldn't have pinpointed the moment. When she realized he was no longer breathing, she had to exercise all her actor's discipline to keep going to the end.

After Beatrice and Benedick agreed to marry, still bantering but no longer able to conceal their love, Kenzie as Benedick spoke the last line of the play. "Strike up, pipers!"

Remembering that she was the accompaniment, Rainey sang, but gay, matrimonial music was impossible. What came from her heart and lips was the traditional song "Amazing

Grace." Though often played by pipers, it was a haunting tune, an elegiac thanks for divine forgiveness. Clementine had often sung it to her daughter.

The silence after she finished was broken by a sob. She turned, and was startled to see a small group gathered by the door. The matron, staff members with name tags hanging around their necks, and several residents stood solemnly listening, and an elderly woman in a wheelchair dabbed at her eyes with a handkerchief.

Expression rigidly controlled, Kenzie stood and rested his hand on his friend's forehead before drawing the blankets over the still face. "Charles asked us to toast his death, not mourn. Mrs. Lincoln, can that be arranged?"

The matron nodded and whispered an instruction to one of her assistants. After the girl left, the silver-haired woman in the wheelchair said unsteadily, "Whenever Charles Winfield was in a play, I was there on opening night. He was always worth seeing, even if the play wasn't. It was such a thrill when he came to live here." She gave a watery smile. "He made me feel like a duchess."

A male staffer said, "He was always a real gent, no matter how bad he felt."

One by one, people contributed their memories. Rainey spoke last, saying, "I never met Charles Winfield before tonight, yet he made me feel like a friend. I wish I'd known him better."

As she spoke, the assistant entered the room with a tray of champagne-filled wine glasses. Rainey accepted one, unable to imagine such a scene in the United States.

Kenzie waited until everyone had been served, then said in a voice that filled the room, "You asked to be toasted, not mourned, Charles, but I must do both. 'Now cracks a noble heart. Good-night, sweet prince, And flights of angels sing thee to thy rest!' "

He swallowed his champagne in one gulp. Then he hurled the wineglass into the fireplace. As it shattered into bright splinters against the brick, he said softly, "When one drinks a toast from the heart, one must break the glass."

"To Charles Winfield." Tears in her eyes, Rainey followed suit, as did the others. The wheelchair-bound woman rolled close enough to smash her glass into the pile.

As people wordlessly began to depart, Mrs. Lincoln approached Kenzie and Rainey. "It's very late. There are some visitor rooms upstairs, so you can stay here if you like."

Rainey glanced at Kenzie. Her throat was raw and she was weary to the bone. The thought of staying at Ramillies Manor was much more appealing than looking for a hotel at this hour.

Seeing her expression, he said, "We'd both like that, Mrs. Lincoln." After a last look at the mortal remains of Charles Winfield, Kenzie followed the woman out.

An elevator took them to the top of the building, where several doors opened off a narrow corridor. "These were servants' rooms once. They're small but pleasant, and convenient when someone needs to stay over." Mrs. Lincoln indicated one door for Rainey and the next one for Kenzie. "Sleep well. If you like, you can join us for breakfast in the ground-floor dining room."

"Thank you, Mrs. Lincoln. You've been very kind." Fingers clumsy, Rainey turned the old-fashioned key in the lock, then pulled it out and took it inside.

Closing the door, she leaned against it with her eyes closed. She was glad she'd come, but every shred of strength and emotion had been used up.

She opened her eyes to a pretty, gabled room such as might be found in a nice country bed-and-breakfast. There was also a connecting door to Kenzie's room. She smiled tiredly. How very clever of the matron to make this arrangement for two people of uncertain marital condition. She crossed the room and opened the door to Kenzie's room.

He stood at his window, looking blindly at the lights of London, but he turned when she came in. The composure that had carried him through the long night was gone, leaving him dark and hollow.

She opened her arms, and he walked into them. "I'm so sorry," she whispered, aching for him.

"It was time." He buried his face in her hair. "Charles had lived a full, long life."

"That doesn't mean losing him shouldn't hurt." Too tired to talk, she guided them the couple of steps to the bed, kicked off her shoes, and drew him down beside her. In a few minutes, she'd get up and take her clothes off, but for now, she needed so much to rest. . . .

✖ 24 ✖

Kenzie woke when the morning sun struck his eyes. It took a groggy moment to recall the last sixteen hours. The drive up to London, the time with Charles, ending up in bed with his head pillowed on Rainey's shoulder. They were both fully dressed, though during the night someone had pulled the bedspread over them. Probably Rainey—he'd been nearly comatose.

Stiffly he got up and tiptoed to the bathroom. It was small, but had a shower, a terry cloth robe on the hook behind the door, and fresh toiletries, including a disposable razor. The servants who'd once lived here had never been so lucky.

A quick shower and shave helped clear his mind, though his emotions felt . . . flattened. The last good link to his early years was now gone.

He put on the robe and emerged from the bathroom to find Rainey blinking sleepily at him from under the bedspread. Her hair tangled across the pillow like spun amber, and she looked good enough to eat. It was a measure of his heavy spirit that he didn't feel even a trace of sexual response. All he wanted was to put his arms around her and go back to sleep again.

Since that wasn't practical, he sat next to her on the bed. "Thanks for coming, Rainey. It . . . helped."

"I'm glad for that, and glad I met Charles Winfield." She covered a yawn. "How lovely that you were able to give him the actor's equivalent of a Viking funeral—sending him off in a blaze of glory."

He hadn't thought of it that way. "I owed him more than I can ever repay."

"He's the first piece of your pre-Hollywood past I've ever met." The statement was without inflection, but she watched his face carefully.

"Charles and Trevor were the best part of that past."

"Trevor?"

Kenzie must be even more tired than he'd realized to say that. "Trevor was . . . a friend of Charles's. He's shown in some of the pictures downstairs."

"I don't suppose I'll ever fully understand how much Charles meant to you," she said tentatively, "but it occurred to me that I can put a dedication to him at the end of *The Centurion*. Would you like that?"

His throat tightened. "Yes, and Charles would have, too."

He rolled Rainey onto her stomach and began rubbing her back. She gave a sigh of pleasure and stretched like a petted cat. "That feels so good."

The massage benefited him, too. Touching her always did. He gave silent thanks that Charles had died while he and Rainey were sharing this last interlude of intimacy, and not just because her support was a blessing. It was good that she and Charles had the opportunity to meet.

As Rainey's tight muscles softened, she asked, "Did Charles have any family?"

"None that would acknowledge him." Kenzie pressed his thumbs under the edge of her shoulder blades, looking for knots of tension. "He was the black sheep of an upperclass family. When he left Cambridge to act, they said that if he insisted on following a dissolute, disreputable life, he should take a stage name and leave them alone. So he did."

"Sounds as if you had a lot in common."

Ignoring the implied question, he said, "I'm the executor of his will. He wanted cremation and a small memorial service. He said once that he'd had his time in the spotlight, and an actor should know when it was time to leave quietly."

"I think English actors are much saner than American ones."

"So much of America is larger than life. Here, centuries of history are everywhere. It keeps things in proportion." He patted her elegant backside and stood. "Ready for a shower and breakfast?"

"I am now. Thanks, Kenzie." She got out of bed and leaned into him for a long hug. "Will they serve the classic British breakfast with eggs and bacon and fried bread and tomatoes and all those other wonderful cardiac killers?"

"Probably. Being saner than Americans, the English are much less obsessive about what they eat."

"I could get into that. Maybe I should buy a flat here." Yawning, she returned to her own room to shower.

After dressing, he stood at the window and gazed over London. On a Sunday morning, it was as quiet as it ever got. Thank God he'd have today before he resumed work on *The Centurion.* The sound stage scenes they were going to shoot would be the most searing in the whole movie.

God only knew where he'd find the emotional energy to get through this last week. He'd barely been managing even before Charles's death. If not for his nights with Rainey, he wouldn't have made it this far.

His mouth tightened. Charles would have said the show must go on. As a private tribute to his mentor, he must dredge up whatever it took to make these last scenes the best work of his life.

Then, thank heaven, he'd have two months to go into hid-

ing before his next picture began shooting. Ordinarily he'd
have Seth Cowan look for some small jobs to fill the time between pictures, but this time he wanted inactivity. He'd go to
Cíbola, where the Gradys had already moved into their new
home. He'd be able to fix up the old ranch house the way he
wanted, recover, and explore the spare, beautiful land he'd
bought.

Explore, recover, and try not to think of Rainey.

Breakfast in the Ramillies dining room was as cholesterol-
laden as expected, and Rainey relished every bite. Sometimes,
a woman just had to live dangerously.

The residents were too well-bred to stare at the celebrities
in their midst, though after they'd finished eating one woman
shyly asked for autographs for her granddaughter, and several
other residents stopped by to offer sympathy and share memories of Charles Winfield. Kenzie handled the condolences with
his usual graciousness, but she could see signs of strain. Deciding it was time for the anonymity of The Dorchester, where
they were booked for that night, she gave Kenzie the wordless
signal that married couples develop, and they said their good-
byes.

Realizing her hands were too empty when they left the dining room, she said, "I think I left my purse in Charles's room
last night. Which way is it?"

Kenzie led her down the corridor and opened the door for
her. Winfield's personal belongings hadn't been touched, but
the bed was mercifully empty, and had been remade with a
fresh bedspread. Rainey crossed the threshold, then halted at
the sight of the trench-coated man studying the photos around
the fireplace. He turned toward her, quickly sliding one hand
into his pocket. Nigel Stone.

Seeing the reporter, Kenzie swore, "You damned vulture!
Have you no shame?"

"Just a journalist doing my job," Stone said piously. "A
washed-up actor dying isn't newsworthy, but you and your es-

tranged wife spending the night reading plays to him is a great story."

"Get the hell out of here right now." Kenzie stalked forward, looking ready to remove the other man bodily.

"He may have taken something of Charles's," Rainey warned. "He shoved his hand into his pocket when he saw me."

Kenzie's eyes narrowed dangerously. "Robbing the dead. You're even more despicable than I thought."

"I swear I took nothing that belonged to Winfield. She saw me put away a tape recorder I use for notes." Stone pulled a small voice-activated recorder from his deep coat pocket.

"Is he telling the truth, Rainey?"

"What I saw was about that size and shape."

Accepting that, Kenzie said, "Out. Now. Unless you want to give me the pleasure of dragging you out."

Stone ambled toward the door, taking his time. "Don't get your knickers in a twist. I just wanted to look around."

Rainey grabbed her purse from under the bed and followed the men toward the front door. Just before stepping outside, Stone paused, his hard gaze on Kenzie. "I've only seen eyes that shade of bright green once before," he said meaningfully.

"Haven't you ever heard of colored contact lenses?" Kenzie yanked the front door open, and found a group of reporters and cameramen waiting.

Rainey groaned. Running a press gauntlet was the last thing they needed. As Stone joined his colleagues, she moved to Kenzie's side. "Let's get out of here."

Face like granite, he draped a protective arm around her shoulders and they started for his car. Reporters stepped back to let them through, intimidated by his expression, though questions came from all sides. Rainey bowed her head, wishing the small car park was closer.

Pamela Lake, a reporter she knew slightly, shoved a folded newspaper into Rainey's shoulder bag. "Take a look at this, and call me if you have any comments." Intent on escape, Rainey barely noticed.

A harsh voice rose above the others. "Is it true Charles Winfield died of AIDS?"

From behind, Nigel Stone laughed nastily. "Probably. Everyone knew he was queer as Dick's hatband."

Rainey could feel the fury that blazed through Kenzie. He spun around, and for a moment she feared he would strike Stone.

Instead, he placed a hand on the reporter's shoulder in a gesture that looked casual, except for the bruising power of his grip. Stone gasped and tried unsuccessfully to jerk away. "Charles Winfield did not have AIDS," Kenzie said in a voice that could cut glass. "Nor would it have been relevant if he had. Judge him by his fine acting, his wit, his generosity, and the friends who will mourn his passing,"

Kenzie released Stone so abruptly the other man staggered, then pulled out his keys and used the remote to unlock the doors. Rainey dived into the safety of the Jaguar gratefully, and within thirty seconds they were off the grounds of Ramillies Manor.

She exhaled slowly. "Your eyes really are that shade of green."

"I didn't say they weren't. I just asked Stone if he'd ever heard of colored contacts." Kenzie's voice was blackly humorous.

"I wonder if he'll recognize the weasel wording." She thought about the reporter's comment on Kenzie's eye color. "Do you and Stone have a history?"

" 'Twas long ago and in another country and besides, the lad is dead."

She suspected that answering with another fractured quote meant that Kenzie had known Stone, and didn't want to talk about it. Next topic. "Did Charles have AIDS, or did that reporter just ask because he was homosexual?"

"Technically I told the truth—he didn't have full-blown AIDS, but he was HIV-positive, and that contributed to his overall condition. He chose to drift out of touch with many of his friends, not wanting pity, or to have them uncomfortable around him." Kenzie slowed until he could safely pass a bevy of bicyclists. "Charles grew up in a world where gays stayed solidly in the closet. He wouldn't have liked being outed posthumously."

"Between HIV, smoking, and British breakfasts, it's a miracle he survived as long as he did." Survived, and flourished, and died on his own terms. Not a bad way to go. "Did his family cast him off because of his sexual orientation?"

"I'm sure that was a large part of it. He found the theater far more welcoming."

Where people like Kenzie would protect Winfield's privacy even after his death. "The theater has always been a world unto itself. From what I've read, even in Greek times actors were outsiders. People like us were considered weird and wild and surely immoral, but accepted because of our talents. That's as true in Hollywood as it was twenty-five hundred years ago in Athens."

"Accepting diversity is perhaps the best thing about show business. No matter how strange one is, there's room if one has talent."

Kenzie's words were general, but the way he said them sounded very personal. "Even if one of those reporters does out Charles, he's beyond being hurt by it. I expect he'd prefer being buried in his closet, though."

"There's much to be said for closets. If Britons are saner than Americans, maybe it's because we don't feel compelled to air our dirty linen in public."

"There are Americans who will tell you more about their personal lives than you really want to know," Rainey admitted. "Heck, they'll do it at high noon in front of television cameras. But some problems really do need to be aired, or they'll fester." Would it have helped if Kenzie had been less secretive? Perhaps. But she had her share of things she'd rather not talk about. "I suspect that actors who talk too much about their addictions and sex lives risk harming their careers. A little mystery, that sense that there is always more to know, is an asset to a star."

"The secret of my success." His smile was ironic.

"You laugh, but I think it's true. For someone so famous, you've done a terrific job of being an enigma." After she'd married Kenzie, her movements had become vastly more interesting to media gossips. Knowing she could soon return to relative obscurity was a silver lining to the divorce. "Where are we heading—The Dorchester?"

He nodded. "I'd just as soon not drive down to Devon again."

"I'm sure Josh and Val packed us both very efficiently." Her gaze fell on her purse, which she'd dropped on the car floor by her feet. The rolled newspaper made her curious why Pamela Lake had stuffed it in her bag.

The tabloid wasn't the one that employed Pamela, though the reporter's card was clipped to the front page. Definitely a response was hoped for.

Rainey's gaze dropped to the photograph that dominated the front page, and she gasped with shock.

"What's wrong?" Kenzie asked sharply.

"Some bastard with a telephoto lens was spying on us in Devon." She stared at the picture, feeling ill. There was Kenzie leaning over her, one arm braced against a tree to shut out the world. She laughed up at him, too much of her soul in her eyes. "There's a big, romantic-looking picture of us together, and the headline is screaming, 'Kenzie and Raine Make Up!!!' "

"Damnation! Are there any facts, or is it all hot air?"

She flipped to the story inside, which included several more pictures. Though the photographer hadn't been able to invade the bedroom, he'd been wickedly good at capturing private moments that spelled out intimacy as emphatically as a kiss.

Feeling ill, she read the text. "Some unnamed employee of the hotel claims to have seen us creeping into each other's rooms late at night, and a local girl I never heard of says she became my 'confidante' over afternoon tea and clotted cream. Allegedly I told her that you and I have reconciled, and that I'm pregnant with your baby." Her voice cracked. "I hate this, Kenzie, I just *hate* it."

He swooped the Jaguar to the left and parked illegally in a bus stop zone. Taking the paper, he skimmed the pictures and headlines. "The self-proclaimed confidante is delusional, but the sleeping together part is accurate, so there's no grounds for libel."

"Even if it was, a lawsuit wouldn't make this go away. I *loathe* having speculation about my private life smeared across the globe." She wrapped shaking arms around herself. "I feel like . . . like I've been groped by perverts."

His expression turned to granite. "And it's my fault it happened." He refolded the newspaper with military precision. "I'm sorry, Rainey. I should have kept my distance."

"As I recall, everything that happened was by mutual consent." And to their mutual pleasure. They'd both been happy, she knew it in her bones.

Worn down by the stress and fatigue of the last day, she blurted out, "Why are we getting divorced when we get along so well, Kenzie? Both in and out of bed."

He drew a harsh breath. "Because you can't trust me, Rainey. Not then, not now, not ever."

✎ 25 ✎

Rainey stared, chilled, as she felt him pulling away from her emotionally. "I don't understand! It would be different if you were a sex addict who has to boff every woman in sight, but you're not. Isn't what we have good enough for you to keep your pants zipped when we're apart?"

A red double-decker bus pulled up behind them, honking

indignantly. Ignoring it, Kenzie said flatly, "You want and deserve more than I have to give, Rainey."

"That's not an answer."

He ignored her words as completely as he ignored the looming bus. "The time together in Devon was good, but it's over. Even in the country, we couldn't keep what we were doing a secret. In London, it will be impossible."

"So that's it? Sex is starting to be a nuisance, so enough already?"

The bus roared around them in a cloud of diesel fumes. "There was an element of therapy in what we were doing. With only a week of shooting left, we should be able to survive without that." He put the car in gear and pulled into traffic. "Every day we're together will increase the media feeding frenzy, which means more invasions of privacy. It's time to end things, before it gets worse."

"So you're making the decision for both of us."

"Yes." His mouth was hard. "I've damaged you enough. If I'm to live with myself, that has to stop."

"Don't give the little woman a vote. How very arbitrary and Victorian." She stared blindly out the window, thinking that she'd been cheated. She'd been prepared for things to end in a week, but not yet. She wasn't ready.

"John Randall is making me more Victorian every day." He pulled up in front of The Dorchester. "I'm going to be busy the rest of the day with arrangements for Charles's cremation and memorial service. I'll see you on the set tomorrow."

With a uniformed hotel employee approaching, there was no privacy for a good-bye kiss. Though probably Kenzie wouldn't have wanted one. How had they gone so quickly from the emotional intimacy of the night before to this? She felt as if a limb had been severed.

Pride came to her rescue. She'd be damned if she let him see how much she hurt. "You're right, the cost-benefit breaks down in London." She slid on her sunglasses. "The sex was great, and sneaking around was good kinky fun, but I don't need more reporters raping my life."

The doorman opened the door and she swung gracefully from the low car, a dazzling movie star smile on her face as she thanked the man for helping her out. Then she sailed into the hotel as confidently as if she hadn't slept in her clothes the night before, and checked in. *Yes, Miss Marlowe, your suite is ready, such a pleasure to have you back. Your luggage will arrive later? Very good, Miss Marlowe. Here are your messages.*

The manager personally escorted her to her suite, where fresh fruit and flowers waited. With her movie budget tight, she disliked spending so much money on her hotel, but Marcus had insisted. If she was the boss, she had to live like the boss, just as Kenzie had to be treated like a star even if he'd agreed to do the movie mostly as a favor to her.

The manager left, bowing in old-world style, and finally, mercifully, she was alone. Not bothering to admire the splendid view over Hyde Park, she sank onto the hard, elegant sofa and curled up like a hedgehog. She and Kenzie had been separated and on the way to a divorce for months now. How could the pain be this fresh? This intense? She'd known from the beginning that their Devonshire intimacy was strictly temporary.

Bleakly she recognized that in some deeply stupid corner of her brain, she'd been hoping for a reconciliation. She'd wanted Kenzie to beg her forgiveness and promise never to betray her again. When she was younger, she'd sworn that no man would ever hit her, or cheat on her, more than once. Yet she'd actually been on the verge of giving her faithless husband a second chance. Despite all her efforts to be different from Clementine, she was certainly her mother's daughter. Her forbearance wasn't going to be needed, though. *You can't trust me, Rainey. Not then, not now, not ever.* He could hardly speak plainer than that.

She lay numbly on the sofa for an indefinite period of time. Maybe Kenzie was right to end things now. How would she have handled the rest of the week, knowing how quickly their time together was running out? How could she have endured spending the last night with him, knowing it was the last night?

Her paralysis ended when Val let herself into the suite. "Rainey? Oh, sorry, I didn't know you were napping."

"I wasn't." She pushed herself to a sitting position. "But it was a long, tiring night watching Kenzie's friend die."

"I'm so sorry."

"Charles Winfield died in peace. We should all be so lucky."

A bellman appeared in the doorway hauling a cart piled high with personal and business luggage. Val supervised the disposition of bags and boxes, then dispatched him with a generous tip. When they were alone, she said hesitantly, "I assume you don't want me to use the second bedroom this week. I checked downstairs, and they can find me a single."

Rainey rubbed her temples, not quite following. "Why would I want you elsewhere? I've enjoyed having you in the next room."

"Maybe before, but now . . . well, I'd be a third wheel."

So Val had known about Kenzie and their Devonshire affair. "You won't be in the way. That little fling is over." She found the tabloid and tossed it to her friend.

Val frowned as she read the article. "This is certainly an inducement to celibacy. How do you stand this, Rainey?"

"Very badly."

"Shall I call this Pamela person and deny the story? I assume she's after a quote from you."

Rainey's brain began to function again. "No, I'll call her myself. She'll give me more ink than she would you."

Val's gaze went to the stack of waiting messages. "I'll start on these, then."

"Don't. Weren't you planning on sightseeing today with Laurie, the line producer?" Rainey glanced out the window, where the sun shone as merrily as it had before everything went to hell. "Go. It's Sunday, and you've earned some time off."

Val looked at her doubtfully. "Are you sure?"

"Positive." She managed a smile. "Frankly, I'd rather be alone."

"Okay. We're going to have dinner out, so I'll be back late." Val vanished into the other bedroom with her rolling suitcase.

Rainey unpacked her personal belongings, mentally preparing herself to call Pamela Lake, who clearly wanted an exclusive interview that could be headlined: "Raine and Kenzie: The Real Story." But Pamela was a decent sort, and this would be a good place to start spiking the guns of gossip.

Rainey closed her eyes and spent a couple of minutes thinking herself into the proper frame of mind: bright, casual, amused by the grossly inaccurate story. Once you can fake sincerity, you can fake anything. Then she called Pamela's cell phone number.

When the reporter answered, Rainey said in a voice that oozed charm and woman-to-woman friendliness, "Pamela, this is Raine Marlowe. Thanks so much for giving me that paper. Isn't it amazing what some people will invent to fill pages on a slow news day?"

Pamela Lake caught her breath when she recognized her caller. "So the story isn't true?"

"Of course it's not true! Trust me, there is no reconciliation in the works. Kenzie and I enjoy working together, and we'll probably always be friends, but marriage?" She laughed at the absurdity of the idea. "For the record, I've never even heard of the woman who claimed to my confidante, much less had tea with her."

A scratching sound indicated that Pamela was taking notes as fast as she could. "What about the hotel employee who saw you going into each other's bedrooms?"

"The rooms were directly opposite each other, so of course we were both seen going in that direction. But sleeping together?" Rainy laughed again. "Do you have any idea how exhausting it is to both direct and act in a movie? By the end of the day, my fantasies were of a hot bath and a nice glass of wine." And one night, she and Kenzie had shared just that . . .

"What about your visit with Charles Winfield? You did look awfully friendly when you left Ramillies Manor this morning."

Rainey rubbed her temples, but maintained her smooth tone. "Kenzie had just lost a close friend, so it was an emotional time. I'm glad that I was able to be there for him."

The conversation continued, with Rainey enthusing about what a great movie they were making, how smoothly shooting was going, how amiable the divorce was, and other official lies. By the time she signed off, she was assured that Pamela's newspaper would have headlines refuting the reconciliation story the next morning. Maybe that would calm things down a bit.

Methodically she began returning her phone calls. During the production of a movie, Sunday was seldom a day of rest. She worked till dusk on autopilot, ordered dinner from room service, then went back to work.

When she was tired enough to sleep, she took a bath, then popped and swallowed the last birth control pill from the flat plastic disk that held a month's supply. She was about to toss the holder in the trash when a thought struck her.

Today was Sunday. Usually she ended a cycle of pills on a Saturday. Since she'd just taken the last one, she must have skipped a day in the last four weeks. *Hell,* why now of all times instead of during the months of celibacy?

Obviously she'd been so busy working that she'd forgotten. But when? Taking the pills was so automatic that she had no idea when she might have skipped. There had been plenty of long, disrupted days when a mistake might have been made.

Even though the chances of getting pregnant from one missed day were infinitesimal, she couldn't stop herself from imagining how nice it would be if she was pregnant. There had been times during her marriage when she'd been tempted to "forget" her pills, yet she'd never done so because it would have been unforgivable to trick Kenzie that way. But this missed pill was a genuine error.

Though her dream had been to raise her children with two

loving parents, not as a single mother, she made good money and could raise a child on her own. She'd never have to ask a thing of Kenzie. He wouldn't even have to know it was his since he didn't want to be a father.

With a sigh, she relinquished the pleasant daydream and crawled into bed, hoping that sleep would come. She'd almost drifted off when the memory of what Charles Winfield had said jarred her back to wakefulness: *Don't let him push you away.*

Was that what Kenzie was doing—pushing her away because he thought he should, rather than because it was what he wanted? Could be—thinking back, he'd always seemed unhappy with himself, not her.

But if he was being noble and self-sacrificing, like John Randall, it was damned effective. It took two to make a relationship work, only one to end it.

As he just had. Again.

✺ 26 ✺

"Mind if I sit down?"

Val glanced up and saw that Greg Marino was hovering with his lunch tray. "Not at all. Glad to have you join me." She smothered a yawn as he sat down opposite. "Do all movie productions feed you as well as this one? These meals make me want to curl up and nap afterward."

He dug into his beef Wellington. "Good food is essential, actually. When people are away from home and working like crazy for months on end, they need as many comforts as can be provided."

"Makes sense." Having finished her curried chicken, she bit into a fresh baked raspberry tart. "If I weren't slaving away like a workhouse child in a Dickens novel, I'd be a blimp by now."

"On you, it would look good."

She grinned. "Coming from a man who's filmed some of the most beautiful women in the world, that's a lie, but a gallant one."

"Beautiful women are just part of the job. A lot of 'em are all bones and hyper as race horses. The camera loves those angular faces, but it's like shooting porcelain dolls—not quite real." He took another bite and chewed thoughtfully. "I like a woman who looks like a woman. You do."

Looking sexy and dim was the curse of Val's life. "Half the reason I went to law school was a desire to shock people who think I look more like a barmaid than a woman who scored eight hundreds on her SATs."

"When I was nominated for an Oscar, I got a lot of juvenile satisfaction thinking about the reactions of all those people who thought I'd never amount to anything." Greg smiled blissfully at the thought. "Now that we're within a couple of days of wrapping up, what do you think of your first moviemaking experience?"

"It's been fascinating and exciting and I wouldn't have missed it for the world. But I'll be glad to go home."

Greg choked on his coffee. "You're kidding, right? You really want to go back to Buffalo or Boston or wherever it is you come from?"

"Baltimore, and yes, I do." She smiled at him fondly. They'd often hung out together at the end of the long work days, and it would have been easy to tumble into bed with him. He'd made it clear he was willing. But she was trying to simplify her life, and men were never simple. "Fantasy is fun now and then, but reality suits me better."

"But you're so good at getting things done. You could make a career in production, no problem. If Raine can't find you another job, I can. You'd be a hotshot producer making tons of money in no time."

"If money was that important to me, I'd have made a lot of different choices along the way. Making movies requires a touch of the gypsy, and I don't have that. Not to mention the fact that there's an awful lot of sitting around and waiting for something to happen, which would rapidly drive me crazy."

"This movie is less crazy-making than most—we're clipping along at a pretty good pace." A craft service girl passed with fresh tarts, so Greg snagged a couple. "I hope Raine keeps directing. I'd work for her again in a New York minute."

"I've watched all the dailies, but I'm a civilian," Val said. "Is *The Centurion* going to be as good as it looks?"

He turned serious. "I hope so. We've all busted our balls on this job. But a movie can be lost at any stage. In the casting, the shooting, the editing, the mixing. So many things can go wrong that sometimes I'm amazed any good stuff is ever released."

"No wonder directors and producers are control freaks." She hesitated, wondering if she should ask her next question. "Are all productions this tense at the end?"

"This one is tenser than most, but I think it's because of the scenes that are being shot." He ate half a tart in one bite. "Real gut-wrenchers. Plus all the press craziness. A couple of times I've wondered if Kenzie was going to freak out, and Rainey is looking pretty frayed, too."

Val frowned. The tabloids were having a field day at Kenzie and Rainey's expense, with Nigel Stone dropping heavy hints of shocking revelations to come about Kenzie's past. Cynically she wondered if some slander was being timed to hit just as production ended.

There was also frenzied speculation on the state of Raine and Kenzie's marriage. The Pamela person had done a good article refuting the reconciliation story and quoting Rainey at length—headlined "Just Good Friends"—but there had been plenty of wild stories, including an American female wrestler claiming she was the cause of the divorce because she was pregnant with twins by Kenzie. Rainey didn't read any of that rubbish, but she knew it was out there, and surely it added to her tension.

But the real source of tension was on the set. Kenzie had already filmed several devastating scenes with Sharif that ex-

plained why he'd returned to England emotionally trauma-
tized, and their climactic scene would be shot that afternoon. In
the morning, he and Rainey would tackle revelations, lovemaking, and reconciliation. Val wondered how that would go.
She couldn't imagine acting a love scene with a man who was
in the process of breaking her heart.

Relationships were hell. Why couldn't people reproduce
asexually like amoebae?

No doubt Rainey and Kenzie would act those last scenes admirably. Professional to the core, they'd rather be carried off in
straitjackets than admit they couldn't fulfill their obligations.
But Val would be profoundly glad when this production was
over so Rainey could get away from Kenzie and start to heal.

Amoebae really had the right idea.

Bare to the waist and artfully decorated with bruises and artificial sweat, Kenzie paced tautly across the set, innards churning, while the lighting was adjusted. Hell was having to choose
between artistic honesty, and showing the deepest scars of your
soul to a camera. Why was he doing this?

Because of Rainey. Because of Charles. Because the bloody
show must go on.

"Pictures up, gentlemen," the first AD called.

He entered the simulated tent, canvas on one side and camera on the other, and let himself be tethered to a post with a
long chain. As he settled on the rug that floored the tent, Sharif
watched with dangerous intensity, deep in his character. Playing Mustafa required him to be in control of a complex relationship that stimulated him on many levels, and he was doing
it magnificently.

In contrast, John Randall was just a bleeding victim with a
fractured sense of self. Kenzie should have demanded to play
Mustafa.

The sexual scenes had been merely hinted at, with shots of
a dark hand on pale skin, shadows moving behind canvas, and
other images that made it clear what had happened without

being graphic. More explicit were scenes of flashing debate, a rope securing a bloody, abraded wrist, reluctant admiration, and moments of odd tenderness, including Mustafa nursing his captive through a near fatal fever. Now all those conflicting emotions must come to a head. Kenzie stared at his nemesis, and let himself fall into a pit of despair.

Rainey gave the signal to start. His long robe swirling around him, Sharif stalked across the tent toward Randall. "For months, we have argued and fought and learned to know each other as only two warriors can, yet still you wish to leave? Very well, I shall let you go." His lips drew back from his teeth. "Beg for it."

Mentally and emotionally at the end of his tether, Randall struggled to his feet and managed to say, "A British officer doesn't beg."

"Then you will die in the desert," Mustafa said softly, his eyes glittering with menace, "and the wind and sand will polish your bones."

"Kill me and be done with it! Do you think my life has any value left?" It was a cry from the heart of a man pushed beyond his limits by physical and emotional abuse that had turned his normal life into a hallucinatory memory.

Face twisted with anger and frustration, the desert chief grabbed Randall's shoulder and shoved him to his knees. "Beg, you English swine!"

"No!" Randall snatched the dagger from the sheath at Mustafa's waist and held it to his own throat. "Kill me if you must."

The two men stared at each other, Randall's life weighing in the balance. Then Mustafa wrenched the weapon away and slammed it back into the sheath. "Go then! I'll not taint my blade with the blood of an unbeliever."

The scene ended with the camera zooming in on Randall's haggard face, showing the victory that had come at a price so high it was really defeat.

"Cut and print. Well done, both of you," Rainey said in a

voice pitched softly so as not to break the mood. "Once more, and then we'll do the closeups."

Kenzie stood, the words and emotions of the scene churning in his mind. Love and hate. Antagonism and mercy. Disgust . . . and desire. The culmination of all the painful, difficult scenes he and Sharif had played together. "This isn't right. It's weak."

Rainey blinked. "I thought the scene worked pretty well, but there's always room for improvement. What do you suggest?"

He rubbed his forehead, smearing his makeup. Why the *hell* was he doing this? Crucified by the Muse. "Forcing Randall to beg is . . . too obvious. Too much a 1930s B-movie. There needs to be . . . more between them. More conflict, higher stakes. Vulnerability."

"The scene is based on the book, so the sensibility is late Victorian," Rainey agreed. "What would go beyond that to make it work better now?"

He tried to pace, only to be jerked short by the chain on his left wrist. He pivoted, scowling. "Randall's ambivalence needs to be clearer. Mustafa wants to force him to recognize that on some level he was attracted to his captor." That the upright Victorian officer had experienced a dark, unwilling satisfaction in some of what was done to him. "Isn't that the core of the story? That Randall can't bear to acknowledge that he has ever been less than a one-hundred-percent pure heterosexual, even for a few minutes?"

"That's Randall," Rainey agreed. "How do you think it should be played?"

"Instead of making his captive beg for freedom," Kenzie said slowly, his head throbbing, "Mustafa should say that he'll free Randall, if . . . if Randall will admit that he loves him."

"Yes!" Sharif exclaimed. "I love my upright, maddening English officer, I don't want to lose him. I cannot bring myself to kill him, yet keeping him against his will would be cold ashes in my mouth. I offer him a bargain—I will allow him to go back to his cold northern land if just this once he admits the truth that lies between us."

"That's brilliant, Kenzie. Edgy and complicated and painful, just like their relationship." Rainey's gaze met his, and it was as if she was talking about them, not the fictional characters.

He turned away. "Sharif, shall we try this as improvisation?" He usually avoided ad-libbing since he wasn't sure about coming up with the right words, but this character and this dilemma he knew in his bones.

Since Sharif agreed, Rainey let them go ahead. Instead of angry threats, Mustafa used a raw, tormented voice that revealed more than he intended. Randall retreated as far as the chain would allow, futilely trying to escape that agonized demand. He couldn't bear to admit what Mustafa wanted to hear, yet if he denied this secret, loathed side of himself, he would never be free to return to his real life.

He closed his eyes, imagining Sarah, his touchstone, the bright angel who had moored him to sanity. For the sake of her and his family, he would speak the words Mustafa wanted to hear. What did a small lie matter, if it would secure his freedom?

He closed his eyes and said haltingly, "I . . . love you," speaking the words his enemy—his honored, loved, and hated enemy—wanted to hear. He told himself his "confession" would make no difference to who he really was.

Yet it made all the difference in the world.

There was a hushed silence after Rainey whispered, "Cut and print."

Then the crew broke into applause. It was the kind of spontaneous tribute that did an actor's soul good—but not this time. Wearily Kenzie leaned against the pole, then slid down to the carpet and buried his face in his hands.

Crucified by the Muse.

❧ 27 ❧

Today, karmic justice would be visited on Rainey. It was almost time to play the big love scene with Kenzie in front of a relentless camera. Restlessly Rainey moved around her shabby studio dressing room, the long skirt of her Victorian day dress picking up a dust bunny or two along the hem.

"In the interests of distraction," Val said from her desk in the corner, "shall I summarize some of your mail?"

"Anything exciting there?"

"Not really. Your paternity investigator's weekly report says he may have a line on the studio executive Clementine was involved with, and it appears to have been more than a casual fling."

"A studio executive?" Rainey wrinkled her nose. "The drug dealer is starting to look better. What else have you got?"

"An e-mail note from your grandfather. Apparently he's becoming an Internet addict on that get-well computer you gave him." Val glanced at the printed-out note. "The suggestions we made about where he might be able to link up with some of his old Korean War buddies have borne fruit. He found some, and they chat back and forth daily. Your grandparents have booked tickets to his outfit's reunion in Florida next winter."

"That's very good news." Gradually, at long distance, the relationship with her grandparents was improving. It was an unexpected benefit of her grandfather's accident. She actually looked forward to her next visit with them, after *The Centurion* finished shooting, though she knew better than to expect too much. There could be friendship and respect between her and them. For warmth, she would look elsewhere, as she always had.

Deb, the makeup artist, entered the dressing room. "Time to touch you up before this next scene."

Obediently Rainey sat in a straight chair. With a third person present, Val put away the personal messages and returned to transcribing Rainey's scrawled notes from the previous evening's viewing of the dailies.

Rainey's thoughts returned obsessively to the upcoming scene with Kenzie. Maybe it would have been worse to direct Jane Stackpole in bed with him—but probably not. Being there in that bed herself, with his familiar touch and the haunted eyes that were as much Kenzie as John Randall—she shuddered at the prospect.

"Don't twitch," Deb said.

"Sorry." Rainey needed cosmetic magic to make her over-thirty face look ten years younger. Mentally she rehearsed her lines while Deb fine-tuned Sarah's dewy English complexion.

Then it could be avoided no longer. She left her dressing room and picked her way across the vast, darkened sound stage, avoiding cables and equipment. Kenzie was already on the brightly lit bedroom set, fingers drumming on a tall, carved bedpost.

The scenes with Sharif had reduced him to monosyllables and zero eye contact. She studied him critically, glad that filming was almost over. Both of them were looking haggard and had lost weight. Luckily, that suited the scenes they were shooting. The stress of moviemaking coincided with the stress of their fictional characters.

This scene directly followed the one on the cliff where Sarah had coaxed Randall back from suicidal despair. He'd stammered out enough for her to understand why he was so profoundly wounded. Though Sarah was uncertain of exactly what had been done to him, she had recognized the depth of his emotional pain. Loving her husband, she was determined not to allow his nightmares and shattered self-esteem to drive her away.

The cliff scene had ended with their returning to the house across the fields, Randall moving like an old man, his arm around his wife's shoulders. This take would start with them, windblown from the cliffs, entering his bedchamber. Rainey scanned the set, automatically checking that the details were right before looking at Kenzie. "Ready?"

He nodded and crossed to stand in the doorway. She joined him, saying in a low tone, "You won't be able to do this scene without looking at me a time or two."

Mouth tightening, he met her gaze, the torments of the damned visible in his eyes. She swallowed hard, wishing she could believe that he was merely in character, but sure that much of that bleakness was Kenzie.

To match his intensity, she reached deep inside to release sorrow from the well of pain at her core. The emotion centered her in Sarah, who was frightened and out of her depth, but would not give up. When tension shimmered between the two characters, Rainey gave the signal to start.

The camera began to roll. Clinging to each other, they entered the room. Then Randall pulled away, unsteady but determined to stand on his own feet.

Rainey said, "Rest now, my dear. You'll feel better then."

"You don't understand," he said harshly. "A night's sleep won't cure the past. Nothing will." When she reached for him, he caught her hand, keeping her away. "Which is why you must leave me before it's too late."

His touch sizzled through her. Though a virgin, Sarah knew there was a powerful attraction between them. "Then we won't look to the past. Only now and the future."

"Sarah, we have no future." He released her hand and stepped back. "Since we are not truly married, it will be possible to separate legally. Perhaps an annulment, which will free you in the eyes of society."

"You are the one who doesn't understand, John." Her fear of losing him was laced with anger. "You might not have meant the vows you took, but I did. Before God, you are my husband. I will have no other while you live."

He looked at her as if she were a distant, cherished memory. "You are so fine. So pure. I thought of you as my bright angel when I was imprisoned."

Her anger erupted, making her reckless. "I cannot live on the pedestal where you've placed me, John. Though I know little of the world, I know enough to be your wife. Or is it impossible for you to . . . to desire me?"

The flick of his eyes down her body betrayed him, though he said stiffly, "You should not speak of such things."

He had made himself vulnerable by revealing the shame that scarred his spirit. If they were to be husband and wife, Sarah must make herself equally vulnerable, and the only way she could imagine was by offering herself sexually. In passion, he would be stronger and more experienced than she.

"Words are not helping. You have always been a man of action. It is time for us to act. Together." Fingers shaking, she began to unfasten the pearl buttons that ran down the front of her bodice.

He caught his breath as the dress fell open to reveal her lace-trimmed undergarment and pale, virginal skin. "This . . . this isn't fitting, Sarah."

"What could be more fitting than intimacy between husband and wife?" Seeing his glance go to the door, she turned the key in the lock, then dropped it into a vase of roses that stood on his dresser.

He'd revealed that he desired her. Now she must remind him of the vows they had taken. She began unfastening her cuffs. "I, Sarah, take thee, John, to be my wedded husband, to have and to hold, from this day forward. For better. For worse. For *always*. You swore an oath to me, John. I shall not release you from it." She peeled off her tucked and lacy blouse.

Gaze riveted, he whispered, "With my body . . . I thee worship."

The skirt tied back with a sash at her waist. She tugged the bow loose, then pushed the skirt to the floor, leaving her in lace-edged chemise and petticoats. Though almost every inch of her was covered, the fact that she was in her undergarments charged the air with eroticism. Voice husky, she said, "You must unlace me."

He swallowed hard as she turned, presenting her back to him. As he unfastened her laces, she struggled to control her fear of the unknown, for she knew in her bones that this was the right course. She must put herself in his power to remind him that he possessed power.

Reverently he caressed her, sending liquid heat curling deep inside. The corset fell away, leaving her body unbound and tingling with sensation. As she arched her back, he bent to kiss her neck, his breath warm against her nape. She gasped, frightened now not only of what he might do, but of herself, and the body that no longer seemed fully her own. Rather desperately, she groped for her identity as Rainey. "Cut."

Behind her, Kenzie's breathing was rough as her own. Not daring to look at him, she asked, "Did that look good, Greg?"

Voice a little thick, the cameraman said, "I thought the lens might melt, but it didn't, so I'd say this should be printed."

Kenzie had retreated across the room and was showing great interest in the ivory-backed toiletry articles on the dresser. She hoped he found this as harrowing as she did.

Though she'd give a year's income not to do this scene again, she couldn't risk going with a single take this close to the end. "Okay. One more time for safety's sake."

The rest of the day was taken up with the love scene and the impressionistic closeup images that would keep the movie romantic and PG-13 rather than graphic and R-rated. It was one of the strangest acting experiences of Rainey's life, a false intimacy with a man where the intimacy had once been real and profound.

They filmed silken garments sliding to the floor with a luxurious whisper. Stroking hands, tentative when they belonged to Sarah, taut with barely controlled desire for Randall. Her anxiety spiked with pain, then dissolving into wonder, the awed tenderness as Randall discovered the magic of his bride's unstinting love. She was the Maiden, powerful in her conviction, while he was the wounded Warrior regaining his strength as he remembered what it was that men fought to protect.

After they wrapped for the day, Rainey went to her dressing room, sprawled on her sofa, and slept like the dead.

Rainey awoke stiff and aching, uncertain where she was until Val asked quietly, "Back among the living?"

"Barely." She sat up, glad she'd taken the damned corset off while they were shooting. "What time is it?"

"About nine in the evening." Val looked up from the chipped, wobbly table in the corner where she'd been working. "I figured that if you were that tired, you should rest."

"So you stood guard and kept the world at bay. Thanks." Lurching a little, Rainey went to the dressing table and removed her smeared makeup.

Val had placed a banana, a packet of peanuts, and a container of milk on the table, so Rainey wolfed them down. Preferring to shower at the immaculate hotel rather than the shabby dressing room, she changed into her own clothes. "Ready to escape?"

"With pleasure." Val slid her paperwork into her briefcase and stood.

"What did Kenzie do after we finished shooting?"

"Changed and lit out of here like his tail feathers were on fire." Val joined Rainey as they left the dressing room. "Thank God shooting ends tomorrow, before one or both of you have nervous breakdowns." Her voice echoed through the empty studio.

Rainey thought of the climactic scenes that would be shot the next day. They would grind away whatever reserves she had left. Only then could she could fly home to her little house in the canyon. "You've called the charter company about my flight back to L.A.?"

"Your private jet shall await your pleasure after Charles Winfield's memorial service."

"Want to fly back with me? It's no problem to drop you off in Baltimore."

"Thanks, but I want to take advantage of being in the British

Isles. This morning Laurie and I decided to go to Ireland for a week's vacation."

"She's fun. You'll have a good time." Rainey glanced at her friend. "I've really enjoyed having you on this job, Val. I . . . I don't know if I could have made it through without you."

"You've helped me pick up the pieces of my fractured love life half a dozen times. I'm glad I was able to help you for once."

Outside the studio door their car waited patiently. Rainey climbed inside and sank into the seat as they began the trip back to central London. "If I offered you a permanent job, would you take it?"

"No." Val gazed out the window, her brow furrowed. "This has been a great experience, and it's motivated me to go home and make some changes. But not California, and not the entertainment business."

"You're wise. Sometimes I think that moviemaking is an incurable disease." Rainey smiled self-mockingly. "The business makes me crazy, but I wouldn't want to do anything else. Especially if I can make movies on my terms, not Hollywood's."

"*The Centurion* will make that possible," Val said confidently. "But success and wild acclaim are months away. Tonight I have a better solution to the world's ills."

Rainey grinned. "Ice cream?"

"Right." Val fished out her cell phone. "I'll call room service so they can get started on our dinners right away. After you've showered and eaten, we'll find out if these Brits can made a decent hot fudge sundae."

Feeling less drained, Rainey settled back in her seat. Old friends and ice cream were cures for a good number of the world's ills.

As Kenzie opened the classic Victorian straight razor, light glittered menacingly off the hollow ground blade. He'd borrowed the razor from the set, where it had rested innocently among Randall's other toiletries.

In recent years, the strange form of self-mutilation that drove people to cut themselves had come out of the closet and onto the airwaves. He'd watched a talk show on the subject once, where young girls rather proudly explained how the physical pain of cutting themselves had mysteriously relieved their unbearable inner pain. He understood, having cut himself sometimes when he was young.

He rested the blade against his arm. Not the inside wrist, where a cut could cause bleeding to death, but higher up, on his forearm. He imagined the razor slicing through skin and muscle. First there would be shock at seeing the severed flesh and knowing it should hurt. Then the pain would explode, throbbing, so overpowering that for a time it would obliterate everything else in the world.

He increased pressure on the razor, wondering how hard he'd have to press to break the skin. Then, exhaling roughly, he snapped the razor shut and tossed it onto a chair. He wasn't that hard up.

Not yet.

❧ 28 ❧

Dinner, shower, and a very respectable hot fudge sundae restored Rainey to the point where she could watch the dailies and note the best scenes. Great stuff. If everything came together as she could see it in her mind, they'd have a fine movie. Not a blockbuster, but a moving, well-crafted film that should find an appreciative audience.

But her long nap left her awake and twitchy after Val had gone yawning to bed. Restless and wanting to stretch her muscles, she quietly left the hotel for a walk. The killing production schedule had meant less exercise than usual, and the sessions she'd managed had been early and abbreviated.

As she stepped out onto Park Lane, she drew the cool English air into her lungs. It was good to be alone and anonymous. Brooding was more difficult when there were other people around, and she was in a broody mood for sure.

Tomorrow they'd finish shooting the movie. The wrap party would be that night, and the next morning, a small, private memorial service for Charles Winfield. Then she and Kenzie would go their separate ways once and for all.

Of course they'd see each other occasionally in the future. There would be a premiere for *The Centurion,* probably joint publicity appearances. Since they traveled in similar circles, there would be casual meetings now and then. She'd pretend that seeing him didn't make her feel kicked in the stomach, even if he had some gorgeous female on his arm. They'd chat. Terribly civilized. Then she'd probably go to the nearest ladies' room and throw up. Her stomach felt queasy just thinking about it. Eventually, the pain would fade to a dull ache, but she didn't expect that to be soon.

Loss was still a day and a half away, though. Tomorrow she must endure her most challenging scene yet, with Sarah and Randall resolving their problems in the bed where they'd finally consummated their marriage. Having affirmed their love and commitment, they would decide that their best hope for a new life was to leave England and its suffocating restrictions and expectations. Australia was an easy choice. Randall's uncle had settled there many years earlier, and his letters to the family described a raw, energetic land where a man could be free in ways impossible in the Old World.

Traveling halfway around the world appealed to the adventurer in Sarah, and her intuition told her that their marriage would prosper there. Nonetheless, the thought of leaving home and family was wrenching. When he realized that, Randall would say there was no reason to emigrate. They could manage very well in England.

Sarah, at her most noble and self-sacrificing, would quote Ruth's Biblical speech to Naomi in perfect King James prose.

"Whither thou goest, I will go; and where thou lodgest, I
will lodge.
Thy people shall be my people, and thy God, my God.
Where thou diest, will I die, and will I be buried.
The Lord do so to me, and more also, if ought but death
part thee and me."

From the creative point of view, Rainey knew that speech was
exactly right. A product of her time and place, a young woman
coming into her strength, Sarah would freely and gladly follow
her husband anywhere.

But as a modern woman, Rainey hated the way Sarah gave
up everything for a man. When and if she produced and directed another movie—a horrific prospect at the moment—
she'd use a modern setting, and a relationship where a man and
a woman had to struggle to achieve a balance between them.
Equality was more interesting, and more difficult, than a relationship with one party dominant. In fact, she'd read a novel a
couple of years earlier that might serve as the foundation for a
really good screenplay. . . .

Between horror and amusement, she realized that she was
actually considering future projects. Moviemaking really was
an incurable disease.

Her path eastward took her past Buckingham Palace and St.
James Park, then down to the Houses of Parliament, a dramatic
sight at night. Turning north, she started along the Victoria Embankment, a handsome walkway that edged the Thames.

As she walked, she wondered why Sarah's self-sacrificing
nature irritated her so much. Rainey believed in a woman's
right to choose her path in life, and a man's right to do the
same. So why did Sarah's submissiveness make her crazy?

With a jolt, she recognized that her reaction was really
about Clementine. Even as a little girl called Rainbow, she'd
known her mother was too anxious to please the men in her
life. Clementine would become so involved with her current

lover that she often neglected her career and her daughter. A classic "woman who loved too much."

Some of those lovers treated her in ways that would drive any self-respecting woman out the door, and Rainbow had been furious on her mother's behalf. No wonder Rainey had grown up swearing she'd never, ever let a man take advantage of her. She'd kept that promise, too, which was why she disliked playing the obliging Sarah.

Beginning to tire, Rainey sat on a bench and gazed across the water. Next up the river was Waterloo Bridge. Whenever she saw it, she thought of the old movie with Vivien Leigh and Robert Taylor. She and her friends had watched it on television one night in high school. They'd all been outraged by the story of a gentle English ballerina who fell in love with a handsome, aristocratic soldier during wartime.

The pair became engaged, but the dancer lost her job by cutting work to bid her beloved adieu at the train station. After hearing a false report of his death, she'd become a prostitute to support herself. Then her fiancé returned from the dead and took her off to meet his family, not knowing what she'd done. Riddled by guilt, the dancer later killed herself by jumping in front of a bus on Waterloo Bridge. In 1940, it wasn't enough for a woman to repent of her sins—she'd had to die messily.

The twit. If she feared the truth coming out, she should have confessed her fall from grace to her fiancé, who might have loved her enough to marry her anyhow. And if not—well, the girl was young, she could have built a new life. The movie was supposed to be a great romantic classic, but there was nothing romantic about stupidity and guilt. Rainey much preferred stories of redemption and reconciliation.

Of course, Sarah was not the dancer of *Waterloo Bridge*. Her head was screwed on much better. Better than Rainey's, probably.

But she didn't envy Sarah's admirably level-headed personality. What she admired, and resented, was Sarah's ability to make an absolute commitment to a man.

Raine Marlowe, twenty-first-century woman, had never made such a commitment in her life. She'd been so determined not to be the victim of a man that she'd approached love with her list of conditions raised like a shield. No man would hit her, or cheat on her, or take advantage of her, or take her for granted, or marry her for her money. If a man broke one of her rules, she'd take off.

Given her doubts and suspicions, it was amazing she'd actually married Kenzie. Of course, she'd gone into the marriage knowing it was doomed to fail—and that had become a self-fulfilling prophecy, hadn't it?

How much was a woman supposed to give? Clementine gave too much, Rainey surely not enough.

She began to weep, feeling more alone than at any time since her mother's death. Despite all her defenses, she'd fallen heart over heels for Kenzie, but she hadn't made a true commitment. All the time they'd been together, she'd been waiting for him to betray her, so she was always ready to leave. She hadn't even sold her house.

> *Thought this battered heart of mine would never mend.*
> *Yet here I am, heart over heels again.*
> *Heart over heels, moth to the flame.*
> *Maybe this time, Lord, maybe this time . . .*

Her mother had picked the wrong men, and that had contributed to her death. But she'd had the courage to love with her whole heart, a courage Rainey lacked.

Not long before her mother's death, Rainbow had asked why a moth flying into a flame was in a love song. Clementine drew her daughter onto her lap, saying, "The moth is consumed in the fire, but don't you have to envy it for wanting something so much?"

Young and already pragmatic to the bone, Rainey hadn't understood, but tonight, finally, she did. She had never dared let herself want anything—or anyone—that much.

Her reasons for seeking a divorce were clear cut and entirely justifiable. No one blamed her for leaving a man who'd been unfaithful. She was in firm possession of the moral high ground.

Yet now she blamed herself for not trying to understand why it had happened. The more time that passed, the more she doubted that Kenzie had betrayed her from simple lust. Moviemaking was grueling, and playing intimate scenes with an attractive member of the opposite sex could create the illusion of a love, or at least lust. Kenzie probably succumbed to Angie Greene's silicone-enhanced charms from sheer, exhausted loneliness after months of work on a demanding movie with only brief visits to or from his wife.

Though Rainey had never been unfaithful to Kenzie, she understood how such a lapse could happen. She'd experienced that kind of desperate loneliness when working on location. Before her marriage, she'd also succumbed to that craving for warmth and physical comfort when the stress of work grew overpowering. Separation and strain were a major reason why so many Hollywood marriages didn't last long.

She couldn't blame herself for turning around and flying back to California immediately—the shock and pain had been devastating. But looking back, she questioned her decision to immediately file for divorce. She hadn't made the least attempt to salvage her marriage. She'd never suggested counseling, or even asked her husband if he was sorry and wanted to try again. She'd just walked away, following her personal rules of disengagement.

Kenzie hadn't contested the divorce, and had said repeatedly that she was better off without him. But like John Randall, he'd never said that he didn't want his wife. Making *The Centurion* had drawn them into intimacy over and over again. When he was at the breaking point, he'd come to her, and she'd offered comfort without question. He'd done the same for her.

Wasn't providing shelter from the storm an important part of marriage? Despite the legal wheels grinding away in California, they were still deeply connected to each other. Maybe not enough for a real marriage, but enough to make her question her original belief that divorce was the only possible choice.

Shaking, she buried her face in her hands. She thought of loyalty as one of her virtues. She'd been loyal to her friends, her principles, to people that had helped her when she needed it. But she hadn't shown much loyalty to Kenzie. She'd been determined to preserve her pride, and her fragile heart.

Her jumbled thoughts calmed as a decision emerged. Maybe Kenzie was incapable of real intimacy. Maybe she was, too. But she would not be the one to break their marriage.

As of this night, this moment, she was finally making a commitment.

Footsteps passing by paused, and a deep voice asked, "Are you all right, miss?"

She looked up into the concerned face of a policeman. Wiping her eyes, she said, "I've been better, but I'm okay. Really."

He nodded and continued on his way. Rainey glanced at her watch. Nine hours time difference between London and Los Angeles, so it was still business hours there. She found her cell phone and pushed the autodial code for her lawyer. She was put through immediately. The lawyer greeted her warmly. "Good timing, Rainey. The paperwork is finally done, so the divorce can be finalized when you return to California."

"That's why I'm calling, Ann. Pull the plug on it. I've changed my mind."

The lawyer caught her breath. "You and Kenzie have reconciled? That's great! At least, I hope it is."

"No, we haven't reconciled." Rainey sighed. "I don't think we will, either. But for various complicated reasons, I've decided to knock the ball into Kenzie's court. If he wants a divorce, he'll have to be the one to get it." She would be passively cooperative, exactly as he had been. Would he immediately file for divorce? Would he take her gesture as an olive branch, and try to resolve their differences? Or would he let matters drift, with them separate but still married?

It would be interesting to find out, in a macabre sort of way.

❧ 29 ❧

Kenzie arrived at the wrap party a little late, as tired as if he'd hiked across Death Valley in high summer. Actually, that would have been less draining than spending a good part of the day in bed with his estranged but infinitely desirable wife. Wearing minimal clothing, emoting madly, and with a camera and crew watching every move.

Crossing directly to the open bar, he ordered a double shot of single malt whisky. He hadn't been drunk in decades and wouldn't be tonight, but he figured he was entitled to one really good, stiff drink. Hell, he was entitled to have a bottle of champagne cracked across his head as if he were a bloody battleship. He'd actually made it through Rainey's wretched movie.

After a deep, scorching swallow of whisky, he turned and leaned back on the bar. The wrap party was being held in a function room attached to an old London pub. The spacious, high-ceilinged room was decorated like a gorgeous medieval banquet hall, complete with smiling waiters and waitresses in colorful period costume. It was a handsome place for a celebration, and the Americans in particular loved it. Rainey had used her tight budget for *The Centurion* well, not wasting a penny, but not stinting when it came to making her colleagues feel appreciated.

He took a slower sip of whisky. Wrap parties were always bittersweet. For the duration of a production, cast and crew were like the crew of a ship, sometimes at each other's throats but bound together by their mutual mission. He'd been in the business long enough so that there were always familiar faces from the past, and people he'd see again in the future, but each production was unique. Never again would exactly the same group come together to make a movie.

Still, by the end of shooting there was often a desire to have the blasted thing over with, especially if the production had been plagued with problems. Kenzie had worked on one film where the director had been changed twice, insanely expensive mechanical props had refused to work, the weather had been killingly hot and humid, and the leading lady was a screaming, coke-snorting hysteric. All that plus a scene-stealing dog eager to bite everyone but its handler. He'd certainly celebrated the end of that one.

Given the strain of working with Rainey, this should have rated as a production he wouldn't miss, yet in most ways, it had been a good experience. First-rate people had done their best, with minimal interference from egos. Moviemaking at its best.

The script supervisor approached, a wicked light in her eyes, and gave him a smacking kiss on the cheek. "I've been wanting to do that for weeks."

He grinned and patted her ample rump. "I'm glad you finally let your inner tiger loose, Helen."

She moved off, laughing. He glanced around the room and spotted Rainey in the middle of a knot of people. With her hair loose around her shoulders and garbed in a flowing green gown, she looked like the ingenue, not a tough, determined producer and director who'd worked tirelessly to bring her story to life. He hoped she was feeling pride in what she'd achieved.

Tomorrow she'd be gone for good.

He began to circulate, speaking to everyone at least briefly. Doable with a cast and crew of about seventy-five. Small by Hollywood standards.

He suspected that his reputation for being courteous and down-to-earth had taken a beating on this production. There had been days on end when he'd barely been able to manage civility. No one seemed to hold that against him, though. Arrogance would have been resented, but he'd been so obviously stressed that his coworkers had been downright protective.

Halfway around the gilded hall, he'd finished his drink and was considering going for another when a pretty redheaded waitress approached. "Excuse me, Mr. Scott, I know I shouldn't do this, but when I heard you'd be here . . . well, my little boy would really like to meet you." She glanced around. "Would you mind awfully coming to the cloakroom to meet him? Only for a minute. It would mean ever so much to Evan."

"Of course I don't mind." He followed her from the hall and down a short passage to the empty cloakroom. Evan was about eleven, with great blue eyes, his mother's red hair, and a thin body confined to a wheelchair.

As the child's face lit up, Kenzie dropped to one knee so their faces were level. "Hi, Evan. You know who I am. I gather you like the cinema?"

"Oh, *yes!* You're my favorite actor, sir, and *Sky Quest* is my favorite movie, especially the final scene when you have to battle both the villain and your own dark twin." His words tumbled over each other as he delivered a detailed analysis that would have done credit to a film school student.

When the boy paused for breath, his mother said firmly, "That's enough now, lad. Mr. Scott will be wanting to get back to his friends."

"I'm in no rush," Kenzie said. "Why not get back to work and return in ten or fifteen minutes?"

She gave him a smile that brightened the room, and complied. By the time she came back, Kenzie and Evan had discussed *Sky Quest, The Scarlet Pimpernel,* and were well into *Lethal Force.* Kenzie signed a movie poster Evan had brought, then shook hands and said good-bye.

As he and the boy's mother returned to the hall, she said softly, "I don't know how to thank you enough, Mr. Scott. For the first year after Evan's accident, movies were the only thing that made him smile. Meeting you is a dream come true."

"It was my pleasure. He's a fine boy, with a mind like a steel whip." And how lucky he was to have a mother like this one. "Don't discourage him if he wants to work in the film industry someday. There are jobs that can be done from a wheelchair."

Her eyes widened. "Really, sir?"

"Really." If Kenzie could make it in show business, a boy

as clever as Evan could. "He has the passion. Skills can be learned."

A man who looked like the hall's supervisor stepped up, glowering. His gaze on the waitress, he said ominously, "Come along, Mrs. Jones. You know our rules."

Suspecting she was on the verge of being fired, Kenzie said to the supervisor, "Sorry, was I out of line? I heard that Mrs. Jones has a son who's a cinema fan, and asked if I could meet him. We had a fine time. I'm sorry that I took her from her work."

The supervisor's expression changed. "You asked to meet the lad, Mr. Scott?"

"Yes. I find it very useful to keep in touch with my fans." He gave a full-wattage movie star smile. "I'm dreadfully sorry to have interfered with your staff. It isn't easy to create an event like this and make it seem effortless."

"Got that right, mate." As the supervisor began detailing the difficulties of running a catering operation, Mrs. Jones gave Kenzie a swift, grateful glance before slipping away to help re-plenish the buffet tables along one wall. After listening intently to the supervisor, Kenzie signed an autograph for the man's wife, then excused himself and returned to circulation.

He was close to finishing his task of talking to everyone when Josh arrived at the party, late and harried. "This was just faxed in from California, Kenzie." He drew out a folded paper. "I thought you should see it right away."

Wondering what could be so important, Kenzie looked at the paper. At first glance the letter was a chaotic, indecipher-able jumble of letters, a sure sign of fatigue.

He closed his eyes for a moment, forcing his mind to slow down and concentrate, then tried again. The letterhead was his lawyer's. A word at a time, he started on the text. When he reached the end, he read through the letter again. The words re-mained the same. "Good God," he said blankly. "Rainey has withdrawn the divorce?"

"So it seems."

Kenzie's mental circuits melted under a clash of mixed emotions. Shock. Anger. Grief. Fear. "Don't tell anyone about this."

Josh looked offended. "Of course I won't."

"Sorry." Expression grim, he went in search of Rainey. He found her locked in a long, wordless hug with Rabbit, the hirsute sound man. There was a lot of hugging at wrap parties.

When Rainey disentangled herself from Rabbit—named for his uncanny sensitivity to sounds—Kenzie asked tersely, "May I have a moment?"

Rainey stiffened and looked as if she wanted to bolt. "Of course."

Rabbit gave Kenzie's arm a friendly punch and ambled off toward the buffet. Taking Rainey's elbow, Kenzie steered her away from the food and the casual circular dining tables. "Josh just gave me the most remarkable fax from my lawyer. What the hell kind of mind game are you playing? Or is this some peculiar kind of joke?"

"Neither. It's just what it looks like—I dropped the suit."

His temples began to throb as if he'd drunk five shots of whisky. "Producing movies is an expensive hobby. Did you decide you wanted some of my money after all? Dividing my last three years of income by community property would certainly finance your next movie or two."

"You *bastard!*" She jerked her arm free. "What have I ever said to make you think I want your damned money?"

Nothing. In fact, when she'd first filed, he'd had his lawyer offer her a substantial cash settlement. She'd flatly refused to take anything from him. Well on his way to a rare migraine, he said wearily, "Sorry. That was uncalled for."

"More like unforgivable."

"That, too. I'm . . . not good with surprises." Another dyslexic coping mechanism was to plan and organize as much as possible. Surprises that scrambled his hard-earned strategies were never welcome.

"I'm not fond of surprises myself," she said more moderately. "The sign of a control freak."

"Why did you change your mind, Rainey? Surely you can't want to stay married."

Her gaze went across the room to the glittering ice peacock that presided over the salads. She had the starkly beautiful profile of an exhausted angel. "The honest truth is that living inside Sarah Masterson's skin made me realize how . . . how heedless I was to race back from Crete and immediately file for divorce. I didn't spend a single second considering whether I was doing the right thing. Since I don't like seeing myself as thoughtless, I canceled the lawsuit. Don't worry, this doesn't change anything. You've made it clear that you don't want to be married, so go ahead and file your own petition. I won't contest it."

He stared at her, baffled and off balance. He'd counted on her determination to end the marriage. God knew that he deserved to be left. "I . . . don't know what to say."

She sighed, her gaze coming back to him. "This isn't the time or place to talk. After we're both back in California and have caught up on our sleep, we can sort this out with a phone call. Most of the legal work has already been done, so a new petition should go through very quickly."

The reasons to divorce hadn't changed. She'd just laid the burden of it on him. Diabolical, even though that hadn't been her intention. "Whatever you want, Rainey."

"What a pity I don't really know what I want."

Not daring to wonder what that might mean, he said, "Are you going to the memorial service tomorrow?" When she nodded, he continued, "Shall we go together?"

Accepting his olive branch, she said, "That would be nice. I wouldn't want to miss it." Very erect, her soft gown rippling like spring water, she turned and walked to the buffet, where she was welcomed with another long hug, this time from Laurie, the line producer.

So he was going to have to get the divorce. It would be easier to gnaw his arm off like a fox caught in a trap.

Charles Winfield's memorial service packed the small chapel to overflowing. He'd made many friends over the years, and a dozen distinguished members of the British theatrical community had asked to speak in his honor.

As executor and organizer of the service, Kenzie spoke first. He kept his remarks short, saying only that he owed his career to Charles Winfield, then recounting an anecdote that showed Charles at his most charming and generous. Struggling to keep his voice from breaking, he ended with, "Charles told me once that he had no family, but he was wrong. The British theater was his family, and today we all mourn his loss."

Rainey gave a smile of approval when he returned to his seat beside her. She wore a severe, tailored black suit, and looked even more alluring than the night before.

As the service unfolded, she quietly took his hand. He squeezed hers gratefully. Saying good-bye to his mentor and oldest friend was a painful reminder of all of the other losses of his life. For better and worse, Charles had been the last link to his childhood.

The service ended with a powerful organ rendition of the hymn "Jerusalem." Slowly the crowd began to leave, with knots of people reminiscing and making plans for lunch. Several, including Dame Judith Hawick, paused to exchange memories of Charles and to thank Kenzie for organizing the service.

Just before they reached the carved double doors, they were intercepted by Jenny Lyme and a man who looked vaguely familiar. She hugged Kenzie hard. "That was perfect, Kenzie. Charles would have been delighted by the turnout." She gestured to her companion. "You remember Will Stryker, don't you? He was with us the first year at RADA, then dropped out to study set design. He's the best in London."

"Of course I remember." Kenzie offered his hand. "Good to see you again, Will."

Jenny turned to Rainey and said warmly, "You don't know me, but my name is Jenny Lyme, and I'm a huge admirer of your work."

If her aim was to counter any jealousy caused by the tabloids' stories, she succeeded. Rainey extended her hand, saying with equal warmth, "As a matter of fact, I do know you, or at least, your work. Your ITV series, *Still Talking,* was wickedly funny. I had a friend in London taping episodes for me every week. I wish I had your talent for comedy. Have you considered doing movies?"

Jenny shook her head. "No, I'm the approachable girl-next-door type that does best on television. I can't do larger-than-life the way you and Kenzie do."

Kenzie suspected that given half a chance Rainey and Jenny would become friends. After a few minutes of chatting, they said their farewells and stepped outside.

It was an overcast morning, and mourners leaving the chapel were hit by a barrage of electronic flashes and television lights. "Damnation," Kenzie muttered under his breath. "I'd hoped the service wouldn't be noticed by the press hounds, but I suppose that was too much to expect."

"At least they have plenty of celebrities to choose from," Rainey said as she took his arm. "Look suitably sad for the camera, and we'll be out of here in no time."

Since the occasion was a memorial service, the reporters were well-behaved. Kenzie spotted the hired car waiting nearby at the curb. The plan had been to drop Kenzie at the hotel, then take Rainey directly to London City Airport, but maybe he'd go with her to the airplane. The longer he could put off saying good-bye, the better.

They were nearing the car when a harsh, familiar voice barked, "I know the truth now, Scott."

Blood chilling, Kenzie turned to see Nigel Stone bearing down on them, flanked by a photographer and a television cameraman. The last few days had been so demanding that he'd half forgotten about the reporter and his bizarre crusade. Josh monitored the tabloids daily, and had assured him that Stone was saying nothing Kenzie needed to know.

Stone's eyes gleamed with vicious triumph. He *knew*. This was no longer a ploy to increase circulation, but a full-blown, malicious attack. The reporter had remembered their early acquaintanceship. The whole, vile truth would come out, and there wasn't a damned thing Kenzie could do. His vision began to blacken and his stomach twisted with the sick knowledge of inevitable destruction felt by a man plunging from a cliff.

With one hand Stone shoved a microphone in Kenzie's face while the other held up a copy of the *Inquirer*. The headline screamed, "The Queer Truth about Kenzie!" "Would you care to comment, *Jamie Mackenzie*," the reporter sneered, "on your first career as a male whore?"

ACT III
Walking the Labyrinth

Rainey gasped. How dare *Nigel Stone say some-*thing so slanderous!

Then she felt Kenzie's arm spasm under her hand. Glancing up, she saw that his face seemed to have turned to granite. Something was disastrously wrong.

She gripped his arm hard, digging in her nails in an attempt to jolt him from his paralysis. "That's almost as wild as some of your own stories, Kenzie," she said lightly. "Though I think your claim to be the true king of England is more believable."

She gave him a quick glance. Kenzie had the rigid expression of a man who'd been mortally wounded. Guessing that he wouldn't be able to come up with a coherent response, she swung her gaze to the reporter and said with delicate contempt, "Have you considered writing a novel, Mr. Stone? Obviously fiction is your strong point."

His eyes narrowed with malice. "While researching your husband, I discovered that your mother was Clementine, rock star and drug addict. Father unknown. Care to comment on why you're so ashamed of her you've kept it a secret all these years?"

"My mother's identity has never been a secret, Mr. Stone." She managed, barely, a cool smile. "I'll admit I don't make a point of mentioning who she was. I never wanted to trade on her fame to help my own career, particularly since I lack her musical ability."

Anger at her calm, controlled reply sparked in the reporter's eyes, but there was no opportunity for further talk, because pandemonium had broken out. Other reporters crowded around shouting questions while mourners emerging from the chapel demanded to know what was going on. The twenty feet to the hired car looked like a mile.

Behind the television camera, Rainey saw Jenny Lyme, her expression appalled. Rainey sent her a fierce mental plea: *If Kenzie is your friend, help him!*

Jenny seized her escort's arm and the two of them pushed between Kenzie and the television camera. "How bizarre!" she said with her famous husky laugh. "I've known Kenzie since our first day at RADA, and trust me, Nigel darling, he's *not* gay." She batted long, dark lashes at the reporter, her voluptuous and totally feminine figure angled to the best advantage.

"Sadly true." Will Stryker became deliberately flamboyant. "Every gay student at RADA tried to seduce Kenzie at one time or the other. I mean really, who could resist? He was the most gorgeous man." The set designer gave an exaggerated sigh. "He always declined and went off with a girl. Polite but terribly, terribly straight. Near broke my heart."

That kicked off a new round of questions directed at Jenny and Will. Was Jenny sleeping with Kenzie again? Did they have plans for the future? Who were some of the other gay RADA students?

Desperately grateful for the distraction, Rainey fought her way through the crowd, holding Kenzie's arm in a death grip. Her burly driver, Jack Hammond, surged into the mass of people to meet them, forcing open a path to the car.

As Hammond threw open the door, Dame Judith Hawick joined Jenny and Will in front of the camera. Her stern gaze on Stone, she said in a voice that sliced through the tumult, "Have you no shame, sir? I had thought your kind couldn't possibly become more contemptible, but I was wrong. You're like those fools who claim Jane Austen was a lesbian because she and her sister shared a bed, as people often did before central heating." She shook her head sadly. "What a world we live in."

Rainey slid across the backseat of the car, pulling Kenzie in after her. He moved as stiffly as a marionette. Hammond slammed the car door, then leaped behind the wheel, started the engine, and pulled away from the shouting reporters.

Kenzie slumped into the corner of the seat, his eyes closed. He seemed to have shrunk, as if his flesh had drawn defensively close to the bones.

She took his hand. It was icy cold. "You're in shock, Kenzie," she said, trying to sound calm. "Can you talk?"

He opened blinded eyes. "Aren't you going to ask . . . if it's true?"

"Later, maybe." She chose her words carefully. "I don't much care what you did in the past, Kenzie. I care a lot about what happens in the present."

"Now comes the media crucifixion."

"Not if I have anything to say about it." But what could she do? Take one step at a time. "Is there any chance Nigel Stone has any evidence of what he's claiming?"

"I . . . doubt it."

She was painfully aware that he hadn't denied the charges, only the probability of evidence. "You need to get out of London. Better yet, out of England. If you stay here, the reporters will make your life hell. You won't be able to set foot outside your hotel without being mobbed."

A muscle in his jaw jerked. "I could not . . . endure that."

"Then you're leaving England." She opened the sliding door to the driver's compartment. "Skip the hotel and head straight to the airport, Jack."

"Will do." He hit his left turn signal.

She closed the sliding door again, thinking hard. Her baggage should already be on the jet, and her passport was in her purse. What about Kenzie? Damn, since he was a British citizen, he wouldn't have his passport on him.

He could do without clothes, but not a passport. She found her cell phone and punched in Josh's number, waiting impatiently through the English double rings. She was about to give up when he answered, sounding half asleep even though it was almost noon. He'd left the wrap party late, and had definitely had himself a good time.

Not bothering with small talk, she said, "Josh, it's Raine. A hellacious tabloid scandal is breaking out—utter nonsense, but Kenzie has decided to fly to the States with me to get out of the firestorm. He's not coming back to the hotel because reporters might try to intercept him there, so pack his things as fast as you can, and bring them to the airport. If you think that will take too long, just bring his passport."

Coming awake fast, Josh said, "I can do the packing, though his clothes will be wrinkled like crazy. I'll call a car now and be on my way in twenty minutes. London City Airport?"

"Right—the one you and Kenzie flew into. And thanks, Josh."

She shut off the phone and closed her eyes, shaking. Stone's highly public disclosure about Clementine was upsetting, but basically old news. The claims about Kenzie were inflammatory and dangerous, though. It was the sort of sex scandal the tabloids loved most—a famous man with a good reputation accused of breathtakingly sordid behavior.

What could be done to kill this in its cradle? If Stone had evidence of his charges, nothing could save Kenzie. If he didn't have proof, though, maybe the story could be spiked before anyone took it seriously.

Though Kenzie's friends had started damage control, heavier guns must be brought to bear as quickly as possible. From what Pamela Lake had said, Stone was disliked even by his colleagues. If he couldn't document his claims, they'd turn on him like jackals ripping apart a wounded member of the pack.

Time to summon the publicists. Though part of a publicist's job was getting attention for clients, equally important was scotching negative stories. Chloe, the smart, experienced unit publicist who'd worked on *The Centurion* set, was based in London. She must be called before the plane took off so Chloe could use her local media contacts to undercut Stone's reports.

Next call: Barbara Rifkin, personal publicist for both Kenzie and Rainey. Barb was tops in her field, with some of the biggest stars in the business among her clients, and the protective instincts of a tigress. An entertainment reporter who ran a story that Barb didn't like risked never getting another interview with any of Barb's clients.

Then alert Naomi and Marcus Gordon. They also had tremendous influence in Hollywood. A lot of people owed the Gordons favors, and God willing, they'd use their clout on Kenzie's behalf.

Rainey glanced at her watch. It was the middle of the night in California, so she'd hold off calling Barb and Marcus until a more civilized hour. As she looked up the private number of the unit publicist, she mentally rehearsed what she'd say. Outrageous charges by a reporter known for his malice. Complete nonsense. Make it go away.

If Nigel Stone could prove his story, she'd look like a gullible fool.

The phone rang in her hand, blasting adrenaline through her system. She raised it. "Yes?"

"Raine, Pamela Lake here. Is Kenzie Scott with you?"

Rainey stared at the phone. "How did you get this number?"

"You gave it to me."

"Oh, of course." Remembering that she mustn't sound too concerned, she continued, "It's been such an exciting half hour that my wits are a bit scattered. Kenzie is here. Were you covering Charles Winfield's memorial service?"

"Yes, but I was off to one side interviewing the man who directed Winfield's last performance. Too far away to be part of the riot." Pamela's voice was sympathetic. "Kenzie didn't respond to Nigel Stone's charges. Does he want to make a statement now?"

Kenzie was in no shape to speak to anyone. "Of course he didn't reply—he'd just been yanked from grieving for one of his oldest friends by a journalistic ambush. Let me check if he's willing to talk to you."

Covering the phone with one hand but not enough to completely block sounds, she dropped her voice as low as it would go and muttered a string of barely intelligible curses. Reverting to normal, she said, "If that's all you have to say, Kenzie, you'd better not say it." Speaking to Pamela again, she said lightly, "His comments on Nigel Stone's accusation aren't fit to be printed in a family newspaper."

The reporter chuckled. "That bad?"

Rainey lowered her voice confidentially. "Usually Kenzie lets these wild stories roll off like water from a duck's back, but this time he's completely exasperated. You know how reasonable he is. He understands that reporters need to make a living, and he'll always allow pictures and give comments when he's interviewed in public. The stories he's made up about his past have been a way to provide copy while maintaining his privacy. Don't you think he's entitled to that?"

"I do, though not all reporters agree with me." Pamela paused, probably taking notes. "Is it fair to say that he denies Nigel Stone's story?"

"A loose translation of his statement is that sensationalist rubbish shouldn't be dignified by an answer." Her voice lowered. "My personal, off-the-record opinion is that Nigel Stone was inspired to this lunacy by one of the plot threads of *The Centurion.*" Any entertainment reporter who tried to read Sherbourne's original novel to figure out what that meant would be bogged down for days. Victorians wrote long and heavy.

"Kenzie is probably wise to avoid a slanging match over this," Pamela agreed. "Can't imagine what dear Nigel is going to produce as proof."

"Did Stone give any hints about that?"

"He claims Kenzie was born in London and named James Mackenzie, and he has a birth certificate to prove it."

"I'm sure he could produce the Prince of Wales's birth certificate if he wanted to, but that wouldn't put Kenzie in line for the throne," Rainey said dryly. "There are a whole lot of boy babies born in Britain every year. A birth certificate proves nothing."

"My thoughts exactly." Pamela's tone changed. "Are you really Clementine's daughter?"

"Yes. As I told Nigel Stone, it's not a secret. I simply decided that I didn't want to trade on either her fame, or her tragedy." Nor did she want the pain that always followed discussing her mother.

"I grew up listening to Clementine's records," Pamela said nostalgically. " 'Heart Over Heels' got me through more than one broken romance when I was single. She really conveyed the pain of loving, but also hope for the future. I cried for days when she died. I think she was the greatest female rock singer ever."

"I agree, but I'm not exactly impartial."

Pamela's manner turned professional again. "While we're on difficult subjects, are you still saying there's no reconciliation in the wind between you and Kenzie? The two of you looked very much together this morning."

Rainey hesitated. She was already using the reporter, and she didn't want to lie any more than necessary to a woman who had been decent and helpful. "The honest truth is that I don't know what's happening, Pamela. If there should be any dramatic announcements in this area, I promise I'll call you first. But don't hold your breath."

"Fair enough. Good luck at making a getaway."

Rainey said good-bye, then called Chloe, the unit publicist. After going through her prepared spiel and securing Chloe's fervent cooperation, Rainey turned off the phone, unable to bear talking to anyone else, even Val. The rest of the drive to the airport was in silence. Kenzie stared blankly out the window, nearly catatonic.

With nothing to distract her, questions about Kenzie's past circled compulsively through her mind. Could his intense secrecy be because he really had been a gay hustler? Every fiber of her body protested that it couldn't be true. The passion between them couldn't possibly have been faked, not for almost four years. While it was theoretically possible he was bisexual, she'd never seen him show a hint of interest in another man. He'd always behaved like a straight male who was entirely comfortable with his own sexuality.

Yet even if Nigel Stone had lied, there had to be some connection to Kenzie's mysterious past. Kenzie's reaction was so violent.

Could poverty have driven him to turning tricks to survive? She supposed it was possible. She even wanted to believe it, but the idea just didn't ring true. Kenzie would have found some other way to survive poverty.

How would she feel if it turned out that Kenzie really was bisexual? Starkly she recognized that she didn't want it to be true. She had plenty of gay friends, had worked with gay and bi people and never thought twice about what they did on their own time. This was . . . different.

Reluctantly she acknowledged that if Kenzie was attracted to men as well as women, it would explain his conviction that he shouldn't have married her, and would never marry again. It also explained his reaction to playing Randall, a man ambivalent about his feelings for another man.

Perhaps Kenzie had been so caught up in the white heat of their early affair that he thought he'd be straight forever, only to realize later that he'd been wrong. Maybe drifting into a meaningless affair and letting Rainey be the one to leave was his way of letting her down as gently as possible.

It was all horribly logical.

She wrapped her arms around herself, shaking. She didn't think that anything could stop her caring for him, but dear God, she didn't want this to be true!

❧ 31 ❧

Awareness returned in sluggish fits and starts.
Vibration surrounded him. An airplane, he decided.

Hazily he reconstructed what happened after Nigel Stone
had tossed his bombshell. Thinking of Charles, assuming Stone
was no longer a threat, he'd been caught completely off-guard.
His brain had splintered, leaving him as paralyzed as he'd been
when starting school and a teacher demanded answers he
couldn't give. As an adult, he'd learned enough clever, self-
deprecating sound bites that he was almost always able to give
a ready reply. Not this time.

Luckily, Rainey's brain didn't crash the way his did. She'd
responded beautifully, then taken him away before his disintegration was public. His memories of what followed were frag-
mentary. His friends rallying to confuse the issue. Honest,
incorruptible Rainey lying like a trouper on the phone. Boarding the jet. Josh arriving with his luggage, panting and un-
shaven, but still efficient.

Those events seemed so distant they might have happened
to someone else. The encounter with Nigel Stone was different—the moment when the reporter smashed the fragile,
blown-glass illusion that had been Kenzie Scott was acid
etched in his brain.

He rubbed his aching head. Rainey had given him some
kind of pill, which had seemed like a good idea at the time. In
retrospect he regretted it; medications always left him dazed
and disoriented.

"Returning to the real world?" Rainey's quiet voice asked.

"Only because I can't think of an alternative." Wearily he
swung his feet to the floor and buried his face in his hands.
He'd removed his jacket and tie and kicked off his shoes before
crashing, but he still wore his formal white shirt and dark suit
trousers. James Bond after a bender.

Across the cabin, Rainey was curled up in a deep seat with

a book in her lap. She'd changed from her tailored suit to silk slacks and a tunic, but the bruised shadows below her eyes revealed how much she was suffering.

He stood and made his way to the well-stocked bar in the main cabin. The damned airplane looked like the same one they'd flown home in after *The Pimpernel*, at the start of the purest happiness of his life. The irony of being in the same plane now was too heavy to miss.

He poured a triple shot of scotch into a glass. Not a single malt, but he wasn't feeling picky.

Rainey followed him, trying to sound casual when she said, "Drinking might not be a good idea after taking a tranquilizer."

He knocked back a third of the whisky. "Frankly, my dear, I don't give a damn."

She sighed. "Then I'll have to hope the amount of time that's passed will save you from yourself."

He dropped into one of the wide leather seats. Where the hell did he go from here? For that matter, where the hell were they? Light showed outside the window, but since they were following the sun westward, that would be true for a long time to come. "Where are we?"

"About an hour east of New York." She took one of the facing seats. "I had the pilot change the flight plan from Los Angeles to New Mexico. I thought Cíbola would be a lot more peaceful than California."

Rainey was a genius. The thought of the secluded ranch was like a beacon in endless night. A place where he could hide from the world forever.

He swallowed more scotch. Alcohol, one of the oldest and most disreputable of crutches. He'd worry about the wisdom of it later. "Your restraint in not asking questions is impressive."

"I figure you'll tell what you want me to know when you're ready to talk about it. If you ever are." She hesitated, then said slowly, "One possibility that occurred to me is that you were a runaway teenager who turned some tricks to keep from starving. A lot of kids do that. The lucky ones escape."

He closed his eyes, drifting in limbo, so detached that the horrors of his childhood seemed to belong to someone else. That made it easier to speak, since Rainey deserved to know the truth. "Not a bad guess, but more charitable than I deserve. I was exactly what Nigel Stone claims: a gay whore."

After a long silence, she asked, "For how long?"

"Five years. From age seven to age twelve."

She gasped. "Dear God, that isn't prostitution—it's child molestation! How did it happen?"

"My mother was born somewhere in rural Scotland. Around age seventeen, she ran off to London. She might have been pregnant already, or maybe that came later. There's a lot I don't know about her."

"Do you know who your father was?"

"Haven't the foggiest."

She laughed without humor. "Something we have in common."

"Among other disasters we both suffered." He finished his first drink and went for another, this time filling the glass with ice first.

As he took his seat again, she said, "I've never seen you drink so much."

"If the plane were equipped for it, I'd run the alcohol directly into my veins." He pressed the icy highball glass against his forehead, remembering his mother. She'd been tall, dark-haired, and green-eyed. Beautiful, and terribly, terribly fragile. "My mother called herself Maggie Mackenzie, though I suspect that wasn't her real name. Since I look quite like her, only God knows what paternal genes might have been involved."

"So Nigel Stone's birth certificate for James Mackenzie is legitimate?"

"Probably."

"You said there was no evidence tying you to Stone's accusations."

"He can't prove I'm the person listed on the certificate. There isn't a shred of documentation on me from the time

Jamie Mackenzie was seven and dropped out of a London council school, and when Kenzie Scott started at RADA eleven years later. I didn't exist." He didn't really now. His whole life had been smoke and mirrors.

"How did you go from being the child of a single mother to . . . " Her voice faltered. ". . . to prostitution, then studying at the world's most famous drama school?"

"Whoring was the family business. My mother didn't have any other skills," he said bluntly. "She raised me the best she knew how, even after I started school and the teachers told her I was retarded. Of course, by then she was hooked on drugs so maybe she simply didn't care that I was hopeless. Drugs are expensive, and there was only one way she could afford them. She had a pimp boyfriend called Rock. He supplied her with drugs, took her money, and beat her up. When I was seven, I think one of the drugs he supplied must have been contaminated or more potent than usual." He drew a ragged breath. "It killed her."

"Did . . . did you find her body?" Rainey asked, her voice trembling.

"I watched her die, and couldn't do a damned thing about it." He drank more whisky, thinking this was easier than he'd thought it would be, because he felt nothing. Nothing at all. "Rock came several hours later to beat her for not working. He was quite casual about finding her body. It probably wasn't the first time he'd lost one of his girls to drugs. He took care of everything very efficiently. I don't know where she was buried—there was no funeral service. She was just . . . gone." But not forgotten.

"Did the pimp take you to the authorities so you could be put into foster care or whatever the English equivalent is?"

"Not Rock—he was too sharp a businessman to waste an asset. I was a nice-looking boy, and there's a market for those. He explained that he'd take care of me, but because my mother owed him money, I had to work to pay off her debt. And he knocked me across the room to demonstrate what would happen if I didn't cooperate."

Jamie had been terrified of the pimp, but the fear was less paralyzing than the knowledge that he was stupid and worthless, and deserved whatever punishment Rock chose to inflict. He'd been the perfect, obedient slave, never imagining his life could be any different.

The first step in creating a slave was to break the will.

"The family business." Silent tears ran down Rainey's face. "He forced you to be with pedophiles and perverts and God knows what."

"It was the best training in the world for an actor. I learned how to cower in terror from johns who liked that, and how to be seductive. I learned how to pretend affection, and how to abuse those who wanted to be hurt. RADA was child's play by comparison."

Rainey swallowed hard, imaginative enough to understand all that he wasn't saying. She'd never be able to think of him again the same way, which was perhaps best. "Did you live with Rock?" she asked.

"He preferred to keep his private and business lives separate, so he set me up in a flat with a rotating list of his whores. They made sure I was fed and had clothing and took baths. Some of them were even rather kind."

"How did you escape? Did you run away?"

Rainey didn't—couldn't—understand how completely hollow Jamie Mackenzie had been. No will, no soul, no hope. Hollow people didn't run away. "As I got older, I realized that I was definitely straight, and it became harder and harder to pretend I was a passionate little hustler. One day when I was twelve, I snapped when I was with a German who came to London regularly on business. He liked playing rough. Instead of going along with it as usual, this time I provoked him. He beat me bloody. Enjoyed it so much that he left twice the usual fee."

After the German left, young Jamie had lain weeping on the

bed in the sleazy hotel room, racked with agony, and bitterly disappointed that he was still alive.

Face ghostly pale, Rainey asked, "Then what?"

"I was passive to the end. Another regular client, Trevor Scott-Wallace, was scheduled to come an hour after the German. He was a decent old duffer who'd always treated me kindly. The German had left the door unlocked, so Trevor came in and found me battered and bloody. Being the responsible sort, he took me to a hospital instead of running away. I was delirious, and started babbling about my life." Jamie had pleaded for death, which had horrified Trevor most of all. "When he realized that I was basically a sex slave rather than a willing whore, he took me home and kept me, like a stray dog."

"You were adopted by a pedophile?" Rainey's voice shook with revulsion.

"It was . . . more complicated than that. Trevor was a professor of literature, a Shakespeare specialist with an international reputation. We never had a physical relationship—instead, he'd pay for my time and watch me while he quoted poetry and masturbated. My role was to look enthusiastic and ardent."

Rainey kept her composure despite the weirdness of what he was saying. "Was that better than having him touch you?"

"A little. It made it possible for us to live under the same roof. He told people I was a distant cousin with no other relatives, so he'd taken me in. He and Charles were former lovers who'd stayed friends. Trevor was comfortably off but not rich, so it was Charles who paid for the surgery. He had the kind of offhand generosity that didn't think twice about spending tens of thousands of pounds for procedures that weren't covered by the National Health."

Rainey pressed her hand to her mouth. "Surgery?"

"The German had been very thorough. The broken bones of my face needed to be rebuilt, which is how I became the unutterably handsome Kenzie Scott." Bitterly he touched the faint, perfectly sculpted cleft in his chin, brushed one of his high, dramatic cheekbones. "The basic shape and structure didn't change, but they were enhanced. This beautiful face the camera loves, the subject of countless gushing journalistic words, isn't mine. It's as much a lie as everything else in my life."

"No wonder you have no vanity," she whispered.

"How can I be vain about something that isn't mine?" The stranger's face had been his mask, and his shield against the world. People saw the chiseled, too-handsome-to-be-real features, not the hollow core.

"Did . . . did Trevor make you continue to act out for his sexual fantasies?"

"Luckily, he was wise and kind enough to realize how destructive that would be. Besides, even more than a lover, he wanted a son. Someone to love and be loved by." It was another role the young Jamie had learned well. And if simple filial love had been impossible, there had been genuine affection and profound gratitude. "He took care of me, and in return, I kept the secret of his pedophilia, since that would have disgusted most of his friends."

"Secrets and lies." She closed her eyes for a moment. "Did you lead a normal life after you recovered, or was it too late for that?"

"There has never been anything 'normal' about my life." He finished his second scotch. "Trevor was appalled to learn he'd taken in an illiterate, but he was an educator, and realized fairly soon that I was dyslexic. One of his academic friends was a pioneer in the study of learning disabilities, so between them they created a private tutoring program that helped me overcome my weaknesses and learn to use my strengths."

Trevor and Charles had been part of a circle of aging, highly cultured gay men. All had grown up in the days when homosexuals stayed deep in the closet, and they preferred to stay there even when society became more tolerant. The plastic surgeon, one of the best in Britain, had been part of the same circle. They'd delighted in giving their battered boy a perfect face. They'd probably thought they were doing him a favor.

Living quietly at the edge of Trevor's life, listening to the talk of clever, well-educated men, young Jamie had learned how to behave. "I ended up with a patchy but decent education, and the ability to fake being well-bred. Trevor died just before I turned eighteen. Charles Winfield had been encouraging me to study acting. He pulled some strings to get me an audition to RADA. I was admitted, and with a little fudging of the records, Kenzie Scott was born."

"How did you manage that?"

He shrugged. "One of Trevor's friends was high up in the government security establishment, and I presume he knew where to find the best forgers. I'm not sure exactly what he did, but I ended up with a passport in the name Kenzie Scott, and RADA got records that satisfied the bureaucrats."

"What an incredible story." Her brow furrowed. "That's why you think no one could connect you to your past—because you didn't grow up with the usual paper trail, and your appearance had altered enough so that no one who knew you as a child prostitute would recognize you now?"

"Exactly. Nigel Stone, known as Ned, knew me then. A pity my eyes are a distinctive color. If they'd been generic blue, he'd never have figured it out."

"So there is a connection with Stone! Was he another hustler?"

Kenzie thought back to the first time he'd seen that sneering face. "He was the son of Rock, my mother's pimp."

"Rock—Stone. I see." Looking ill, Rainey asked, "Did his father force his own son into prostitution, too?"

"No, even Rock wasn't that depraved. Or maybe he thought his son wasn't attractive enough to be worth selling. Ned lived with his mother, who was a couple of steps up the social scale, but sometimes Rock would use him to run errands—collecting money, delivering drugs, things like that. Ned was several years older than I, and mean to the bone. I think he felt some weird kind of sibling rivalry because he thought his father cared more for me than him, the real son. He might have been right—I was more valuable. Luckily, we saw each other very seldom, because he did his best to make my life miserable when he had the chance."

"And once he guessed that Kenzie Scott was the boy he'd hated, he tried to destroy you," she whispered.

"Not just tried." He closed his eyes, contemplating the shattered remnants of his life. "Succeeded."

❧ 32 ❧

"But he hasn't," Rainey said, *wanting to erase* some of the bleakness from Kenzie's face. "While you were sleeping, I talked to Barb Rifkin and Marcus Gordon, and they're already taking steps to quash Nigel Stone's story. No one seems to believe there's a word of truth in it."

"And yet there is. Ironic, isn't it?" He set aside his empty glass and rose to pace the small cabin, his balance unaffected by the amount of whisky he'd put away. "No matter how well they succeed, this kind of stain always lingers."

He stopped by a vase of flowers secured in the center of a small table, his fingers drifting over the petals. "Movie stars are creatures spun from dreams and fantasy. Reality means nothing compared to how people think of us—and they'll never think of me the same way."

She thought, aching, of the horrors he'd experienced. What incredible resilience he possessed, to have built a successful life after such a ruinous childhood. "Even if the stories linger, you have nothing to apologize for. You were a *child*. No one can blame you for what you were forced to do."

"So the world can see me as a victim? Charming. I think I'd rather be considered a sinner."

Kenzie played heroes. Sometimes his characters were larger than life, other times they were ordinary men who rose to the occasion and triumphed against terrible odds, but never were they helpless victims. That's why he'd had so much trouble playing John Randall. "I wish I'd known," Rainey said. "I'd never, ever have asked you to star in *The Centurion.*"

"My life as a pedophile's plaything isn't a subject one raises voluntarily. Even now, I couldn't speak of this if I weren't three-quarters drunk." He pulled a daisy from the vase and studied it intently. "But I thought you deserve to know, and I trust you not to tell anyone else."

"As you wish." She swallowed, trying to ease her dry throat. "But maybe you should consider talking to someone else, like a really good therapist. Secrets fester."

"Acting *is* therapy. To be any good at all, an actor must know himself well. Even the most neurotic of our breed have a deep understanding of what makes them tick." He was pacing again, the smooth, athletic movements masking his inner turmoil. "I know what happened to me, and the ways I've been permanently warped by my experiences. I doubt a therapist can tell me anything I haven't already thought of."

"Therapy isn't talking for the sake of talking. The whole point is to find a way to heal the pain."

"Did you ask a therapist to help sort out your problem childhood?"

"You've got me there," she admitted. "There were times when I considered therapy. I know people who have benefited greatly by it. But for me, it seemed best to work through my problems in my own way."

"You've done a good job of it. You're functioning, sane, especially by Tinseltown standards, and doing what you love, so I'd say your instincts were sound."

He overestimated her. "Since we're being honest, why did you marry me in the first place? And why did you suddenly decide it had been a mistake after three years?"

"When we met and clicked so well, I . . . I didn't want to let you go. Even though I knew marriage wouldn't work for me, I decided to hell with logic." He shrugged. "You've probably noticed that I spend a lot more time in my right brain than the left."

"What went wrong?" she asked, fighting the tears that threatened to spill over. "I thought we were getting along well. Did you get bored?"

"Remember that phone call where you raised the subject of children? Even though you tried to make a joke of it, I realized how much you wanted a baby. Until then, I'd thought you were as uninterested in having a family as I was, and probably for the same reasons. When I saw that I was wrong, I knew our marriage had to end."

Her jaw dropped. Looking back, it was blindingly obvious. "So you succumbed to Angie Greene's bountiful charms."

"You may not believe this, but I never had sex with her."

She thought of her surprise visit to Crete, and the way Angie had been climbing all over him. "You're right, I have trouble believing that."

"I was certainly considering it. She was more than willing, but I wasn't interested—it was you I was missing. You popped into my trailer just as I was trying to decide whether to go through with it. I knew an affair would end our marriage, but it was such a . . . a cruel, vulgar solution. When you showed up and jumped to the obvious conclusion, it was too good an opportunity to pass up. It also spared me from having to actually sleep with Angie. I was rather relieved."

She didn't know whether to laugh or weep. "Why didn't you just come out and say you don't want children? I suspected that from your reaction, and after some soul searching I decided I could live without them. But you never gave me a choice. Did you think females are such hopeless breeding machines that I'd want a baby more than you?"

He smiled without humor. "No, I thought you'd be loyal to our marriage—and live to regret it. By the time you left, it might be too late for you to have children."

She stared at him. "So you decided to destroy our marriage for my own good? You arrogant bastard!"

"That did sound arrogant," he agreed. "Tell me how wrong I was."

She hesitated, furious but unable to say he'd been entirely wrong. "You were right that I wouldn't have divorced you over the issue of children, but leaving you was not inevitable. Isn't it possible we could have stayed together and lived reasonably happily ever after?"

"In a marriage where neither of us once dared to say that we loved the other?" he said gently. "The end was just a matter of time."

She was as shocked as if he'd slapped her. No, love was never mentioned. There had been occasions when they were at their closest that she'd come near to saying she loved him, but she couldn't bring herself to do it when she was unsure what he felt for her. She knew he liked and desired her, but she wasn't at all sure she was loved. "You . . . noticed," she managed to say.

"I noticed. Though I'm hardly an expert on emotional intimacy, I understand that it's impossible without a willingness to be vulnerable. We let our barriers down with each other a little—you more than I. But we were both too wary to reveal much." He stopped pacing to regard her with compassionate eyes. "You're less damaged than I, Rainey, but you won't be able to overcome your fears and find the love you deserve unless you're with a man who's healthier and braver than I."

She knotted herself into a fetal position, shaken by how well he understood her. He saw himself, and her, with no illusions. It had taken Sarah Masterson, fictional Victorian maiden, to make her recognize that she'd never fully committed to her marriage. Raine Marlowe, thoroughly modern woman, had always had one hand on the doorknob.

Everything had changed in the tumultuous hours since they'd stepped out of Charles Winfield's memorial service. It was time to be brutally honest about what she wanted from Kenzie, and for herself.

The answer to the first was blindingly clear: She wanted him with her always as lover and husband. Today he'd revealed more of himself than in the four years they'd known each other. Surely the fact that he'd acted out of concern for her showed a kind of love, even if he couldn't bring himself to say the words?

As for her—she wanted to have the courage to make a commitment, no matter what the risks. She wanted to live life as passionately as Clementine, but with more wisdom. She wanted to be able to smash the defenses she'd hidden behind her whole life.

That meant handing Kenzie her heart, even if he threw it right back at her. "I can't deny that I have fears, Kenzie, but I . . . I do love you. Enough to marry you even when I was sure it couldn't last. Enough, finally, to say so out loud."

She uncoiled herself from her seat and crossed the cabin to him. "And I think that maybe you love me, too, because you did what you thought best for me even though you were wrong. If we love each other in our own battered, defensive way, isn't that a foundation for building a future?"

"It's too late, Rainey." His voice was raw with anguish. "Maybe we could have continued indefinitely the way we did for three years with a relationship that was limited, but rewarding within those limits. Not now. The illusion that was Kenzie Scott has been shattered, and the pieces can't be put back together again."

She placed one hand on his shoulder, her gaze searching. "Learning about your past hasn't changed how I feel, except that I love and respect you more than ever. The last weeks have been hard on both of us, but maybe now we have a chance to build the kind of marriage that will last for as long as we both shall live."

In his eyes she saw despair, but also a terrible longing. She stood on her tiptoes and kissed him.

For an instant he responded, his hand sliding down her arm. She leaned into him, amazed at the power of a simple kiss when it was made with love. How could she have been willing to let him go without a fight? She felt her shields crumbling, her bruised spirit slowly opening to allow him in.

He grabbed her arms and pushed her away. His breathing was harsh, and despair had won the battle for his soul. "This won't *work*, Rainey!"

He swung away and headed for the rest room in the rear of the plane. After the door closed, she heard sounds of violent retching.

Shaking, she sank into a seat. She wanted to believe that he was ill because of too much alcohol and not enough food. Instead, she thought of the wedding night scene between Sarah and her new husband. Kenzie had come up with that powerful bit of business where Randall had become ill, torn by the conflict between the abuse he'd suffered in captivity, and the reality of the young bride he idolized.

She felt ill herself now that she knew Kenzie's idea had come from his own experience. No wonder he believed their marriage couldn't go on. For over twenty years he'd managed to function by suppressing the horrors of his childhood. He'd become a master of detachment, sublimating his emotions into his acting, and doing it brilliantly.

But that was no longer possible. Nigel Stone had destroyed the defenses that had enabled Kenzie to function.

Now the horrors that had shaped him were free to ravage his soul.

After Kenzie spilled his guts, in every sense of the word, he and Rainey hardly spoke for the rest of the trip. They went through customs and refueled in New York, then flew on to New Mexico in almost absolute silence. Rainey had spent most of that flight sleeping, curled in a ball on the bed.

He'd been tempted to open the bar and drink himself sense-less, but his stomach churned at the thought. Instead, he summoned the attendant who'd been exiled to the front of the plane during the transatlantic flight, and asked for food. Though he'd been unable to eat much, at least his hands were no longer shaking.

Like a homing pigeon, he yearned for Cíbola. Odd, considering he'd never spent so much as a single night there. Yet those wild acres represented sanctuary.

It was near dusk when they landed at a private resort airstrip not far from the ranch. A wide-eyed young man told Kenzie that his rental vehicle was ready. Rainey must have arranged it by telephone.

Kenzie signed the paperwork and accepted the keys, then went outside and found that Rainey's luggage had been loaded into the SUV along with his. He pulled out the nearest of her suitcases. "Careless of them to transfer all the baggage."

"They didn't make a mistake." She scowled at him. "I'm going with you."

He stared, startled and not sure whether he was glad or sorry. She probably thought he'd self-destruct if left to his own devices. "Don't be ridiculous. In London, you said several times how much you wanted to go home. That jet can have you there in a couple of hours."

"Home is where the heart is."

Her meaning was unmistakable. He felt yearning so sharp he could taste it. If only it were that simple. But she didn't understand. How could she? "You've got months of high-intensity post-production work ahead of you, and that means Los Angeles."

"I need a vacation," she said. "Even God took a day off after creating the world, and my stamina is way less than His."

"Rainey . . ."

She glared like an angry cat, pulling her *Centurion* jacket tight as cool mountain wind gusted around them. "Unless you use physical force, I'm coming with you."

He closed his eyes, feeling his pulse hammering in his temples. Did she want him to spell out that the kiss she'd given him, and the arousal he'd felt, had triggered unbearable images of forced sex? For years he'd been able to bury those memories in his worst nightmares, but no longer. The evil genie had escaped its bottle, and it was an open question whether Kenzie would ever be able to bear having sex again, with anyone. "Proximity isn't going to fix me or our marriage, Rainey."

She sighed, her belligerence fading. "You're not the only one who understands human nature, my dear. I've been thinking about what you've said. I can't really know what it's like to be you, but I've accepted that it would take a miracle to salvage our marriage, and I don't believe in miracles. But give me an honest answer here. You've been all honorable and noble, pushing me away for my own good. Forget being noble. Would you rather have me around for a few days, or not?"

When he hesitated, she said tartly, "The truth, Kenzie."

The truth? She'd have to return to California soon to begin the immense task of editing and scoring the raw footage into a finished movie. But for the next few days . . . "It would be nice to have you at Cíbola, Rainey. Just . . . don't expect much of me."

"I don't. Most of the reason for going is to have a few days of relaxation a long way from La La Land." She eyed the car keys in his hand. "Are you up for driving, or should I?"

"The alcohol has burned off." He opened the passenger door. "Last chance to change your mind and be reasonable."

She smiled as she climbed in. "How often does either of those things happen?"

"Almost never." He got into the driver's seat, feeling a little better for the fact that in spite of everything, they were still friends.

❧ 33 ❧

The mountains of northern New Mexico might have been on another planet from the London sidewalk where Nigel Stone had ambushed Kenzie. Rainey relaxed into the bucket seat, content to admire the molten colors gilding the austere landscape as the sun slid behind the hills. Still trying to process all he'd told her, she asked, "Did your mother's pimp try to get you back?"

"No, even if Rock had known I was with Trevor, he couldn't have traced me. It's a furtive, cash-only kind of business. Neither buyers nor sellers use real names and addresses. From Rock's point of view, I just vanished. He might well have decided I wasn't worth bothering with—I was almost too old to appeal to the pedophile trade."

Rainey shuddered. Even Kenzie's supreme detachment couldn't reduce her horror at the life he'd been forced into. "Do you have any idea what happened to Rock? A really long jail sentence would have been nice."

"A couple of years after I escaped the life, Rock was knifed to death in a bar. I wouldn't have known, except by then I was doing well with my reading lessons, and my tutor had me reading a daily newspaper. Rock was just a small story on a slow news day."

"How did you feel when you saw he was dead?"

His mouth tightened. "I was so happy that I totally lost the ability to speak for about ten minutes. My only regret was that he probably died quickly."

So he wasn't completely detached. "I don't suppose Nigel is likely to be knifed."

"I don't hate him the way I did his father," Kenzie said slowly. "The poor devil had a miserable childhood. His father was a monster, and his mother a drunk who knocked him around. He used to hide in movie theaters just like I did. It couldn't have been easy for him to claw out an education and become a successful reporter."

"You're amazingly forgiving."

"Not forgiving, exactly, but I'm aware that in many ways, I was luckier than Ned. Despite all her problems, my mother was a loving person, when she wasn't strung out. Once Trevor took me in, I was raised by wise, cultured old men who took pride in teaching and guiding me. It was like having a dozen kindly godfathers. I doubt there has ever been much kindness in Ned's life."

"Given how vicious he can be, who'd want to get close enough to be kind?" She wondered if Kenzie was as free from anger as he seemed, or whether a molten river of rage flowed through the depths of his soul. Maybe he owed his survival to an ability to let go of what couldn't be changed.

Since the atmosphere was relaxed, she asked, "Why do you hate the idea of children so much? You're great with kids, both fans and the child actors you've worked with. I'm not trying to change your mind, just trying to understand. You thought I wouldn't want kids for the same reason you didn't."

He slowed and turned left into a narrower road. "From what I've seen of people who've survived wretched childhoods, some react by wanting to have children of their own. Raising their kids as they wish they'd been raised is a way of fixing the past. Others can't bear the thought of revisiting childhood under any circumstances. I fall into that category. I thought you did, too."

"I did when I was younger, but in the last few years, I've realized that I want to fix the past, just as you said." She gazed out the side window. "Like your mother, Clementine could be wonderful and warm, but she spent most of her time on the road, performing. Even when she was home, she always seemed to be busy with work and her . . . overactive social life." There'd been a succession of nurses and housekeepers to take care of little Rainbow, but none had been her mother.

"I'd lie awake at night, hoping to see her. If I heard her

come in, I'd patter out to say hello." Though first she'd make sure Clementine wasn't high or with a lover. "She'd laugh and put me to bed, and sing a song if I was lucky." Rainey sighed. "I've sworn that if I ever have children, I'll take them along when I do location work. I want them to feel loved and protected. I want them to know that they matter." She stopped, realizing how much she revealed. Well, if she wanted to be more open with Kenzie, this was a good place to start.

"It takes a lot of giving to raise a child well. I don't have enough in me to do that," he said bleakly. "The thought of having children is . . . painful beyond description."

Any hope she'd cherished that he might change his mind died. Wanting to drop the subject, she asked, "Did you used to wonder what it would be like to have a real father? I did all the time." Her cold, critical grandfather hadn't been much of a role model for fathering. "It was only after talking with you a couple of months ago that I found the courage to hire that detective I told you about."

"Has he found out anything new?"

She told him about Mooney's latest report. When she was done, Kenzie remarked, "A studio executive is on the list? That might explain your desire to run your own show."

"A hereditary desire to give orders? Maybe, though I suspect that most actors fantasize being the one in control. Don't you?"

"Not really." His voice roughened. "I hate being controlled, but I don't want to control others, either. Too much responsibility. I just want to be . . . *free*. Not in anyone's power." More moderately, he continued, "One thing that appealed to me about acting was being my own boss. If I didn't want to take a role, I could always support myself driving a taxi or working as a bicycle messenger."

The thought made her smile. "Instead, you were so successful that you now have the freedom never to work at all unless you want to."

"Which is fortunate, because I may never act again."

His voice was so low that it took a moment for his words to register. "Not act? Surely you're not serious! You're an actor's actor—so good, and so committed. How could you stop?"

In the dark, all she could see was his profile faintly illuminated by the dashboard lights. "Acting was my way of escaping myself. Now . . . my self has caught up with me. I don't know if I can act anymore. Or if I want to."

Chilled, she recognized bleak conviction in his voice. The work that had been his joy and his passion might have been stolen from him as surely as his mother's pimp had stolen Kenzie's trust and innocence.

With so much taken away, would there be anything left of Kenzie Scott?

Kenzie halted his SUV on the rise that looked across the valley to the ranch house, anticipating the serenity of the place. "I wonder why the lights are on. The Gradys moved into their new house several weeks ago, so the ranch house should be empty."

Rainey covered a yawn. "When I called Emmy Herman to arrange for the car rental, I also asked her to let the Gradys know you were coming. My guess is that Alma stopped by to unlock the door and turn on the lights to make it look friendly."

He headed down into the rutted road. "Having good assistants is like having invisible elves smoothing out one's life."

He hoped Rainey was right that the lights were just a friendly gesture. Though he liked the Gradys, he was in no mood to deal with anyone else. Hard to believe that it was only this morning that Nigel Stone had revealed his sordid past. It had been an endless day covering eight time zones. A third of the way around the world.

Tired to the bone, he pulled up in front of the house and turned off the ignition. A low-powered outside light illuminated the area as they climbed from the SUV. He lifted the two largest suitcases from the back of the vehicle and crossed to the house.

Pulling a wheeled case, Rainey opened the door into the

kitchen for him, then gasped. "Have we come to the right place?"

He stepped inside and set the suitcases down on the mellow, well-worn tile floor. "I called Callie Spears, the interior designer I used on the beach house, and asked her to fix the place up. The kitchen was pretty dismal."

"You were right about elves taking care of life's hassles." Rainey ran her hands over the oak cabinets, then stroked the vanilla-colored countertops. "This particular elf really knew her business—the kitchen is simple but gorgeous. Just right for this house. Smart of Callie to keep the tile floor and stucco walls and exposed beams—the good stuff." Her eyes narrowed as she studied the room. "But the old hutch, table, and chairs look like the Gradys' furniture. Those wonderful Indian rugs are awfully familiar, too."

"Alma said they might seem charmingly authentic to outsiders, but to her they were worn rugs and beat-up old furniture, and she was looking forward to going out and buying exactly what she wanted for once in her life. She only took a few items that had sentimental value to her."

Two furballs tore into the kitchen, skidding on a rug as they rounded the corner. They were the gray and tabby kittens from the litter Rainey had visited weeks before. These two had doubled in size, and were utterly fearless.

He scooped up the gray kitten, a male who wriggled ecstatically at the attention. Noticing a note on the table, he said, "If we're hungry, there are enchiladas and frijoles and salad in the refrigerator."

"Alma is a genius. A saint. Bringing the kittens to greet us was a master stroke." Rainey caught the dancing tabby kitten, rubbing her cheek against the soft fur. "I'll put the food in the oven. By the time we're settled, dinner should be nice and hot."

"Which bedroom do you want? The two at the end of the hall are the largest." It was the most tactful way he could say that he couldn't bear to sleep with her.

Rainey got the message. She walked down the hall and

checked out the bedrooms. "I'll take the one on the right—the velvet and brocade patchwork quilt is spectacular. I've always liked the Southwest interior design style, but there's no substitute for the real thing."

He took his bags into the other bedroom, glad Rainey had left it for him. He liked the antique quilt pieced together of whites and faded blues that Callie had found. The designer had also bought a dresser and wardrobe made from a silvery weathered wood that suited the house perfectly.

Curious, he moved through the other rooms. The two smaller bedrooms were clean but empty. The sofa and reclining chairs in the living room were new, upholstered in soft tan leather that invited touching, while a tiny powder room had been tucked into a hall closet. He made a mental note to give Callie a bonus for achieving so much in such a short period of time, most of it with local labor. He'd specified that, knowing that the area needed the work.

The last major project had been to renovate the bathroom. Rainey caught up with him there. "Oh, *bliss,*" she said reverently. "A thoroughly modern bathroom, with whirlpool **and** separate shower. This place is a gem, Kenzie."

She was right; it was a house he could live in forever. And probably would.

After a very long day and a good meal, he thought he'd sleep well, but no such luck. He couldn't even blame the bed, since Callie had installed the same type of mattress he used in the beach house.

Whenever he closed his eyes, nightmare images assaulted him. Incidents that he thought forgotten returned in a flood of horrific detail. Suffocating, gagging, at the mercy of sweaty male bodies. His desperate need to please. Terror at being dominated, body and soul—and the utter hopelessness of believing he deserved nothing better.

He'd survived by separating his mind from the body of the powerless child compelled to perform on command. During the ordeals, he'd mentally fly away to better times. Afternoons in the park with his mother, visits with her to the cinema. They'd both loved movies, and would watch double and triple features at cheap rerun theaters.

That detachment had kept him sane, but behind the wall of separation churned a holocaust of emotions. The wall had been built so high and wide that in time he'd managed to almost forget the details of his early years. Then John Randall cracked the wall, and Nigel Stone had smashed it to splinters, releasing the horrors as irrevocably as Pandora when she'd opened her box.

How could he survive the agony saturating his mind? He thought of asking Rainey for another tranquilizer, then rejected the idea. The earlier one had knocked him out but hadn't relieved the pain. No more drugs. Having an addict mother had taught him the danger of seeking peace in a pill.

He tossed and turned, his anguish increasing as his mind spun from horror to horror. Sweating despite the cool night air, he gave up trying to sleep and rose. After yanking on clothes, he found a flashlight in the kitchen and went outside in search of fresh air and oblivion.

The emptiness of the night was as vast as the emptiness within.

> *Alone, alone, all, all alone;*
> *Alone on a wide wide sea;*
> *And never a saint took pity on*
> *My soul in agony.*

But the Ancient Mariner had killed an albatross, and his ordeal had been punishment for unnecessary cruelty. What had little James Mackenzie done to bring such suffering on his innocent head?

When his eyes adjusted to the darkness, he saw there was enough moonlight to make the flashlight unnecessary as long as he stayed out of the shadows. By luck, he found the path that started behind the farm buildings and led up into the hills.

He began to climb. The cool mountain night was sharp with the scent of pines and aspens and things he couldn't identify. Just above the ranch buildings was a shallow, saucer-shaped meadow surrounded by pines and carpeted with pale wild-flowers that fluttered in the moonlight. Too agitated to admire the subtle loveliness of the sight, he continued upward.

Fragments of plays and poetry buzzed through his mind. Some were relevant to his situation, others less obvious. Living with Professor Trevor Scott-Wallace for more than six years had been an advanced course in British literature.

> *Full fathom five thy father lies;*
> *Of his bones are coral made:*
> *Those are pearls that were his eyes;*
> *Nothing of him that doth fade,*
> *But doth suffer a sea-change*
> *Into something rich and strange.*

But he hadn't a clue who his father was—what nation owned him, whether he was living or dead, whether he had any idea that he'd made a son with a beautiful girl too young to understand what she'd been doing.

As a boy, he'd liked to imagine his father as a Highland lad who lay with Maggie among the heather, then joined a regiment and went off to see the world, as Scottish youths had done for centuries. Even today, the regiments sent recruiting units marching into Scottish towns with pipes and banners flying to capture the imagination of bored young men who yearned for adventure. Maybe Maggie's lover had gone off promising to return for her, then died overseas in one of the nasty little skirmishes that regularly flared up around the world.

Of course, Kenzie's father might have been a drunken clerk who'd paid Maggie five quid to spread her legs. Or an incestuous relative who'd molested her and sent her fleeing in terror from the only home she'd known. There was no way to know. He prayed that she'd found some pleasure in his begetting. She'd had little enough joy in her life.

> Break, break, break,
> On thy cold gray stones, O Sea!
> And I would that my tongue could utter
> The thoughts that arise in me.

Tennyson had known grief, too.

At the top of the hill he halted, panting from the steep climb. What the devil should he do about Rainey? He'd bought this retreat partly to have a home with no memories of her, yet now she slept under his roof.

He was desperately alone, and she was the only person he could bear to have near. But she wanted to give their marriage another chance, and that was more impossible than ever. He was so knotted up sexually that he wasn't sure they could ever again share the glorious, healing passion that had been the bedrock of their relationship.

Seven long, celibate years had passed between his sexual servitude as a child and his first relationship as a mature male. Those years had let him see himself as a different person. In fact, he'd felt like a nervous virgin with his first lover, an actress fifteen years his senior who had taught a workshop at RADA. Her unselfconscious sensuality had helped him make the transition to an adult sexual identity.

But now he could no longer separate Jamie from Kenzie. The merest hint of a sexual thought about Rainey caused his stomach to clench as images of degradation rose and obscured her.

Agonized, he looked down over his valley. He was high enough to see the glint of moonlight on the small alpine lake, and the A-frame contours of the Gradys' new home beside it. The house was dark, since sensible people were asleep at this hour.

Physically drained but no more at peace than when he came outside, he started back down the path. Tomorrow he'd have to tell Seth Cowan that he would not do the thriller he was slated to start shooting in Australia in two months. He hadn't signed the contract yet so they couldn't sue, but Seth would still go through the roof. Better to leave a message early, on Seth's voice mail, so he wouldn't have to discuss his decision.

What the devil would he do with the rest of his life? To be an actor was to bare parts of oneself, and he felt too raw, too exposed, to ever act again. Most people dreamed of what they'd do if they ever had the time, but his only desire at the moment was to become a hermit and never interact with the world again. But how did hermits fill the empty hours?

Between one step and the next, he found the perfect angle that turned the almost circular lake into a moon-silvered mirror. His mind flashed to the labyrinth at Morchard House. It was strange how walking that winding path had relaxed him. He supposed it was because physical motion used up restless energy, allowing the mind to be still.

He tried not to think of the passion he and Rainey had shared beside the labyrinth. That was another issue, one he couldn't deal with. But the labyrinth itself called to him.

Why not build one here? The work would keep him busy for a few weeks, and when it was done, walking the mystical path might calm his wounded soul.

A jangling sound heralded the appearance of a dog. It was Hambone, the Gradys' friendly mutt, tongue lolling. Kenzie rubbed the dog's head and ears, grateful for a companion whose needs were so easily satisfied. As he resumed his descent of the hill, Hambone trotted amiably by his side.

He'd get a dog of his own. A hermit needed a dog.

❧ 34 ❧

Yawning, Val made her way down the narrow staircase of the bed-and-breakfast where she and Laurie, her travel partner, had spent the night. She'd seen enough of Ireland to realize that yes, indeed, the Emerald Isle was green, and the musical accents made her want to whimper with pleasure. Laurie was sleeping late, but Val was up early and raring to start acting like a tourist.

"And how are you this fine mornin', Miss Covington?" Mrs. O'Brien, the landlady, asked cheerfully as Val entered the breakfast parlor. "Will you be having a wee pot of tea with your breakfast?"

"That would be heavenly." Mrs. O'Brien returned to her kitchen to fix Val's breakfast and brew the tea. Alone in the breakfast parlor, Val picked up the newspapers set on the sideboard and settled down to read.

Most of the headlines were routine, until she found the London tabloid underneath the sober Dublin paper. A huge picture of Kenzie and Rainey dominated the front page of the *Inquirer* with the headline, "Kenzie Scott: A Gay Blade?"

Dismayed, she skimmed the first paragraphs of the story, then returned to the photo to study it more carefully. Kenzie looked frozen with shock, as well he might. Rainey radiated surprise and fury.

So Nigel Stone had hit the grand crescendo he'd been building toward for weeks. Val's lawyer instinct made her want to dive into the fray. She'd become rather fond of Kenzie, and it went without saying that this kind of scandal would hurt Rainey deeply.

From habit, she paused to consider whether Stone might be telling the truth when he claimed that Kenzie was gay. Nope, she still didn't believe it. She was good at picking up male vibes.

What about bisexuality? Possible, but that didn't feel right, either. She hadn't sensed any interest on Kenzie's part when he was around men, even though the movie crew had included a couple of good-looking gay guys. She'd stake her right to practice law that Kenzie was exactly what he seemed—an unconflicted heterosexual male.

The next page detailed Stone's evidence. He had a birth certificate for one James Mackenzie, allegedly Kenzie's real name. That meant nothing in itself, unless he could prove in some other way that Kenzie Scott and James Mackenzie were the same person.

Nigel also claimed to have spoken to men who swore they'd paid to have sex with Jamie Mackenzie. Again, that meant nothing unless they were willing to go on the record under their own names. Which they probably wouldn't, since few men would want to admit publicly that they'd solicited sex with a minor.

She swore when she read the next paragraph. Stone claimed to have a child pornography video that Kenzie had made. A carefully cropped image showed a desolate-looking child. She scrutinized the blurry photo. There was a general resemblance to Kenzie, but the features weren't quite right. It was like the best of the photos sent in by readers responding to the *Inquirer*'s call for information—close but no cigar. If this was Nigel's best evidence, he was on thin ice.

Mrs. O'Brien returned with a tray that held a pot of steaming tea and a plate piled with bacon, sausages, eggs, and a grilled tomato. Val's appetite had diminished sharply, but she managed to eat about half the food. She was going to need her strength.

When she finished her meal, she retreated to her room and dug out her cell phone. It wasn't yet midnight in California, so who should she call first? Emmy Herman would be the most tactful choice, and she'd probably know exactly what was going on, but pregnant women needed their rest. She'd have to call Rainey directly.

Though Rainey should be home by now, the call to her private home phone was picked up by an answering machine referring people to her office number. Val left a message, then tried the Gordons. She'd become friendly with Naomi and Marcus during filming since she'd been the major liaison to the producers.

Naomi Gordon picked up the phone. "Hello."

"Naomi, this is Val Covington. I'm in Ireland, and I just saw the *Inquirer.* What's going on, and what can I do to help?"

"Val, I'm so glad to hear from you. Hang on a second and I'll get Marcus on another extension."

A minute later Marcus said tersely, "Glad you checked in, Val. Maybe you'll be able to think of something we've missed."

"All I've seen is Stone's article, which naturally tells it his way. Can you fill me in on what really happened?"

"Nigel Stone jumped Kenzie with this about six steps outside the church where Charles Winfield's memorial service was held," Naomi said acidly. "The British tabloid reporters really are worse than the Americans."

"That *bastard.* Then what?"

Marcus picked up the story. "Rainey and Kenzie got away ASAP without making any comments. She was still shaking when she called us and the publicists to let us know what happened. We're doing our best to kill the story before it turns into a major media feeding frenzy."

"I wish I understood the British establishment better," Val said with frustration. "I'm good at digging out facts, and in the States I'm sure I could find some useful defensive ammunition, but I wouldn't know where to start in London."

"We can hire good researchers," Naomi said. "What should they look for?"

Val considered. "For starters, I'd check out dear Nigel's career in Australia. He worked there for years. See if he was ever accused of fabricating stories or evidence, or if he was ever sued for libel. Even if he won a suit, several incidents like that would really undermine his credibility."

"Good idea. I hadn't thought of investigating his Australian past, but I've got contacts in Sydney," Marcus said. "I'll get right on it."

"Have you seen any stills taken from the porn movie that allegedly shows Kenzie as a boy?" Naomi asked. "We haven't seen anything from that yet."

"The paper I just looked at had a still, and I don't think the boy is Kenzie. Right coloring and eyes, wrong chin, wrong cheekbones. It must be some other poor kid."

"So Stone hasn't got much. The problem is that this kind of thing can be hard to disprove unless we can clearly place Kenzie elsewhere at the same time he was supposed to be selling himself in London," Marcus said soberly. "Maybe Kenzie will finally talk about his early life to prove he couldn't be this kid hustler."

"Then again, he might say that he'll be damned if he'll be coerced into giving up the privacy he's protected so long," Naomi said dryly. "Underneath those lovely English manners, he can be pretty stubborn. Why should he have to talk about his private life, now or ever?"

Val frowned as she thought about early lives. "Get someone to look through a bunch of London school yearbooks from the right time and pick out half a dozen boys who looked like Kenzie. Then track them down and persuade them to appear at a press conference. Kick off the conference by showing a picture of the first man and announce, 'This is James Mackenzie.'

"Then bring out the man whose photo it is. Ideally, he'll now be short, fat, and balding. Then you say, 'Actually, this is Reggie Smothers of Croyden, but didn't he look a lot like James Mackenzie?' After the reporters get through laughing, repeat that several times. By the time you're done, you'll have demonstrated there's no connection between the birth certificate, a fuzzy picture of a pre-adolescent, and Kenzie Scott."

Naomi chuckled. "Val, Val, are you sure you don't want to work for us? That's brilliant. If you don't want to do law or production, we'll put you in publicity."

"No, thanks. I actually rather like the law. I just need to find the right place to practice it." Val frowned. "I'd also make sure the reporters realized that whoever the boy was, he was so young then that he qualifies as a victim, not a callous hustler."

"I shudder when I think of how many exploited children there are living on the streets," Naomi said softly. "Don't get me started, or I'll be ranting."

The older woman's comment triggered a hunch. "There probably was a real James Mackenzie who was a boy hustler," Val said. "Maybe Nigel Stone genuinely believes that boy grew up to be Kenzie. But street life is hazardous, especially for someone who got into it so young. It's a long shot, but I'd look for a death certificate for the real James Mackenzie."

Marcus whistled softly. "If we could find that, it would certainly close Stone down. Great ideas, Val. Now you get back to your vacation and put this out of your mind. I think we're going to spike Stone's guns without any damage to Kenzie or to Rainey's movie."

Val sighed. "You really think I can put this out of my mind?"

"Call for daily updates," Naomi replied. "Trust us, Val. In a week or two, this will be ancient, discredited history."

Val hung up, praying that the Gordons were right. The movie might survive unscathed, but would Rainey's husband?

Chunk! Chunk! Chunk! Gradually the banging sounds penetrated Rainey's fogged mind enough to draw her from sleep to hazy wakefulness. She lay with her eyes closed as she pieced together where she was and how she'd gotten here. A pity she couldn't convince herself it was all a bad dream, but she was definitely in New Mexico. With two kittens purring on the patchwork quilt beside her, so it wasn't all bad.

The sounds and timing of the *chunking* noise varied somewhat, but overall were pretty regular. The world's largest woodpecker?

Aching in every muscle, she hauled herself out of the deep,

comfortable mattress and headed to the bathroom, kittens ricocheting off her ankles. Good grief, was it really two in the afternoon? "Jet lag" was too gentle a term. "Jet victim" came closer.

A quick shower revived her some, though she was still bone-weary from accumulated fatigue. After dressing in khaki shorts and a jade green tank top, she made her way to the kitchen, accompanied by kittens who earnestly assured her that they hadn't eaten in days, possibly weeks, and were now hovering on the brink of starvation.

A search of the cupboards produced a bag of cat food, and the knowledge that Alma Grady had stocked the kitchen well. There were plenty of staples and a good selection of perishables in the fridge. Leaving the kittens diving into their food, Rainey poured herself a glass of orange juice and wandered outside to find the woodpecker.

The ranch had a number of outbuildings, including a barn and a bunkhouse. All were thick-walled adobe, like the main house. In a paddock behind the barn were two horses. She wondered if the Gradys would mind if she or Kenzie rode them occasionally. It would be heaven to get up into those hills on horseback.

On the far side of the bunkhouse, she discovered the source of the noise. Kenzie was chopping wood. Quite a lot of wood. The sun was hot, and he'd peeled off his shirt, showing the powerful, crisply defined muscles of his back and arms as he swung the ax. The sight of him weakened her knees with yearning that was as much emotional as physical.

It seemed like forever since their last night together. She wanted to walk into his arms and kiss the salty sheen of his skin, hoping that the sweet intimacy of sex could heal the searing wounds of his past, and salve her own bruised and exhausted spirit.

Yet desire was overlaid by a horrific image of a helpless child being molested by a sweaty, panting pervert. Knowing where he'd learned to be such a wonderful lover made her almost vomit the orange juice she'd drunk.

Keeping her voice light, she said, "Stockpiling firewood for winter?"

Chunk! The ax swung wickedly through the air, and a half round of wood split into two kindling-sized pieces. He tossed them on the pile stacked against the bunkhouse. "This is about the only kind of ranch work a city boy can do without training."

There were blisters on his hands. He may have figured out the way to swing an ax, but his palms weren't hardened for this kind of work. Of course, firewood wasn't the point. Channeling his rage into productive violence was.

"You chose well when you bought this place, Kenzie." She looked across the valley. "It's beautiful. Serene. A place to be sane."

"Maybe. Let's hope none of the gossip reporters will leave the city and hunt us down here." He set another length of log into chopping position. "They'd have a bad effect on the sanity."

She peered in the window of the bunkhouse, and saw a sizable room with four single beds and wide-planked floors. A door led into another room beyond. "This will make a nice guesthouse."

Chunk! "I don't plan on having any guests."

Did he regret allowing her to stay here? He was avoiding eye contact, and the vulnerability he'd revealed on the flight to New Mexico had vanished behind an impenetrable shell. The trouble with loving an actor is that you never had the least idea what he was thinking if he chose to shut you out.

"Have you had any breakfast? Or I guess lunch would be more appropriate." Assuming his shrug meant no, she continued, "How about I scare us up an omelet? I can't remember my last meal."

He hesitated. "I suppose I should eat."

"An omelet won't take long. If you want to shower, the food will be done by the time you're finished."

He retrieved his shirt from the stacked logs where he'd left it and rubbed it over his sweaty face. "That sounds good."

Side by side but not really together, they returned to the house. She told herself it would take time for him to recover enough to relax with her again. She'd have a week before she had to be back in Los Angeles to start postproduction.

But in her gut, she knew a week would not be enough.

❧ 35 ❧

Rainey savored the scent of frying onions as she tossed chopped pepper in the pan. How long had it been since she'd done any real cooking? No child could be raised by Virginia Marlowe without learning her way around a kitchen. Rainey had enjoyed cooking, despite her grandmother's critical comments when the sugar and butter weren't being creamed together properly, or some other sin. They'd even shared some fairly companionable moments when working together for a holiday dinner.

But movie stars didn't have a lot of time for cooking. Kenzie had a housekeeper who cooked like a dream, while Rainey used a personal chef who would drop wonderful, healthy meals by the house with precise instructions for reheating. She hadn't made anything more complicated than cappuccino in years.

The hashed brown potatoes she'd found in the freezer were crispy and golden, so she combined them with the onion and pepper mixture to make the omelet filling. She was whipping eggs with a fork when the phone rang. Since she could hear that Kenzie was in the shower, she lifted it warily. "Hello."

"Raine? It's Marcus."

She relaxed. "Good. I worry that some reporter will find this number."

"So far, only Naomi and I, Val, and Emmy know where you are, and none of us will talk."

"You'd better tell Kenzie's people," she suggested. "They'll have a heart attack if they don't know where he is."

"I'll call Seth Cowan, and he can handle Kenzie's end."

"How is the world responding to Nigel Stone's grand revelation?"

"About as you'd expect. The more respectable news outlets are ignoring the story since at this point it's basically hearsay, while the sensationalist press has pounced with glee. A couple of tabloids have dug up so-called experts who've never been closer to Kenzie than the local multiplex, but who are quite willing to speculate that his macho movie roles might be a way to cover up the fact that he's secretly gay."

Rainey sighed. "Why am I not surprised?"

The producer laughed. "One idiot even claimed that you're secretly gay, too, and you married each other to provide mutual camouflage."

Her mouth tightened. "Such rubbish. What are the white hats doing to make this go away?"

"Barb Rifkin has been cracking heads among her media contacts, which is probably why the story hasn't been picked up widely. Also, Val called from Ireland with some good ideas for counterattacking." Marcus summarized Val's suggestions. Rainey nodded through most of it, but frowned at the end.

Kenzie entered the kitchen, hair wet and expression unreadable. "It's Marcus," she said. "Do you want to talk to him?"

When he shook his head, she said good-bye and hung up. "Sorry the omelet isn't quite done. Would you like some orange juice?"

This time a nod. She poured a tall glass of juice. Noticing that he hadn't shaved, she asked, "Growing a beard for anonymity?"

"Maybe."

He was definitely not in a communicative mood. "I thought it would be nice to eat in Alma's walled garden. Would you set the table, please?"

Another nod. Juice in hand, he opened the door to the garden, kittens skittering out with him. She poured the beaten eggs into a skillet, then started the coffee and toasted Alma's sourdough bread.

By the time Kenzie had scouted the garden and located placemats and silverware, breakfast was ready to go. Rainey divided the omelet with two-thirds for Kenzie and the rest for her, slid the pieces onto plates warmed in the oven, then added the toast and a jar of honey. As she lifted the tray, she asked, "Could you pour the coffee and bring it out?"

He filled the mugs and followed her out to the garden, which was at the height of late summer glory. Flowering vines covered one wall and the air was heady with high desert scents. She noticed a small, weathered statue of St. Francis lurking beside a sage bush. The circular table and chairs were pleasantly cool under the arbor, and decorated with a hopeful-looking gray kitten.

Kenzie set down the coffee mugs and removed the kitten from the table. "Sorry, gray guy, that's not allowed."

"Is Gray Guy his name?" Rainey placed the plates on the table and set the tray aside, then took one of the chairs.

"It might as well be. Do you want to name the tabby, since she's just leaped on your lap?"

Rainey petted the little cat, who purred ecstatically at the attention. "She says her name is Honeybunny, since her fur is bunny soft, honey-colored, and she certainly is sweet." Gently she returned the kitten to the weathered quarry tile floor. "I hope the food is okay. I'm feeling vastly proud of myself for remembering how to turn on a stove."

Kenzie sampled the omelet. "This is good. I'm not sure I knew you could cook."

Glad he was eating and speaking sentences, Rainey started

on her eggs. They had turned out pretty well, and the food steadied her. How long had it been since she'd eaten? She bogged down on the time zones, but knew it had been too long.

Under the influence of dappled sun, fragrant flowers, and wrestling kittens, the knots in her shoulders slowly eased. Peace radiated from the earth itself. Los Angeles and London both seemed like different planets.

It felt so right to be sitting here quietly with Kenzie. Despite their hectic lives, there had been many pleasant times spent sharing meals and each other's company in some remote, beautiful spot. For a few minutes, she allowed herself the luxury of pretending that all was well. After they finished eating, she poured second cups of coffee. "I'm beginning to remember what it's like to have a life."

"Enjoy it while you can. I should think you'll be as busy in postproduction as you were doing the shooting."

She contemplated the return to Southern California without enthusiasm. "You're probably right."

Kenzie rested his elbows on his knees, turning his mug restlessly in his palms. "What did Marcus have to say?"

"Things are looking pretty good." Rainey briefly summarized the producer's remarks. She hesitated before adding reluctantly, "Apparently Nigel Stone has also produced a child pornography video he says you were in."

Kenzie shut his eyes, face twisting. "I'd almost forgotten about that. Rock gave me some kind of drug, a form of Ecstasy, maybe, then took me to this grimy little studio. I don't remember much about it, and never saw the finished product. Nigel probably found a copy among his father's things after Rock's death."

"Val saw a still picture from the video, and said it didn't look like you—right coloring, wrong features. So Nigel can't hurt you with it."

Kenzie's gaze went to a pair of butterflies dancing above a bush. "He's already done quite enough damage."

"It's hellacious to have everything you wanted to forget stirred up again, but it will blow over in a few weeks."

"It didn't for Humpty Dumpty. All the king's horses and all the king's men couldn't do a damned thing for him." Kenzie glanced up at her, expression taut. "Don't look so worried. I won't kill myself on your watch."

Her blood froze. "Is killing yourself an option?"

Too much time passed before he said, "It's not very likely."

"For God's sake, Kenzie, don't even think of that!" She leaned forward and clasped his wrist. "This will pass."

His gaze dropped to her hand, then traveled down her body, lingering where the tank top fell away from her breasts. She felt a strange heat between them—desire so tangled with complications that it was impossible to act on.

Grateful he hadn't wrenched away, she released his hand and leaned back in the chair, trying to look normal even though she was shaking inside. If she freaked out, he'd stop talking to her altogether. "I'd like to be sure I understand this. You're saying you're too considerate to off yourself while I'm around to find the body?"

"That's pretty much it." His voice dropped to a whisper. "No one should have to do that more than once in a lifetime."

She winced as she thought of Clementine, and the hapless girl called Maggie Mackenzie. "Given the horrible effect of suicide on one's nearest and dearest, can I get you to extend your promise to the point of saying it's not an option? You'll get over this depression, Kenzie, I'm sure of it. You're so strong. You've survived too much to be brought down by a vicious little weasel like Nigel Stone."

"Not depressed. More . . . hollow," he said, choosing his words slowly. "It took so much time and energy to create Kenzie Scott out of such unpromising material. He was like a blown glass Christmas ornament—impressive until it shatters, and there's nothing inside but emptiness. Building again would take more stamina than I have. But I don't intend to do anything rash. At the moment, my thoughts are running more toward never setting foot outside of Cíbola for the rest of my life."

She raised her gaze to the mountains soaring above the adobe walls. "That I could understand. But what would you do with yourself? I have trouble seeing you as a serious rancher."

"I'm going to start by building a labyrinth. There's a little meadow on the hill above the house that's perfect for that."

At least constructing something was productive. "A turf labyrinth like the one at Morchard House?"

"Too dry for that. I thought some kind of tile or flagstone."

"Shall we go into Chama and see if they have a building materials supplier?"

He shrugged. "Callie Spears, the decorator I used, can pick something out and get it delivered."

So much for getting him away from the house. He might claim he wasn't depressed, but she had her doubts. Whenever she was depressed, she wanted to crawl under her bed and hide, which was pretty much what Kenzie was doing now.

"Back to the woodpile." He stood and collected the plates, then left.

She watched him enter the house, thinking that he might doubt if he had the strength to rebuild himself, but he certainly had more energy than she did. For days, she'd felt like a limp dishrag. A pity his energy was fueled by anger and frustration.

She closed her eyes, feeling the blood pound in her temples. She couldn't leave him when he was in this strange, dangerous mood.

But what about the damned movie? Investors had risked their money, cast and crew had knocked themselves out to make it. She had a responsibility to all of them.

Feeling a headache coming on, she went inside to her bedroom to call Marcus again. Too tired for tact, as soon as he answered she said bluntly, "I can't come to L.A. to edit the film, Marcus. I don't dare leave Kenzie alone."

The producer sucked in his breath. "If he's in that bad

shape, we should get him into a good clinic until he's stabi-
lized."

"No! That would be the worst possible thing for him. He's
not raving or anything, and I'm sure he could convince any
shrink he's fine. It's just that he might, in a perfectly rational
way, decide that he's tired of having to work so hard on his
life."

She expected an argument, but Marcus surprised her.
"Okay, stay in New Mexico. No movie is worth risking a person's life, especially if losing Kenzie meant losing you, too."

How well he understood her. "Thanks, Marcus. Eva Yañez
is the best editor in the business for this kind of character-driven movie, and my scene notes are so complete she can do
most of the job without me. I'll fine-tune after she's through
cutting it."

"Whoa, girl! You can stay in New Mexico, but I'm not letting you off the hook for postproduction. With the right com-
munications and satellite hookup, you can work with Eva and
the sound people as if you're in the same room."

"I can do this by computer?"

"Sure. It's not ideal, and it's certainly not cheap, but the
technology has been in place for several years now."

"I'll have to ask Kenzie for permission to set up all that
equipment," she said uncertainly. "He is the owner of this
place, and it's not beyond the realm of possibility that he might
very politely say it's time for me to leave."

"Play cat—quiet but companionable. Sometimes the best
thing you can offer someone is your presence. Don't press him
to bare his soul—being English and male, he won't want to."

She smiled a little. "I'll try not to be too touchy-feely Cali-
fornian."

"Get his permission to set up shop as soon as you can. I'll
make the arrangements to get the equipment together and
trucked to you. It should be in place by the beginning of next
week. The installers can be in and out in a day, so it shouldn't
be too intrusive."

"Marcus, this will cost a fortune, and every penny in the budget is spent or committed already!"

"I'll put in whatever extra is needed."

She ran her fingers through her hair, hopeful but anxious. "What happened to never investing your own money?"

"A man's gotta do what a man's gotta do." There was a chuckle in his voice. "This has the potential to be a truly fine movie, Rainey, but it needs your vision every step of the way, or we risk losing what will make it special. I'll be damned if I let a terrific movie be lost for the sake of a couple of hundred thousand dollars."

She rubbed her eyes. After years of never crying, now she felt on the verge of tears constantly. "No wonder you're the best independent producer in Hollywood."

"Damn straight. In return, I expect you to bring your next project to me first." He turned serious. "I mean that, Rainey. The world has enough blockbuster special effects flicks. What it needs is movies with heart. If I can't support the kind of project I love, what's the point of being in the business?"

"Bless you, Marcus." After she hung up, she closed her eyes and uttered a silent prayer of thanks. Maybe she could honor her obligations to both the movie and Kenzie—if she could persuade him to let Hollywood invade his sanctuary.

He found the paving tiles in a corner of the toolshed when he returned the ax. Eight inches square and made of an unglazed clay that matched the soil of Cíbola, they were exactly the look he wanted for his labyrinth. He was laying a few of the pavers out on the ground when Rainey found him. He glanced up. "What do you think?"

It took her a moment to recognize what he had in mind. "For the labyrinth? Perfect. They must be made here in northern New Mexico. In fact, these look as if they were left over from paving the area under the arbor." She knelt and brushed her fingertips across the reddish brown surface. "Callie Spears is good, but for something as personal as a labyrinth, you should choose the materials yourself."

He agreed, as long as he didn't have to leave the ranch to do it. "I'll ask Jim Grady where these pavers came from so I can order more."

She looked up at him through tousled apricot hair, biting her lower lip the way she did when she was going to say something she wasn't sure he would like. "I talked to Marcus again."

With a sinking feeling in the pit of his stomach, he wondered if she was going to tell him that she had to return to Los Angeles right away. Lord knew he was the worst possible company, dour as an old bear. She should leave—but he'd thought she'd be here for a week or so longer.

"When I told Marcus how much I hated the idea of coming back to the smog and traffic, he suggested that I edit the movie from here." Her words tumbled out in a rush. "It would require a lot of computer equipment and a satellite link and probably another phone line or two, but Eva and I can talk and watch the images on the screen at the same time just as if we're in the cutting room together."

When he sat back on his heels, startled, she began twisting a lock of hair around her index finger. "Would you mind terribly if I stayed on and worked from here? I'll keep out of your way. You wouldn't have to see any of what's going on. The equipment can be set up in the bunkhouse."

When Rainey wasn't consciously acting, she was transparent. "Are you suggesting this because you're afraid to leave me alone?"

"That was the original reason," she admitted, giving up on subtlety. "But I truly don't want to go back to Tinseltown."

He frowned, torn. The last thing he wanted was to have John Randall around again, and the sooner Rainey got back to her real life, the better.

Yet if he was honest with himself, and these days he seemed unable to be anything less, he would love to have her near. She was the only one who understood why he was in such a state, and she was wise enough to leave him alone. "The bunkhouse isn't air-conditioned. It would be better to set up in the two empty bedrooms."

Her expression turned bright with relief. "You wouldn't mind?"

"I sincerely hope I never have to see a frame of that film again. But I do like having you around. Just . . . don't expect much from me."

"I won't ask much," she said softly.

He looked into her marvelous, changeable eyes, blue from the intensity of the New Mexican sky, and told himself that he really had to call his lawyer and refile the divorce suit.

But not yet.

✿ 36 ✿

Suppressing a yawn, Rainey said, "Time to break for lunch, Eva, and maybe a nap as well. I can't imagine how professional editors keep up the pace. This is grueling."

"We practice sitting still for hours on end, and have the butts to prove it," Eva explained. "You eat and take your nap. I'll call in a couple of hours, after I've had lunch and worked up those three versions of the farewell scene for us to compare."

"Thanks. Talk to you then." Rainey hung up, then stood and stretched. The long-distance editing was going well, but it took one hundred ten percent concentration to study the images and discuss the possibilities with Eva. Marcus had been right to insist that Rainey stay involved every step of the way. As good as her film editor was, God was in the details when it came to moviemaking, and editing was nothing but details.

She'd worked every day in the two weeks since Marcus's techies had arrived and installed the equipment, then taught her how to use it. Their presence hadn't disturbed Kenzie, because he'd saddled a horse and ridden into the hills for the day to avoid them.

She wandered to the window and looked up the hill. The labyrinth wasn't visible from the house, but she knew Kenzie would be working away up there. He was as obsessive about his project as she was about hers.

As soon as the computers were installed, he'd found Internet instructions on how to design and build a labyrinth. He'd leveled the ground, then laid out the concentric circles with powdered chalk. Now he was painstakingly setting each tile in a bed of sand for stability, teaching himself how to do it as he went along.

Their lives hardly touched except once or twice a day at meals. Kenzie was unfailingly polite, but they might have been strangers living in the same boardinghouse rather than husband and wife. Conversation never got beyond the superficial, if they talked at all. She did as Marcus had suggested, playing cat, quiet and undemanding, hoping her presence had a beneficial effect. And very frustrating it was, too.

Maybe he'd like a picnic lunch, since otherwise he'd probably forget to eat. She packed a tote bag with food and drink, then hiked up the hill.

Kenzie was on his knees setting pavers in place, watched solemnly by Hambone. Both glanced up at her approach.

"Hi," she said cheerfully. "I thought you might like some lunch."

"Thank you. That would be nice." Kenzie stood, stretching the kinks from his muscles. He'd lost weight, and there'd been no fat on him to begin with, but he looked healthy enough otherwise, as long as his eyes were covered with sunglasses. He'd acquired a beautiful tan and a beard several shades redder than his long dark hair. Soon he'd be able to play a convincing mountain man without benefit of makeup.

She hadn't been up here in several days, and she was startled by the progress he'd made. The concentric circles that doubled back and forth, twining their way to the center, were almost complete. "You've worked fast. How long until you're done?"

"Later today or tomorrow morning."

"What will you work on when this is finished?"

"Landscaping, I think. Shifting rocks around and planting tough native bushes will enhance the site." He wiped his sweating face with a towel. His hands were grazed and bruised from the manual labor, but still beautiful in their shape and strength.

Accepting a tall glass of Alma's fresh, cold lemonade, he asked, "How is the editing going?"

"Pretty well." She spread a bright embroidered tablecloth on the pallet of remaining pavers, which was down to the height of a low table. Then she set out utensils, a bowl of Southwestern bean salad, and a couple of pita sandwiches filled with tomatoes, lettuce, and chicken salad. "It's fascinating how easily we can try different scenes, different cuts, different optical effects, but it gives too blasted many choices. A good thing I had a pretty clear idea of what I wanted before starting, or I'd be paralyzed by all the options. Even so, it's hard to make the film match the story in my head."

" 'Story is all,' Trevor used to say."

She scooped bean salad onto her plate. "What was Trevor like, besides being a good teacher?"

Kenzie's face blanked. "He was a brilliant man torn between what he knew was right, and urges he couldn't suppress."

She gave him a swift glance. "You said that he didn't have a physical relationship with you."

"True." His expression made it clear that he wouldn't say any more.

She changed the subject. "When you walk the labyrinth, can you feel the energy getting stronger as it comes closer to completion?"

"I haven't walked it yet." He bit into the pita sandwich, chewing and swallowing before he continued. "I'm waiting until it's finished."

"Why? I'd have thought that once the pattern was laid out, you'd be walking it at least once a day."

"It's . . . magical thinking, I suppose," he said slowly. "The hope that the longer I delay, the more powerful the calming effect when I finally do walk it. I need to conjure all the peace I can get."

She put down her sandwich, dismayed. "Kenzie, I don't know if a labyrinth is going to be enough to do the trick. Maybe it's time to consider stronger measures."

His expression darkened. "Have you and Marcus been debating whether to haul me off to some discreet, expensive clinic with soothing drugs and well-paid doctors?"

"Marcus suggested it once, but that will happen over my dead body." She sipped lemonade to lubricate the sudden dryness of her mouth. "No drugs, no committing you for your own good. But surely there's some middle ground between doing nothing and getting checked into an upscale asylum."

He tossed the remainder of his sandwich to Hambone, then began to prowl restlessly along the curving edge of the labyrinth, his body tense as a drumhead. "God knows I've thought about it, but I'm not going to talk to some shrink, Rainey. I couldn't bear to tell anyone what it was like to be Jamie Mackenzie. The memories churn like the evils released from Pandora's box, stinging and biting like poisonous snakes. I can't sleep, can't bear the thought of touching you, can't imagine this ever ending."

The raw emotion in his voice seared her. She'd hoped he was making headway in coming to terms with his demons, but obviously not. He wasn't even able to sweep them under the carpet again.

It seemed particularly horrible that his ravening memories had made it impossible for him to accept touch, the most basic of human comforts. Having him so close without being sleeping partners was miserable. Quite apart from the lack of sex, she missed the skin-to-skin contact of being with her mate. In the past, that intimacy had soothed them both, but no more.

"Time may be the only healer," she said hesitantly, "but perhaps small, careful steps can speed the process a bit."

She rose and intercepted him, laying one hand on his right wrist. He stopped, the muscles tensing under her hand. "Just a touch, Kenzie," she said softly. "Nothing sexual about it. A touch between people who have known and trusted each other for years."

Slowly his arm relaxed under her palm. Though she guessed that it was an act of will rather than genuine relaxation, at least he wasn't ill. Progress of sorts.

He raised his hand and caught hers, squeezing briefly before releasing it. "It's a start. Thanks for understanding, Rainey."

Knowing she'd pushed enough for one day, she started packing up the picnic. "I'll leave the lemonade in its cooler. See you at dinner? Alma's going to town, and she promised to pick up some of those great ribs from the barbecue shack."

Then she left, wondering how one could close Pandora's box.

He laid the last paver in the row with hands that had almost stopped trembling. He had hoped that time would bring a measure of peace. Having lived with his past for over two decades, he should be able to again. Instead, every day deepened the pressure of corrosive memories. He couldn't even name the volatile mix of emotions bubbling like lava inside him.

Worst was the way his thoughts about sex were so intertwined with pain and fear and degradation that he couldn't remember the joyful, tender lovemaking he and Rainey had shared. Childhood horrors now contaminated what had been perhaps the most satisfying part of his life. He wondered with despair if he would ever experience such intimacy again.

Which was why he was building a labyrinth. Three tiles across, the labyrinth path was about eighteen inches wide, with another eighteen inches between one circle and the next. Enough so that a number of people could walk at the same time without crowding each other, though he doubted that this particular labyrinth would ever host more than one or two walkers at once. It was coming into existence mostly as his private attempt to maintain sanity through physical labor.

Laboring in the scorching noonday sun gave him a vague, satisfying sense of penitence. It was absurd to feel like a sinner when he'd been the one sinned against, but the mind was not a particularly logical instrument.

He laid pavers for the next row, thinking of how Rainey had touched his wrist. His nerves had jangled like an electrical overload, and he'd had to control the impulse to flinch. Ironic that he couldn't bear physical closeness, yet he was intensely grateful that she had stayed near him. She was his anchor in hurricane winds.

It was good not to be alone.

Brooding, Rainey returned to the house. She needed a dose of her old friend Kate Corsi's sunny good nature and unconditional sympathy. Kate's remarriage to her ex-husband made her a role model of sorts. If Kate could rebuild a badly damaged relationship, maybe Rainey could, too.

Luckily, Kate was in her office. She and her husband were co-owners of the world's top explosive demolition firm, and her biggest complaint in life was the time she had to spend on paper shuffling rather than working in the field, blowing up buildings.

Just hearing her friend's familiar *hello* made Rainey feel better. "Hi, Kate, it's me. Is this a good time to talk?"

"Perfect. You'll give me an excuse to delay some number crunching," Kate assured her. "Val tells me that you and Kenzie are in the high desert. Have you recovered from location shooting yet?"

That had been the official explanation for this retreat to New Mexico, but Rainey was too frayed to maintain the façade. "We're suffering from more than movie fatigue, Kate." She hesitated, wondering how much she could say without be-

traying her husband's confidence. "Being in England stirred up
a . . . a lot of childhood issues for Kenzie. He's going through
a very bad time."

"I'm so sorry, Rainey. Is there anything I can do to help?"

"Not unless you and Donovan devised a magic formula for
sorting out the past and getting on with life."

"That wasn't magic—just a lot of talk, and years of growth
between our divorce and when we met up again," Kate said.
"As hellacious as the breakdown of our first marriage was, now
I'm glad for it. We know ourselves and each other so much better than we would have otherwise. We appreciate each other
more now, too. On our second honeymoon, we laid out new
ground rules, chief of which is that the marriage always comes
first. Next to that, nothing seems important enough to fight
about."

Which did sound like magic, but not of a sort that would
help Kenzie. "Since Englishmen don't talk about their feelings,
that won't work here." She meant the remark to be humorous,
but her voice cracked.

"You sound seriously stressed. Why don't you visit Tom?
He's probably only about an hour or so away from you, and it
sounds like you could use a big brotherly hug."

Tom Corsi, Kate's brother, had been a surrogate sibling to
all of Kate's friends. He was also one of the kindest, wisest
people Rainey had ever known. "I didn't realize his monastery
was that close. Can he have visitors?"

"Yes, though you'll have to wait if they're in one of the
seven daily prayer services Benedictines are so fond of. Why
not drive over? It's a beautiful trip."

"Maybe I will. Where is this monastery?" Rainey wrote
down Kate's directions, then hung up when her friend had to
field a phone call from Saudi Arabia.

The thought of getting away from Cíbola was appealing,
but Rainey hesitated. It would take all afternoon to go to Our
Lady of the High Desert, talk to Tom, then come home. Time
she should put into *The Centurion.*

To hell with the movie. She'd worked seven days a week for months. She was entitled to a half day off.

After leaving a message on Eva's voice mail, she wrote a note to Kenzie and stuck it on the refrigerator with a magnet on the off chance that he might notice she was gone. Then she changed into an ankle-length, navy blue cotton skirt and a matching tunic with long sleeves and a hood. It seemed suitably sober for a visit to a monastery.

To find the keys to the SUV, she had to enter Kenzie's painfully neat room. He'd left no mark of his presence here.

The keys lay on the dresser, untouched for weeks. As she pocketed them, she noticed a framed photo of Kenzie, Charles Winfield, and Trevor Scott-Wallace. It must have come from the memorabilia Charles had left to Kenzie.

She lifted the pictures and studied the faces. Having met Charles, she could see his irony and humor easily. Kenzie was . . . himself: young, handsome, contained, with haunted eyes that she understood much better than the first time she'd seen the photo.

Reading Professor Scott-Wallace was harder. In his own way, he also looked haunted. From what she'd read about pedophilia, it was an unalterable sexual preference. How horrible to have those yearnings while knowing they were deeply wrong.

She set the photo back on the dresser, and gladly headed out into the mountains.

❧ 37 ❧

*She'd worried that Tom Corsi would have be-*come a pious, unrecognizable stranger, but his dark hair was still untonsured and unruly, and his white robe hadn't changed his smile. He'd always been so patient with his little sister and her friends. Always tall and good-looking, he was now also tanned and serene.

"Am I allowed to hug you?" she asked uncertainly.

"Of course. You're family." He engulfed her in a brotherly embrace. She relaxed against him, painfully grateful for the simple animal warmth.

As they separated, he said with a smile, "Are you here to gather atmosphere for playing a nun? That outfit you're wearing looks like it's trying to be ecclesiastical."

She pulled the hood lower over her forehead. "A priest once told me in all seriousness that the color of my hair was an invitation to sin, and I didn't want to cause any trouble."

"The monks here have moved beyond that medieval tendency to blame women for being female," he assured her. "Though the hood might be useful protection against the sun if you'd like to go for a walk."

"That would be great." She fell into step as he led the way through the cluster of adobe buildings that surrounded the church. "Kate suggested I talk to you. Even if you haven't any words of wisdom, it's wonderful to see you again."

He opened a wooden gate for her, revealing a path that wound up the mountain. "Is this a secular form of confession, allowing for the fact that I'm not a priest and you're not Catholic?"

She smiled. "Close enough."

They started up the well-traveled walkway. The monastery property was in the middle of a federal wilderness area, and the scenery was spectacular. When they were well above the monastery, she said, "This canyon is magnificent. Beautiful and rather savage, with a harsh, clear light unlike any I've ever seen. A good place to seek God. Are you happy here, Tom?"

"Yes, I am."

She glanced up at his face. "I hear a 'but' in your voice."

"I love the land, the community, and simplicity and spirituality of the life," he said slowly. "But I'm not sure if what I feel is a true vocation."

"I thought Kate said you'd taken vows?"

"Simple vows only. They can be renewed annually for anywhere up to nine years." He grinned. "If I can't decide if I have a true vocation by then, I deserve to be thrown out."

Rainey was panting when they reached the top of the path. Sage-scented wind whipped her loose garments. Tom gestured to a flat, wide stone in the shade of half a dozen tangy pines. "This is a popular site for contemplation. How about if we sit down and you tell me what's troubling you?"

She settled on the stone and drew up one knee, wrapping her arms around it as she gazed over the rugged red stone canyon. How much could she say, should she say? "I'm very worried about my husband, Kenzie."

When she paused, Tom asked quietly, "What is he like?"

"Forget anything you've seen on a movie screen. In real life, he's a quiet, wonderfully talented man made up of kindness and shadows. Making a movie in England stirred up his memories of a childhood that was . . . about as bad as a childhood can get. Now the memorics are eating him alive. He can't bear the idea of hashing over everything with a therapist, and he avoids drugs, even legal ones, like the plague, for reasons that are similar to mine. He's in agony, Tom, and I don't know what to do. *I don't know what to do.*" She hid her face in her hands.

Tom waited patiently until she collected herself before he said, "If he can't talk to anyone, suggest that he write a journal chronicling whatever is tormenting him."

"A journal?" She stared at him. "How would that help?"

"Studies have shown that most people benefit from writing down traumatic experiences," Tom explained. "The act of writing seems to put distance between the sufferer and the original incidents."

"Kenzie is dyslexic, and writing doesn't come easily for him."

"This kind of writing isn't easy for anyone, but there's no need to worry about spelling and grammar and sentence structure. What matters is digging down into the pain as deeply, and as honestly, as possible." He frowned, trying to make the concept clearer. "Words are a way of gaining control over the past. Some people later burn the pages as a way of releasing the pain. It works pretty well, too."

"Have you done this yourself?"

He nodded. "I had a lot of anger after my father threw me out of the house and told me I was no longer his son. In San Francisco, I took a journaling seminar and decided it was worth a try. Amazingly, it worked. I was able to feel compassion for my father, who was torn between what he'd been raised to believe and his love for his only son. Eventually, I was able to get past the anger and get on with my life."

"In other words, confession really is good for the soul, even if it's on paper. This is certainly worth suggesting to Kenzie. Maybe he can write what he can't say out loud."

"How is he using his time? If he's too depressed to do anything but brood, it could send him into a dangerous downward spiral."

"He's building a labyrinth. It looks sort of like the patterns on the surface of the brain." She tried to remember what he'd said. "It's a classic eleven-circuit labyrinth, the same as one that's set in the floor of Chartres Cathedral."

"A labyrinth? Interesting. He has good instincts," Tom said thoughtfully. "In the Middle Ages, believers who couldn't travel to the Holy Land made symbolic pilgrimages by walking on their knees around the cathedral labyrinth. There's a labyrinth in the desert garden behind our chapel, actually. It's a very powerful meditative device. A way to find God, and sometimes healing as well."

"But first the pain has to be cleared away."

"The labyrinth can help with that, too. Walking to the center is a journey into oneself. The center brings release, and the journey out represents integration. It's not unknown for people to have intense emotional reactions if they've been laboring under great stress."

"Kenzie hopes his labyrinth will bring him the kind of peace a labyrinth in England did."

"Maybe it will. But suggest the journal, too. It might be the only method private enough to help him now." He regarded her gravely. "Stay close to him, Rainey. Powerful tools release dangerous emotions. Some therapists carry twenty-four-hour-a-day beepers so that patients who are journaling can reach them at any time if they have a bad reaction."

"In other words, 'Kids, don't try this at home.' " She stood, feeling a little lighter at the prospect of being able to offer Kenzie something that might help. "Thanks so much, Tom. I'll let you know if your suggestions work for my husband."

Tom stood also, his body a protective barrier against the wind. "Is he going to stay your husband?"

"I surely hope so." Hope had been left in Pandora's box, which was why it sprang eternal.

Kenzie laid a final circular paver to complete a rosette at the heart of the labyrinth. He had the odd thought that the earth welcomed the stone, as if the ancient pattern he'd created in the desert expressed a profound natural harmony.

Muscles and joints protesting after hours of kneeling, he stood and stretched, mentally preparing himself to test his creation.

He stationed himself at the entrance of the labyrinth, his gaze tracing the pattern. Eleven concentric circles, with the pathway turning back on itself as it swung unpredictably through all four quadrants of the labyrinth. As in life, sometimes one seemed to be nearing the center only to have the path swing away to an outer circle. The road must be walked with attention and diligence.

Breathing deeply, he relaxed muscle by muscle, then took his first step onto the walkway he'd laid with blood, sweat, and care. Three steps in, the path swung sharply to the left.

He'd never believed in God. His childhood hadn't included religious education, and later he decided that no decent God could allow the atrocities that were commonplace in the world. If a divine being existed, it had created the world, then abandoned humankind to pursue more interesting projects.

A labyrinth worked for more earthly reasons. The mind was a drunken monkey, he'd once heard. Movement could channel off that restless energy, allowing the mind to slow to a meditative state.

Yet instead of calming, his emotions intensified. Tennyson's words echoed in his mind again.

> Break, break, break,
> On thy cold gray stones, O Sea!
> And I would that my tongue could utter,
> The thoughts that arise in me.

Though his tongue couldn't utter them, the emotions were flame bright, searingly real. Despair. Grief. Most of all, anger. Rage at the pimp who'd destroyed hapless Maggie Mackenzie, and immediately dragged her son into degradation. Fury at the uncounted men who'd chosen to believe that a child was willingly selling his body. Loathing of those who'd known better, and enjoyed feeding on a child's pain.

He wanted to confront his mother, who'd loved him but hadn't the strength to care for him. He wanted to curse Trevor, who'd saved his life but damaged his soul. He wanted to strike out at the men who'd abused him, teach them what it was like to be terrified and alone, but there was no one within reach of his punishment.

Most of all, he raged against himself, despising his pathetic weakness. He could have walked up to any kind-looking woman on the streets and begged for help, and been saved years of horror. Yet because he'd believed that he deserved pain and degradation, he remained a passive victim.

He wavered, then forced himself to continue. At some point he would have to hit bottom, and then the tidal wave of pain would begin to ebb.

But it didn't. The wave continued to build until Jamie's sobs echoed in his ears, Jamie's fear choked him, and Jamie's hopelessness stood revealed as the foundation of his whole misbegotten life.

Despairing, he stumbled into the center of the labyrinth and fell shaking to his knees as he gasped for breath. Kenzie was Jamie and Jamie was Kenzie and he could no longer separate the two.

The midday sun blazed like hell's own fire as he slumped onto the newly laid stones. He'd worked so hard to build a life, but nothing he'd achieved, not success, not money, not fame, could heal the primal wound at the center of his soul.

Ashes to ashes, dust unto dust . . .

It was dinnertime when Rainey arrived back at the ranch, but there was no sign of Kenzie. Maybe he was close enough to finishing the labyrinth that he'd decided to work on until he was done.

As Honeybunny and Gray Guy leaped around her, she read Alma's instructions for how long to heat the barbecued ribs the older woman had deposited in the refrigerator. Rainey read the note fondly, amazed at how natural it seemed here to leave the house unlocked so a neighbor could drop in and leave dinner.

She'd fed the kittens, poured a lemonade, and started for her bedroom when the phone rang. She picked up the call in the living room. "Hello?"

"Raine, I've got two pieces of great news," Marcus said with rare excitement.

She flopped full-length on the sofa. "Speak. I'm up for great news."

"Val's hunch paid off. One of our London researchers found a death certificate for the James Mackenzie that Nigel Stone claimed was really Kenzie."

Rainey gasped, wondering how that could be. "How old was he when he died?"

"The poor kid died of a beating when he was twelve. Assailant unknown, probably a trick who turned violent." Marcus sighed. "After I got that call, I went out and hugged the first grandchild I could find."

Trevor's friend, the intelligence officer, must have created a false death certificate to sever all connection between Jamie Mackenzie and Kenzie Scott. "What is Nigel Stone saying?"

"He's issued a public apology to Kenzie, saying that obviously he hadn't done enough research and he'd made a mistake. The unofficial word is that he was told by the *Inquirer* to grovel or find a new job. Kenzie is very popular in England, and a lot of people were unhappy when someone so widely respected was attacked by a mudslinging tabloid. Val's brainstorm about producing other men who looked like a young Kenzie wounded Stone's case mortally, and this drives the final nail into the coffin."

"So it's over." At least, the public ordeal was. Lord only knew when Kenzie might recover from what Nigel Stone had done to him personally. "Thank heaven. I'll tell Kenzie. What's the other good news?"

"Universal's big chick flick for the holidays has officially gone *splat* after months of rumors about trouble on the set. Problems with stars, script, budget, directing, you name it. No way can they get anything releasable by Thanksgiving, if ever. So the studio has decided to put *The Centurion* in that slot."

"Ye gods, how did that happen?" she gasped.

"I showed the execs a half hour reel, and they loved it. The movie will get a level of promotion it never would otherwise, and with Kenzie as lead, a profit is guaranteed, which will put you in a strong position for your next project."

"Fantastic! But can we finish the movie on time?"

"I've sworn on the head of my first-born grandchild that it will be ready. I once produced a movie that started shooting in July and was released the first week in December. We were all exhausted, but we did it, and it was a damned good movie. This one will be even better."

Honeybunny had jumped on Rainey's stomach, so she

scratched the kitten's head with tense fingers. "I'm glad I took the afternoon off. It sounds as if I won't get another holiday for months."

"Probably not, but this is worth it. This evening, think about how you want to handle the sound and music editing. We'll talk about a new schedule in the morning."

"Okay." She said good-bye and hung up, nerves jumping. With *The Centurion* committed to a major release, there'd be no time to tweak the editing until it was exactly right. On the plus side, the suits wouldn't have time to make her crazy with minor objections.

Setting the kitten down, she headed outside to tell Kenzie the news. The sun's rays were long at this hour, and when she reached the edge of the meadow, she had to squint as she looked for him. Where the devil was he?

She froze when she saw the unmoving figure crumpled in the center of the labyrinth. Oh, God, no. He wouldn't have . . . He *couldn't* have . . .

Powerful tools release dangerous emotions.

Heart pounding, she raced into the labyrinth.

❧ 38 ❧

*He was sliding down a spiral to hell, dragged in-*to into the abyss by the weight of his past. Then he felt Rainey's cool hand on his forehead, her arms strong as she pulled him onto her lap. He clung to her, so emotionally shattered that he was beyond even the tortured memories that had made touch impossible for weeks.

At first her urgent words were unintelligible. Gradually he recognized that she was saying over and over, "It's all right, love. It's all right," as if he were a child.

Strange how such simple, meaningless words could reach him. He whispered, "Rainey."

She hugged him so close he could feel her heart beating beneath his ear. "What happened, Kenzie?"

"Walking the labyrinth . . . made everything worse." He struggled for more breath, as short of oxygen as if he'd run five miles. "Anger. Pain. Confusion."

"Why confusion?"

How to transmute raw pain into words? "Looking into the mirror at a face that isn't mine. Knowing that even though I loathed what was done to me, sometimes I . . . I felt physical pleasure, and despised myself for it." He had to stop to breathe. "Owing Trevor so much, yet I couldn't forgive him for being what he was."

"Is that ambivalence why you seem to have been closer to Charles Winfield than Trevor?"

"Charles and I could be mentor and student together without the ugly undercurrents there were with Trevor. Even though Trevor never touched me the wrong way or asked me to role-play for him again, I could feel him watching and wanting. I hated that because it reminded me of every man who'd ever abused me. Yet how could I complain when he'd saved me and never asked anything in return?" Kenzie shuddered. "Except to be loved, and I . . . I deliberately withheld that because I was so angry."

"And you feel the guilt of that still." She stroked back his hair, her fingers cool on the throbbing veins of his temple. "This afternoon I visited Tom Corsi, my friend Kate's brother. He's a novice at a monastery not far away, and he knows about labyrinths. He said that in periods of great stress, walking a labyrinth can trigger emotional upheavals. Having had your life stirred up by Nigel Stone, everything was ready to erupt this time."

"So I was playing with a loaded gun, and it went off."

"Luckily Tom had a couple of good suggestions for dealing with past horrors. He says that writing down the ghastly memories will put distance between them and you, and make the past easier to bear. It worked for him." Her gaze went to the surrounding tiles. "He also said that walking into the labyrinth takes a person inward. The center is for release of emotions, while walking out integrates the experience. It's worth a try. I'll walk with you if that might help."

He closed his eyes. "It . . . might. But first walk to the center yourself. Then we'll go out together."

"If you want me to." She rose, fingers tenderly brushing his beard.

Cutting across the circles to the outside, she turned and composed herself at the entrance as he'd done. Then she pulled the hood over her hair and entered the labyrinth, walking straight toward him until the first sharp turn to her left. Her lowered gaze and dark, flowing outfit reminded him of a medieval nun, or an ancient pagan priestess.

He clambered to his feet and watched as the path took her back and forth. Twice she came so close he could have touched her, only to move away again. The labyrinth as metaphor for their marriage.

Her pace gradually slowed. At the center she lifted her head, tears coursing down her face. He raised his arms, and she walked straight into them.

"Tom was right," she said unsteadily. "This is powerful medicine. I don't know why it affected me so much more this time."

"We have too much in common, Rainey." He rubbed her back, trying to ease her trembling. "Operatically dreadful childhoods. Not knowing our fathers, losing our mothers young. The drive to be performers, you to prove yourself, me to lose myself. We connect on so many levels that whatever affects one affects the other, I think."

"Maybe that's why I just remembered something I haven't thought of in years." She drew a ragged breath. "Once one of my mother's druggie friends put me on his lap and . . . and touched me. I was horribly uncomfortable but didn't know how to say no to an adult. Luckily Clementine came in before he went too far. She attacked him with the fireplace poker when she saw what he was doing. I think she'd have killed him if he hadn't run away. She held me and cried and said that I was safe and it would never happen again. It was a minor incident, nothing compared to what you endured, but I had nightmares about the man for years." She hid her face against his shoulder. "Remembering gives me a faint, horrible idea of what it must have been like to be you. Dear God, Kenzie, how did you survive?"

"Because it didn't occur to me that I had a choice." He rocked her in his embrace, wishing she'd never had to endure an event that had given her so much empathy.

She sighed. "I want to be angry at my mother for not protecting me better, but there's no point in anger for anger's sake. What matters is learning how to release the pain." She stepped back and caught his hands in hers, raising her tear-stained face. The hood had fallen back, revealing the tightly drawn flesh over her exquisite bones. "Why stir up the past if we can't let it go?"

"I don't know if I can let it go," he said with painful honesty.

"Try." She closed her eyes and began to recite. *"I will lift up my eyes unto the hills, from whence cometh my help. My help cometh from the Lord, who made heaven and earth."*

He involuntarily looked up at the mountains, magnificent in their austerity. *I will lift up my eyes unto the hills, from whence cometh my help.* Even if he didn't believe in religion, the idea of God was appealing.

She continued through the psalm, the poetic words flowing like music, until she reached the end. *"The Lord shall preserve thy going out and thy coming in from this time forth, and even for evermore."*

"Amen," he whispered.

Wrapping his arm around her shoulders, he guided her onto the outward-bound path. What had Rainey said about this part of the labyrinth journey? Integration. He'd lived his life in a state of separation—Jamie cut off from Kenzie, childhood divided from adulthood. His deepest feelings severed from the life he'd created with painstaking care.

Since starting *The Centurion*, integration had been forced on him, and it had been disastrous. Was it possible to accept the whole of himself without madness or paralysis?

It had to be possible, because he couldn't continue to dwell in the abyss. Rainey had thrown him a lifeline. It was up to him to summon the courage and willpower to rebuild without the suppression and detachment that he'd used as a shield for too many years.

By the time they left the labyrinth, he was calmer than he'd been in weeks. He glanced down at Rainey. "How are you doing, TLC?"

She managed a smile. "Better. Tom was right, I think. The outward path does help integrate what's been stirred up. The spiral can lead up as well as down."

Tucking her close to his side, he turned to the path down the hill. She slid her arm around his waist, her closeness a blessing. As they walked, he said, "Three years of marriage, and I haven't the faintest idea of your spiritual beliefs, if you have any."

"Needless to say, Clementine didn't believe in fettering my childish mind with dogma, but when I went to live with my grandparents, they promptly enrolled me in the Sunday school of their church. They also sent me to the local Quaker school. Though I've never thought of myself as religious, whenever life has gotten difficult I've been supported by a kind of bedrock faith that's kept me from going off the deep end, so I guess that early training worked."

He looked up at the mountains again, the peaks tinged with molten gold from the last of the sun. "Faith sounds like a good thing to cultivate."

"Walking a labyrinth is a form of seeking. Maybe faith will sneak up on you someday." Hambone had joined them, so she paused to ruffle the dog's ears. "Will you try writing a journal? Tom said it doesn't matter how well you write, and no one will ever have to read it. In fact, he suggested burning the pages. The idea is to make your journal a cheap, disposable therapist."

He'd heard about journaling. The point was to dig as deeply into one's horrible memories as possible. Charming. But maybe effective. "I will if you will."

"You drive a hard bargain, but it's a deal. By the way, Marcus called. A death certificate for James Mackenzie has turned up. An example of Trevor's intelligence friend at work?"

He whistled softly. "It must have been. Sir Cecil was an amazing chess player who always saw a dozen moves ahead. When he was creating new papers for me, he must have done a death certificate as well, to sever all links between James Mackenzie and Kenzie Scott. What about Nigel Stone? Is he standing by his story?"

"Marcus said he apologized, with his newspaper's metaphorical gun in his back." She slanted a glance up at him. "You probably could get him fired rather easily."

Kenzie thought of the hell Stone had put him through, then shook his head. "I'll have Seth issue a statement accepting Stone's apology, along with the suggestion that next time he have his facts lined up before he goes public with his suspicions."

"You're generous. I'm all for chopping him up and leaving the bits for buzzards."

"Bloodthirsty wench. But considering that his story was true, it would be unfair to use my influence to cost him his job." Kenzie smiled faintly. "Besides, you know the old saying: Love your enemies—it will drive them crazy." After another dozen steps, he said quietly, "Thanks for being there, Rainey."

"I will be for as long as you'll let me."

He was too emotionally bruised to consider the future. But at least now he felt that he had one.

❧ 39 ❧

In a movie, Rainey would have cut away after they left the labyrinth. In real life, high drama inevitably descended to the mundane. When they entered the house, she asked, "Shall I heat up the spareribs Alma left?"

"Please. I'll shower while they're warming." Scooping Honeybunny onto his shoulder, he headed for the bathroom. He looked drained and far from happy, but the brittle tension she'd felt seemed to have dissipated. Though the marriage might not survive, Kenzie would, and so would she.

Feeling lighter than she had in weeks, she enjoyed puttering in the kitchen. Besides heating the ribs, she made a salad and set the table with candles and the checked tablecloth. Since there was nothing elegant about spareribs, she opted for the effect of a cheerful bistro. Several leaves and blossoms in a narrow vase completed the look.

Over a lazy dinner, she told Kenzie about the accelerated schedule for postproduction on *The Centurion*. He knew a lot about production, and made several shrewd suggestions that would save precious time. If he was dismayed that the movie would receive a wider release than originally anticipated, he didn't show it.

As they cleaned up after the meal, she said hesitantly, "It's pretty cool now that the sun has gone down. If you built a fire in the living room, we could both work there."

"Might as well use that mountain of wood I've chopped," he agreed. "I'll bring some in."

She made coffee and carried it into the living room. Outside the wide window, a rim of color edged the craggy horizon. Not a single artificial light was visible. They were a long, long way from Los Angeles.

Inside, Kenzie had turned on the reading lamps placed by the leather recliners, and was adding wood to the first crackling flames in the fireplace. "I love the smell of burning wood," she remarked. "Piney. Tangy. The scent of the Southwest."

"Jim Grady supplied several different woods for chopping. Cedar. Juniper. Mesquite. They tend to burn fast, but they're wonderfully aromatic." He sipped his coffee, the firelight flickering over his features in a ridiculously theatrical way.

"Your face might not feel like your own," she said hesitantly. "But most of it is. Plastic surgery didn't alter the shape of your skull or the fall of your hair or the texture of your skin. The beautiful green eyes that got you into trouble with Nigel Stone are certainly yours."

He stood and gazed into the circular mirror that hung over the mantelpiece. "If I'd chosen to have plastic surgery, it would be different. Having my face rearranged without my consent was . . . alienating. Every time I look in the mirror, I think of how helpless I was."

"It's hell to be a kid with no control over your life," she agreed. "That's probably true even with wise, loving parents. But you're not helpless now, Kenzie. You're in a position where you can work or not work, pick only projects you like, live where you want, when you want. No one has power over you."

"No one?" He glanced at her obliquely before intercepting Gray Guy, who was showing an unhealthy amount of interest in the fire. After drawing the metal mesh screen across the fireplace, he asked, "Do you have any lined yellow tablets? I might as well start on my journal."

They spent a quiet evening working on opposite sides of the fireplace. Rainey organized her production schedule while Kenzie wrote. Occasionally his blue felt-tipped pen raced across page after page. More often there were long silences while he stared into the flames, or petted whichever kitten had settled, or rose to put wood on the fire. His profile was like granite and he never spoke . . . but he kept writing.

When she finished her planning, she reluctantly picked up another yellow tablet to start her own journal. Where did one begin? She gnawed on the end of her pen. Chronological? Free association? Whatever issue bubbled to the surface?

She set pen to paper, and found herself writing.

As a child in my mother's house, I always felt as if I was raising myself, despite the nannies and housekeepers and hangers-on. Like Clementine, they came and went, though at least Clementine always came back, eventually.

Lolly was my favorite nanny. She promised me a special fifth birthday party with clowns and balloons. A week before, she and Clementine had a big fight and Lolly was fired. I ran crying into her room as she packed. She was crying, too, but she didn't stop packing. She gave me a hug, told me to be a good girl, and left. No birthday party that year. Clementine flew off to sing at a big concert in Central Park. She brought me back a wonderful music box with a twirling ballerina on top, but on my actual birthday, she didn't even call.

Rainey stopped writing, paralyzed by a wave of desolation. For an instant, she was five years old again, weeping alone in her bed because no one cared that it was her birthday. She might have cried now if Kenzie hadn't been sprawled on the sofa, writing down experiences that had to be a hundred times worse than a forgotten birthday.

No wonder I felt I was raising myself. No one else could be relied on. I've never fully trusted anyone, have I? Well, maybe my friends like Val and Kate and Rachel and Laurel. Those are relationships of equals. But I didn't trust Clementine, or my grandparents, or Kenzie. Anyone who might be assumed to have some emotional responsibility for me.

She gnawed at the end of her pen, thinking, before she continued.

I didn't trust them because I was sure they couldn't be trusted. Trust makes you vulnerable, so don't trust.

Yet without vulnerability, there can be no true intimacy. Being untrusting didn't mean that I escaped being hurt, but it sure guaranteed that I'd never develop a really deep relationship. The classic example is the way I expected the marriage not to last. A self-fulfilling prophecy.

She smiled wryly.

Must work on this.

The fact that she could smile was a sign that Tom was right: The act of writing helped create a sense of distance and control. She was no longer a desolate five-year-old, but a grown woman looking back on her five-year-old self with compassion.

Despite Clementine's failings as a mother and the anger I've felt toward her, I loved her desperately. Sometimes she was so very much there. Loving, playful, beautiful. So driven by her talents and demons. Rest in peace, Mama. I know that you did your best. It's not surprising that you couldn't run my life well, when you couldn't even run your own.

Blinking back more tears, she stroked Honeybunny's tummy. Pets were definitely therapeutic.

She was on the verge of quitting for the night when Kenzie rose and crossed to the fireplace. Drawing the screen open, he knelt and began feeding pages to the flames, one at a time, his expression unreadable. Tearing the pages from her tablet, she joined him.

"Ritual magic," he said. "It seems to work, too."

"Thank you, Brother Tom." She laid her journal pages on the fire at a ratio of one of hers to three or four of Kenzie's so that they finished about the same time. As the yellow sheets curled and blackened before exploding into flame, she felt a surprising lightness of being. She rose, suppressing a yawn, feeling that part of her life had been purified by fire.

Kenzie pulled the glass doors shut so the fire could burn out safely, then followed her down the hall. She turned to say good-night, one hand on the knob of her door, then paused, startled by his rigid posture as he watched her. As clearly as if the thoughts were her own, she sensed that he wanted to be with her, but wasn't sure he was ready for a greater level of intimacy.

The relaxed mood vanished. She wanted to be with him so much it hurt, but she'd be a fool to ask too much, too soon.

Wordlessly she extended one hand.

A muscle in his jaw jumped as his gaze locked on her hand, but he didn't move to take it. Softly she said, "Only to sleep. Nothing more unless it's what you want." She smiled a little. "I'll even wear the most decent nightgown I own."

Movements jerky, he clasped her hand. His fingers were cold. "I can't promise that I won't freak out again."

"I understand." She lifted their joined hands and pressed them to her cheek. "Thank you for daring to try."

Side by side, they entered her bedroom to risk the night.

He awoke rested. A miracle. Or rather, the effect of having Rainey burrowed against him, her head on his arm and her bright hair a silky cascade. It was early, the sky not yet fully light and the air in the bedroom chilly, but under the quilt was all the warmth a man could ever ask.

Though she'd kept her promise and wore a cream-colored, lace-trimmed nightgown, the fabric didn't disguise her desirability. In fact, the gown made the curves of breasts and hip more tantalizing, riper than a few weeks earlier, when she'd been working herself to the bone in England. Now she was re-laxed and sweetly provocative.

Arousal was instantly accompanied by stabbing images of sexual violation. He closed his eyes and held himself ab-solutely still, fighting to control his frantic reaction.

Rainey's hand skimmed down his body, familiar, deft, fully and delicately female. "Don't think anything else, Kenzie," she said quietly as his pulse accelerated. "Only us. Only now."

With absolute certainty, he recognized that reclaiming his sexuality would never get easier than this moment. The more he obsessed and worried, the more difficult physical intimacy would become. When her hand slid inside the shorts he'd worn to bed, he surrendered to passion, and learned that concentrat-ing on the moment pushed the horrors of the past to the edges of his consciousness.

All his attention was on his wife. Her eyes, misty gray in the morning light before they drifted shut. The luscious softness of her skin as he pulled the nightgown over her head to reveal her dearly loved body. The beat of her blood under his lips as he kissed her throat, her breasts, the tender curve of her waist. Her rapturous sigh as he entered her, every muscle straining for control so he could make this joining as wondrous for her as it was for him.

When she cried out, he let himself dissolve into searing re-lease. This was how lovemaking was meant to be. A passion-ate joining, a bond of trust, an annihilation of self beyond the shadows. *With my body, I thee worship. . . .*

It was full light when Rainey woke again. She wanted to laugh out loud, except that might wake Kenzie up. Emotional healing was a patchwork process, but based on the way he'd made love, he was well on his way to unraveling the emotional knots that had kept him at a distance since they'd left England.

Her well-being diminished as her stomach began to churn. She fought the nausea, but it increased with violent speed. *Hell!* She slipped from the bed, praying Kenzie wouldn't wake, and darted into the bathroom. She barely made it in time. After vomiting into the toilet, she curled into a miserable ball, her cheek pressed against cold porcelain.

Kenzie was so quiet that she didn't know he was there until he wrapped a warm robe around her shivering body. His, apparently, since it was huge on her. "What's wrong, Rainey?"

Panicked, she pulled the voluminous fabric close. "A touch of food poisoning, I think. Or the spareribs were too spicy. I shouldn't have eaten so many." She tried to stand, then doubled over dizzily, retching again.

When there was nothing left to throw up, he put a glass of water in her hand. She rinsed her mouth and felt better, though not so good that she was ready to leave the bathroom yet.

Clad in jeans and nothing else, Kenzie sat on his heels, one arm around her shoulders. In a carefully neutral voice, he said, "This has all the elements of a cliché."

Her first instinct was to lie, but that would be a temporary reprieve at best, assuming he even believed her. "I'm pretty sure I'm pregnant," she said wearily.

As she expected, he went rigid. Near hysteria, she blurted out, "Don't worry, it isn't yours. I was having nooners with one of the crew guys in England, and it's his."

The arm around her shoulders was trembling. "You're a poor liar, Rainey. Even assuming you wanted to sleep with two men at the same time, you didn't have the time or the energy to be carrying on another affair."

She began to weep uncontrollably. "I'm so damned sorry, Kenzie. It was an accident—I was so crazy busy that I missed a pill." She'd thought missing a pill was no big deal, until she'd researched the subject as her suspicions of pregnancy grew. It turned out that the directions for her low-dosage pills warned that a single missed day meant using another form of protection for the next seven days. And she hadn't. "I never would have gotten pregnant deliberately, but don't worry, you needn't have anything to do with this baby. I'll deny that you're the father and raise it myself."

He swore under his breath, but kept his arm around her. "Do you think I'll abandon my child like my father abandoned me? Or your father abandoned you? I . . . I don't know anything about being a parent, but if you think I'll walk away because you're pregnant, your common sense has been scrambled by hormones."

She gulped for breath. "Your sense of responsibility does you credit, but you said yourself that the thought of having a child was painful beyond description. Sticking around from duty won't benefit either the baby or me."

He began massaging her back, his large hand rubbing around her neck and between her shoulder blades. "You're right, the idea of having children terrifies me. I should have had a vasectomy, but doctors, especially those with knives, also terrify me. The price of cowardice is that I have to take responsibility for the consequences."

"Me wanting kids and you horrified by the idea is a really basic difference, and not likely to change." She'd thought enough about this so that she was clear on what was right. It was just her stupid hormones that were making her want to collapse into his arms and hold onto him at any price. "Why put ourselves through more torture until we get to the place where we have to admit that staying together for the sake of the child isn't working? You are what you are, and I am what I am, and ne'er the twain shall meet. Your turn to file for the divorce."

He slid his arms under her and pulled her onto his lap, leaning back against the wall as he cradled her. "A lot has changed in the last few months, including a rearrangement of my brain. The one thing that hasn't changed is that I like being married to you, Rainey. I like it a lot." He rested one hand on her belly. "We made this baby together, and unless you've changed your mind, you also want to stay married. Your desire to avoid trapping me is admirable, but how can we not at least try to do this right?"

She rested her head on his shoulder tiredly. "Maybe it's my

lifetime theme song playing here: 'I don't trust you to stay, so I might as well push you out the door now.' "

"Could be. Lord knows we both still have issues to sort out, but at least we have a pretty good idea of what they are, and now we have another incentive to get it right." He kissed her brow. "Oddly enough, I'm terrified, but . . . not sorry. Now I can stop being noble and just be with you, which is what I've wanted all along. Not a bad compensation for terror."

She gave a shaky laugh. "That's kind of romantic, actually."

He got to his feet while holding her, a tribute to the fitness advantages of chopping wood and building labyrinths. "I'll try to be more romantic when you aren't on the verge of being sick. Is it a deal then? We're married, we're staying married, and we'll both do our damnedest to raise this child better than we were raised."

She caught his gaze. "If we're going to give marriage and parenthood our best shot, we can't spend so much time apart, Kenzie. Separation hurts too much."

"Agreed." His mouth twisted. "One reason I was always working was to stay too busy to think. No more of that in the future, I promise."

"Then it's a deal." She put her arms around her neck and kissed him. "I love you, Kenzie. Always have. Always will."

He smiled down at her, weary but tranquil. "I must love you, too, Rainbow, because no one else can tie me in knots the way you do."

As a declaration of love it needed work, she thought as he carried her off to the kitchen to find something she could stand to eat. But not bad for a first time. Not bad at all.

❧ 40 ❧

There was nothing like recommitting to one's marriage to settle life down. For the first time ever, Rainey felt that she and Kenzie were truly moving in tandem. She loved it when she had time to think, which wasn't often. Most of her waking hours were spent editing like crazy.

While she worked, Kenzie took care of general life. He'd come out of his shell enough to leave Cíbola to buy food and supplies, and haul her off to the nearest obstetrician for checkups and vitamins. He no longer minded business calls from his manager and assistant. Compared to his mood when they'd first returned to New Mexico, he was calm and in control.

Nonetheless, in spare moments she worried a little, suspecting that he was suffering low-grade depression—which would make sense, given that he spent his evenings writing down his childhood memories and burning the results. Journaling was every bit as difficult as Tom Corsi had said it would be. She just hoped that when he finished processing his past, he'd lighten up again.

She worked on her journal as well, but less productively, since she had a tendency to fall asleep by the time she got to it. Editing, gestating, and journaling were too much to do all at once. She promised herself, and Kenzie, that she'd work harder once *The Centurion* was finished.

Alma Grady proved to be as reliable a resource for impending motherhood as she was for cooking, gardening, and New Mexico. From the gleam in her dark eyes, the baby was going to become an honorary Grady grandchild about ten seconds after it was born.

The dedicated skills of Eva Yañez, the sound editors, and other postproduction specialists meant *The Centurion* was almost finished in record time. With the deadline only a week away, she appealed to Kenzie over dinner. "Can you stand to watch the movie? Mostly it's done, but something about the pacing isn't quite right, and Eva and Marcus and I can't figure out what. Maybe you can."

His face tightened, but he nodded. "I suppose I'll have to see *The Centurion* sooner or later, so it might as well be now."

Hoping the movie wouldn't trigger more emotional up-heavals, she led the way into her workroom, turned off the lights, and began to run the current cut on her giant computer monitor. The opening credits rolled over the scene of Sarah darting across the green gardens of her home with Randall in pursuit so he could propose to her. "The look is lush and very English, but the resolution isn't great," Kenzie observed. "Is that a limitation of the computer monitor?"

"Yes. Marcus has promised to fly out here with a film ver-sion when we think we've got the final cut." She made a face. "I'm hoping that film won't show me a zillion bad things that pixels disguised."

"Eva wouldn't let that happen."

They both fell silent as the movie continued. Rainey, who'd watched till she was sick of it and no longer knew if it was any good, kept one eye on Kenzie. His face was unreadable, but he occasionally jotted a note on the tablet he'd brought along.

The movie ended with Sarah and Randall setting sail for Australia. As they stood side by side on the deck of the ship, her wistful regret showed how much she was giving up for the sake of her marriage. Then her husband took her arm, and she turned toward him with a smile that proved that Sarah Randall believed she'd gained far more than she'd lost. The last image of the movie showed the ship sailing into the sun.

"What did you think?" Nervous as a cat on a hot griddle, Rainey asked Kenzie as he turned on the lights, "I don't expect you to like it, but in your professional judgment, is it at least okay?"

He smiled at her as if she were a toddler impatient for Christmas presents. "It's a lot more than okay, Rainey. You re-ally are a born director. Amazingly enough, I even like it." He frowned. "It was hell to make this movie, as you know, and that was in my mind as I watched. But seeing the finished product on a screen is rather like journaling—it puts the experience at a safer distance. Now I can look at *The Centurion* and see John Randall, not me."

She exhaled with relief. "Thank God for that. I think it's the best performance you've ever given. I promised you a shot at an Oscar, and here it is."

He shrugged. "An Oscar means less to me than it used to, but this movie will certainly open doors for you. It's going to do solid box office, and there's a chance it will be one of those surprise hits that exceed everyone's expectations."

"You think it's cut right?"

"I didn't say that." He glanced down at his notes. "I think you've cut it a little too tightly. You've got a lot of wonderful, powerful moments. Too many—the viewer needs time to recover in several places. Here's a list of the spots where I thought you could add a little more time. I know the footage was shot, so it shouldn't be difficult if you agree."

She scanned his carefully printed notes, nodding as she saw which scenes he'd flagged and the suggestions he'd made for augmenting them. "I think you've hit it, Kenzie. Damn, you're good."

He put an arm around her shoulders. "If you're not too tired, I'll prove it later."

"That kind of good has been well proven already." He really did have a wonderful understanding of moviemaking, that mysterious blend of story, character, and medium. Watching from one corner of her eye, she said, "I keep thinking what great partners we could be—making movies together like Marcus and Naomi Gordon."

She felt him subtly withdraw. "I don't know if I want to be involved in any aspect of moviemaking again."

"Not even acting?"

He smiled without humor. "At the moment, acting has no appeal whatsoever. I rather like the idea of living on my investments and playing househusband."

Rainey rested her head on his shoulder. She had trouble imagining that Kenzie could be happy without using his tremendous talent and energy. She'd pray that when he finished rearranging his mind, he'd be ready for new challenges.

Rainey was dozing in her recliner when Val called. "Hi, girl-friend," Val said. "Good time or bad?"

"It's a fine time. The movie's basically done, and we all think it's pretty damned good. The sound guy flew out so Kenzie and I could loop dialogue for places where it wasn't clear. Any minute now, Marcus Gordon will be arriving from Los Angeles with a film version for us to go over one last time." Rainey suppressed a yawn. "After he leaves, I'm going to sleep for a week, minimum. How are you doing? I can't wait for you to see the final version of the movie!"

"I'm fine." Val hesitated. "I'm calling at the request of Mooney, your private detective. He asked me to break some news you might find a little . . . surprising."

"He's located a possible father worse than a drug dealer?" Rainey said lightly. "Imagination boggles. Did Clementine manage to find herself a space alien?" Outside the house, she heard the sound of the SUV pulling up. Kenzie returning with Marcus from the airport.

"No space aliens. On a hunch, Mooney kept digging to learn more about the studio executive alleged to be one of your mother's flings. He learned that the affair was more serious than preliminary reports had indicated. The dates are perfect for this guy to be your father, and apparently she wasn't sleeping with anyone else at that time."

Rainey had thought she was beyond caring much about the results of her investigation, but she pushed the recliner upright. "Mooney thinks he's identified the bastard?"

"Yes, and the candidate is alive and well." Val took a deep breath. "Rainey, it's Marcus Gordon."

"Marcus?" Rainey froze. That couldn't possibly be true. His marriage to Naomi was famously devoted.

And yet—he'd always been around. The friend of the family who'd put Rainey on the plane to Baltimore after Clementine's death. The producer who'd given her opportunities, including the amazing chance to direct her first movie with almost no restrictions.

And he had the same kind of small-boned build she did. She felt so dizzy that for a moment she wondered if she was going to pass out.

Marcus Gordon entered the living room, Kenzie behind him. Marcus smiled broadly and headed toward her for a hug.

How many times had he hugged her over the years? And what the hell had been in his mind when he did? Confusion turned to ice. "I'll call you later, Val. Kenzie and Marcus have just walked in, and there's work to be done."

"Stay calm, Rainey," Val said with a rush. "Give him a chance to talk."

"Don't worry, he'll talk." Carefully Rainey returned the handset to its cradle and stood, raising her hand to keep Marcus away. "I've just received some remarkably interesting information. Are you my father?"

Marcus turned dead white under his California tan. "I . . . might be."

"I suggest you sit down and explain." Rainey watched with gimlet eyes, like a cat ready to pounce on a mouse that showed signs of fleeing.

But he didn't flee. He dropped onto the sofa, looking ten years older than when he'd come through the door. "Naomi and I were going through a bad spell. When I contacted Clementine about starring in a movie I was putting together— well, one thing led to another. She was so lovely. So full of life. I . . . I might have left Naomi for her, but Clementine refused to consider marriage. She said she'd been a lot of things, but never a home wrecker, and besides, she didn't want to marry me. I was a nice change of pace, but no more than that." Pain showed in his eyes for an instant.

Rainey stood over him, arms crossed belligerently. "What about when you found out she was pregnant?"

"I asked if I was the father, and she just laughed and said of course not." He raised his gaze, expression stark. "I went almost crazy wondering after you were born. Sometimes I thought you looked a little like me, other times I was sure you didn't. By this time, Naomi and I had worked things out, so I never pressed the issue with Clementine. I settled for keeping an eye on you when I could, just in case."

"In other words, she made it easy for you not to take responsibility, and you were happy to go along with that. How very convenient. A DNA test should prove the relationship or lack thereof pretty quickly."

Marcus turned even whiter, but didn't look away. "If that's what you want. You have every right to be angry. I'm so sorry, Rainey. If it's any comfort, I've tortured myself plenty over the years. When I look at what you've accomplished, I'm so proud to think my blood might be in your veins. But if you are mine, I've failed you." His mouth twisted. "As Naomi says, there's no guilt like Jewish guilt, and I've carried that about you for over thirty years."

Rainey's hands clenched into fists. "How do you think Naomi will feel to learn that you cheated on her, and maybe fathered a child with another woman?"

Marcus flinched. "She might throw me out. She's entitled."

Before Rainey could say more, Kenzie's arm came around her, warm support in a world turned upside down. "You don't need a DNA test. Compare your hands. Look at the overall shape, the fingers, the nails."

Startled, Rainey spread her hands in front of her, then looked at Marcus as he did the same. Kenzie was right, allowing for the difference in age and gender, their hands were very nearly identical, right up to the slight inward bend of the little fingers. She lifted her gaze and examined Marcus's small-boned build, the shape of his skull. Here was the genetic missing link, the traits she hadn't inherited from Clementine.

He was studying her with equal intensity, and in his eyes she saw the same certainty she felt. "So it's true," she said unevenly.

Kenzie's arm tightened around her shoulders and he drew her out into the hall for a private talk. "Before blowing up a long-term marriage, step back and take a few deep breaths, Rainey. Clementine was the one who insisted on keeping your father's identity a secret, and it sounds as if she did that at least partly to save Marcus and Naomi from splitting up, which would have damaged both them and their children."

"I wanted a father so much," she whispered, her voice raw.

"You've got one now. Think about what you want from Marcus before you say something disastrous. I think he's a much better choice for a parent than the drug dealer."

She focused on Kenzie's concerned face, remembering that he of all people could understand. "How would you feel if you found out that your father was someone you'd known your whole life? Someone like Charles Winfield."

"I'd be shocked speechless, and probably as angry as you are at first. Then I'd be glad. I wish to hell Charles *had* been my father."

But he would never find out the truth of his parentage. Reminding herself that she was lucky by comparison, she returned to the living room, Kenzie's hand on her shoulder. Marcus was staring out the window, his face haggard. He turned as she entered the room. "I wanted to be your father, Rainey, but I didn't think I had the right."

Her anger began to fade. She'd had a fantasy of a father who would always be there for his little girl, giving the unconditional love and support she'd craved. But she was a grown woman now. When she needed a reliable man, she had Kenzie. There was no point in blaming Marcus for failing her when Clementine had never given him a chance. And no point in hurting Naomi and the rest of Marcus's family over an ancient indiscretion. "I wish Clementine had told you, or somebody, the truth, but I like the idea that she was being noble rather than merely careless."

"She didn't have you from carelessness." Marcus shook his head ruefully. "I've sometimes wondered if Clementine slept with me because I came from healthy peasant stock and would give her baby good genes. She wanted you very much, Rainey."

She might as well believe that was true, since it felt better than to believe she was the product of casual adultery. Deciding to get all the hard questions out of the way at once, she asked, "When you cast me in my first lead role, and when you got financing for *The Centurion* against the odds—how much of that was because you thought I might be your daughter, and how much was it on merit?"

"It was both," he said seriously. "I did give you special consideration, but I never would have made a bad business decision that would cost investors millions if you weren't up to the job."

Marcus had known exactly the right answer to give without getting into trouble. Her father was a smart man. It was an odd, exhilarating thought. Marcus Gordon was *her father.* Dear God, she had three half-brothers! She'd met and liked them, too. Wistfully she realized they couldn't be told the truth, because they'd be bound to resent their father's infidelity. But she knew.

She pressed her fingers against her forehead, fighting a desire to cry. Pregnancy definitely turned her into a watering pot. "This is going to take getting used to, but . . . I think I'm glad."

His face lit up like a sunrise. "I know that I am."

A gentle push from Kenzie, and suddenly she was in Marcus's arms, crying. She'd always wanted a father.

Better late than never.

❧ 41 ❧

Indian Blanket. Kenzie sat back on his heels to admire his latest transplant. According to the desert handbook he'd bought, it would have a splashy red flower with yellow edges during its late spring blooming season.

Though he didn't know a damned thing about gardening, he'd discovered that he quite enjoyed it. For weeks he'd been landscaping around the labyrinth, moving in tough native plants with the goal of making the area look natural, only better.

Since it was time for lunch, he stood and poured water around the base of the transplant. Was there time to walk the labyrinth before going down to the house? No, he didn't like being rushed.

After his first harrowing attempt, it had been a week before he'd had the nerve to walk the spiral path again. Luckily he'd never again had such an intense reaction. Overall he found it calming, and sometimes even uplifting.

He was almost to the house when Rainey raced out the back door, her ankle-length skirt swirling around her legs. She'd caught up on her rest since signing off on the movie, and it agreed with her. The pregnancy didn't show yet, but she assured him that any minute she was going to start ballooning. Despite his anxiety about impending fatherhood, he found the process interesting, and he and Rainey had never been closer.

Her eyes were gleaming wickedly when she bounced into his embrace. "Have I got a deal for you!" Grabbing his hand, she towed him toward the house. "As soon as you finish lunch, we're going to Santa Fe."

"Why do you want to go there?" He had no trouble visiting a small town like Chama, but he wasn't sure he was ready for Santa Fe.

"Remember Dame Judith Hawick?"

"Of course I remember Dame Judith." He washed his hands

at the kitchen sink. "Is she visiting Santa Fe and we're going to meet her for dinner?" That he would enjoy.

"Sort of. She's a guest director at the Santa Fe Shakespeare Forum this fall, and she's putting on *Much Ado about Nothing.* Tonight is her opening."

He frowned, not liking the idea of being in a large crowd. "I've seen the play, thank you very much. If we're meeting her for dinner, another night would surely be better than on her opening."

"Oh, this isn't about seeing the play." Rainey darted him a glance that clearly said she was up to something. "It's about you playing Benedick to my Beatrice."

"What!" He stared at her. "Rainey, you've convinced me. Pregnancy makes women insane."

"Not this time. The production was all set to go, until most of the cast went out for a late supper after last night's dress rehearsal. Dame Judith says this is clear proof that a good dress rehearsal is a disastrous omen." Rainey steered him to the table and sat him down in front of a chicken Caesar salad.

Ignoring the food, he asked, "I presume there is a point to this?"

"Today half the players, including her leads *and* their understudies, are down with food poisoning, way too sick to set foot on a stage." Rainey sat opposite him and started on her salad. "Dame Judith can cobble together most of a cast. She's going to dress in drag and play Leonato herself. But she desperately needs two good leads. She'd heard we were in New Mexico, so she tracked us down through Marcus and called me."

"If that many people are sick, they should cancel the performance."

"The show must go on," she said piously.

"Rubbish. Sometimes the show shouldn't go on, and this is one of those times."

Her expression turned serious. "This is really important to Dame Judith, Kenzie. It's her first time directing in this country, and she's frantic for it to go well. She almost cried with relief when I said we could fill in." Rainey's changeable eyes were pleading. "I owe her one for acting in *The Centurion* at a price I could afford. That's my obligation, not yours, but you know the part, and you're available. Please—will you do it?"

Mouth dry, he said, "I haven't done live theater in over ten years."

"You don't have to be great, just competent. The audience will be so blown away at having Kenzie Scott fill in that they'll be very forgiving."

"Shakespeare is usually presented in an edited form, and we don't have her script."

"Dame Judith e-mailed it to me. It's printing out now. You can drive while we run lines, and I tell you where the variations are. Plus, if we leave in the next half hour, we should reach Santa Fe in time for a fast run-through with the rest of the cast."

She'd thought of everything. He closed his eyes, struggling with fear. "I don't think I can do this, Rainey. I'm not at all sure I'll ever be able to face a camera again, and live theater is a hundred times more terrifying."

Her hand came over his where it rested on the tabletop. "I know this will be hard for you, but even though you feel stripped to the bone and vulnerable, no one but me knows about your past," she said quietly. "This is a good chance for you to decide if you want to continue acting, Kenzie. The stakes are a lot lower than on a big-budget movie, and you'll be helping Dame Judith out at the same time."

He'd loved live theater when he was at RADA, but that was a long time ago. Now the thought of standing in front of hundreds of staring eyes made him want to lock himself into Cíbola and never come out. But Rainey was right, dammit. He needed to find out if he was still an actor. More than that, he owed Dame Judith for standing up for him after Nigel Stone's ambush. "I can't really say no, can I?"

"Not really." Her smile was tremulous. "I'm scared, too, Kenzie, but I think we can do this."

"Your faith exceeds mine." He regarded the salad. Appetite had vanished, but it was going to be a long, long day. He picked up a fork and began to eat.

Dame Judith greeted them with extravagant hugs. "Thank the heavens you're here! Today has been a nightmare." She frowned at Kenzie. "Would you consider shaving off the beard?"

"No, I would not," he said firmly. The heavier his disguise, the happier he'd be.

"I suppose there's no reason why Benedick shouldn't have a beard." Taking each of them by one arm, Dame Judith marched them to the back of the theater. "First we'll let the wardrobe mistress have at you, since she'll need time for alterations. It shouldn't be hard to costume Rainey, but some improvising will be required for you, Kenzie. My regular Benedick was rather smaller."

The controlled chaos that always marked an opening night was multiplied by the food poisoning disaster. Cast and stage crew members, most very young, buzzed in all directions. Adding two Hollywood stars to the mix brought the brew near the explosion point. On the whole, Kenzie was glad for the confusion. It distracted him from his own rampaging nerves.

After the wardrobe mistress swiftly devised costumes for Kenzie and Rainey, they walked through the play. It was less a rehearsal than an attempt to work out blocking and stage business. The newly recruited friar kept tripping over the hem of his robe, while the very young Hero's deathlike swoon after being repudiated at the altar led her to fall off the stage, luckily landing on a well-upholstered musician.

The third time the stately but inexperienced Don Pedro, Prince of Arragon, ran into another performer, Dame Judith caught the man's gaze and said in a blood-chilling tone, "The basic rule is remember your lines and don't fall over the furniture. Do you think you can manage that tonight?" Blushing beet-red, Don Pedro promised to do better—and promptly backed up into a large wine jug, which fell over with a hollow boom.

When the run-through ended, Dame Judith said with a sigh, "If Shakespeare weren't dead, this production would put him in his tomb."

Rainey said encouragingly, "A bad final rehearsal is a good omen for the actual good performance."

"Except when it isn't," Dame Judith said dourly. "I've booked the two of you a room at a charming bed-and-breakfast around the corner, but there isn't time for you to go there to rest before the performance. Since space is rather tight, would you mind sharing the largest dressing room?"

"Not at all," Rainey said. "Just point us in the right direction."

A junior assistant stage manager took them to the dressing room, which was reasonably furnished and had a shower. When they were alone, Rainey flopped full-length on the sofa. "You were right—my hormones have made me mad," she said dramatically. "We'll be lucky to leave Santa Fe alive."

He sat at the end of the sofa and draped her legs over his lap. After removing her shoes, he began massaging her feet. As she moaned with pleasure, he said, "Do you have the energy to make it through the play tonight?"

"I'll be fine." She grinned. "Actually, I'm having a wonderful time. It's been years since my playhouse days and I'm frightened half out of my wits, but there are no real consequences for failure. I can do terribly and still get credit for being a good sport."

The consequences were higher for him, and they both knew it. Even if he made it through the evening without disgracing himself, this might be the last performance he ever gave. Acting had sustained him for years, but he was no longer the same man. Luckily, he could get through tonight's performance with skill, even if passion was missing. Dame Judith and the people who paid their hard-earned money for tickets deserved at least a competent performance.

None of his rationalizations prevented his muscles from knotting.

Rainey sat up and swung over to straddle his lap, her long skirt pooling around her. Cupping his face between her hands, she said, "I have a really good idea for dealing with opening night jitters." In case he didn't get the idea, she wriggled against him.

He had to laugh. Catching her around the hips, he asked, "Are you sure this is good for you?"

She leaned forward and kissed him, her lips warm. "I really do like your beard. It's so lovely and male. As to your question, one of the books on pregnancy I read said that basically, there are two kinds of people when it comes to sex during pregnancy: those who like sex more, and those who like it less. I've figured out that I'm the former type. How about you?"

"I certainly find you sexy." He slid his hands under her skirt, caressing her thighs. "Good grief, when did you abandon your underwear?"

"Advance planning." She kissed him again, doing interesting things with her tongue. "I figure we have half an hour before we need to shower and do costumes and makeup."

"Less if we shower together." He began moving against her.

"Excellent improvisation," she murmured.

Rainey was right. This was a terrific way to deal with opening night jitters.

There was an absolute aloneness before stepping on stage. Kenzie waited in the wings, and wished he'd had the sense to refuse Rainey's pleas. If he wasn't so close to being physically ill, he might have walked out of the theater.

Onstage, Rainey as Beatrice, Dame Judith in a false beard as Leonato, young Hero, and a Messenger were tossing the opening lines back and forth. Dame Judith was marvelous, of course, her trained voice pitched to a convincing tenor.

Rainey, a consummate pro, gave her opening line perfectly, her question about Benedick's survival betraying how much she cared for him even though their prior affair had come to nothing. Flanked by experts, Hero gulped, and spoke well.

Then it was time for Kenzie to enter with the Prince of Arragon and three of the other main male players. As he stepped out, he felt the pressure of all those eyes staring from the darkness. Dame Judith had announced to the audience before the performance that food poisoning had required numerous substitutions. She hadn't mentioned any names, promising to introduce her performers at the end of the play.

The audience began murmuring, and he saw people looking from him to Rainey and back again. A piercing whisper said, "It's Raine Marlowe and Kenzie Scott!"

The murmuring intensified, completely paralyzing poor Don Pedro. Under his breath, Kenzie prompted, " 'Good Signior Leonato, you are come to meet your trouble: The fashion of the world is to avoid cost, and you encounter it.' "

After a panicky glance at Kenzie, the prince managed to croak out his line. Leonato responded, and suddenly the play began to fall into place.

Kenzie had always loved Benedick, who hid his feelings behind banter, and the role fit like a well-worn glove. Rainey tossed her first teasing dart at Benedick, Beatrice doing a preemptive strike. At the same time she was his wife, who'd had as much trouble trusting as the character she played.

As the play unfolded, slow joy began to move through him. He'd forgotten the electric intensity of a live performance, the excitement of being fueled by the emotions of the people who watched so raptly. What actors and audience created tonight would never be repeated in quite the same way. This night was unique and intimate, immediate in a way that film could never match.

Inspired by Kenzie, Rainey, and Dame Judith, the rest of the cast members surpassed themselves. Kenzie wanted to laugh out loud at the sheer pleasure of performing. This was what he'd been born for, but had forgotten amidst the pressures of Hollywood fame, the unnatural stop-and-go nature of filming.

Beatrice, like Rainey, must be won by a man who was her match. At the end, when Benedick had accepted his fate and proclaimed, "Strike up, pipers," Kenzie caught Rainey around the waist and swept her high in the air, holding her over his head like a dancer. Time slowed while he revolved in a circle, looking up into Rainey's laughing face as her gauzy skirts floated around her slender figure. "Thanks for making me do this, Rainbow," he whispered.

As thunderous applause threatened to blow the windows from the playhouse, she gave a smile more intimate than a kiss. "You're welcome, my love."

There was no exhilaration quite like that of taking bows in front of an audience giving a standing ovation. The clamor was beginning to subside when Kenzie stepped forward and raised one hand for silence.

When the crowd quieted, he said in his most resonant voice, "Thank you for being here tonight, and reminding me why I became an actor." He caught Dame Judith's hand and pulled her forward. "Thanks also to Dame Judith, one of the grandest ladies the British theater has ever known, who took a chance on bringing in two Hollywood hacks for tonight's performance."

As the audience rumbled with laughter, he drew Rainey forward. Her apricot hair was trailing wisps and her cheeks were flushed with exertion. "Most of all, I want to give thanks to Raine Marlowe. My wife, now and forever." He bowed and kissed her hand. His gesture brought down the house again.

Charles Winfield would have been proud of him.

❧ *Epilogue* ❧

Rainey shifted restlessly in the backseat of the limousine. It had been weeks since she'd been able to get comfortable anywhere, and tonight she was as twitchy as a bored two-year-old.

"Are you sure you're up to this?" Kenzie gave her the worried glance of a man about to become a first-time father. She rather missed the beard, but he did look gorgeous in a tuxedo.

"Pass up the Academy Awards ceremony when my movie is up for nine Oscars?" she said with a grin. "This is never going to happen again." She glanced down at her flowing black evening gown, trimmed with black sequins and designed to take advantage of her cleavage, which was pretty impressive at the moment. "No way will I miss it even if I do look like a high-fashion version of the Goodyear blimp."

He took her hand. "You look beautiful." A charming lie, since it had taken massive efforts to get Rainey up to looks-pretty-good-for-a-woman-in-her-ninth-month.

She relaxed into the leather upholstery, thinking about the amazing months since *The Centurion* had opened. The gods had smiled, and the movie became a critical and popular hit. Reviewers raved about the wrenching, nuanced portrayal of trauma and healing, the luminous cinematography, and what a wonderful alternative the film was to the holiday crop of high-tech, big-budget thrillers.

Success had been sweet, especially when viewed from the safe distance of New Mexico, where it was easier to keep a sense of perspective. They'd decided that Cíbola would be their primary home, though they kept the Broad Beach house for when they needed to be in L. A. Rainey sold her canyon home to Emmy Herman and her husband. With their baby boy, they needed more space.

Over the winter, she and Kenzie had worked out a map for the future. The ground rules were spending at least ninety-five percent of their time together, and doing only work they truly loved. Their new production company had several projects in different stages of development, and working together was an unending source of pleasure.

Dame Judith Hawick was going to direct a West End revival of Wilde's *The Ideal Husband*, and Kenzie had agreed to play the lead with Rainey as the blackmailing Mrs. Chevely. They'd bought a handsome West End town house, since in the future they would be spending more time in England.

Even better than their creative partnership was their personal life. Playing Benedick in Santa Fe had been a catalyst for Kenzie, and ever since then he'd been his best and happiest possible self. Their relationship had reached levels of intimacy and trust Rainey had never dreamed possible, since trust had never been her strong point.

Rainey's grandparents were happy, too. Though they refused her offer to fly them out for the Academy Awards, they'd promised to come when the baby was born. Virginia sounded downright giddy at the prospect of a great-grandchild.

The limo halted, and it was their turn to step onto the red carpet. Kenzie helped Rainey out as the crowd roared with excitement. "You're Hollywood's darling," he said quietly. "The woman who fought to bring her vision to life, and succeeded beyond anyone's wildest dreams. It's the recipe for winning a tribe of Oscars."

"The nominations are a mark of respect, but we're not going to win many of them," she said pragmatically. "Note that I'm a *woman* who fought to bring her vision to life. It's males who actually get declared winners when they do the same."

"Good box office creates jobs, and the rank-and-file craftspeople who make up a large part of the academy love you for that." He tucked her hand in the crook of his arm and they proceeded into the huge theater, collecting hugs all the way.

Their aisle seats were in front of Marcus and Naomi, both of whom were beaming. She and Marcus were cautiously developing a new kind of relationship. Though it was never referred to openly, the knowledge was a warm bond between them.

Across the aisle Greg Marino sat with Val, who had flown out to California to be his date and keep him from going nuts as he waited to learn if he'd won the Oscar for best cinematography. Val looked fabulous in what appeared to be a vintage flapper dress that sparkled with black jet bugle beads and set her red hair off splendidly.

As the ceremony began, Rainey found that under her excitement was a curious sense of peace. The time she'd been up for the Best Supporting Actress Oscar, she'd wanted desperately to prove to the ghost of Clementine that it was possible to be talented and successful without self-destructing. Tonight, she had nothing to prove.

Which didn't mean that she didn't want to win, of course. She clamped her teeth tight when Sharif didn't win for Best Supporting Actor. He deserved it, dammit! He gave her a philosophical glance from his seat. He might not have an Oscar, but his role had put him on the cover of *People* magazine, and brought piles of scripts to his door.

She shrieked when the composer of the *Centurion* music won for best score, sighed when her art director didn't win. Then it was time for cinematography. The presenter opened the envelope. "And the Oscar for Cinematography goes to—Gregory Marino, for *The Centurion*!"

Ponytail flying, Greg leaped into the aisle and strode up to the stage wearing a smile that threatened to split his face in half. *The Centurion* gang howled their support. He gave the usual thanks, ending with, "Most of all, I want to thank Raine Marlowe, a terrific director who knows when to let her DP have his head." Amidst laughter, he left the stage to be photographed and interviewed in the press room.

Then it was time for the adapted screenplay award, for which Rainey had been nominated. Her fingers locked around Kenzie's hand like claws, though she kept her face carefully impassive. It wouldn't do to look disappointed on camera.

When her name was announced, for a moment she was so stunned that she almost didn't believe it. But Kenzie stood and helped her from her seat, beaming as he hugged her. "Way to go, TLC! You earned this one fair and square."

With his firm hand holding hers, she climbed the wide steps to the stage, wondering dizzily how many hundreds of millions of people worldwide were watching her waddle to the podium. Her mind blanked on the remarks she'd prepared, so she kissed the Oscar and said, "Actresses work hard to be beautiful, but what they truly love is being appreciated for their brains!"

As the audience roared, she thanked the Gordons and gave credit to George Sherbourne for writing a novel whose deeply human story still resonated in the twenty-first century. She moved through the press room as quickly as possible, wanting to get back to the audience to watch the other awards.

Rainey felt only a pang when she didn't win for best actress. She had her Oscar, and no matter what happened in the future, when the time came her obituary would read "Academy Award–winner Raine Marlowe . . ."

But she truly, desperately wanted Kenzie to win for best actor. He deserved it hands down. Seeing her expression, he said quietly, "It's okay if I don't win, Rainey, and I probably won't. It's not exactly a heroic role."

"Which is exactly why you should win!" she said fiercely. "How many actors would be willing to bare their souls the way you did?"

He just smiled, but the hand clasping hers was cold. The list of finalists and clips was interminable. Finally the presenter, the glamorous winner of the previous year's best actress award, opened the envelope and blinked near-sightedly at the slip inside. "The Academy Award for best actor goes to . . . to . . . Kenzie Scott for *The Centurion!*"

Rainey shrieked as she hugged him, but Kenzie was coolly composed as he squeezed her hand, then rose and headed to the stage. He was a popular choice, and the applause was slow to die down. His gaze went across the audience, and Rainey knew that a billion people across the world would think he was looking right at them.

When there was silence, he said reflectively, "Truly great roles don't come along very often, but John Randall is one of them. *The Centurion* is a story of survival and growth, second chances and redemption. Too many people have helped along the way to mention them all, but I must give special thanks to the memory of Charles Winfield, my mentor and my friend."

He mentioned some other names before his gaze went to Rainey. "Most of all, I must thank my wife, Raine Marlowe, who bullied me into taking this part"—laughter—"and in doing so, gave me the most profound experience of my life, and a second chance." His voice became intimate, as if they were alone together. "I love you, Rainey." He raised the Oscar to her in a salute.

Even knowing that a billion people would see her crying on camera, she couldn't control her tears. Damned hormones.

When he returned to his seat, she put her arms around him and rested her head on his shoulder. She felt equal parts sick, exhausted, and happy, but having Kenzie's arm around her was so comfortable that she half-dozed despite the strange, wired excitement that pulsed through her.

Then she heard her name. "Raine Marlowe, for *The Centurion!*"

Her head shot up and she stared at Kenzie, stunned.

"You're not dreaming—you've just won the Oscar for best director." He helped her rise, offering an intimate smile. "I am so proud of you, love."

He escorted her to the stairs and was going to retreat, but

she hung onto his arm. "Come with me! I may freak out and need help."

He climbed the wide steps with her, staying out of camera range when she went to the podium. In contrast to her exhilaration when she won for adapted screenplay, Rainey found that this time she was eerily calm.

"This is going to be a really tough act to follow with my second movie," she quipped. "Making a movie is a job of incredible complexity that requires immense hard work by an army of dedicated people. When everything comes together, the result is magic. If I listed the names of everyone who worked to make *The Centurion* what it was, the Academy cops would come and haul me off the stage.

"But I must mention my friend Val Covington, who told me I could do this when I didn't believe I could. This rates the world's biggest hot fudge sundae, Val." She smiled toward her beaming friend. "Thanks also to Marcus and Naomi Gordon, the producers who took a chance on an untried director because they love this business as much as I do. And most of all, to Kenzie Scott, a great actor, and an even better husband."

Would it be just too corny to say how much she loved him? Before she could make up her mind, a fiercely painful contraction swept through her. Dear God, it hadn't been just excitement making her feel so strange! Dizzily she grabbed the podium as the Oscar dropped to the stage and bounced. "I think I'm going into labor," she gasped, "but I'd never write a scene like this. It's such a *cliché*!"

"You can do the rewrite later." It was Kenzie's voice, Kenzie's arms sweeping her off her feet. She clung to him as he carried her from the stage past startled, excited faces. She knew from all the pregnancy books she'd read that some women did go into labor this fast, but why her, and why *now?*

Because there was a God, and She had a wicked sense of humor.

The Academy had an ambulance standing by just for her. Refusing assistance, Kenzie carried her into the vehicle and gently laid her on the bed inside. "Don't worry, TLC, this baby is a born performer, and will play its part flawlessly." He knelt beside her as the ambulance began to move. " 'All the world's a stage . . .' "

She smiled, then crushed his hand as another contraction ripped through her.

What could be better than going forth with Shakespeare?

Even though he was wrung out as if he'd run a marathon, Kenzie couldn't take his eyes off Rainey and their brand-new, red-headed daughter. "Not only did we get the best prize of all, but your timing gave us a perfect excuse to skip all the post-Oscar parties."

Rainey chuckled. She was tired and there was smudged makeup around her eyes, but she looked beautiful and vastly content, her apricot hair tumbling over the white hospital linens. "There's no way I could have managed the parties, but I'm kind of sorry I missed seeing Marcus and Naomi accept our Oscar for best picture of the year."

"We can watch it later on videotape." He hesitated. "Is it all right if I hold her?"

"Of course. She's half yours." Carefully Rainey handed over the baby.

Terrified that he'd break her, he cradled the infant in one arm, studying the tiny hands and dozing red face with awe. His daughter. *His daughter.*

She opened her eyes and blinked at him. His heart somersaulted. He had not known that such instant, profound, unconditional love existed. He was still terrified, but dimly he recognized that terror was a normal condition of parenthood.

He made a solemn vow that this was one baby who would be raised with the love and protection that all children deserved, and so many tragically didn't get. Though he suspected that parenting would be the most difficult role he'd ever tackled, between them he and Rainey would do better than their own parents had.

"Have we decided which name we're going to give her?" Rainey asked drowsily.

"Faith," he said softly as he returned his daughter to his wife. "We'll call her Faith."